ACCLAIM FOR MONA SIMPSON'S

A Regular Guy

"Perfectly pitched. . . . [A] true reflection of our time."
—*The Philadelphia Inquirer*

"[Simpson's] best so far. . . . [Tom Owens] is the 'regular guy' of the title, high irony in that he is hardly regular. . . . He is one of the great fictional creations of our era. . . . Lyrically rendered."
—Vince Passaro, *The New York Observer*

"Simpson is in her element, with her astute eye and compassion for idiosyncratic detail and characters. . . . [Simpson writes] wonderfully about oddballs craving normalcy, about parents so busy pursuing their dreams they forget about their children's."
—*Chicago Tribune*

"Simpson knows the ripple effect that spreads from wealth, the social earthquakes and aftershocks that follow when sudden riches erupt. . . . Like Austen, for whom the nuances of income are more than just numbers, Simpson knows the prices of things. And, more crucially, the prices of people."
—*New York*

"Simpson has never written a novel so teeming, nor one so technically daring. . . . Her language is as compelling as ever, and so is her wonderful way of prying into all the crevices of the human heart."
—*Time*

"What's mesmerizing is the razor-sharp way Simpson unveils delicate levels of human covetousness and greed [and the] lyrical flow of her assured, inventive prose."
—*Elle*

"*A Regular Guy* is rich in scale, funny and bitterly poignant. . . . A beautifully crafted story."
—*Miami Herald*

"The kind of narrative writing—poetic but rooted in the real sights and sounds and smells of living—of which [Simpson's] in total command. . . . My, how imaginative and ambitious a writer is Mona Simpson."
—*Vogue*

"A marvelous chronicler of the fractured American family."
—*Washington Post Book World*

"In her luminous and most brilliantly realized novel to date, Mona Simpson . . . has finally proven Tolstoy's axiom wrong for this age: Not all happy families are alike and not every unhappy family is unhappy in its own way. . . . Simpson never loses her fine command of perfectly tuned speech, nor does she ever falter in her subtle observations about relationships between men and women, friends and lovers, parents and their children. . . . Completely absorbing."
—*Detroit News-Free Press*

"Simpson's intensity and poetic capabilities are as engaging as they were ten years ago. . . . This is indeed Simpson territory, and territory worth travelling."
—*The Boston Book Review*

"Simpson captures the subtleties of personality and syntax in beautifully modulated voices . . . [and] brings emotional surrealism to vivid life with . . . sympathy and intimate detachment." —*Newsday*

"Sparks in its confrontations and provocations."
—*Los Angeles Times*

"Wryly comic. . . . Simpson's most powerful and moving writing is reserved for the fragile, makeshift alliances that sustain her characters, though she turns her deadly irony even on these."
—*Sunday Times* (London)

"*A Regular Guy* is a minor classic. . . . Could it be the start of a wonderful series like Updike's *Rabbit* quartet? . . . Mona Simpson's talent is a match for a task that ambitious." —*Scotland on Sunday*

MONA SIMPSON

A Regular Guy

Mona Simpson's work has been translated into
fourteen languages. She is a recipient of the Whiting
Writer's Award, a Guggenheim grant, and the
Hodder Fellowship at Princeton University. Since
1988 she has taught at Bard College, where she is
now the Sadie Samuelson Levy Professor of
Languages and Literature. In 1996 she received a
grant from the Lila Wallace–Reader's Digest
Foundation and was selected as one of *Granta*'s
Best Young American Novelists. She lives with her
husband and son.

A Regular Guy

A Regular Guy

a novel by

MONA SIMPSON

VINTAGE CONTEMPORARIES

Vintage Books

A Division of Random House, Inc.

New York

FIRST VINTAGE CONTEMPORARIES EDITION, OCTOBER 1997

Portions of this work first appeared in *Ploughshares* and *Granta*.

The Library of Congress has cataloged the Knopf edition as follows:
Simpson, Mona.
A regular guy : a novel / by Mona Simpson.—1st ed.
p. cm.
ISBN 0-679-45091-2
I. Title
PS3569.15117R44   1996
813'.54—dc20   96-2947
CIP
Vintage ISBN: 0-679-77271-5

Author photograph © Gasper Tringale
Book design by Misha Beletsky

Random House Web address: http://www.randomhouse.com/

Printed in the United States of America
10 9 8 7 6 5 4 3 2 1

For Ye, who now has faith

A Regular Guy

Prologue: Monuments

‹‹‹ ‹‹‹ ‹‹‹ ‹‹‹ ‹‹‹

*H*e was a man too busy to flush toilets. More than most people Jane had known, he was oblivious to the issuance from his body that might offend. He didn't believe in deodorant and often professed that with a proper diet and the peppermint castile soap, you would neither perspire nor smell.

This inability, not just to pander, but to see any need to pander to the wishes or whims of other people, was unusual in a man who had political aspirations. It was fortunate, for him, that he was wealthy. Also, he was handsome, so even before his prosperity, he had not been lonely in love. His favorite art was art in the classical mode, particularly public art, in the form of monuments. He was as interested in the Louvre itself as he was in the paintings inside, which, beautiful as some were, and arresting, seemed to him just so many details. If a man wants the face of the earth to look different after his life upon it, he must think on a certain scale.

This afternoon he was taking his daughter to see the Eiffel Tower for the first time. Although he had limited patience for many things, he would never tire of showing places to his children—works, gardens or even states of feeling he had known. Someday, he would show her Italy. Next winter he intended to teach her how to ski. That, for the most part, made up what he believed a father should do for his children: introduce them to the wonders of the world.

And it was true, years later, long after she'd forgotten walking into the powder room while he was talking cross-continentally to his girlfriend too long on the phone, Jane remembered her father's tall form, riding with her in the crushingly crowded elevator, to the second-to-top landing of the Eiffel Tower, then walking up the metal stairs in his slant way, standing on the top balcony, his longer-than-most-fathers-of-his-day hair whipping against his round forehead, lips pressed together in a kind of patriotic awe, a smile breaking down towards her. That was him. His hair disheveled by wind, his voice raised to be heard over nature, he strode at the very end of the balcony like the mascot on a ship, invested in the future of the world. He was an American industrialist, a believer in the potential accomplishments of state, and, in a way he couldn't explain, proud. He was her father. And they saw all of the planned city of Paris spread below them.

He whispered, "I'm kind of thinking of running for office. Hey, doesn't this remind you a little of the Statue of Liberty?"

He had just told her he might run for office. She assumed he meant running for president. It never occurred to her then that the choice would be anyone's but his.

That evening, in the hotel, he picked her book out of her hands, flipped through and then returned it. "Have you read anything by Abraham Lincoln?" he asked, dismissing the book issued by her old school. "You should read his speeches. I feel I can learn from people like Abraham Lincoln. See, I think it's individuals who make history." He paused a moment. "I think sometime when you're older, you're going to understand a lot better."

"Understand what?"

"I don't know, why I'm so busy. Why I wasn't always around when you might have wished I was." He knocked the cardboard cover of her book. "In school you study history; well, Genesis probably made a few of the great inventions of our time."

"It's a company."

"It's a company but it's more than a company." He fixed a look on her. She was too young to break in at the moment an adult would have, to force his own claims upon himself. His eyebrows went the way they did when he was serious. "You'll understand when you're older. A lot more about me.

"Here," he said, on the top landing of the tower, "we'll remember this." He pulled out two candy-colored franc notes, big bills, folded one into a paper airplane and sailed it down, over the metal railing. "Now yours."

"I'm keeping mine," Jane said.

Over the years, he took her to see the Empire State Building, the Lincoln Memorial and his favorite mountain lodge, built in the 1930s. He showed her Yosemite, his favorite place on earth, save home.

She led him, once, to an old abandoned factory at night.

"You like this?" he said, features like an owl's. "Why?"

"Never mind," she said, turning back, face parallel to the ground. She'd found it beautiful, the moonlight on hundreds of half-cracked-out windowpanes.

But he truly was only curious.

He made various thwarted efforts to erect his own monuments. All his life, he was impressed with architects and listened with his head cocked a certain way when they were talking, but each of their collaborations failed because the men he hired fell short of his standards and he did not have the time to direct the projects himself.

He bought a tower once, and he bought an orchard. He also owned a cave in Italy. Usually, he demanded that no statements involving money enter his sphere at all, but because of an odd carelessness of the accountant, Jane had seen a credit card bill on his dressertop. "Grotta," it said, and then converted a phenomenal amount of lire into eighteen thousand American dollars.

When she asked him about it, his face changed, his lips self-happy, remembering. "That's where Olivia and I made love one time. We fell asleep on this little haystack right outside the cave. And then while she was asleep, I hid her dress."

All of these purchases took place when he was living in a drafty upstairs wing of rooms with a roof that leaked and floors that bloomed fungus and an outside terrace where weeds grew up, cracking the tiles. A colony of bees made their home in a corner of the dining room.

He was not—as she had long hoped—a man inclined to ordinary dwelling.

What Existed, Far Away,
While He Never Wondered

◄◄ ◄◄ ◄◄ ◄◄ ◄◄

*I*t would take Jane years to reconcile her father with the man she'd grown up imagining, on the strange dark slide into sleep. One long-ago morning, she'd gone with her mother to a post office in a small Sierran town and seen a picture of a very young man, wanted for armed robbery. He appeared delicate and misunderstood in the grainy photograph, fugitive as an angel.

Her mother found her staring forlornly at that picture among the sad gallery. Jane was still a young child, but her face assumed an expression of concealment. For years afterwards, Jane would stare at certain men on streets and try to follow them. Her mother, Mary, would nod sadly and say no, he doesn't look like Owens at all, because it was the criminal's young face.

Mary wanted to correct the error, but she'd burned every photograph she had of Tom Owens.

Jane was born in Gray Star, a settlement in remote southeastern Oregon, where her cries were lost in miles and miles of orchards, stilled by a constant, omniscient rain. One of the people who lived in the communal house drove to town to wire Mary's message to Owens. Eight days later, she'd heard nothing. Staring out at the endless gray, she wrote a letter to her mother and told her she'd named the baby Jane, the name she'd once given her only doll.

They'd moved many times in the decade since, always because of a man. First there was the one who repaired string instruments and lived with nine cats. He gave Mary a guitar and made a high chair, where he allowed Jane to eat with her hands. Then, for a long time, there was the man who constantly traveled, following the greatest band on earth; he left them a truck, after he'd only begun to teach Mary how to play chords. Then came their months in Seattle, with the man who almost eclipsed Owens because he was beautiful, although he wanted to see them only weekends and said goodbye every Sunday by noon. Though he professed little aptitude for children, he taught Jane to read, because he couldn't stand the garbled language of toddlers and wanted to rush her to the age of conversation. It was this man who first showed them Owens' picture in the newspaper. With the small photograph, composed of dots, Mary tried to prove to Jane that her father was not the thief whose face she'd memorized from a post office wall.

In the article, Owens said he was the father of no children.

The city man's weekends shrunk. He started to come on Saturday morning, still leaving punctually before Sunday lunch. When his visits began at midnight, they moved again. But by then Tom Owens seemed to them the most famous man in the world.

They moved to a place with natural hot springs, where they tried to learn to sit and not think. There, in a mud whirlpool, Jane told a group of children her father was rich.

"And I'm heir to the crown of Curaçao," a boy replied. Actually, it wasn't unusual for the children Jane met in communes and ashrams to claim lineage so distant it would be impossible, ever, to trace, while they lived in trailers and trucks, on bare mattresses. She once befriended a family of Hungarian royalty whose only proof was a rare hereditary disease called porphyria. They had never been to school and their mother taught them out of a book of Elizabethan plays and a video of the movie they watched over and over again in their van.

Finally, a woman called Bixter led them to a mountain town, where they lived in a wooden cabin at a camp once operated, during the warm months, by the park service. Most nights, the men built a bonfire and the women cooked, everyone watching the weather, sniffing for the hidden pith of bread that meant snow in the sky.

Jane understood that no place they had ever lived was where they were from. Auburn was the name of that place, and although she'd never seen it, she knew it from her mother's stories. She drew the one wide Main Street blue with yellow lanterns and ended it in a pink square, where there was a newspaper-and-tobacco shop and a movie palace. She rimmed the town with stunted peach groves and palms full of dates, and set houses in every direction, each with its own yard and fruit-bearing tree. At night, she imagined the town sighing as the sky turned pink, then slowly dark. Jane had seen only one picture, on an old postcard they'd found in a dusty drugstore, showing horses and carriages instead of cars.

Unlike most towns, Auburn had been started by one person who'd had an idea. He had stopped not because the place was beautiful or different. In fact, it so exactly resembled land he'd already covered that only the collapse of his young wife made him stop. She had been called Auburn for the color of her hair, which had grown dark years before. Once she was buried there, he would never leave. Others in his party, however, noticed the kindness of the evening, a faint sweet smell emanating from white flowers in the dark. The man envisioned a clean town, no saloons, where ordinary people could grow their living. Over the next decades, more immigrants arrived, wealthy New Englanders from the long sail around the Horn, midwesterners in covered wagons, off the overland route, and eventually the patient citizens came on Pullman coaches, with modest expectations for the smell of fruit trees wafting through their afternoon rest. By then, Auburn had become an apricot town.

The founder's daughter declared a swap meet every month, where people brought things found or no longer wanted and gave them to anyone who craved. A weekly clemency was instituted to encourage criminals' remorse and the return of the stolen to its owners.

Over the years, the swap meet had grown into a dump. Mary sometimes ached, missing the soft blurry start and end to the days in Auburn, the scent of wild rosemary and sudden mint rising from patches of refuse. When she was a child, the farthest she'd imagined going was San Francisco, the City of Clouds, which was no doubt still beautiful and corrupt. Now, though, when she felt far away, it was the homely valley town she remembered.

But when Jane asked if they'd return, she replied, "That cow town? What do you want to go there for?"

Mary di Natali had grown up on an old road in the part of town where overland settlers had built small brick houses like what they'd left, matchboxes on big yards with ancient trees, and lived for generations without the suspense of weather. People kept chicken coops or tied goats to trees. Mary never knew her father, but she had read his forty-three letters, which in small penmanship complained of a ship's damp cold and relished an imagined future, when he would again be a baker of bread and live his life in front of fire.

Mary's mother supported herself with her husband's small bakery. In later years she became famous as far away as Fresno for her wedding cakes that gave a mysterious happiness, caused by a secret ingredient only Mary knew was wildflowers, broken into the batter.

Although she'd never been there, Jane felt she would recognize the dead-end road near the train tracks, where prim brides of all ages stood in line. As a girl, her mother played in white ruffled dresses, with a bow in her hair. These came from the dimestore or Browns' catalogue, the same as other children's, but Jane's grandmother favored the less durable styles.

Mary had never fit in. But in the places Jane had already lived, she'd fallen in with the pack. In the camp, she was a leader, calling out games and rules. Her clothes, like the others', were muddy colors from being collectively washed. When Jane heard her mother's stories, she wanted that white dress with the white bow.

"Can't you write to her and ask if I can have it?"

Mary sighed. "Someday we'll go back. I don't want you wearing dresses anyway." This was an idea she'd heard once from a man and kept because her own childhood dresses had no pockets and she couldn't collect things except in her skirt, and then her underpants showed.

"By the time we go back, they won't fit anymore."

"I'm sure she saved a few. Like the communion dress. That she'll have."

Jane's grandmother had delivered eighteen intricate cakes with small beans in their pale-bellied centers so Mary could have her first communion with a silk dress and her own wedding veil, cut down. Wax orange blossoms held the lace on her head.

"You look just like a little bride," Phil the milkman had whispered.

It was windy that day and Mary felt so light from fasting, having eaten only paper-thin wafers, that when the old nun led them up a hill by a rope that had hoops for their hands, she believed it was to keep them tethered, to prevent them, in their white dresses, from billowing away.

"Why don't I get to have a first communion?" Jane asked.

"Because the Pope's a liar," her mother said.

Jane's grandmother silently conducted two hundred and eighty-four weddings in Auburn. She baked the brides' cakes, wired mortified bees and pressed butterflies into attendants' bouquets and took the festal photographs. She'd thought about her own daughter's wedding since the day Mary was born and every year, on her birthday, presented her with a silver knife, fork or spoon to contribute to an eventual nuptial set. When Mary announced that she was moving out to live with Owens, her mother immediately disowned her. She had never liked Owens—not then or later, when he appeared on the covers of magazines—because he didn't know decent manners.

By then, Mary had become slovenly and lank-haired, a disgrace to her mother, who tried to maintain the standards of a Frenchwoman in Auburn, wearing a permanent bun so no one could have the slightest apprehension of finding a strand of hair in his cake.

"She *says* she's from France," Mary heard them say, behind her mother's back, "but we all know she's a Belgian."

She was Belgian and the dumpman's daughter.

◄◄

Owens and Mary lived together one summer. In September, he went to Harvard. Mary sent him a twelve-inch nasturtium chiffon cake in the mail and received no letter of thanks.

By Christmas, when Owens returned, he renounced all food but rice and beans and the smallest increment of green vegetables. He rented a cheap house near Auburn's only highway, splitting it with Mary and his friend Frank.

In the house that shook with the rumble of trucks, this was a period of giggling love, repeated chases that ended with her caught on the soft bed, and pancakes for dinner at midnight. But at her job at the dime-store cash register, Mary sometimes cried because she and Owens hadn't known each other as children. Owens had roamed the family junkyard with his father, looking for car parts. Once, they tore a fender off a wreck for a Caddy his father was working on, and that day, Owens told Mary, he saw a little girl in a white dress and a white bow, walking in a path through the debris.

Mary tried to show him bits of nature, because it was hard to talk after he came back from college. One night, she pulled him to the top of a hill, where, among the ancient, broken oaks, they watched the sunset spill for miles over the valley they'd always known. His eyebrows lifted: he was glad to see. She reached for his hand, but even then he didn't acknowledge it. The sunset was the sunset, with or without her.

She wanted to get him off alone, somewhere simple and small. Her dreams at that time were always dreams of closure. And he did sometimes say, "Well, maybe if this thing doesn't work, I'll just go and live on an apple farm. In the mountains somewhere."

Owens wanted to establish a business where everyone was young. He had already proven himself unable to work with bosses. He and Frank both had the nightshift now, at the company that employed half the valley. The nightshift was where they put misfits and Mexicans.

Mary got pregnant accidentally, and from the day she told him, he made it clear that her condition held no enchantment.

He was every day up and out of the house by noon. At that time, Owens and Frank were inventing the business that would later make them famous and put their drowsy valley town on the map of the world.

⤙⤚

The last day of her life in Auburn, Mary did the unthinkable and burst in on him at work. She had never been to the place where he and Frank planned their empire, because it was the basement of Owens' parents' house. She'd expected test tubes, Bunsen burners, petri dishes, chemicals, wires, smoke and possibly a conveyor belt, but instead she found Frank whistling "I've Been Working on the Railroad" while Owens stirred his beans and rice on a hot plate. The only evidence of scientific activity was an open ruled notebook with penciled equations. The rest of the basement seemed to be a woodshop.

"Owens," she said, "we've got to decide what to do."

He lifted his hands to a loose position of prayer while Frank climbed the stairs.

"You can stay, Frank," Owens called, but the whistling became fainter and then they heard the door bang.

"I can't have a baby now, Mare." With one cupped hand, he touched her hair. He couldn't give her anything in words, and this wouldn't count. His voice built the last wall, but for a moment, Mary closed her eyes and basked. Her neck weakened and the weight of her head fell to his hand. It had been a very long time since he was kind to her. But it occurred to her that she would have to choose, between him and his child.

"I've just started something," he whispered. "It's brand-new. I've got to give it time."

"I'm starting something too."

"I didn't ask you to get pregnant."

"But now it's happened and we have to deal."

Their fight escalated until he threw the beans at her. He noticed, as she walked away with the mess on her shirt, that her breasts had become large. The only vanity he'd ever suspected in her was the tendency to wear tee shirts backwards. Some girls in high school said she did it to show off her figure, but he knew now that was a lie. Mary was guileless.

Mary had been pregnant at nineteen with the bewilderment she still carried like a halo of bees. She had gone with her predicament and asked strangers for advice, as if carrying the small globe of her life and offering it to them. This made a mission of a youth that had previously lacked direction. Mary kept asking until she found someone to tell her yes.

She had her tea leaves read by an old woman near the railroad tracks, who told her that life is a long time and good-for-nothing young men are always abundant, plenty to pick from, like weed flowers. The milkman's daughters, who went to church every Sunday, their heads covered by thin veils of spiderwebs, whispered the ingredients of remedies to flush out the mistake.

Only one person said yes: a Taoist priest who lived on a high ridge of the coastal range, eclipsed half the day and all the night in fog. He had not mastered English and he only said, "Child is miracle," but that was enough to start Mary on the journey that led her to seek refuge on a communal apple farm in southeastern Oregon, where everyone was responsible for cleaning up and every meal included apples.

Forever after, Jane's mother blamed the Taoists, because the priest never sent even the smallest check to help.

Owens visited them once, in the mountain camp that finished the first decade of Jane's life. He came at night, while she was asleep, and Jane remembered the visit afterwards as in a silver dream. She'd heard the racket of a car and felt the milky heat of headlights, but then she rolled over and fell into an embracing sleep like a spot of kinder water in a lake or the first sensation of warmth when she wet the bed.

He and Mary hauled Jane up, opening her from a curled position. He spread her across his outstretched legs, measuring. Mary tilted down to the floor with a candle. Mary had always believed her daughter was a rare beauty, and she had a mother's pride.

Owens put his fingers on Jane's knee, through a hole in her green stretch pants. For a long time, those pants had been her favorite thing; they had once been yellow.

"She has your forehead," Mary said, pulling back her daughter's bangs, to show.

They did that all night, isolating a part of her anatomy and saying it was one of theirs or the other's. And they both looked at her with wonder, because she was a physical marvel—the only thing they had in common now and could agree on.

They played a game on the floor, drawing a grid with their fingers in the dust.

"I'm five ahead of you and eight ahead of Mom," Jane said, grabbing her feet and rocking her small body. Jane competed avidly, sucking her hair for inspiration, shrieking when she won. The score finally finished with him first, Jane second, her mother far behind. And that seemed to settle them all.

The next morning, the floor was swept and there was no trace of him, except the stack of new, unbent money on the kitchen table. It was late but the air still felt early, thin and cool with a lace of frost, as if they had confessed and all was forgiven, for a little while. Jane couldn't remember what he looked like.

Mary believed she'd finally found the cure for love: she'd become more Owens than he was. Passing wishes he'd mentioned were her life. She really had lived on an apple farm.

There was another man now, Mack Soto, who had two boys of his own and a fat short wife who had once been petite. He gave Mary white-bordered photographs of his sons, and from then on, Mary made sure to have Jane's picture taken in a machine booth every season, and she sent these to Owens, with Jane's age penciled on the border.

Mack drove to the wintercamp one night a week, while his wife had her book club. His coming made a party. They lit candles and drank long ribbons of brandy, which tangled in Jane's stomach, her arms and legs loosely knotted, like a doll she'd once seen, held together with rubber bands.

In the deep middle of one night, they sent her outside to walk. She put on her jacket, jammed her hands in the pockets.

"It's safe out there, isn't it?" she heard her mother say, behind the door.

Mack's voice slowed, stony and arrested, in a permanent state of nostalgia. "I used to walk with my grandfather here when I was a boy."

He told them what he'd already told his sons, but his sons never listened fully because while he talked their mother rolled her eyes.

There was noise that was branches swaying, pine.

"We're lucky he has no girl," Mary had said. "He always wanted a girl. She did too, I suppose." The fat short wife who had once been petite took to bed when her second son was born. She got up again two months later wanting no more children and refused to let him touch her, except to rub her head.

Jane and Mary were always like this, knowing intricate stories about other people while the other people knew nothing about them, not even that they were alive. Jane wondered if her father understood how they ran out of money and worried what they would eat. The time he came in the middle of the night and they played checkers on the dusty floor, she asked for his phone number. He shrugged and said, "You already have it." She made him write it again, with his finger on the floor, but it was only the number of a phone at an office and other people answered; they sometimes left five messages and still didn't hear.

Jane walked the long road, her shoes so soft the bottoms of her feet felt pine needles. Stars touched the tops of her hands like bites, and trees on both sides drew up tall, tilting. She pulled the caps off acorns with her fingernail and chewed the bitter green meal.

She was drunk too. Her mother didn't like to leave her out and Jane craved the taste of liquor, like harsh dissolved candy. She fingered uncurled pine cones in her jacket pocket to steady herself under the close stinging stars.

Beneath trees taller than any cathedral, Mack had walked with his grandfather quietly.

She ended up shivering and vomited, heaved out like an animal, then, cold, curled up by the side of the dirt road. Her mother came later, scratching the ground with a flashlight, her slippers whispering and the red wool plaid robe itchy when she gathered Jane in her arms.

"Look," she said, turning Jane to the millions of small stars, which seemed to fleck the sky with chalk. "Do you believe in God?"

"Yes," Jane said cautiously, as if she'd guessed the right answer but didn't know why.

Mack's feet hung blunt off the edge of the bed, pointed stiff, like a butcher animal's. She had touched the hoof of a hanging cow once—it was dry like that.

The next morning, the liquor woke them hard and early. Mack was gone and there was no money on the table, only white cinching rings where glasses ate the wood near drops of candle wax.

Jane could tell from the rhythm of Mary's heels on the floor, her steps wound tighter than what usually meant mother. Her orbit went smaller and smaller, cranked erratic wishes, steps of a carousel, the bed exhaling a final puff of hate.

She lay down for a long time without anything, looking into the repeating wood of the walls, her circle shrunk to the size of a pineknot. She said her hands felt fizzy, hard to move. "I give up, you win," she said, not to Jane.

All day, they never left the cabin's one room. But the outside lured Jane. Bright-colored insects ticked against the screens, high pines slowly waved.

"Can we get something to eat? I'm hungry."

"Mom, do you want me to bring you a glass of water?"

"When are you going to get up?"

There was never any answer, only the breathing, the snagging torn breath that seemed to fill not only the space of the small cabin, but time itself, with hooks and debris.

Jane watched the green day tempting, effervescent, behind the screen. But she couldn't live without her mother. On the sheet, Mary's saliva formed a coin. Jane touched it—it smelled metallic—and fell in.

It seemed hours they lay there, turning on the sour sheets. The busy optimism of the world passed. They heard the habits of civilization roll by, the important weight of semis, rushing the highway, delivering food and milk to apartment dwellers on patios in distant cities, and the whistles and confetti shouts of children outside.

Mary and Jane had always been different anyway. They never read the newspaper or heard radio—they couldn't keep the daily habits when they tried, and often were slow and late.

As the noises outside leapt and grew, Jane discovered the suspended pleasure of resignation.

Her mother woke, rubbing her own head. "I can't anymore," she said, smiling down haplessly, the way the man had said to her, on his hands and knees when their affair was young, "I can't help it," and the same way he had said, the night before, "She knows everything and she's forgiven me."

"Do you want me to go outside?" Jane asked.

The mother nodded, her eyes wise now as miles of travel.

The Driving Child

⤛ ⤛ ⤛ ⤛ ⤛

*B*ixter owned an old black pail she used for everything. While Mary took the Greyhound bus to her mother's funeral, Bixter and Jane scoured the woods with it for wildflowers to make a pie.

"Won't it be bitter?" Bixter asked.

"We sugar them," Jane explained.

They washed the frail petals in rainwater, let them dry on a screen in the breeze. Then they mixed them with eggs, milk and a dust of nutmeg, and poured it all into the crust. This was the first time Jane had ever been away from her mother.

When the smell from the tiny oven rose, Bixter said, enigmatically, "A crust must be made in the morning."

"Why. Why can't it be made in the afternoon?"

Bixter frowned. "Because of the air."

Jane would remember that all her life. While somewhere in cities children were chanting the names of all the presidents in order, the collected odd convictions of solitaries became Jane's education.

Two days later, they heard Mack's car outside. Mary burst in the door just as the sky cracked and rain started. Mack had cried, she told Jane. "He was so big and he cried."

"If it wasn't for the kids," he'd said.

Sunday, Mary stayed in bed and a pink cup of coffee floated before her. They hadn't eaten anything for days now, since the tart pie of flowers. Jane stood in the cool air like a statue, holding the cup. Clouds outside meant evening. Mary sat up on the bed and sipped, then began to move. The world was soft, as it always was when she first rose late in the day. Perhaps here hid the lush secrets of indolence, but that was knowledge she couldn't use. She collected the candles, saving the wax in an old milk carton.

They drove out to Tastee-Freez, half an hour away. Back at the wintercamp, women were boiling root vegetables with seaweed, but they sat at a table on the tar lot, cluttered with dry spills and autumn flies. The highway spread serene, lavender, the land quieting, tall grass blurry at the top. They ate hamburgers, warm grease darkening their yellow wrappers, and drank malteds, thick and hard to suck through flimsy straws. Jane stuck her fingers in and licked off the sweetness. She never used knives and forks, and Mary blamed the long-ago violin maker, who'd let her eat with her hands.

Time returned to Jane's body, drop by drop, through the straw. Tomorrow would be school again, the bus. She put one hand between her rump and the metal bench. Her mother would write a note. The teacher would nod once and take the scrap of paper without reading it, put it in her left top drawer. The teacher was used to children from the camp; most of them fared poorly in school and, like Jane, came for the chocolate milk they gave out. Jane had never met her grandmother, but now it was as if some clock far away that was always ticking for her had stopped. Even as long as she'd been gone, ten days, going back to school didn't frighten Jane. They did the same things every day anyway. The minutes passed slowly, as if they were sorting sand into its constituent elements: granite, crystal, lava.

When her hand fell asleep, she blew on it.

Mary watched her daughter with exhausted relief. Jane was not a sensitive child, she was not. She was mainly this—eating with her fingers, slowly, after thirty hours of dizzy hunger, without regular days or school. This was the way she knew happiness, her foot on the bench, the other heel kicking metal, the bite of wet gold-brown meat against the cold.

Mary's own childhood had been all rules: napkins at table, a dessert served on flowered china, with her glass of milk. She'd wanted anything but the sameness of that house, though now when her mother was gone she missed it.

A highway-side wind slipped in her sleeves and touched her ribs, shivering her. They both wore old soft clothes. "Honey, I'm going to send you to your dad," she said. "I'd take you myself, but I can't. I just don't think I can."

Her daughter knew when not to say anything. But she pulled her knee closer, softening a scab with her tongue. "I don't even know him," she finally said.

A train horn started too far away to see. Her mother's round face looked out into distance. "You met him that once."

"Was at night. I don't remember."

"He's got a house and all now. And a lotta lotta money. He's an important man down there. He might even be governor someday. *Governor*. Wouldn't you like to be the governor's daughter?"

Jane tried to keep her top lip straight. "No."

"Yes you would. Later, you would." Mary sighed. She unclasped her purse and gave Jane final money for two swirled ice cream sundaes with nuts. "I'm going to teach you to drive."

The only car they had was a truck and it was old.

Teaching Jane to drive took a long time. She stopped going to school. As the fall progressed, they absorbed themselves in the nesting of the truck. Mary fitted pillows to the seat, sewing telephone books in between padding and basting on a slipcover, so Jane sat fifteen inches above the cracked vinyl. They had to strap wood blocks to the brake and gas and clutch pedals, so Jane's feet could reach. But the blocks slid and they couldn't trust the straps and they finally borrowed a drill from the Shell station and attached the wood with deep barnum screws. Never once did Mary call Mack, although his long letters arrived every day, small forlorn script in blue ink on yellow lined paper.

"They're probably having some bad times," Mary said, "but little contentments too, I suppose." The two of them were silent, reverent to the idea of marriage, the boys, Mack and the fat, displeased wife sitting down to supper around one table. They perched high in the truck eating Arby's, down the block from his house, where a strangled tricycle waited in the driveway.

"He says she's on a diet." Mary read from the letter. Mack used to tell them stories about his wife's weight. *When I married her she was a wisp of a thing,* he'd said softly.

"Remember the time she ate the big zucchini?" Jane said. Once, he'd made a week's worth of stuffed zucchini, a huge oversized squash as big as an arm, and she'd come in after her book group and scarfed it all down.

"She tries to diet and then gets mad at herself." Mary pondered. "She should just accept that's the way she is."

The fixing of the seat took six days, sewing, adjusting the padding so the phone books wouldn't slip and the sides rose up to enclose Jane. Fortunately, the truck's long stick shift was easy for her to reach. Mary taught a little every day and tested Jane. Where is the choke? Okay, do it. Lights, brights, wipers, emergency brake. They fixed the broken back window with tape and a piece of cardboard. Mary sealed the seams with clear nail polish.

Then the real lessons started. They went on an old road, columns of trees on both sides, straight as far as they could see. They practiced starting, the gradual relay of clutch and gas. Jane found the brake again and again until it was easy. When the car sputtered and died on the late-afternoon road, no one knew.

Clouds bagged huge and magnificent.

In the rosy, cricket-loud dusk, Jane pedaled and shifted, as naturally as the woman they'd seen once playing the organ in an empty church.

Mary made her do it all again with her eyes closed, which was like swimming in rain.

❖

Braids, piecrusts, flowers in a vase, require talents that yield only themselves, nothing more than those passing pleasures. But Mary didn't have the knack. She'd asked people fifty times to show her how to braid, and she still couldn't do it deftly. Jane's braids always looked uneven, at once too loose and too tight. Girls who lived in town with their grandparents came to school with braids like this, to keep the hair off the face. Only the young mothers seemed to understand that girls need a little flair, like the girls far away on television.

On Thanksgiving, Jane sat on the end of the mattress while her mother brushed her hair straight up from her head, pulling it tight, then braided it into a basket around her ears. She dressed Jane warmly, with two pair of socks in her new shoes. The truck seat was packed with a grocery bag, Jane's clothes, her bear and her old shoes. They'd quarreled over those shoes; they had holes in the soles, and Mary wondered what people would think of her, sending a child with shoes like that, as if these same people would accept it as perfectly normal to send her in a truck over mountains.

"What do you care?" Jane had argued. "I need them."

Mary rolled down the top of the grocery bag, with Jane's four Twinkies, Fig Newtons, an apple and a banana.

Then everything was done. Jane's braids were tight and her scalp still felt as if someone were pulling her up by the hair. She sat on the bed, hands clutching under the mattress.

Her mother knelt on the floor. She slid off Jane's left shoe and rolled down the double sock. Then she took a breath and lined her words along one edge, her attempt to be firm. She felt it was necessary to warn Jane about life's dangers.

"Now, I'm giving you money," she said without smiling. "That's twenty, forty, seventy. And one, two, three, four, five ones. That's a lot of money, do you hear?"

Jane noticed that her mother kept no dollars for herself, and this frightened her.

"Don't, whatever you do, let anyone see you when you take that out." Her mother folded each bill into a small triangle, like a flag, and put them in the bottom of her sock. She pushed the shoe on over Jane's heel, tied the laces and patted it finished.

"Get just what you need. Because it was hard to save that. And here." She pulled the special undershirt over Jane's chest. She'd sewn in a pocket to hide her ring—as proof. Years ago, Owens had given her the ring, hidden inside a cherry pie. She'd sent him pictures of Jane every season, but he had never acknowledged them so they couldn't be sure.

They watched the sky change, waiting. Finally, stars glittered against black, and Mary clapped a hat on Jane's head. With the hat and the height of the telephone books, no one would see Jane was a child.

Mary fixed a glass of coffee the slow way and fed it to Jane with a spoon, as she had when Jane was a much younger child. From the first taste, Jane knew her mother had used the last sugar.

"Now I don't want you to go." Mary laughed a little.

"I don't want to go either," Jane said, her hands lifted, soft on her mother's shoulders.

"But it's the best thing, my little paw. He'll have a house and you'll get your own bedroom. He'll probably buy you your own bike."

For a moment, Jane lapsed to imagine. She'd seen a television show once where children ran around an obstacle course hammering bells, winning a prize with each ding. But in less than a minute, Jane went from being someone who'd always wanted many things to someone for whom prizes, if they rained on her now, came too late. "I won't have a mother," she said plainly, as they walked under the high cloudless sky.

"But you had me. And we've always had a better relationship than I had with my mother, ever. You can remember that I went as long as I could for you. And I always will love you, wherever I'm sitting." They stopped at the truck. "If I had the money I'd buy you a little locket you could have around your neck."

"I'll get one someday." For a long time already, Jane assumed she could do things her mother only wished for.

"And it'll be from me. Whoever pays."

In a tree above the truck, Jane saw an owl, stiffly lurching. She pressed closer to her mother, listened to her heart like the far sound inside a shell and felt the pull of an empty immensity, the attraction of wind, the deep anonymous happiness of sleep. "I want to stay with you."

"No," her mother said, separating their bodies, the way a lover might.

Through the window, her mother pulled on the truck's lights, illuminating the invisible before them, and Jane had the sensation of being pushed, as she had been years earlier, trying to learn to ride a bike. In no time at all, she was down the road, wobbling until she caught her balance, past her mother, the cabin contracting in the small rounded mirror. She stopped the truck, leaned out the window and cried, "Mama!"

Her mother's choked voice echoed back through trees. "Go on ahead, Jane. Go now."

Jane drove. Her mother had taught her patiently and well, at dusk while others ate their supper. Jane saw her own leg, long for a ten-year-old, reaching the wooden block pedal, and she thought of her mother and the man who was her father marveling over her parts and understood, for the first time, *this is why.* The world seemed for a moment to have become clear, and remarkable uses for her brow, arms, cheekbones and widow's peak would soon become apparent: she could use them to cross mountains, to collapse distance and to fly back in time.

She rounded a curve and felt herself flying already—sitting so high in the truck she could feel the velocity and whistling air—but her hands without her steered the wheels back into chronological time and she drove down a long simple road. Her mother's pencil-drawn map lay on the seat next to her. She was traveling west, with an old sense of which way west was.

The envelope labeled *Owens* poked into her side. "I better safety-pin it on," her mother had apologized.

Jane understood she was driving at night so shadows would conceal her childhood. Her mother had put her to bed six afternoons, waking her late and leading her on stumbling walks outside, to prepare her dreams for daylight and accustom her eyes to the dark.

There was no heat or radio in the truck, there never had been, and the sounds that entered through cracks were sounds of the world repairing itself in its sleep. Animals moved in the distance, water seeped somewhere invisible, and there was the etching work of wind on branches, ticking. Jane listened to the sounds people almost never hear and forgot about driving and then snapped erect at attention when she caught herself swinging hammocklike into the lurching swoon of sleep. She opened the window and drove rigid, eating the air.

No one passed but, twice, mile-long semis, and then it was just clutching the wheel hard, through an arc like an amusement park ride, the noise so whole it carried you in it. And it wasn't up to her if it let you down again or not. But it did and she was still there, her teeth chattering loose, the truck wobbling on the plain dark road.

For the rest of her life, moments from that night would rise into Jane's memory to haunt and enchant her, though the sequence of the drive itself remained a mystery, so that finally she could only claim what her great-grandmother had once said after lifting a Ford off the junkyard ground to save her only child's back: "I don't know how I did it. I couldn't do it now again if you paid me."

Jane wanted to stop and lie down in the seat, but she was afraid of day: if she couldn't make herself wake up. She had the clock, she could put it by her ear or inside her shirt on her chest. She decided to pull over and eat just one Fig Newton. That would help. But it tasted dry and strong; she didn't really like them without milk. Water from the round canteen tasted metal, sticking to the back of her teeth. She finally let herself sleep, holding the clock against her chest, then woke with a start and it was only a quarter hour. On her knee she had a scab. She picked it off and ate it, liking the tough opening taste of blood.

Her mother had warned her not to let the gas go down to empty. She had painted a red line on the glass gauge with fingernail polish. But now the needle was hovering below and there was no filling station. When Jane felt frightened, she pulled on the wheel and made herself sit up straight. "I will always sit up straight from now on," she told herself.

She made numerous promises to any God that night. By the end, she'd promised her whole life away to goodness.

Later, the road widened and she stopped at a ten-bank gas station, got her money out and put on her hat. She was trembling and her knee jumped when the man came over to help her. He was an old man and small.

"Fillerup?"

She handed him one of the twenties.

"Okeydokey."

She picked a scab from her elbow, watching. When he put the hose back in its slot she drove away. That was done.

At one point, Jane began singing all the songs she knew, the night everywhere around dimensionless and still beginning, and she came to understand that she knew very few songs, and of those she remembered only one verse and a scattered mess of words with spaces between. Most were from camp meetings and she despised them. After "The Farmer in the Dell," she tried the Beatles songs her mother liked to hum.

She did numbers then—picturing them, the line, the carry-the-one—and for a while she named the things she knew. Capitals lasted nine states, history was little better, and she remembered only the first two lines of a poem she'd once had to memorize: "By the shore of Gitche Gumee, By the shining Big-Sea-Water . . ." She now understood the point of memorization. Rhymes and numbers and state capitals and presidents could keep you out loud at a time like this. All Jane knew was what she hated.

But she had been doing other things while her classmates chanted their gradual multiplication tables. In the tree hollow she had placed seven acorns, unfitted their hats and sprinkled each with salt: that was for Mack to come back with her mother. She'd made offerings too for weather and the end of weather. She didn't plan. Each commandment came complete, sometimes in school, and she had to obey. One time, she took a nest down and put in the three broken parts of her mother's sparkly pin. These were her small duties that guaranteed nothing. Only, if she did not do them, it could be worse.

She drove that night in a straight line, through storm, the crack of lightning, trees of white, sheets of water dividing, spray on both sides, and it came to her that she had passed into the other world, where her mother was dead. Jane felt sure her mother was going to die, because that was the only reason she could imagine they had to be apart: her mother so pretty and, everyone always said, so young. "Yeah?" Mary questioned, with a strange expression, whenever Jane reported a compliment. Mary didn't trust people talking about them. She felt always alert to the possibility that they were making fun of her.

Jane had never had a death yet. Mary had told how she'd leaned down and kissed her mother in the coffin. And Jane had the picture now of her mother dead. She would be dead the same way she had been a thousand times on the bed, sleeping, the way her face went, lying down, everything draped from her nose. Jane started crying for herself because she didn't even get to kiss her mother.

In the beginning, more things were alive: plants felt, something commanded, creatures lived in the sky. The morning after her trip to her father, she woke up in a hole of dirt, her mouth full of stones, her hands smelling for a long time of gasoline.

The most terrible and wondrous experience in Jane di Natali's life was over by the time she was ten, before she'd truly mastered the art of riding a bicycle.

Dawn began long before light. There was less in the air. Sooner than she expected, the first turn came.

She thought again of her acorns and what she'd forgotten. She was supposed to glue the caps back on over the salt, but they had no glue. This was to be sure Mack Soto helped her mother in time. Last night, this lapse made her wince, but now it seemed nothing, a breath on air. She understood she would never believe in her childish powers again.

The sky was lightening in thick bands of color. Highway signs worked. She would find his house today. And she would discover the town she had been promised since she was born. She would use signs and numbers and songs of outside now. But she would have to learn them, system by system, in a new school.

For the first time, Jane wondered who built the roads and if there was one person sprawled somewhere, as she had on the floor with her crayons, and drawn the whole world, plotting the highways, and then how that one person got the people to build them and where would the money come from and was that person God when he made the lakes and the dry land or was it the President. They were still building new highways all the time. That was what those striped mixing trucks were that you sometimes got stuck in back of at a traffic light. One of them had dropped a glop on the road where she went to school and kids ran up to write their names with sticks and put their handprints forever in the sidewalk. There in the mountains was an uneven corner with the imprint of Jane's smaller hand.

When she finally saw the town, it was alive with order. A flock of children walked in sunlight to their everyday school. Men sat outside a tobacco shop, reading newspapers. It had all been going on without them.

Then, at a corner, she saw the man she recognized from the picture long ago, wearing a brown uniform. Against all orders, she stopped the truck and jumped out.

He seemed to be delivering a dolly of milk crates, cartons of different whites and a few chocolate.

"Do you know me?" she said.

He shrugged, smiled and said, "No hablo inglés," then walked on.

After her drive, when she became a passenger again, she always buckled her seat belt without being asked. Danger had little allure for her, no music. In fact, she seemed to retain almost no desire for her earlier life: the whisper of a dawn wind, the cold promise of an autumn moon over the High Sierra, when all the tourists have gone home and woodsmoke spikes the air and the ones who are left are those you will know your childhood with. Her only remnant of nostalgia seemed to rise with inclement weather. Storms reminded her of the years when she inhabited a larger region. Less than a forest but in every way different from a home.

Then she would find herself—no coat, no umbrella, soaked shoes— running across roads, darting and slanting, daring cars, gauging the density and smear of headlights. She yearned to live unsheltered again and to recognize: This rain is the voice of the world. When teeth chatter and the body shivers beyond control, this is the real cold, the real hunger.

In the mountains, she had eaten her scabs. It was a habit she could never quit.

Here, she vowed to become normal. She would walk right up to her father's door and knock.

The Proposal

✦✦✦✦✦

*N*oah Kaskie was not satisfied with his musical education. He wished he'd paid more attention in elementary school when his music teacher had played Bach's Little Fugue in G minor. Her heels had lifted out of her shoes as she conducted along with the record.

Thomas Edison invented the phonograph, Owens had told him that. He probably also knew who made the compact disk.

Noah shook his head. Even in fifth grade, it seemed he was supposed to know more than he did. He'd been afraid to ask the simple questions. And opera. Noah knew almost nothing about opera.

He always meant to take a music appreciation class, but he was busy right now and life was life, so when Noah bought a new tape, he listened to it eight or ten times until he could whistle the melody. He vaguely remembered the music teacher doing this, lifting the needle back to the same passage to identify theme and variations. She played the same recording for the entire spring; at the end, the class took a bus to hear it at a concert. The Alta Concert Hall had two beautiful curving stairways. Worried, Noah's parents had wanted to send his older sister along with him. But Noah had insisted on going alone. His same friends who gave him a lift every day in school carried his chair up the grand stairs. Dressed up and scrubbed, though, for the first time they seemed solemn, like little pallbearers, as if only here they realized he was different.

Noah felt better when he was teaching himself something. Now he was listening to the clarinet concerto for the eleventh time while he checked over a graduate student's dissection. "Caviar," he said. "Now I'm going to filet it. Watch."

A zebra fish egg was only slightly larger than a pinhead. Kaskie pulled out a hair from his eyebrow. He attached the one hair to a tool the rough dimensions of a matchstick and proceeded to cut the embryos with this homemade knife. Under the microscope, the mutant cells were elegant, like winter trees.

The next thing Noah knew, Owens was filling the doorway. It was nine o'clock in the morning. Owens seldom called ahead. He liked to just drop in. Noah suspected one of the things Owens found comforting about him was that he was so easy to find. He hovered over another minute dissection, and Owens seemed happy to wait. Owens liked the atmosphere of the lab. Its equipment and cheap furniture and productive messes made him think of an artist's loft. Mozart, was it? Mozart.

A young man of indeterminate European origin stood in the corner, staining pieces of embryo with an antibody that recognized proteins expressed when the cells began to turn into a brain. Europeans generally intrigued Owens. This one turned out to be from Denmark.

"I'll make you coffee in a sec," Noah said. Though he often wanted to do things for Owens, he seldom let you.

"Or we could walk to the Pantheon."

"I'll make it here. And even breakfast." Noah rubbed his hands. "Caviar. Sweetbreads upstairs. No, seriously." In the lab and at home, he had elaborate setups for coffee, all the paraphernalia, the apparatus of an addiction. His cups and tin measure were not fancy. But he bought his dear beans from Switzerland, at seven ninety-nine a pound. A luxury, but one he'd long ago deemed essential to his daily contentment. He measured the beans and then measured the water. Precision, Noah believed, made all the difference in both cooking and science;

the difference between the mediocre and the sublime was often a matter of proportion. Coffee involved a whole chain of procedure, and every day it came out a little different, with new complexities. In a life without sex, you had to guard your few pleasures and relish them.

Noah had been told many times that he had good hands, the highest compliment for a young scientist but revealing the paradox of the career, for the further you go in biology, the less time you spend doing experiments with your own hands. He was already thirty-one and had been doing this job for three years.

"Smell," he said, holding the grinder up to Owens' face.

"Good," Owens conceded.

Kaskie began his measurements for the oatmeal. But Kaskie was never completely Kaskie with Owens there. He was a Kaskie minus or a Kaskie added to. Possibly because Owens had the air he often carried of being either in a hurry or bored or not particularly happy doing what it was you were causing him to do, Noah, who'd made this same breakfast every morning for six months, now dutifully read the instructions on the side of the tin. They called for salt, which he never used, but he grabbed some sodium chloride and added it. He made the oatmeal on a burner and heated up maple syrup over another flame, putting the whole glass jar in boiling water. In his own way he was hospitable. He had two mugs, which he used when alone for oatmeal and coffee, and so, with Owens here, he would serve oatmeal first, wash the mugs, and then make coffee.

Noah believed he'd discovered the breakfast he would eat for the rest of his life and serve his wife and children, when he had them.

When he served the cereal at last, after stirring the dented pot for half an hour, Owens flustered him by refusing maple syrup. The whole secret of Noah's oatmeal depended upon hot maple syrup.

Owens took a bit of the oatmeal on the end of his spoon, closed his mouth around it, testing. "This is very salty," he concluded. His eyebrows formed the broken line they often made in judgment. He was a man used to judging.

Probably he judged in bed, Noah thought, moving a-jitter in his mistake, realizing at that moment that the combination of salt and hot maple syrup was noxious.

"I've got an idea," Owens said, setting his mug down on the counter. "Let's walk to Café Pantheon." For Owens, walking formed a necessary element of conversation between friends. He liked seeing the land, smelling it, appreciating trees. The other kind of talking, across a table, sitting down, with its inherent filterings and concentration—that to him was business, and it was impossible not to negotiate, to somehow want to get more. He understood this, so with his friends often suggested an activity to put him in motion. Owens was tall, long-legged, and his pace exceeded most people's. But he and Noah in his chair were evenly matched.

"I'll take you out for some breakfast." Owens' voice lowered, kind but authoritative. He seldom restrained himself from clearly stating his desire, regardless of its intensity. In his life, he hadn't seen many reasons to defer. And it was probably a pleasure, however minor, to convince others to follow his whims.

On the way out, Noah stopped to give instructions to the young Dane. They were not yet trying to find the gene that caused their mutant but were still tracing the signals to find the tissue next door. Louise would do an in situ hybridization, with fish that had no eyes, if she wasn't too busy with her damn flies. The amount of DNA from the four-hour-old embryo was so small it would have to be amplified, using a procedure called PCR.

PCR changed the world, Noah thought.

Outside, they had to pass a row of animal rights protesters. "Did *you* get the polio vaccine?" Noah shouted, a taunt particularly jarring, he noticed, for the dumber ones, whose eyes flickered as they wondered if *he* had polio. Oops, he just remembered that Owens' girlfriend, Olivia, was involved with animal rights now, something to do with Latin American parrots.

"Hey, why don't you ever get any *women* biologists from Denmark in your lab?" Owens asked. Because he was seldom outside at this time of day, he associated morning hours outdoors with love. In the first few months with Olivia, he'd snuck away from the office for picnic lunches in the hills. Not many CEOs of Fortune 500 companies, he thought, made love on the ground before noon.

There was a particular smell of bark the ground released when, later, it was going to be hot. Owens walked through the fields of palm and live oak in the hiking boots he'd been wearing whenever he wasn't in a suit for the last five years. Kaskie wondered how he kept them clean. A strange thing they had in common. One thing about a chair: shoes stay new.

"Or do you know any French female scientists? Sort of like Madame Curie?"

"I haven't met many Marie Curies."

"Have you ever seen a picture of her? Oh, Kaskie—God, she was beautiful." Owens' voice had reverence and heartbreak, as if he was talking about a whole era of life from which he would be forever excluded: mothers seen from outside windows, bending down over tables, cleaning for love. "You've got to see her. I'll show you a picture."

"Not my type." Noah smiled. It was like Owens to want to show you things. This impulse led to some graces. He was always willing to see a movie again, if he could introduce you to it. As Owens often told the same stories without remembering, Noah thought it was interesting that his opinions didn't change. But he and Owens never agreed on women. Except Olivia, who, as luck would have it, happened to be Owens' girlfriend, since Owens had the corner on luck.

"Well, Olivia's pretty pretty," Noah said.

Owens sighed. "I wish she'd *do* something with her life."

Though Olivia was undeniably beautiful, Noah tried not to envy Owens. He'd known her for years and secretly believed she wasn't that smart. This didn't prevent him from being half in love with her. It was distinctly possible to be in love with a woman and also find her faintly stupid. But it enchanted him that Owens would choose Olivia and then expect her to have some sort of heroic career. Even among friends as close as Noah and Owens, it was important that each man be able secretly to prefer his own life. This small and unacknowledged snobbery allowed Noah to flatter his friend, trying to make it easier for Owens to bear the life Noah himself would not truly want.

"I just don't know if, in the end, Olivia's really smart enough."

"Smart enough for what?" Noah asked, privately agreeing.

"You know how sometimes you're with someone and stay up all night talking? Well, we never do that." Owens shook his head.

Noah was celibate, though he would have been disturbed to hear himself described as such. His condition, in all its aspects, embarrassed him, and while he relished and craved intricate discussions of love, he became vague and abstract about his own circumstances.

Years ago, in college, a girl sat on his lap at a party. She'd ridden with him later on the uneven sidewalks and they'd kissed. Their kissing seemed important to him, as if she were lifting a curtain he always had assumed was the real world and shown him something behind, a secret party where others were already laughing and sighing, even the trees. It seemed for this once easy, as if all he had to do was relax. She kept telling him he had a beautiful face. Like a fat person, Noah thought. "She has such a pretty, pretty face," his mother and sister were always saying of fat women. It was very late when he finally stopped at the girl's dorm and she jumped off his lap and sprinted inside. She was beautiful running. There were more nights, less than a dozen in all, and Noah remembered each in preserved detail. But she'd told him the first night she thought she might be gay. He'd seen her afterwards, riding on a bicycle seat holding the waist of a taller girl, who stood pedaling.

Noah still thought about this girl often, but he didn't mention her. It had ended so long ago, and anyway, not much had happened.

Noah didn't think it was impossible that he'd find love. In fact, he usually felt in love with someone. He needed to think of a woman in order to fall asleep at night. And to work as hard as he did. He told himself if he worked hard enough, work would win him love. He had a hunch that the woman who could love him would not be like Olivia. More the pretty-for-a-smart-girl type. She herself would look down, in a slight way, on women like Olivia. And, as if in deference to his future wife, Noah adopted this mild prejudice. Certain women did go for him, like the X-ray crystallographer upstairs. Rachel was motherly, and he could picture her large body in an apron even though she knew more about hydrogen bonds than anyone in the world. "I'll marry you in five years," she'd joked, "if you don't find anyone else." He was intimidated by her size.

"So tell me what you're doing in the lab."

Owens asked this same question at least once a month, too short a time for much to change. And these broad questions reminded Noah of his parents' friends, who knew nothing about science, or of certain girls who assumed everything to do with laboratories was evil. "I told you about progenitor cells?"

"Mmhmm." Owens had the uncertain air of someone who didn't really remember.

But then, as Noah talked about cell fate, he remembered the article he'd read the night before in *Nature,* and his own excitement took over. In a bracing way, he was in a race with opponents who were also his friends—one lab in Seattle, another had just moved to New York, and he'd heard that Manloe in Copenhagen had begun using zebra fish. But he was late. As a postdoc, he'd discovered a great, promising mutation, fish that learned things and then forgot them, which got him grant money and the job here. Now, halfway to tenure review, he still hadn't found the gene. And he'd let Louise, one of his postdocs, talk him into studying the mutation in drosophila, fruit flies, when she'd noticed something in the footnotes of a Caltech paper. The things were supposed to be in bottles all the time, in the one closet he'd allotted her, yet they were constantly in his hair.

Owens walked with his hands in his pockets, head bent down. He seemed chastised, as if he were ashamed and a little sorry for his own life. He was also, of course, a multimillionaire. Even science couldn't intimidate him for long.

Noah was in the middle of saying that surfaces of all cells were extremely polymorphic and that the major histocompatibility complex proteins explained how the cell recognized the difference between self and other, a recognition that thrilled him.

Owens interrupted. "What's your ultimate objective?"

That stopped Noah, for a moment. Owens, it occurred to him, thought like the people who wrote the essay questions for college applications. But then he blurted, "To see how it all works. To figure out how a heart cell knows to be that and not something in the foot."

"Aren't you interested in sequencing the human genome?" Owens asked this question, too, every time they were together.

Noah flipped his wrist. "I personally don't want to. Even if you know the structure, you don't know how it folds, what it does. It's too slow for me. It took Rachel seven years to get the structure of her protein. You met my friend Rachel. Rachel's famous now. Her enzyme's on the cover of a textbook." Noah rubbed this in because Owens had once pestered him for a month, wanting to meet the female scientist upstairs. When Noah finally capitulated, Owens had reported back: "I could never fall in love with someone like her." Noah had found himself babbling, "I think she has a really pretty face."

"If I were a biologist," Owens said, "that'd be what I'd want to do. I'd want to sequence the genome."

The two men were odd friends for each other. They both had known Frank. Noah had gone to graduate school with him. Then Frank left academics and started Genesis with Owens, but eventually he left that too. When Owens let himself think about it, which he only rarely did, he felt keenly, and with a flat acceptance, this loss of Frank. The day-to-day quality of his life was lower and there was nothing he could do about it. It troubled him that Frank belonged to a world he'd chosen over theirs. Most people Owens knew worked for Genesis and were, in one way or another, being paid by him. Noah understood that Owens had intended for a long time to make him one of those people and perhaps today he planned to close the deal.

They walked through the university square, its sandstone arches copied from a four-hundred-year-old mosque in Egypt. Frank and Noah had been graduate students here, partners. Owens stood solemnly, looking over the pavilions, as if he had a problem he couldn't fully articulate. In the last five years, he had found himself in the odd circumstance of luck. Everything he touched turned to money. Noah had some inkling of what that would be like: for a while, four years back, his experiments were working. Owens probably experienced the strange apperception of momentum and the courage that came from it; his trajectory was going up and up, and if he multiplied the stakes he could only multiply the gains. Before, he'd been poor— so poor, Frank said, that his currency was not cash but apples. At first his prosperity must have been exhilarating. But the more he experimented, the more he proved himself invincible. Nine hundred people worked under him now, maybe a thousand, including men he considered his best friends and, from what he said, women he'd slept with. People always warned that in science, after you've made a great discovery, it's almost impossible to think the way you did before. And of course nobody believes it's luck when luck happens to them.

"Last night," Owens said, "I stayed at work late, tinkering. I shouted 'Yoo-hoo!' when I went to the refrigerator, but I was the only one left. There were a few cars in the parking lot and I didn't recognize any of them."

Noah pictured Owens standing in the dark, posh conference room, looking out. Across the road, horses stood blank in the night wind.

"So after a while I called Theo; he's one of the old team. And he said, 'We have some people over. Marcia's just serving the salmon steaks.' And I said, 'Oh, okay, I was just running these tests and I thought you might like to do them with me.' "

Noah knew that Owens didn't like to eat fish, but the way he said "salmon steaks" seemed festive, like a waterfront restaurant with paper lanterns in a country that's not your own.

"And Theo burst in ten minutes later, all red-faced, in a zip-up jacket. I told him jokes to try to get him to lighten up."

Noah could imagine them working grimly together.

"Theo and I used to be really good friends."

Owens was probably wondering whom they'd invited for the salmon steaks. Noah suspected he'd eaten artichokes for the last nine nights. When Owens craved a vegetable, he ate it every night and sometimes at lunch until the taste began to disgust him.

The last time Noah went to Owens' house, he'd seen a letter from a guy he must have fired, begging for money. In the letter on the kitchen counter, Todd detailed his obligations; he had a wife now, a mortgage, something else.

Susan and Stephen, the twenty-five-year-old couple who cooked and cleaned for him, wanted retirement benefits, Owens had told him. Even his father called to talk about Owens' sister, and she needed money too.

"So what about *your* work?" Noah asked. "How's Genesis?"

Owens looked at his friend in a way that was intended to impart meaning. He touched Noah's shoulder. Noah was lower to the ground and neither of them ever completely forgot that. "I want to talk to you about that. Let's get some coffee."

"Sometime you have to let me make you coffee." Noah had never once succeeded in getting Owens to accept his hospitality. And among his building's labs and department offices, Noah was renowned for his coffee. Two secretaries came with their own mugs and a carton of milk every afternoon. Kaskie was a man beloved by secretaries. Yesterday they'd brought biscotti from the lesbian bakery. Lesbians are good bakers; why is that? A womanish thing. He remembered the girl on the bike, head on her friend's back.

Owens stopped in front of the old Alta church. Cool air veiled out of the open door. "I'd like to get married here someday," he said, although he'd never attended a service. It waited, orderly and still, the pews symmetrical, the altar plain, evenly patched light from the windows the only ornament. "At five or six o'clock on a summer evening." Suddenly, he turned to his friend. "Where do you think you'll get married?"

"Oh, I don't know. Justice of the peace, probably."

"I can imagine meeting a woman and being married in a month, if I really knew." Owens was always talking about love as if Olivia factored nowhere in it. It was Noah's part to remind him of her existence. The name was met with a sigh.

"You know, one of my considerations is, I have to think: what would Olivia be like as a First Lady? And I'd have to say the answer is: not great."

Noah doubted very much that his friend would marry anytime soon.

Once, the girl in college had said she loved him. He asked her if she'd said that before, and she'd laughed softly. "Yeah, a lot," she admitted. And it had ended after only a few weeks. Even when she'd been with him, Kaskie felt amazed, incredulous, that someone so exquisite could love him. He had never gotten used to it. Maybe she didn't, he realized now, maybe she only said so.

The two men followed the soft, palm-lined road that led to Alta's small downtown. They passed the old movie house, which had been restored by the heir of the Valley Electronics Company; it was shiny and polished, with an outsized marquee. Then they were at the Pantheon, which had great coffee made with Italian machines but a manager who didn't like Owens. He had once tried to bring in a bagel and they'd had a loud altercation, with Owens lowering his voice for the final, gentle statement: "Probably it'd be a lot better for business if someone else had your job, somebody with a very different approach." At that time, Owens was already a local celebrity, and a number of customers clapped. The manager had never been popular because he chased out young girls on roller skates when they came to buy their ices after school.

But this morning, teenagers worked the counter and quiet organ music shelved down from speakers on the ceiling. The coffee was served in thick brown cups.

"So I have something to talk to you about," Owens said. "I think we found a neurotrophin that can regenerate brains. We're in monkey trials now. Parkinson's isn't going anywhere." He shrugged. "Unless we make it. I'd like you to come work with us."

This wasn't the first time he'd offered Noah a job. Noah had no plans of accepting, but he was still glad to be asked. He let Owens go on until a salary was named.

"Whoa, don't tempt me. Listen, I really appreciate it, but I like what I'm doing."

"See, in a couple years, we'd give you a new building and you'd have your own team and you could revolutionize biology. You could leapfrog ten years ahead of all these academic guys."

"I don't think so, Owens." But this talk disturbed Noah. Could industry do all that? He'd always believed the majority of science was hands, experiments, one by one, deciding what needed to go next in the chain. Making discoveries, not using them. After all, Genesis didn't find LCSF. Somebody else did and they took it, figured out how to make it in a recombinant form. They put the gene into bacteria. Industry was always, in the end, about products. Drugs maybe, but never cures. Of course, he might be wrong.

Owens told him about meetings they'd had to discuss how to accommodate him. The salesmanship thrilled Owens a little. Owens liked to overcome objections—this was the game of what he did. But even he seemed strangely reluctant to close the deal he'd spent years idly musing over and the last three days fine-tuning. "So I really can't recruit you, huh?"

"Nope. Not today anyway." Noah lifted his cup with both hands.

Owens sighed. "Well, let me try one more thing. Because I've always had the feeling that we'd be working together someday. And a couple of changes are happening right now. One is that Genesis is going public. Our finances will be subject to review, and we'll have a board of directors, shareholders, all this stuff we don't have now. And so I'm offering you a one-million-dollar bonus for coming on board. But that's a onetime offer. I won't be able to make it again. And, as you know, Genesis has grown a lot and I'm taking a team of the best guys and we're going to go off to a new building to work on our neurotrophin. And you could be part of that."

Noah pulled at his fingers, miserable all of a sudden. A million dollars. Like a trick: either way, he lost. He thought of the immunologist they called Lydgate up at the medical school, who was always frantic because his wife craved mission furniture. He again felt a sensation he'd had two times before in his life, when he'd thought it was possible he would die: the headachy pain of an overwhelming embarrassment, to be leaving such a mess. His zebra fish, his drosophila, his data, his papers—none of it was far enough along to hand on to another person, to survive without him. Then, in a clearing, he remembered a story Louise had told one night in the lab. Her mother had been engaged to a banker. "If you marry him," her father had said, "you'll have an affair with me; but if you marry me, you won't have an affair with him."

"No, I can't," Noah said.

"You're sure?" Owens tilted his head.

Noah nodded.

Owens looked around at various points of the large room, running his palms over his jeans. "Want another coffee?" he asked abruptly. He blinked, no doubt startled at the rare bluff of rejection, but still, he was glad to have Kaskie in the lab. If he'd said yes, a part of Owens would have wished he hadn't.

Noah understood that his friend loved the lab the way he loved the tiny rental cottage, overgrown with roses, where Olivia lived before she moved in with him. There was too little innocence in Owens' life.

Noah tried to restrict himself to one cup of coffee in the morning and another in the afternoon, but he accepted anyway. It wasn't every day he turned down a million dollars.

Owens sat up slightly to pull out his wallet from his back pocket. It was battered leather, bought from a street vendor, that had shined up like a chestnut. Noah reached for his, patting all four pockets. Damn. He wanted to pay. Though Owens had already offered, he always seemed reassured if you paid. It was as if his money had given him a paternity he'd never asked for and that caused him sorrow. But Kaskie had no cash. He didn't like to carry much because when he did, he spent it. Still, the guy hadn't called. How was Noah supposed to know? Was he supposed to carry a twenty in case Owens deigned to drop by and pronounce his oatmeal too salty?

But instead of money, Owens slid out a school-sized picture of a little girl from his wallet. "Do you think she looks like me?"

Noah studied the small photograph. "No, I don't think so. Why?"

"Yeah, I don't either," Owens said, slipping the picture back. He sipped his coffee and held the cup midair, perhaps trying to experience what other people must know as leisure. "It's one of the prices I pay for my life. This woman tried to say she was my kid." As he extracted two bills, Kaskie began to stammer, but Owens raised a hand. "Recruitment effort."

When they left, a girl in an apron ran out after him. "Your change!"

"Oh, no, that's for you. It's a tip. Please tell the manager it's such a pleasure when he's not around."

The girl's face complicated, biting down the grin.

"Hey, seriously, why do you think it's only the young European men who work in your labs? Why don't the young French women and the young Swedish women come?"

Noah shrugged. "A lot of Europeans don't like it here. Most of them stay just for science. That guy you talked to, he sees nothing America has contributed outside of the bomb."

"What about the automobile?"

"Or corn, potatoes, tomatoes, I'm always telling him." Noah's mother was the rare American Jew who'd grown up on a farm. There were pastoral pictures of her posing among rows of cabbages.

"Electricity. The telephone. The personal computer. How about the movie camera?"

"Linus Pauling. The alpha helix."

"George Eastman, Thomas Edison, Alexander Graham Bell, Land and all of Polaroid. Robert Goddard. Rockets. The polio vaccine!"

"The Wright Brothers. Jazz."

"Commercial penicillin."

"I thought that was England."

"We made it usable, during the war. The Brits discovered it but they couldn't make it. What was it some guy said? I think it was, 'This mold is an opera singer.' No, Tishler did it at Merck. He grew it and then he refused to patent it. He always used to say if we discovered a cure for cancer, he wouldn't patent it."

They were still chanting America's contributions when they returned to Kaskie's lab.

"*What* are you talking about?" Louise asked. She was his best postdoc, the most talented and exacting, but she made him nervous. He could usually count on his students to look at him with admiration. But not her. Also, she always wore black clothes, not the usual denim and tee shirts you saw in labs.

When Noah explained, she exploded in harsh laughter. "You've missed the most important one," she said. "Of this century, at least."

"What?"

She snorted. "The pill, of course."

Score one for industry. It made its creators millionaires.

He thought of Louise's parents again. They might have married for love, but they were hardly a glamorous couple now. They'd probably been together thirty, forty years. Her father worked as a postman and walked with a prosthetic shoe.

A Chain Letter

--+- -+- -+- -+- -+-

Owens sat with his feet up on the desk, listening to the girl on the telephone. Her voice was young and impressionable, but she carried a conversation well, not like Olivia.

"To be perfectly frank," she was saying. She then went on to chat about things that didn't require any frankness. She mentioned her aversion to tablecloths that matched the wallpaper and to napkins folded like swans.

"Swans, really?" he said. "I didn't notice."

They were gossiping about the people who had introduced them, the week before. Their hosts had felt honored to have Owens and pleased that Mrs. Maguire brought her daughter Albertine, who seemed to amuse him. They'd gone to great pains over the dinner party. Next to each place card, a bud vase held miniature roses. Owens and Albertine had been happy enough to eat the careful food and sip the wine, and now they were disparaging their hosts. That is the way of the social world and, especially, of flirtation. Owens enjoyed the teasing ardors of his search for Albertine, which involved waking their hostess at midnight and obliging her to climb downstairs to find her book. He'd written Albertine's phone number on the sole of his shoe, to avoid detection. In the past, he'd written girls' numbers on his skin.

Albertine, though certainly not deaf and blind to her hostess's weaknesses, not the least of which she considered to be her face, had nevertheless written her an effusive card. She had been brought up knowing how to secure the next invitation.

Owens did nothing of the sort and in fact planned never to see those people again. "She's just not very interesting," he concluded.

Albertine shuddered with laughter, exhilarated by his lack of social fear. He didn't seem to believe that people could harm him. She lived inside nets and nets of obligation.

She wanted to be a journalist, this Albertine, as she explained from her intern's cubicle at the city desk of the newspaper. In three weeks, Owens learned, she would return to her East Coast hotsy-totsy college, a senior maybe—uh-oh, no, a sophomore.

Outside his office, a row of visible heads, like men in a subway train, gave the impression of passive waitfulness. It would make a good photograph, through this ridged glass. As it was, they seemed almost black and white. There was something eternal in their posture.

"To be frank, I don't *like* the idea of a chain letter," Albertine said. "And you're supposed to send it to ten friends? *Ten*—who has the time?"

"Oh, I'm definitely not answering this thing," Owens said, putting the sheet of paper in his out box, so as never to see it again.

Her laughter was froth, his a lower bell. They lolled. None of what they said mattered much. He knew he had time, the way a soloist knows when he can draw his notes out very long and every soul in the house will gasp when his bow leaves the strings.

"Well, I guess I should go," he said at last, after a long sighing pause that might have meant they'd run out of things to say. A soloist also knows there is a point beyond which he cannot attenuate poignancy. "There's a bunch of guys here who want to see me."

"Really. Who?"

"Oh, one's from *Newsweek,* one's from *Time,* I think there's a guy here from the *Wall Street Journal,* yeah, there he is. And the *New York Times* is here . . . ay-and the *Washington Post.* "

She laughed. There was something good-girl small about her that he liked. She was probably thinking, Well, to be perfectly frank, I wouldn't chat away if the *New York Times* were waiting for *me.*

But that's what makes you so cute, he mused. They never would be. For me they often wait, and this isn't the unmixed blessing you think, Pretty Hair.

The men filed in eagerly, as if instantly awakened to feed.

He'd woken before dawn in the dilapidated mansion, breeze from a broken window cooling his night-sweat skin. Downstairs, he banged on oatmeal. He'd started eating oatmeal every morning with maple syrup. By now he thought of this as his idea. Then he put on the new suit he felt old in. Guys from the bank had told him where to buy it. Slowly he was gleaning names for things. At first the prices shocked him. But he wasn't going to dress like this every day. He thought of himself as a guy in jeans, barefoot in the boardroom. Out on his terrace, where dandelions cracked tile, gummy on his feet, the moon hung over the sharp edges of the mountains. Insubstantial clouds traced by. Being up early felt good; it reminded him of just coming home from the night shift.

Last night, he'd made sure to get gas. *When you need something absolutely, do it yourself:* his father had taught him that without words. Owens was the only one on the wide road. He could drive fast well. This was a small and daily satisfaction.

He was the first person in the office. He stood in the conference room, at the long window, drinking fresh carrot juice from a carton. It was easy to be patient waiting for light. As his life became easy and cluttered with luck, he thought more about before. Frank would be here today. They had to be at their phones when the stock market opened on the other side of the country. Someday that would change. New York was old and breaking; this would be the center, eventually, soon. Civilization on earth was always organized around oceans.

Once it had been the Aegean, then the Mediterranean, and then, for a long time, the Atlantic. But the Pacific epoch had begun. He had decided to stay put, and now it was all coming here to him. Many times in his life already, Tom Owens thought that he'd moved the very capital of America from East to West, because he couldn't bear to leave home. He'd tried once, at Harvard. He hadn't liked it much.

So they'd moved the center to where they lived and remade business in the jeans and tee shirts he'd always worn. "Oh, well, why not the West," Frank once said.

Owens liked being the first one up. Being awake at a time he usually slept made things feel important. The parking lot in the dark looked black and clean, like the playing board of a game.

Money people from the city would be coming down soon. It'd been an uncharacteristic decision to hire the white-shoe firm, but each group was enamored of the other. Especially *them*. Owens had already received six résumés from their ranks.

Light began softly, furring the far hill, and the sky separated, streaked. How far it would go, he couldn't tell yet. For once, he wanted to keep still.

He could see their excitement, bringing him his news; it was pushing their faces into odd shapes. This made him serene.

Many times throughout the day, Owens thought in a detached way about his future and contemplated taking a wife. Though he didn't know who she would be, he imagined her face cool and smooth. He hoped too that she would be a person of talent and accomplishment, an idealistic doctor maybe, or a poet. There would be things she understood, gracious vistas, that he didn't pay enough attention to, and he would follow her slender form down clean corridors. He was almost certain she was no one he knew now. For as long as he could remember, there had been a thread of futility in his feelings for Olivia, which lent their time together an air of poignance or even tragedy.

He thought of Mary di Natali, whom he could hardly remember really knowing. Some people—Frank, for one—believed he should feel some kind of attachment, because she loved him before. She certainly felt that this should be the case.

On a pad of paper, Owens wrote: *For the Next 100 Years.* He wanted Genesis to be self-sustaining into the next century and he wanted the freedom to leave it. He made a note to call the Trappist monastery to book a company retreat.

Years ago, when he'd first gone East, he'd felt the enchantment of Washington. He didn't want to be running a business all his life, the daily totals landing on his desk. He imagined living in Italy for a year. Or maybe in a cabin, high in the Sierra Nevada.

They kept coming to him, their faces stranger and stranger shapes, stretched. Looking at him for reaction, they were amazed to see the detachment in his eyes. Each new number fell. Nothing really surprised him, but finally, at the end of the day, the six goons he'd started with burst into his office, locking the door, and then Frank rolled on the carpet, pulling on Owens' sock, crying and giggling—*can you believe it, we did it, you did, can you believe what you did!*—and it was their imperfect faces, the irregular diamonds, the same but red-rumpled, that finally stirred him to smile.

"Politics are for a moment, an equation is for eternity." This quote was taped to Noah's word processor, under a fortune that said, *You need an extraordinary amount of sleep.*

Since his conversation with Owens, Noah had not slept. He felt nagged in a slight persistent way, like the pull of wrong-fitting clothes. Before, his daily life had not involved many choices, and Noah functioned well that way. He'd come from a modestly passionate family, full of jagged skids and desperate apology, whose greatest legacy to him was the permanent extraction of his capacity for boredom. During his parents' noisy youth, he and his sister had often ended up on his grandfather's alfalfa farm, where they were given chicken and mashed potatoes every night for supper. In Noah, the repetition only instilled a craving for that very same meal. For his sister it was absolutely the opposite.

But since Owens' offer, Noah found himself wondering just how good a scientist he really was. Sunday night, he'd ridden around Alta, on the wide-sidewalked streets where department chairmen lived or the guys who'd started companies. He had the spare time. A lot of what he did every day was think. At the lab, it was easy to forget these houses and the people living in them, who were not much older than he was. Scientists and grad students and postdocs all shared a snobbery about the ones who left. But now he wondered how deep that prejudice really was, how ideological. Maybe the Owenses of the world were this century's Niels Bohrs or Galileos. Didn't Pasteur discover microbes while consulting for the French wine industry?

But the chairman of Noah's department, who lived the conference life of accountable pleasures, did his real work years ago. He still regaled the incoming grad students with forty-year-old phage lore.

The treed streets were quiet; vehicles of family life lay strewn on lawns: the fallen bike, the triangular device recently invented so women could jog and push along their babies. Noah had never ruled out such pleasures for himself. Pleasure—well, life, he supposed—was going to come later, as reward. The only time he hadn't lived like that was with the girl who'd ridden on his chair in college. During those rare weeks, his ambition had evaporated. She'd stepped out of nowhere, perhaps too early in his life. He would have done anything to keep her.

Most of the lots in Alta had remained the same size since the time of the founders, but in the last decade some of the original houses had been torn down to build bigger ones, as the valley had grown affluent. Even though Noah grew up here, now he couldn't afford it. He lived in Auburn, the next town west. Noah liked the smaller houses, the old wood and adobe. He had no idea of prices, but if he went to work for Genesis, he could buy one. Two, even. He could buy his parents a house. They could enter this tranquillity. His parents had always rented. For twenty years, they'd been afraid of the landlord, even though his father had probably put a thousand dollars into the ground. His father still worked at the job he'd always hated: insurance.

Doubts nagged Noah at the lab too. The same tasks that had contained ample excitement a week earlier changed under the weight of their price. Making this library, of the embryo at six hours old, had cost him a million dollars. And was it something so special, that only he could do? Well, no. This wasn't. Louise could map out genes better than anyone he knew. But what was, exactly? What specifically was it that needed his alleged talent?

Noah segregated his day into what was creative, requiring thought and choice and even imagination, and what was just benchwork. A year before or a year later, Noah would have pronounced such a separation impossible; his mind seemed to require the calm performance of precise manual tasks to generate ideas, as if they were born out of the beginnings of boredom. But after Owens' offer, this wisdom, which he had previously expounded to a generation of students, seemed only justification for a mediocre, gutless life.

By Noah's age, Watson had already discovered the double helix and a handful of Noah's friends had mapped their own proteins. A lot of this was luck—Noah's gene didn't seem to live near any useful markers—but he still couldn't help but suspect that it was partly his own fault. He started too many things at once. In this same building, there were steady drudges, content to work for thirty years on one problem, like the structure of a complex molecule, atom by atom. Then there were what Noah called hit-and-run scientists, considered generally more imaginative but of dubious character, who jumped onto the newest compounds and then quickly tired of them, like Louise's boyfriend in the dirty black jeans, who'd just quit viruses for the nervous systems of fruit flies. Noah was neither. His early work on zebra fish had seemed brash and promising when he'd published his short article in *Cell*, but now his production seemed slow, one step forward, two steps back. Then again, Watson had pretty much retired from science; he'd been the administrator of Cold Spring Harbor as long as Noah could remember. He probably decided when to replace the awnings and reroll the tennis courts, then had to eat dinner with somebody he could get to pay for it.

Noah made the decision over and over again, but he couldn't seem to close it. Finally, his circling agitation settled on the girl. Perhaps with the money he'd be what she needed. She'd been poor and in college had worked in the dorm cafeteria. Although he hadn't talked to her in more than six years, he'd always kept track of her phone number. He finally called her at dusk, as if on a dare, though he hadn't thought out, yet, how to word it.

A woman answered. Although his impulse was to hang up, Noah swallowed and left a message. The woman gave no hint that she recognized his name.

Noah moved around the lab, housekeeping for a good hour, and she didn't call back. Samples were labeled, the microscope lens was cleaned and the fish were fed. He sat down at his desk to begin a grant application. But he couldn't concentrate.

He called Owens at work, something he rarely did, figuring someone else would answer. When it was Owens, Noah blundered, "You feel like a movie?"

"Oh, I'd love to do that, but things here are crazy for, I don't know, probably a week. I've had reporters all day. Hey, did you hear about our offering? It went through the roof. And you know how I told you we're moving to another building. So I'm packing up."

"Have you found somebody for that spot you wanted me for?"

"Yeah, we got this guy whose wife didn't want to move from Massachusetts. We flew them both out and Theo took them shopping for a house."

"So I guess I blew my chance to be a mogul."

"But you did the right thing. That's why I didn't push you harder. I was telling Olivia about it, and she'd read some article about a woman who won the Nobel Prize. I guess for thirty-five years, she stuck by her corn. So that's what we said: Kaskie's got to stick with his fish."

"Barbara McClintock," Noah mouthed. He had to hold himself still.

"We've got a really great team for Exodus, and I think we'll make something pretty amazing, but I won't be here forever. You'll be discovering the cure for cancer, probably, and I'll be in Washington, raising the cigarette tax to a dollar a pack. If that cut down smokers by ten percent, say, we'd save forty thousand lives a year. Then I'd do the same thing for alcohol."

Noah mentioned, in a choked voice, that these ideas might not be popular.

"Oh, I know. And I've got a lot more of those. Like, it's pretty clear we spend too much on the elderly. Can't you see getting up there and just saying, 'Let 'em gum it.' "

"Call," was all Noah managed to say.

Noah set water to boil for coffee, then made the rounds. He'd always liked the lab at night, after everyone hired went home. Different music came on and his students seemed closer to each other.

Once he'd set them all going, he sat at his desk with his grant application. He'd done the rote parts over the last two months; tonight he started to write his budget proposal. He was direct, unapologetic, vigorous. He stated the lab's claims and asked directly for further support. When he was finished he looked up, and an hour had passed.

It was after midnight then and he was hungry. He turned off his lamp. Only Louise, who made him uncomfortable even now, still stood at her bench, working. She was wearing her black clothes, and her earrings hung longer than her hair. She was odd but vastly valuable. Perhaps she'd sensed his reaction to her and minded it, yet decided to go about her work for her own sake and only incidentally his. In a moment of hope, he asked if she'd like to go get a burrito. She shook her head. "I'm going to stay and finish."

He wheeled to the old burrito place and sat relishing the ancient solace of tortilla, rice and beans. "Working-class food," his mother called it.

At two o'clock, the phone woke him.

"It's me," the girl said. After six years, *me*. "Is everything okay?"

"I wanted to ask you a question. But it doesn't really matter anymore. I wanted to ask you if it would've made a difference if I had more money. If I worked for a company and we could buy a house, would you ever want to try again?"

"Oh, Noey, we didn't break up over that. And that's not you. You're a scientist."

"I could be happy with other things, I think. A family."

"You'll get that, Noah. And be a scientist. It scares me you'd even think of giving it up. It's what you love."

"No it isn't." He laughed a bitter laugh he later regretted.

"You don't even realize it now, but it is. And it's going to work out for you."

"You don't know that. You don't even understand biology."

"But I know you, though."

She was doing it again. Noah felt wrapped in his life, with happiness possible, even likely.

"And you know, Noah, I've been with someone for a pretty long time now."

Waves of recrimination poured over him after he hung up. He shouldn't have called.

Years later, when Noah defended Owens beyond what his friends deemed reasonable, he was repaying him for this night. He and the girl from college had each given Noah his offered life back to his hands, with a value they recognized when he couldn't.

Okay, science, he thought the next morning, rolling to work. But if this is going to be it, then I better do a lot better.

An opened crate of French champagne lay amidst sealed boxes. Every few hours, Owens' secretary marched through, waving a new faxed clipping, and everyone gathered around the table to read what they already knew about their good fortune. Owens meant for all of this to stop. It was a problem they'd never had the first go-round: when no one's ever heard of you, you don't waste time basking in afterglow.

Eliot Hanson, the moneyman Owens had hired years earlier, picked his way through the confettied hallways, his thumbs stretching out suspenders. When Owens and Frank started Genesis, they had no formal agreement and didn't need one. But eventually, when the company grew, Owens had hired Eliot, whose strategic tip in the second year—switching operating capital into marks and yen—had allowed them to double the manufacturing budget. Owens smiled when Eliot stepped into his office. Every time Owens saw him, Eliot surprised him. Today it was the suspenders. He seemed to Owens a type, like a nerd in high school he'd never particularly thought about at all but who, he was now pleased to discover, genuinely liked his life.

Eliot smiled back. "I enjoy the atmosphere around here."

"Yeah," Owens said. "I think we're going to come up with something really great. Eliot, you've been a lawyer how long?"

"Let's see, I passed the bar in '67, when you were probably still in Little League. So twenty years." Of Eliot's six clients, Owens was the youngest and also the most unsettled. Eliot maintained that he kept his practice small in order to devote himself assiduously to the particulars of each financial portfolio, but he liked to think of himself as doing more for his clients than that.

"And you've probably seen a lot of strange problems in that time," Owens said. "I know with doctors there's a pledge of confidentiality. Do lawyers have something like that?"

"Absolutely. There's no Hippocratic oath, but there are very definite codes of client confidentiality that come into play, especially in criminal cases."

"Well, I have a little . . . I don't know if you'd call it a problem. It's definitely not criminal."

"Good, I'm glad to hear that. That I don't do anymore."

Owens looked at Eliot quizzically. For all Owens' brilliance, Eliot remembered, he was surprisingly slow to get a joke.

"But it's a matter that would require total confidentiality."

Eliot lifted his right hand. "Absolutely."

"Well, as you may or may not know, my biological mother died when I was born," Owens began, his fingertips gently touching those of the other hand. "My father married my mother when I was eight months old. They'd known each other before. They went to the same high school. But I called you this morning because—and I know this doesn't exactly make sense—I'd like to have a picture of my biological mother. I always thought it was a little strange that nobody in her family ever met me. But if my parents ever found out I was doing this, I think they'd be pretty upset."

"I understand. Now, what do you know about her?"

Owens had learned a few stray facts from his father. "I guess she was this rich girl. She went to the private academy outside Auburn. My dad was the grounds guy there. That's how they met." Her father had been something exotic. His father remembered it being Jewish, but sometimes he thought it was Arab. "From over in that part of the world anyway," Nora always said in the end. They thought that was probably where he got his looks.

"I have my birth certificate. You know, it's a strange thing. I've had that one piece of paper since high school. Sometimes I'll lose it for a month or a year, but I always know I'll eventually find it again." He opened the top drawer of his new desk. "And here it is."

They stood staring at the document, which meant so much and said so little.

Boy Owens, it said. "I guess with her so sick, they didn't have time to name me."

"Do you have a copy of this?"

"Nope. Never made one." Owens gave it to Eliot. "You take it. I'll get it from you again sometime."

When he was younger, Eliot had thought about going back to school in another field. He'd considered the ministry, but meeting Hazel had effectively sapped his desire for religious life. Occasionally, he'd thought of psychology, but he had long ago adjusted his vision to the confines of his work. And by now he was firmly convinced that he could do more good from where he sat as a financial manager than he ever could in forty-five-minute sessions behind a couch. He believed that a man's money and his relationship to it ran to the core of his life, and he attempted, through gentle manipulation of fiscal portfolios, to act as both doctor and priest, and to improve not only the value of his clients' net worth but also the quality of their years on the earth and perhaps even the condition of their souls. Though a conservative man by nature, he was given to flights of feeling. He tried to protect his clients' money, yet sometimes also to spend it, to adjust the balance of power and happiness in their lives. Owens was a young man Eliot Hanson worried over, on several accounts. In an extremely quick calculation, Eliot decided that Owens was a youth particularly devoid of maternal imprints. Whether a latter-day history would help him was of course less than certain, but in any event, Eliot couldn't see how it would hurt. He vowed to himself now that he would find out about Owens' mother, whatever it took.

"I'll do what I can," he said, standing.

"Um, you know, I'll pay you for this myself," Owens whispered, fingertips in jeans pockets, "Not through Genesis."

"Don't worry," Eliot mumbled, also embarrassed by the introduction of money to this rare intimate conversation.

Owens immediately sat back down and busied himself with papers from his in box. He opened one stray envelope, typewritten with his name and address, and found only a worn five-dollar bill inside. He shook the envelope, with a bas-relief of his name on its interior, an actual hole made by the period of "Mr." What's this? he wondered, turning the empty envelope over and finding no return address. Then he thought he'd maybe lent it to somebody. This warmed him: the commonness of having a small loan repaid. He slid up to get his wallet from his back pocket, slipped the bill inside and patted it with satisfaction.

The recent statement Eliot Hanson left, chronicling a bond transfer that resulted in a profit to Owens of over a million times this amount, elicited no such response.

Van Castle

-<+-<+-<+-<+-<+

Owens began receiving envelopes with no return address and no letter inside: only five-dollar bills. Some seemed new, others came creased like very old, hardworking hands. One evening, he collected a pile and absentmindedly distributed them in the cubbyholes that served as mailboxes. But like something thrown away that keeps bobbing back, he found a new batch in his next morning's mail. "What is this, some kind of joke?"

By now he realized the error of his original explanation. The memory of that mistaken satisfaction had an unpleasant aftertaste.

Then he buzzed his secretary, Kathleen, the answer to all questions, and she told him that Kaskie's van had come in. "Do you want to pick it up yourself?"

"Nah, I think it'd be nice if he went to get it," Owens said. "Did we pay for that already? Better call Eliot."

For as long as Owens could remember, he'd seen Noah Kaskie around Alta, but it was years before he learned his name. There weren't many wheelchairs when Owens was growing up, and this kid had long blond ringlets.

And everyone in Alta passed the public garden, where a man worked every Saturday and Sunday; his son, with the wheelchair parked by the gate, crawled around on the ground, digging. People brought their seedlings, clippings, bare-root roses and fruit trees, or dropped coins into a tin can attached to the fence. Owens heard that the father experimented with hybrids in his garage and made new flowers. He was the first man in Santa Clara County to create a pink-fruited orange and a persimmon with no bite.

Owens wished he knew them. He and his father often drove into Alta and walked past the garden Saturday mornings, but he stayed close to his father's long legs. The kid crawling on the ground was an Alta kid. He yelled up easily at other people. Owens thought he'd heard that the kid was an artist, but a few years later the Alta *Sentinel* ran a picture of Noah in his wheelchair: "Winner of Elks Science Scholarship." So the kid turned out to be a scientist; Owens thought that fit even better. By then, Owens had met an industrial organic chemist, who traveled the world with petri dishes in his back pocket to pick up stray samples of dirt to screen for microbes. A thin, frowning man, he paced his small living room every night and danced with his young daughters to requiems.

The evening Owens finally met Noah Kaskie, they talked for an hour. Perhaps it was inevitable that they meet and when they did, it happened to be on a hilltop. Neither man appeared anywhere in Alta anonymously; each was always preceded by his reputation. Worth millions, that guy who started Genesis. The one in the wheelchair, he's some kind of genius. Neither man's name came up in conversation without a lowered voice, and to their faces, people strenuously avoided the topics most attached to them in their absence. For each man, there was the hope that no one really noticed and the endless suspicion that everyone did.

In his wheelchair, Noah still had long blond ringlets. Owens imagined his face was what women might find noble. His chest and arms were average, but it was as if the strength drained as it went down his body; his legs were much smaller than his arms, and Owens couldn't tell if they were straight or shriveled.

"So what's your life like?" Owens said, staring at Noah, no hint of laughter on his face.

"Guess about like yours," Noah answered.

"I always passed your garden when I was growing up. And now I know you're a great scientist. I heard about your mutation."

"Thank you," Noah said simply. Generally, it was hard for him to take compliments, although he craved them. But Owens made it easy. He shaped his praise like a small, careful package. Most people babbled on and on, making you stop them. "Is it hard having everyone know you?"

"Yeah, it is. You probably understand what that's like. I mean, I knew who you were. I knew you went to Caltech."

"In the wheelchair." Noah snorted.

"That too. People get all these insane ideas that have nothing to do with who you are. When what they know is one or two things."

"That you're rich."

"See, the word *rich* means a lot of things I'm not. I happen to have a high net worth, but most other people in that category got their money a very different way. I didn't grow up rich. I don't think like a rich person. I don't live like a rich person. It doesn't matter to me very much at all. I just feel like I've been given this resource and I've got to make sure I use it to do something good."

"I feel that too," Noah said, believing, at that moment, that he'd also been given something. Much of the time, he lived in a state of fight. Some days he stopped trying altogether and lay still on his back in the bed, contemplating the wheels' scuff marks on his apartment's white walls. But he meant what he said to Owens and felt closer to him afterwards. Owens had been present for this blare of confidence and hadn't laughed.

"Well, I admire you." Owens was in a state he rarely achieved, which he would have described as the emotion of respect. He believed that Noah was going to be a great scientist, and leave an important human record. He felt, in a way no one else would understand, that they were the same, he and this small, strangely formed young man. He wondered, suddenly, if Noah had ever had sex.

They headed down the hill to where their friends had spread out picnic blankets. Olivia walked up the trail to meet them, her hands skimming the tops of weeds. She had a look that meant: *See. I can lead to where everything is true.*

Owens lurched into her arms, tall-ly, awkward, full of intention. For a moment, he felt he was in love. She nursed his surge of feeling and looked over his shoulder at Noah, who was making his way down the trail with switchbacks.

But their friendship did not maintain its first height. Noah tended towards sarcasm, which jarred Owens, whose customary answer to "How're you doing?" was "Great."

The trouble started when Owens commissioned Noah's father to design a garden for Genesis. He wanted to give people nature to look at while they worked. Owens' childhood attraction to the Kaskie family seemed finally redeemed.

When Norbert Kaskie completed the industrial garden, it filled the lot, as promised, but all the plants seemed too small. There probably was a garden Owens could have admired. Yet these plants didn't look pretty to him. In fact, the flowers seemed too bright and orderly even for Noah. The public garden had not been built this way, all at once; Norbert Kaskie had improvised it over years and years. It depended, as did the yard of their rented house, on seeds, donations, whims and regular moving, digging up, all the things you're not supposed to do. Norbert Kaskie had been an amateur botanist all his life and never once had a gardening job for pay. This time, he'd tried to be good.

It turned out that Noah's sister was the artist, a photographer, and Owens also planned to commission a triptych from her for the conference room. Noah worked as go-between, because Michelle was currently traveling the East Coast, following the fall.

"Can she photograph things other than people?" Owens asked. "For example, if I were a photographer, I think I'd take pictures of the California landscape."

It was the "can" that got Noah, the way Owens raised his eyebrows as if he suspected some flaw in Michelle's education, about which she was, in fact, touchy.

"She could," Noah said. "It's just a matter of wanting to."

"Some of the sequoias are three thousand years old, Noah. They're the oldest living things on the planet."

"So. They don't need Michelle."

"Of course they do, because who knows how long they'll be around? Somebody'll blast them down or there could be an earthquake; anything could happen. You know what they did to the biggest one? They chopped it down to make a dance floor. Oh, and I think with what was left, they carved out a bowling alley."

"Now, *that* I'd like to see," Noah said.

"Anyway, if I were her, I'd make California landscapes."

Noah rolled off in a huff, thinking, So that's what my sister's talent is supposed to be for—a documentary record of trees.

Actually, Noah loved trees. As a child, he'd made a workbook, with labeled sketches of branches, glued-in samples of leaves, flowering seeds and bark tracings. Even then he found himself drawn to old, broken-down oaks, ancient cottonwoods, the close rather than the majestic. Noah wasn't sentimental about big redwoods. He considered refusing the project without telling his sister.

"I've got a problem with Kaskie," Owens told Olivia, in the car. "I don't think I can keep his dad's garden."

"Why? What's wrong with it?"

That night, they walked through it on the bare footpaths.

Olivia shrugged. "I kind of like it."

"But I don't think it's a question of whether you like it or I like it. I just don't think it's great. And I can't be having gardens that are kind of interesting but might be junk. I have a responsibility to the people who work here to give them something inspiring outside their windows."

Olivia laughed. "This could inspire them."

"Well, maybe somebody, but not everybody or even most people. Whereas great art, like Shakespeare or Ansel Adams, would—and I consider the best gardens to be art. I guess I'll just have to tell him."

"Does that make them better than Kafka or Schiele. Or the desert, for that matter?"

Owens had never read Kafka, and he didn't know who the other one was, but he said, "Yes, it does. There's a reason deserts are sparsely populated." He snapped his fingers. "Sissinghurst, that's the name."

"Are you going to pay him anyway?"

"That's a good question." He sighed. "I suppose so."

But as it turned out, Norbert Kaskie turned down the payment. Privately, he blamed himself. He knew he'd been unable to replicate the public garden. No more was ever said of it, and six months later the area was sodded and a volleyball net was erected.

But now Noah was receiving an extraordinary gift, out of the blue. He thought maybe it was the consolation prize for the million dollars he'd lost, though in fact the van had been ordered months earlier. Olivia believed it was her doing. She constantly nudged Owens' generosity. She understood it was essential to his vision of her that she not want bounty for herself, so she felt most animated in her fight for others' portions. Under her influence, Owens' parents received two cruise trips and her cousin Huck got a suit for his birthday. And ever since Noah's father refused payment for the garden, Olivia had been looking for some sort of compensation.

Noah was a member of Olivia's flock. In this period of his life, Owens frequently mentioned Saint Francis and Sister Clare. By the time his daughter knew him well, it was John and Jackie. But do not be too hard on him. It is why movie stars marry movie stars. Great men look to other great men because, in most cases, they cannot model themselves, in the simplest and most common way, upon their parents.

Noah was at work when he received the call from Owens' secretary.

Freckled, nice, green-eyed Kathleen,

Who comes from a state where kitchens are clean.

She had a fresh, clipped voice on the telephone, but he knew she was married. "Your van's in," she told him. "Just waiting for you to go get it."

"Promise me one thing," he remembered his grandmother saying, holding his chin in her hard fingernails. "That you'll never buy German." She'd meant a Mercedes. "You're Jewish and don't you ever forget it."

Noah had promised; it was easy. He was a seven-year-old Noah then, in a wheelchair, and he'd already had thirty-one fractures. Though his favorite toys for years had been cars, no one knew if he could ever drive.

And now Noah was getting a German custom-made van. It was Kempf, not Mercedes, but if she knew, she'd ask what Kempf was building during the war. He could have explained this, he supposed, but Owens was dumb about ethnicity. All he knew was that one of his ancestors was an Arab or a Jew, he didn't know which. He could seem vaguely charmed if a guy he was thinking of hiring or a woman he wanted to date was Lebanese, but if the guy wasn't that good or the woman wasn't that pretty, it was Lebanese Schnebanese. And Kempf made the best. Noah didn't want Everett Jennings. He'd used their chairs most of his life.

The car lot was in San Jose, and his mother drove him. When they saw the van, it was everything. "We never had a car this nice," she whispered, though the salesman had left them alone. She ran her hands down the sides. She seemed greedy, pulling lights on, gingerly searching for the brake with her pump (it braked manually). His mother appreciated fine things. Noah had to ask her if he could be alone with it.

"Do you want me to go and come back?" she offered. "We could have a sandwich."

When Noah was young, every time she bought him a new chair, they went just the two of them, without Michelle. And each chair, the first day, felt wonderful and strong, as if there'd be no more afternoons roaming Telegraph Avenue on a loaner while they waited for repairs. She wouldn't take him back to school. She gave him the day to get used to it. They always went out for crab sandwiches. He no longer had his three old chairs, but he still thought of them.

The van was deep navy blue, sleek, male, automatic. At the press of a button, a ramp drew down from the driver's floor, grip bars on both sides. Noah leveraged himself up, pushed the chair to the back. The ramp would lift automatically, but Noah decided not to use more than he needed. Little eases were the first treats on the long slide down to the bed. Brake and gears, everything was manned on top. He'd have to teach himself here, on the lot. Noah had learned to drive on his parents' old Chrysler, with metal extension bars, which was like driving while working string puppets. The last years, he'd just used buses.

Owens had ordered the van complete with every option, but Noah didn't touch the phone. He'd heard that the bills were outrageous and didn't know when the charges started; maybe when you picked it up. Noah had an underdeveloped sense of money; he thought a call from a car could cost ten dollars or a hundred. But good for an emergency, he thought.

He remembered the place where he and his mom had always gone for the sweet crab sandwiches. But he was too old for that. "I've got to get back to work," he told her.

Sometimes he had to make himself be alone.

When Noah sat high up, he clapped, *I lucked out.* He felt full with gratitude. Or maybe I deserve it, he considered, but the idea couldn't hold. Too many people deserved. He touched the leather seat, which smelled of something recently alive.

"She's all yours," the dealer said, tapping the roof.

The gas tank was full, and Noah started driving, slowly. Working the manual brakes and gas was like juggling; it required all his concentration. Noah was afraid he'd wreck the van before he even got back to the lab. He'd have to park it in the lot there. But he wanted to get used to it now, in the daylight. And there were certain places he'd never been alone. He drove all the way to an ice cream stand at the beach, where he'd once stopped with Olivia. They'd bought drumsticks and eaten them outside, peeling off the sticky paper before a white-barreled surf. He'd often wanted to return, but not enough to talk someone into driving. Whims were different when you could satisfy them without help. Yet as he sat dutifully eating, sand blew onto his drumstick, opening in his mouth like paper flowers, and all of a sudden he had to show someone. Olivia lived at Owens' house, so he got back into the van and drove there.

As he wound past rich people's land, it occurred to him that this was his first charity. He should have tried it a lot sooner. He'd always assumed that charity humbled you, as being carried weakened the body. The van was new and clean. He lurched over the road, controlling motion. It felt due him, even overdue, this power.

But elation cannot last. Getting in and out of the van meant work. He'd build up muscles, he decided, in his arms, his favorite parts. He was weak now from years in a chair with pneumatic wheels.

Owens' place was like an untended cemetery. Gates creaked and banged, loose on old hinges. It had once been the weekend estate of a copper king, who'd planted the now huge copper beeches. He'd lived hard and died in San Francisco. No one had lived here year round before; it was built to be a party house. Architecture was a joke.

And whatever Owens was, he wasn't a party. All his celebration tied to business and occurred in rented places. Once, he'd told Noah, he had nine Japanese businessmen for dinner; when they'd arrived, the couple who cooked for him had the places set, but one setting was without a chair. So the nine Japanese men sat around the table and Owens stood. Before the meal was over, one of the chairs broke and a businessman fell to the floor with a loud thud. The meeting had not gone well, Owens said. Now twelve new wooden chairs waited around the table.

Huge trees swayed like ferns, making the sounds you hear only in an abandoned place.

Sometimes gardeners worked the yard, but no one was around today. Owens' talent for hiring was nowhere apparent in his household. He always seemed to find people who took advantage, an idea that inspired new outrage in Noah because today, for the first time, someone could think that of him.

The whole yard lay dug up. They were supposed to be putting in an orchard. Trees slanted on the driveway, their roots in burlap bags. Before the Genesis garden disaster, Noah had thought of this as a job for his father.

Owens intended to plant his own garden, with two of every kind of tree. He planned to walk out in the evening and pick his vegetables for supper. But Noah just knew it was going to be a long time, years, before Owens bit into his own apple, and when that finally happened, a hundred thousand dollars from now, the apples from the A & P would taste better.

He went in the front door—they didn't lock—and wheeled through the vast, dim living room to the kitchen Owens had never fixed. A triangular piece of ceiling had rotted out. About a hundred cherry tomatoes, yellow and red and orange, spilled over the counter. Noah popped one; it tasted warm. "Olivia!" he shouted.

She was gone or asleep. If she was sleeping upstairs and couldn't hear him, there was nothing he could do. The closest this house had to an elevator was an ancient dumbwaiter. Normally you could trace Olivia from her car, an old black Bug, but it was in the shop again. Olivia worked at the Alta convalescent hospital. He'd try there.

He went out the back door. Overgrown runners for squash scored the ground, the yellow flowers limp and browned. Bees accumulated free around the berry bushes. And in the dip where the garden fell to a carrot patch, among the huge lacy tops, a child lay curled in the dirt. A girl, with matted hair and torn clothes. She was pale and thin, with a wide face and freckles spanning her nose. Noah nudged her with his wheel.

She sat up, most of her weight in her butt, like a top settling. "Are you a midget?" she asked, rubbing her eyes. She bent over, hugging her calves, hair over her face, kissing her own knee through a hole in her pants.

"How old are you?"

"Ten."

"You're ten and you don't know the difference between a midget and a man?"

"There's no difference. A midget or a dwarf is a man."

"So why ask if I'm a midget if I'm a man?"

"I'm sorry. It's just what I thought of." Her stomach growled. Noah looked over the garden. There really wasn't much to eat. "Those strawberries have snails," she added, picking at a bump on her ankle where there was a scab. Once she'd lifted it off, Noah was surprised to see her put it in her mouth. "Do you live here?"

An envelope was safety-pinned to her sleeve, *Tom Owens* penciled on it. Noah pointed at it. "He lives here, but he's not home now. What do you want him for?"

"He's my father," she said, looking down.

The picture. That child. She might be, he thought. Then he wondered if Olivia knew about this. "My name is Noah Kaskie, by the way. So where do you live?"

"Up in the mountains. I'm Jane."

Noah looked at the foothills. There were no mountains around here. "Where's your mom?"

"She's there still."

"She's still there. Then tell me something: how did you get here?"

"That's kind of a secret."

"Well, listen, he's probably at work now. He works a lot. So why don't I take you somewhere and we'll call him. We can even go get you some new clothes. You got a little dirty sleeping here."

"Okay, great," she said. "I love new clothes."

She walked with a hand light on his shoulder to the eucalyptus grove, where an old Ford truck waited like a ruin, rusty as something in a junkyard. She used her hands and a knee to shimmy onto the seat, then jumped back down with a brown grocery bag folded down at the top, like a huge lunch.

"Who drove this?"

"I did."

Noah looked at the ancient truck. He didn't believe her at all. He hardly believed the thing still ran. Then he showed her his van.

"Oh, neat," she said, when the ramp descended. "Like a drawbridge to a castle. You should call it Van Castle. And that makes you Count Van Castle."

"Listen, do you want to try calling Owens first or go get something to eat?"

For a moment, just a moment, Jane forgot her mother. Then it all came back, a dark wink. "Eat," she said.

Now Noah didn't want to see Olivia. He wanted to keep his discovery to himself.

He drove to an old soda shop where Olivia would never be. Olivia and Owens were health people. Except when it came to ethnicity. Olivia'd eat Mexican-food fat but she wouldn't touch a potato chip. Owens wouldn't get near either. You had to grant him consistency, but it made him even more of a pain in the ass. Noah ate anything, particularly anything cheap. It pleased him to buy Owens' alleged daughter a bacon cheeseburger.

Then he took her to the mall. He'd never bought a girl clothing before, and the shop was wonderful. He'd been on the boys' floor of department stores to buy his trousers. But these dresses and shoes were not miniatures. They had a whimsy all their own. Noah had had a credit card almost a year now and still not used it. Now he would. He'd applied for emergencies, but maybe this was what it was for. Borrow for happiness, not safety.

Jane skitted from outfit to outfit. Even Noah recognized the poor quality of what she had on, stretch pants muddy from washings, shoes split at the sole. He wondered about the mother. She had to be someplace nearby. But why would she hide?

He told Jane to fetch what she wanted. She brushed the sleeve of a velvet coat, picked up the price tag, then relinquished it. Then she stood staring at a dress. She wanted it but she couldn't have a dress now. Her mother hadn't let her wear dresses. Jane chose overalls that went with a shirt. "Is it too much?"

"Not at all," Noah said, relieved. "Go try it on." While Jane ran back to the mirror, he motioned the saleswoman to include the velvet coat.

Noah had wanted to stop at the grocery store in case Owens didn't come home before dinner, but they still had to climb into Van Castle and out again. He felt a fatigue coming. He wasn't used to any of this yet. He decided to take Jane to his place instead.

"We're the Van Castles," she said. "Sounds like royalty."

An hour later, she was murmuring in the bathtub while Noah called Owens. Kathleen told him he was at the plant and then had a meeting with architects.

"This is important." He wanted to tell her, but Owens was very private. "Say it's urgent, would you, Kathleen?"

He got off the phone because the girl was hollering, did he have any bubble bath, which he didn't. "How about dish soap?" Noah found a bottle under the sink and with it she conjured a spa of bubbles overflowing onto the floor.

Noah listened to her small, rising hum from the other room. He remembered being washed, sitting in the old, deep porcelain kitchen sink. Or was that because of me, the way I was? he wondered. No, he recalled his sister too, sitting up there by the window, her legs crossed at the knees. Michelle had red hair, and her legs were pink with freckles and small scars.

Jane emerged, her hair still matted in a cloud. "You didn't know that—that detergent's like bubble bath? Sure, Noah, it's just suds."

"Do you drink tea?" He didn't really know what children ate.

"Okay.".

She had tea with a box of graham crackers at his kitchen table, while he sat behind her and tried to comb her hair. A tangle eventually came out, like a burr, but she told him it hurt and he stopped trying.

"I called his office. Is he expecting you, or are you a surprise?"

"Surprise. Definitely surprise. Do you have any games?"

Games were things a person should probably have, Noah resolved right then. He had movies, though, taped from television. She picked *Peter Pan.* Noah made a batch of Jiffy Pop as the sky outside darkened. A carpet of wind swept through the house, and it began to rain. Noah gave her one of his sweatshirts and a pair of his wool socks.

Before the movie was over, she fell asleep on his bed. He covered her with a blanket and wondered about dinner. Owens wouldn't necessarily call, and it was an evening to stay in. He opened the refrigerator: he had eggs he could scramble and oatmeal. Rachel had given him a large jug of maple syrup last Christmas. He had only breakfast foods because he tended to eat supper in the lab. But she'd liked the tea. He looked out the window at Van Castle in the rain.

"What if he doesn't call?" she said in a normal voice from the other room.

"You'll stay here. Are you hungry for some supper?"

"In a little while," she said.

Jane was asleep when Owens finally called. "Hey, have you seen Olivia?"

"I haven't seen her all day," Noah whispered.

"Really? 'Cause I thought she might be with you. You know, I'm a little worried, Noah. She's not here, she wasn't at Huck's, I even called her dad. We were gonna meet for dinner, and I got to the restaurant fifteen minutes late and she'd left."

Owens made no mention of Noah's messages.

"They told me she left. I couldn't believe it."

"Owens, listen. I wasn't calling you about Olivia." Noah heard the light tap of computer keys in Owens' background. "But I went looking for her today at your place and I found a kid who says you're her father."

"Oh, no, that kid. Did you see the mother? Woman about thirty, kind of crazy."

"No woman. There's a truck in your yard, but no mother."

"Yeah, they've got a truck. That's them. And she's not my kid. I'm sure I'll hear from her mom soon and see what she wants, but I can't deal with it tonight, I've got to find Olivia. Can you just keep her there for a day or so?"

"Sure, I guess so. But why does she think she's your daughter?"

"Well, it's a long story." He sighed. "And not a very interesting one. But her mom decided I was the dad. And I had to think, if I didn't agree to be her father, she wouldn't have a father. So I help them out some."

"So she's always known you as her father?"

"She said that?"

"Yeah. Sort of."

"Do you think she looks like me?"

"I don't know. No, not really."

"I know. I don't either. Kaskie, do you have *any* idea where Olivia might be? You'd tell me the truth, wouldn't you?"

"Of course," Noah huffed. "If I hear from her, I'll tell her you're looking—"

"If you hear from her, tell her I love her. Tell her I love her a lot."

As Noah put the phone down, he made out Jane, standing dense in the dark. "What did he say?"

"He said to tell you he loved you a lot." Noah saw her shoulders drop, and he smarted for the lie.

"Is he coming?"

"Probably not for a couple days. He asked if I'd take care of you until then. Is that all right?"

"Yes. But I don't know why he doesn't just come."

"I don't know either," Noah said. "But we'll have fun. You watch and see."

And for three days Noah worked at fun. He took Jane to the Mechanical Museum. Outside, they put quarters in telescopes to see overlapping seals on rocks. They watched Golden Gate Park's last buffalo move slowly in their paddock and then they collapsed at the Japanese Tea Garden, ordering double portions of cookies. Noah fell into the habit of thinking about meals in advance. He worried about money in moments of darkness, at night and in the movies. He was spending more than he ever did. But they laughed together in the theaters and their plastic spoons scraped the waxy cardboard bottoms of sundaes. Sometimes, between pleasures, the girl's face fell to blankness. Noah was beginning to understand how people spent money. Money was worth a laugh.

But he wasn't sure how long he was budgeting for; you never knew with Owens. He was trying to figure out if they could keep on forever. Her food wouldn't cost much if they ate at home. He could quit restaurants, bring lunch to the lab. He'd have to get her into school; they couldn't be out celebrating every day. This was just for now, when they didn't know. And by the third day they were wearing out from fun. Noah missed the lab. He could go a day without it, but after three he wasn't right. He had applications in at Cold Spring Harbor for next summer and at MIT next year. Now he didn't feel like going anywhere. She must miss her life too, he thought. He could tell she was tired. When they'd driven out of the park, full of warm tea, they passed a school where kids in brown uniforms poured out of double doors, jumping in the cold. She turned away from the car window.

"What grade were you in?"

"Third," she said. "But I din go much."

"Well, tonight we should call your mother." Noah had been waiting to say that, but she just shook her head.

She was too old for third grade. At Mitch's bookstore, he bought a math book and what seemed to him a decent volume of fairy tales. That night, he made grilled cheese sandwiches and cleared the table for her to work. He took out a clean notebook to sit with her and think with a pencil. He sketched diagrams of his fish brains, drawing arrows for signals. He'd talked to Louise a long time on the phone, but not enough had changed in the lab. At the tea garden, he'd said he had to go to the bathroom and called Kathleen. She'd sighed, her voice low with apology. But whatever Owens did, he couldn't have a kid. He was never home. He only allowed about five vegetables in that kitchen. They didn't have milk, he didn't believe in flour, he forbade meat and most things you need for a regular life. And the house was too cold.

"Why don't you want to call your mother? Did you have a fight?"

She looked at his notebook. "What language is this?"

"That's biology. You can use the phone whenever you want. Maybe I'll drive to the lab, and you can be alone in the van for a few minutes and call."

"I'll come in too. I always come in too."

The way she said that, he began to think he could keep her. There was a school ten or eleven blocks down. Maybe she could walk to the lab after school and do her homework there. They could eat dinner together. And then what? Could he put her to bed at home and then come back to work? Before, he'd thought he'd move East. He'd wanted to go to conferences, join the capitals of science, get in the long line for the big prizes. But there were a thousand reasons to stay, and Jane was the last, the one that tipped him. And he was from here. He'd shop on Saturday mornings and cook every night. It would be harder to have a child and be a scientist, but he could do it. Women did. He'd buy milk, bread and ice cream. She could have friends over, maybe a birthday party.

"Jane, I'm thinking we should get you registered in school. He's pretty busy, and I'm wondering, whatever you two decide, you could always stay here. Would you mind that?"

"No," she said. "Can I go brush my teeth now?"

Registering a child in school was not easy. They wanted proof. They wanted paper. Noah had the distinct impression the principal thought he'd kidnapped her. They needed her birth certificate, which, incredibly, Jane retrieved from the envelope she'd come with, safety-pinned to her sleeve. The worn paper verified that Jane was born to Mary di Natali. Two inked whorls of baby feet marked the page. "Where is Mary di Natali?" the principal asked.

"We've got to call her," Noah said, sternly. "Tonight, Jane."

Jane shook her head. "There's no telephone."

"Think, Jane. We have to reach her. I can send a letter registered mail. What about a neighbor who has a phone?"

Jane turned to him as they left the school hallway. "My mother's dead, Noah."

"When did she die?"

"She would have kept me if she could've."

"Comere." He hugged her into his chair. He had been trying to puzzle it together, the truck, her journey. "But who really drove?"

"I really drove, Noah," she said, and that moment he believed her. There was more then he didn't let himself ask.

When they returned home, two envelopes waited in Noah's mailbox. One was from Sperry's lab, the other from Cold Spring Harbor. He slid then unopened into a drawer.

Owens came that night, in jeans and hiking boots, loping across the lawn. "Hel-*lo*," he called, reaching a hand in through their open window. Jane's head shot up from her book, but all she said was, "Hi, Owens," as if he were the most average thing in her life.

"Hey, bud," Noah said, knocking his elbow. "Want coffee?"

"Do you have any fresh juice?"

"Nope. Tea and coffee. Bourbon."

"Oh, no, thanks," Owens said. "I'm pretty tired. I've been meeting all day with political types. The mayor was here. Experts."

"So what'd you learn?" Noah said.

Owens had listened with full consideration to the planners of mass transit systems. But try as he did, he couldn't work himself into the idea of taking the bus. It has something to do with freedom, he thought. After a two-day presentation for a subway system throughout Greater Los Angeles, Owens concluded, "I'd rather ride a bike." He sighed. "There should be a moratorium on all cars for a year, until they can clean up the air."

"Fat chance."

"I know. But that's probably what we should do. So, kid, you want to get your stuff and I'll take you home with me? I'm really tired. I talked to your mom, and she's—"

"You talked to my mom?" Jane stared at him.

"Yes, I talked to your mom. She's coming down in a week or so and we can figure out where you two want to live. But tonight I'll take you home and maybe we'll watch a movie. And then this weekend I've got to go to Europe. So I'll probably take you with me. Have you ever seen the Eiffel Tower?"

"No. But when did you talk to my mom, though?"

"Maybe an hour ago. Would you like to see the Eiffel Tower?"

"Yes," she said, suddenly calm. She assimilated the idea that he could make the terrible fall, as just a small part of his day. She looked at Noah, bashful and ashamed. She wasn't lying—it had been that way. But now this was more true, the relation of day to a dream.

In five minutes they were gone, Jane strapped into the low passenger seat of his small car, her few belongings in the back. Noah still hadn't shown her the velvet coat. He'd taken it out of the bag several times that week, while she was sleeping. He'd wondered if the woman would give him the money back or just a store credit. When he was budgeting for her to stay, he'd thought they couldn't afford frivolities like velvet coats. But tonight he'd tucked it in the bottom of the brown paper bag she'd come with. Jane's fingers opened and closed Owens' glove compartment, which was stashed with five-dollar bills. The car fired up and then sped off into the night.

Noah sat in his doorway. Then, left with his future, he felt the depression come on again, a way he'd forgotten. Before, every time Noah had relinquished something expensive he'd wanted, he'd felt a great relief afterwards, as if he'd narrowly missed a disaster. But tonight no relief came. This was an altogether new dimension to money: sometimes you could regret not spending. He stayed in the doorway, the envelopes from the drawer on his lap. One envelope was thick, one thinner. Why should Owens have everything, just because he already did? Owens didn't deserve her, he wouldn't know how to cherish a child. Noah had often envied Owens' love, but now he didn't feel strong enough for sex. He was tired. Fog lingered on his forehead; he could feel his curls tightening. I could take care of a child, he thought. I would have shaped my days around her. And I had things to teach.

What would Owens give? He had slept with a woman, then tried to get her to go away. And that was what made men fathers and men in this world.

He sat there for a long time, looking out at the sky. Now he was free to go anywhere and didn't want to. He rubbed the paper of the envelopes, still sealed. Out at the end of the lawn, the van was still there and it was his.

In the House of Women

⊰⊱ ⊰⊱ ⊰⊱ ⊰⊱ ⊰⊱

*J*ane's mother was never the same to her after the long night drive. She patiently answered Jane's questions, but for Jane some mystery adhered.

Mary shrugged. "I guess it seemed like a good idea for the three of us to be together."

By now Jane knew the exact story, how Owens called the sheriff forty miles away to jeep up to the cabin. Bixter drove her to the airport, a bucket of bait sloshing against her legs through new nylons. An envelope with Mary's name on it was waiting at the counter, and she was the only passenger on the plane. The one stewardess kept refilling her hot water.

Owens took them out to dinner her first night in Auburn, to a square room where they tasted sushi for the first time.

"Inside food," Jane said, as it lay on her tongue, like another tongue.

He suggested that Mary get a part-time job, in a pet store or at the library, even her mother's old bakery, someplace Jane would enjoy visiting.

In Paris, Owens had taken Jane for a haircut. It was the first time her hair had ever been cut. Insect wings and parts of leaves had fallen into the French beauty shop's basin. Owens handed Mary a little bottle labeled *Kwell* and told her to shampoo Jane's hair twice a week.

Mary sighed. "Well, maybe you can control her now."

In the mountains, Jane had done what she wanted. She cracked open nuts with her teeth and on the school bus sucked the white soft end of a weed. She ate and slept by her own clock. Mary had never been stern enough to establish a bedtime. They had an old shower, but Jane didn't allow water on her head. The only thing Jane remembered of Seattle was the old deep tub below a window. It murmured and sang as the water ran.

Owens lifted Jane's arm, to show Mary the scars. "What are these?" he asked.

"Well, there were squirrels in that cabin," Mary said.

He stared at her, keen and still.

The flat apartment building stood perpendicular to the street, and theirs was the last door. It looked like a motel. Owens explained that each month a man named Eliot would bring them three hundred dollars. They felt hidden, as if he wanted to keep them his secret.

Jane asked her mother everything except what she really wanted to know, which was: Why didn't you keep me with you? Or, if you were sick and going to die, then what made you better? Instead she watched her mother's positions, the way she sat or bent over, the hang of her neck, a wilt of clothes off her shoulders.

It was the rainy season and they stayed inside, waiting for they didn't know what. Mary liked to sit in the dim rooms without turning on the lights. She made tea again and again with the same bag, so that by the end of the day she seemed to drink cup after cup of only water. Jane finally understood that her mother was afraid to go out. "He wants us to wait," she explained. "Besides, we're resting."

For Mary, this was a time when they were one, she was we, she and Jane and sometimes Owens. She felt a calming happiness almost indistinguishable from fatigue when the three of them were together, as if a huge burden she'd been carrying for a decade had been lifted and forgiven and she could finally rest.

But Jane grew bored. Somewhere she had learned the gestures of impatience. Her toe and heel tapped. For the first time, she listened to her mother and judged.

"Were you going to die?" she finally asked.

She sighed. "I just wanted to lie down. I was so tired."

"Just from me?"

"You were a lot."

After two weeks, Jane demanded knives and forks and in the long afternoons practiced setting imaginary tables on the floor. That first night Owens had taken them out, Jane began studying other children. In the small apartment, she practiced their voices. For hours in front of the cracked bathroom mirror, she tried to inspire her hair to imitate. Now she wanted to master cutlery and asked her mother to go get her childhood birthday silver.

"Learn chopsticks," her mother said.

And finally, when the rain stopped, Jane insisted on being taken to school.

This occasioned calls to Owens and another dinner, at which he offered her a tutor. "Schools are like prisons," he said. "They teach you to be like everybody else." Owens wanted to keep her safe, until he had time to decide what was best.

"You'll have all kinds of opportunities I won't," Mary whispered, not to instill guilt, but marveling. At the same time, she didn't want her daughter to go out into full rooms, not yet.

"You two both went," Jane reasoned, "and I should get to go too."

Jane had discovered the school in a small pink stucco building. She climbed up on an eaves pipe and listened from a window as the children sang their multiplication tables. At lunchtime, Jane saw them eating with knives and forks. She disciplined herself not to crack nuts with her teeth anymore.

Mary met two old women in a park, picking persimmons off the public trees. Years earlier, she'd met Bixter this way, in a park in Portland, filling her pail with daffodils. These women's names were Amber and Ruby, and they turned out to be retired schoolteachers.

The teachers lived in an old white wooden house, which was like Christmas inside: polished and perfect. Jars of preserves hoarded light on the table.

All at once, the first time she saw it, Jane wanted to live there. Sometimes she wanted a thing so much, she couldn't fathom why, if she stared and complimented, the person wouldn't give it to her.

"Would you be willing to tutor?" Mary asked.

"Could we live here?" Jane blurted.

"Jane," Mary said with a giggle, but she looked up for an answer too. Ruby set her teacup down quickly, trembling the saucer. Amber tugged at the gloves on her lap. They excused themselves to the kitchen to confer.

Jane and Mary sat waiting, looking around the full room. The teachers smelled dry, like chalkboard erasers and the insides of school closets. They were nothing like Bixter. It turned out their grandfather had been a minister from the American Home Missionary Society and had come from Massachusetts on a year-long boat ride around Cape Horn. He had planted those persimmon trees. Mary sighed. "It's a great big house and they're probably always fixing something on that stove."

The teachers walked back in briskly and said they'd telephoned the niece whom they'd raised and there was a bungalow for rent right next door to her cottage.

"You young people would have more fun there," Amber said.

Mary looked down. She hadn't known they had a niece.

"We go to bed so early," Ruby added.

Jane left a message for Owens, saying they'd found two tutors and could they move.

Though he agreed to cover the rent, he gave them no budget for furniture. Mary liked the bungalow best the first moment, when she saw it empty, before they carried their junk in. They owned six boxes of things but no furniture.

When Owens came to visit, he said, "I grew up in a house a lot like this."

Just then, Jane saw the woman out the window again, who was probably *her*, the niece. One night, they'd seen her silhouette as she stood on a ladder, hanging a chandelier. Today she was carrying a big bench up the lawn, wearing neat beige clothes like in a catalogue. The woman had her hair up, tied with a scarf, and she didn't wear her oldest thing like they did for moving furniture. Unless that *was* her oldest thing.

"Should we offer her some lemonade?" Mary asked.

Jane wished she and her mom had the cottage. It was just cuter. But Mary's favorite part of the bungalow was the lemon tree in the front yard. Mary loved citrus. The teachers had already been invited to pick, and they'd left a Mason jar of marmalade on the porch. Jane shimmied up the tree to the first limb and shook the branch. Mary stooped below, gathering the lemons in a paper bag.

Owens stayed inside, lying on the floor, enjoying the lace of breeze on his arms.

Together, Mary and Jane squeezed the lemons and stirred in turbinado sugar, but just when it was finished and Mary stepped out with a brimming glassful, the pretty lady streaked from her door, carrying a purse.

From the window, Jane watched them talk. After a minute, the woman folded into her small car, without the lemonade.

"It's her," Mary said, when she came back. "But she seemed a little cold."

Jane brought Owens the glass of lemonade meant for their neighbor and set it on the floor. "You didn't even see her!" she said.

"Was she pretty?" he asked, barely lifting his head.

"Very pretty."

When Owens left, he said, "Enjoy the house," in a way that somehow reminded them it was his and not theirs. It was a word he said in the mild imperative, as if he vaguely understood the faculty for enjoyment was one he truly did not possess. Enjoy, he said to his employees, with a merry expression like that of a man toasting, when he left them to work on his life's love as he strode out to the tedium of luxury, silvery laughter, dinners. He often said Enjoy, as if he truly couldn't, and when people did, he watched them with faraway reverence, never begrudging, but looking on quizzically with an abstract smile.

The next morning, Jane walked over to give the pretty lady a banana bread they'd baked. Light bounced and splashed against the white walls of her kitchen, and violin music came from a radio. Julie stood making tea in a teapot. She served Jane cornflakes in a china bowl with a heavy silver spoon that pinched into Jane's third finger; she tried to remember again how you were supposed to hold spoons. For the rest of her life, she would feel self-conscious when people watched her eat.

Jane looked around the cottage, wondering, Just how is ours different? Julie's cottage seemed rich. Little things matched: a tiny cream pitcher and a bowl of white sugar both had violets painted on. "How did you get your house to be like this?" she asked.

Julie offered to take Jane and her mother to the flea market. When she talked it seemed easy, but it wasn't easy, or it was easy for her and not for them.

When she got home, Jane asked her mother again to go get her childhood silver.

That Sunday, when Julie knocked on their screen door, they woke up in startled bolts. They dressed in a drill and Julie drove them out of town to what had been the old dump, where now there were rows and rows like streets—a village made of junk.

"It's still dirty," Mary whispered to Jane.

They drank coffee out of cardboard cups, and sharp leaves rasped against their ankles. The sky still held night clouds. Trees swayed widely as vendors were setting out their wares.

Julie pulled a bedspread from under a table. Mary and Jane both said it was nice but they didn't really think so. Later, on Julie's bed, it became beautiful, though it hadn't seemed that way there.

They spent thirty dollars on an iron tiered votive candleholder. Mary and Owens agreed that Jane wouldn't go to church, but sometimes Mary missed the mass. "We'll fill it with candles and light it up for a party," Mary declared.

The large candleholder sat all that summer and the next winter in the long grass. After the rains, rust furred on it, and they didn't return to the flea market.

That evening, they went to Julie's house while she moved around her new furniture. When you walked inside the cottage there were nice shapes, clean alleyways, and you felt like sitting down and having a cup of tea. When you stepped into the bungalow, the natural expression was to raise a hand to your face.

"You're doing it again," Jane told her mother, coming back home. "Stop it with the lip." It took concentration not to be distracted when you first came in.

Jane could never tell anymore what her mother wanted. "Why didn't you come along with me?" she suddenly asked.

"I don't know. Maybe I thought he'd be happier with you alone. Stop asking that."

Jane asked a lot, she knew, but she wanted to. Because it was a different answer every time. Tonight's was entirely new, and Jane wondered if her father was happier. Maybe not. Maybe her mother was disappointed.

Owens traveled out of town a lot, and they never knew when he'd call. They tried to forget about him until he was there. They tried but they never did.

Owens couldn't believe that Jane was his daughter because they didn't have the same color hair. Although he understood the fundamental principles of genetics, he'd always assumed that his genes would dominate.

"Do you think she looks like me?" he would occasionally ask a friend or a colleague, extracting a white-bordered photograph of an ordinary child with front teeth in varying states of progression. He never mentioned that the child's mother had volunteered to give the baby a chromosomal test, accurate within ninety-seven percent, or that in response he'd screamed, "Oh, great! So three percent of the world population—figure about half are women, that's seventy-five million—could be her father, and I'm one of them."

This was precisely how he flummoxed Mary. He had the numbers and the dates of things, but underneath it all, in a way she could never prove, as her family had lived for generations never proving, she knew her side was right.

One day, Owens stopped by Noah's lab. "Hey, Jane said you bought her that coat. That was really nice of you."

"Well, she picked it out," Noah said, his long fingers bouncing on the wheel of his chair.

"She *really* likes it. She wears it every day."

It was a hot morning, and the two men took an outside table at Café Pantheon. Noah loved hot black coffee on a hot day.

Owens looked at him over the rim of his cup. "So do you think she looks like me?"

Noah felt little patience this morning, and he was aware that Owens liked people who didn't let him get away with anything. "She's yours, Owens," he said, "so don't act like a lout."

"A lout?" Owens' face formed a question. "What's a lout?"

"An asshole."

"So you really think she looks like me?"

"Not much. Some. But it's not looks."

Owens nodded. It would take a while, and then he might begin to believe. Sometimes Noah thought Owens trusted him because of his capacities; other times, it seemed he listened because Noah was stunted and small, no threat.

"So you really think she's mine?" He seemed to be waiting, as if Noah's answer mattered greatly. He lost his handsomeness, his face going trapezoidal. Perhaps he'd wanted to love her all along but hadn't let himself believe she was his.

But why couldn't he love her, whether or not she was his? Owens himself was raised by a stepmother. "Yes," Noah said. "And she's a great kid."

"I think so too." Owens now was more at ease. "I got her mom and her this little bungalow."

"I'd like to meet the mom."

"Oh, I'll introduce you." Owens wasn't greedy, not with his house, not with his daughter. He was too accustomed to being busy.

"Hey, I have a chance to go back East. Do my time in the capital." Noah made his voice nonchalant, when in fact he felt tormented.

"What capital?"

"Cold Spring Harbor." Noah shrugged. "For better or worse, New York's our capital."

"Not for long," Owens said. "I mean, wouldn't you rather be in a new culture as it's rising rather than the ruins? New York's over, Noah. Look at how many western presidents we've had. The center of the country's here now."

"Not for science," Noah said.

"Science follows money. Like everything else."

"Then how come the people at MIT and Harvard win all the Nobel Prizes?"

"Don't forget, Linus Pauling went to Oregon State."

Noah laughed. There was a tensile strength to their friendship, which allowed for and even insisted on a good deal of criticism. Neither was quite right for the other in his original form. He gulped down the rest of his coffee. Having convinced Owens that Jane was his daughter, he understood Owens would forget he had anything to do with it. Today he'd gladly let him pay.

I'm no wanderer, Noah thought as they parted on the bumpy sidewalk.

The east door to his old high school was open, and Noah rolled down the clean corridor. The janitor, Jim Clarke, was a friend of his father's. His sister had loved geography, he remembered, passing a classroom lined with maps. She'd always wanted to leave. "Michelangelo hands," she'd said, holding his hands when she finally left. She had stubby fingers. I do have good hands, Noah told himself, checking them on the gritty wheels. My sister is a jar of secrets.

"Noah, my man." His old chemistry teacher, Mr. Riddle, touched his shoulder. "What can I do for you?"

High school seniors buzzed at lab stations, noticing his arrival. Noah told Mr. Riddle about the fellowship while he took Erlenmeyer flasks out of a cabinet for the students.

"Go," Mr. Riddle said. "The line'll be there, whether you're in it or not."

In the bleak schoolyard, Noah sat still. Very little moved. Alta was a stationary place, unlike the city of foghorns and regret only twenty miles north. He hadn't said anything about Jane, her being a reason to stay. She wasn't his.

⋘

From the beginning, Owens could talk to Jane. He was always himself, but Jane felt awkward around him and even the simplest thing seemed hard to say. "I have to excuse myself," she finally said one afternoon, in his factory, when he'd been telling her how machines resembled the inside of the human body. He didn't seem to hear.

"I need to pee, Owens," she said, more loudly.

"Oh, wait. I'll alert the media," he said, and that became a refrain between them, his expression of boredom with the endless, additive, sonorous details of childhood.

That afternoon, he took her to buy new sneakers, and she had to call her mother from a pay phone. "Well, they have ones like mine, but instead of three bumps—you know where I mean—they have two bumps."

Her mother apparently did know what she meant, and they continued a spirited discussion. Owens drifted off to gaze at globes in a store window, concluding that it was a good thing he'd been born male, because he could never in a million years be a mother.

It didn't occur to Jane to thank him for the sneakers. She was a vivid child, full of life, but lacking in what her tutors called refinements. Her manners struck them as indelicately blunt. She was missing those graces a patient mother instills slowly, stitch by stitch. And Owens never bothered with manners, which he considered to be the frills of civilization and a waste of time. He didn't notice if she wiped her nose with the back of her hand or expect to be thanked for sneakers.

In the car, Jane talked incessantly about their next-door neighbor, while Owens listened with a small fraction of his attention until a phrase lifted out at him.

". . . because we're poor," he heard his daughter say.

"You're not poor," he said.

"Yes we are. My mom and I are."

"You and your mom live on the same amount of money as most college professors. I'm sure the woman next door—what's her name, Julie?—has no more money."

"She's a lawyer!" Jane said, as if that proved it.

"At most she makes the same. You might even have more."

Jane didn't know how. Every day, Julie went out in suits; they just wore tee shirts and jeans.

"I have this coupon for a free meal," he said. "It'll probably pay for more than you and me and your mom. Do you think your neighbor might want to come along?"

Jane raced ahead of him to the bungalow, yelling, "Can we go to dinner with Owens?"

"Sure," Mary called from the back, where she often sat with the doors open.

"And can Julie come too?"

Mary thumped into the living room and saw Owens standing there, surveying. The house seemed darker and smaller, as if the room no longer had angular corners, but round ones, like the inside of a ball. "I don't think that's a very good idea."

"Oh," he said. "Well, why not?"

"I just don't, Owens. So if you want to eat with us, that's fine. But if you want a date, then maybe you should go over and ask her yourself."

"It was just an idea," he said, shrugging. "Forget it."

When Mary and Jane met him in the restaurant, Olivia was there too, and a man who was her cousin. Jane had heard about Olivia before. She'd expected her to come down slowly on a winding staircase, in a long red dress with a slit on the side. But she just sat there in the booth wearing jeans. It was like once in Portland when she saw a movie star on the street—blinking, a little pale, with small bites or a rash on her skin.

Jane had often imagined the time she'd finally meet Olivia. But instead Owens just brought her along, and Jane had the feeling that from now on she'd always be there. And that first night, Jane felt they weren't even properly introduced, with their real titles. She had no way of knowing this was how Owens presented everyone in his life. Of course, what she really wanted to understand was how he felt about *her*, if he'd told Olivia she was his daughter and her uncertainty was not unfounded. Much as Olivia was there, a girlfriend, though probably not the *great love,* as if he were still deciding, Jane was only a girl, sort of his daughter but not completely. He seemed to be still deciding that too.

Jane knew Owens' mother hadn't held him until he was eight months old. She thought maybe for him love came from being along together, *as* son or daughter, rather than really being it for sure in the first place, the way she and her mom were. But that made her nervous, and she bit her thumbnail. If that was the way he was, why couldn't she see him every day, then?

Owens showed them all the coupon, which Theo had given him. It had come in the mail addressed to "Resident" and was good for forty dollars any Wednesday before nine, but Theo's wife didn't like foreign food.

Things took a turn for the better. He turned his attention on Jane, with everyone looking. On his lap for the first time, Jane assumed the position of a small queen, legs dangling. He said, "Maybe Jane'll be our country's first woman president. Let's say she decides to go to college, then after that maybe she goes to law school like her neighbor—what's her name—Julie? But say she doesn't want to practice for a while, she wants to live in the real world. So she decides to work at Genesis for a few years. After a little while, she might even take over and run it for a decade or so. Then, when she's forty, forty-five, she runs for president."

Owens looked full and satisfied that night, enclosed by two parenthetical women, with his daughter on his lap. That morning, he'd met with five bald men in suits, who'd offered to plan his campaign for him should he choose to run for governor in three years. He had not said yes, but he had not said no.

"And because of her Persian heritage," he went on, "she'll have certain sensitivities to that region."

"I'll help homeless people," Jane said.

"Yes. Maybe she'll figure out some tax incentives to help the poor. I think it'd be really great if you did that, Jane."

Olivia's voice assumed the slow, deliberate tone often used with children. "Jane, is that what *you'd* like to do when you grow up? What do you think *you'd* like to be?"

"I don't know. Maybe dancer or president."

Huck, Olivia's cousin, exploded in a loud, jagged laugh. He was bulky, square-shaped and, up until then, mostly quiet. He was an eighth-grade teacher, and Jane wanted to ask to be in his class. She'd never had a man teacher.

Mary caught Olivia's eye, then looked down. Both women felt jealous of Jane in a prickling way. They envied her the only thing she knew she had on her fickle throne: a future. Owens was now expounding on educational policy, as Huck passed the rice.

"You work in Alta Saint John's?" Mary asked. When Olivia nodded, she squinted. "And you're a nurse?"

"No. Just a CNA."

"Oh," Mary said, not knowing what that was. "My mom died there."

The dinner continued, sparked with small conversations that easily went out, only Owens and Jane feeling somehow free to talk. When they finished, Owens paid the bill with his coupon, leaving a twenty for a tip.

"I look in the mirror and see what I look like," Jane said, skipping on the sidewalk in her new sneakers, "but I don't know what that is, if it's pretty or not."

"Know what I'll get you for your birthday?" Owens said, his hand clamping her neck.

She hadn't thought he even knew when her birthday was. She began to imagine the presents, five months away, larger and larger ones.

"I'll take down all the mirrors in the house!"

But Jane and her mother didn't own any, and they couldn't take down the ones attached to doors in the rented bungalow.

"Yes!" Mary said, catching up from behind. "She shouldn't even be *think*ing about these things. It would be so good for her to go to India or Mexico for her birthday."

"Yeah," he said wistfully. "You're not turning out to be much of a hippie, Jane."

Olivia pulled her stomach muscles in against her spine as she walked along behind Jane. Although they didn't know it, tonight was her doing. "Let's really try," she'd said to him more than once. "Let's set one day a week Jane can come to dinner and really stick with it."

Unlike most of the women Owens knew during the years of Mary's exile, Olivia had heard of Jane. She'd always wanted to meet the woman and the child she said was his daughter.

"She looks exactly like him," Olivia said to Huck, in the parking lot. But he only half agreed. "Mary's very pretty too," he mentioned.

She made one more effort. "Does anybody feel like ice cream at Café Pantheon?"

"I do!" Jane's voice belled out.

Owens' renown in Alta was such that most people in the café smiled when he picked Jane up so she could see the ices. Mary lifted her arm to grab Jane's foot. For her, too, he provided a certain position. She was, after all, the mother. Jane looked down and wondered, What does she want? Also, glancing around the café with its polished wood surfaces and marble round tables ringed with people, she wanted to be able to wear a dress.

Olivia seemed somehow less at this public moment, waiting behind with her cousin. Only the girlfriend. She sometimes imagined people looking at her, picturing the act.

When they all stood with their cones, Owens' hand slid into her back pocket, and she reciprocated. Olivia vowed to talk to Jane often, the way she brought Owens' mother flowers twice a week since she'd been sick. Owens approved of Olivia's efforts, but he didn't help much. Of the Tuesday night dinners with Jane she set up that first year, he only made it to three.

Nevertheless, that night he thought of them all as family. He threw his arms around whichever two fell on either side, crushing them against him, looking down from face to face, exhaling: "Ah, the women in my life." On a walk with Noah the next day, he'd announced, "If Olivia got pregnant and we weren't ready to get married, I'd go ahead and have the child. I'd get them a little place to live. It's a more European way."

In the bungalow later, Jane declared that when she was president, she would make every kid go to school and let every girl pick out a dress.

"Jane, you don't like politics," Mary said. "You don't even read the newspaper."

"So? Neither do you."

"But I'm not saying I'll be president."

"Well . . ." Jane paused a minute. "Just because I don't read the newspaper, that doesn't mean I couldn't help people."

"Jane, people who do things like that are interested in elections and bills passing."

From then on, Jane demanded a subscription to the newspaper, and for a month, she and her mother spent all day Sunday making their way through the sections.

One calm Friday in April, Mary walked the long mazelike path back to the old bakery, letting the soft wooden screen door bang. In the kitchen she found Rosie, the milkman's stout daughter, dripping liquid frosting crosses on a tray of Sunday buns.

Rosie moved slowly to the drawer under the telephone, where Mary's mother had kept scratch paper and finger-sized pencils.

Mary had flown home to the funeral and stayed up all night, sorting her mother's things into piles. But her mother's possessions were so familiar that at dawn she left them all, taking the bus back after only one day.

Rosie led her down the narrow staircase to the basement, where one cardboard box remained. "Rest we gave away," she explained. Near the top of the box was the wooden case of her silver. *Made in France,* it said. Opening the lid, Mary saw all the cutlery stacked evenly in the slotted felt like keys, blackened from lack of care. Then she carefully closed the small latch, marveling that it was intact, despite her neglect, suddenly and silently grateful to her mother.

"You're lucky that's still there. Them across the street wanted to sell it. She took all your ma's doorknobs." Rosie nodded. "My dad had to wrestle it out of her mitts. Your ma told him, 'Someday she'll come back and want it.' "

Mary understood then that her mother had been not too strict but too lenient and had given her too much when she was young, imposing the lifelong burden of regret. Following the wide, white swathed buttocks of Rosie—whom she'd known all her life—she climbed back up into the flour-infused air. Mary had let the bakery go too. She could have worked here every day, in the warm yellow room that smelled of yeast and sugar.

"Are you coming out to see the neighbors?" Rosie asked. There was a strangeness to her adult voice, of virginal curiosity.

"I will sometime," Mary said. She couldn't bear to think what else was thrown away because she'd been in a hurry. Maybe nothing is worse than knowing you have hurt your own self.

Mary bought a morning roll and Rosie took her money, the cash register ringing its cheer. A young man came in and asked for two buns with nutmeg flowers on top. He was wearing a shirt that could have been a pajama top, the collar ripped from washings.

"You look like you need a cup of coffee," he said to Mary.

They sat down on the steps outside. As he lightly drummed the cement, she told him what she'd told no one else, how she'd left at nineteen and never come back in time to see her mother. Then the funeral, when she abandoned the house full of childhood.

"What did you go back to?"

"I have a daughter," Mary said.

"There you go," he said, fisting her hand inside his.

As they talked, Mary remembered the times she'd wanted to give Jane away. Once, Jane stared at her straight up from the dusty plank floor of the apple farm. It was before dawn, and Mary's body—ninety percent fluid, she'd once read—felt hopelessly watered down from being up every hour to feed. She was contemplating adoption. She sat at the small desk in the room, examining a pamphlet she'd picked up from the local church, then carefully wrote the address on a plain envelope. But her daughter kept staring at her, as if she knew something about Mary no one else did. They made a silent pact that morning, and Jane never again woke up in the night.

"See, she knew. She slept because she knew I couldn't take it."

But she had kept her daughter. She had. A hundred times, maybe a thousand, it had been so hard—the ghost of a butterfly flickered in her back, a permanent weakness felt even now—but she had gone through it and she still had her. That was the one thing she did.

"Your mom'd understand," the man said. "That's what she did, right?" Mary had received a card and a check from her mother, the only present attending the birth.

His name was Eli and he played drums in a start-up band that practiced every night. For money, he ran a gardening team.

"I knew your mom. I used to trade her birds. I'd give her a pair of quail and she gave me a tab at the bakery. This new one, Miss Hips, wiped me out. I still go because I like your mom's nutmeg rolls."

That night, he came to visit after his band practice. He brought a triangle, which still hung on their front porch years later. When Jane stood in front of him, asking her mother a question, he rubbed her shoulders and said, "Hey, man, what's going down?"

Jane couldn't tell about Eli. He was nice, but she didn't think he was what Mary wanted. He was like a boy, more of a friend. He'd tickle and make her mother laugh, sort of at him, sort of with him.

The truck finally gave out, and after they left seven messages, Owens took them to buy a new car. Mary chose the make and model. With Owens, she was discovering, you had a moment of chance, and if you said what you wanted, sometimes he said yes. She could glean no particular logic to his decisions. So she asked for more than felt really right, and it gave her a high strange giggle when he assented. She felt he was letting her in too, not just Jane. But maybe not. She got the model she wanted but not the color. Only one was there on the lot, and Owens didn't want to wait; it was maroon and she'd been hoping for blue.

Driving home the first new car they'd ever owned, Mary and Jane still felt joyless. Jane didn't know if it was her father's way of giving—he'd looked grim, writing the check—or her mother's tendency to suspicion, but they drove straight home and parked and Mary never trusted that car. Almost always she smelled a faint trace of oil, and they drove with the windows open, even in the morning. Now, two months later, it wouldn't start. And Mary had to get to the city to give blood. Rosie had walked all the way to the bungalow the night before, delivering an envelope addressed in light pencil to Mary di Natali, Auburn. "Here's the letter I said came to the bakery." It was from Bixter, who needed an operation on her one eye. She sent the name and address of the hospital where the blood could be forwarded. "It's a funny thing. I'd been thinking of you two for a couple weeks, and then I remembered we have the same blood." Mary and Bixter each prided themselves on being RH negative.

Mary and Jane decided over and over all day that they'd ask Owens to lend them a car. He owned three. Mary wanted him to take theirs back and get the truck again or a new new car, the one that was blue.

He was late, but that didn't mean anything. When he finally came, Jane shuffle-tapped across the floor. "Now that you're together, will you guys please decide like you said you would how old I have to be to be allowed to wear a dress?"

Owens considered this. "I guess we did say we'd get back to you on that, huh?"

"And also how old for dangly earrings."

"See," Mary said, "I don't think she should be thinking about these things."

Owens held a finger to his lips, pondering. "Well, I'd have to say eighteen."

"Yes," Mary said, solemnly, her long neck bent.

Jane moaned in a way that was mostly pleasure. It was nice like this, when they agreed. They were her parents and they were making rules. Impossible rules.

Mary's face filled with what only Owens could recognize as guilt. "The car isn't working again, and I have to go into the city."

"Bixter's having an operation," Jane said.

"Did you take it in?" he said absently. He knew no Bixter.

"I wonder if it's just a lemon, so much has gone wrong already." Mary was repeating what Eli had said, but they didn't mention his name around Owens.

"The last time was a cable, Mary. Cables are little things." He'd bought it. That was the end.

"But I have to get there tomorrow, and so . . ." She lapsed into a fragile smile, which she expected would delight no one, like a poor tap dance.

"We wanted to know could we borrow a car from you," Jane finished.

"Just for tomorrow," Mary added.

He shook his head slowly. "No."

"Why not?" Jane snapped.

His jaw made a hard angle. "I don't have a car to give you."

Jane sprang up. "Come on, Mom. If we're going to ask Julie, let's do it now. It's late already. I'll go with you." She stood under the porch light, waiting with her hand out to take her mother and cross the yard to ask of neighbors again.

After they asked to borrow his car, Owens didn't call for three months. The first weeks, they didn't say anything, even to each other. On the sixth Sunday, they woke up feeling bad, so they decided to treat themselves. Eliot Hanson had come with the check on the first, like every other month. At the mall, they bought a black velvet headband for Jane and found a hooded sweatshirt for Mary on sale. They both needed socks and underwear. And they bought themselves a fondue pot and had it gift-wrapped, then ate lunch in a restaurant that made crepes. It was easy for Mary to make Jane laugh. Her aunt Alma never cut her hair in her whole life, she said. She could sit on it, but she wasn't vain at all. "She hardly knew it was there," Mary said.

"Mom, no one has hair that long by accident. Not nowadays anyway." Mary was more like a grandmother when it came to hair.

Jane added up the purchases and announced that they'd spent one hundred and six dollars. "Everything's so expensive," Mary said.

In the late afternoon, when they parked in their driveway, Julie was hauling a long table in over the lawn. They helped her manuever it through the door and then let it down gently by the front window. Julie arranged the chairs she already had around it, then took out candles and placed a pitcher of flowers in the center. Now she had a dining room, and Jane thought you could just see that every night, dinner would be different.

"A hundred bucks," Julie said.

And all they'd had was their day. Julie bought big things, Jane thought, and we buy little ones that clutter up or else don't last.

"It's confidence," Mary said. "I'd be afraid it wouldn't be right when I got it home."

That was true, Jane understood. Her mother didn't know how to do anything with her hair, and when she had to dress up it took her a whole day. Jane had started caring how she looked even before she came to Alta. In the mountain town, she'd studied herself in store windows. "Why don't you have any?"

Mary's lip lifted on the left. Her jaw was slightly uneven and her teeth didn't line up. She was considering braces to correct them. "I don't know. I guess I was born that way. Because my mother always asked me the same thing. But honest, Jane, I was popular in high school. People liked me." She said this shyly, as though Jane wouldn't believe her. She shrugged. "I was just nice to everybody. And now I'd like to try and do something in art again. It's hard, though. I love having the chance to learn, but it's not easy on your confidence." In Seattle, the man who'd taught Jane to read suggested that Mary collect in one place all the things she'd learned in her vagrant life; he told her the book would be a best-seller. Back then, she'd played guitar and memorized popular songs for children's parties, songs Jane found herself still humming. And now Mary was trying to paint again, because that was what she was best at in high school.

"If it's so hard, though, why don't you be something else? Like a teacher? Or a lawyer?" For these things she'd have to go to school, and she wasn't a school person, but at least she could get a job and wouldn't have to cry every time she didn't think she was good enough.

"Why, honey? This is my own chance to have a life and feel it, and that's the most important thing."

"More important than me?"

"As important. Everybody loves more than one person in their life."

Jane sighed. An hour before, she'd been entirely happy.

Then the phone rang, and Julie invited them over to supper on her new table.

"See?" Mary said. "Even if we spent a lot today, dinner's free!"

So many times, Jane noticed, her mother's most positive emotion was consolation. But her mother's relief in the free meal—that was Jane's destitution. Years later, when she was trying to determine if their poverty had been necessary, she thought Mary hadn't fought against it very hard, taking too much pleasure in saving the cost of a dinner, as if that meant they were getting ahead a little.

Julie used mixes and cans to cook with, but soup arrived in a special tureen and you ate on a different dish for every course. Jane felt, I am definitely having a meal. At home, they often ate parts of things, standing up.

Julie said she was dating, and what she described sounded as pretty as the noises of the silver and the glass. Jane decided that she would date when she was older.

Peter Bigelow owned pumpkin fields and an orchard in Half Moon Bay. He was a kind person, Julie could tell, but she didn't know if they could really talk. He'd given her an article he'd written about the economics of organic harvesting, and she was trying to make her way through it. "But I don't know. I'm thinking, a lifetime of talking mulch and phytopathology?"

"What's that?" Jane asked.

"Tree disease."

"He gave me this," she said, holding out her arm to show a watch.

Neither Mary nor Jane had ever received a present like that from anyone but each other. And Julie said he sent her three dozen white roses after the first night. But she wasn't sure. She had to just wait and see. Maybe by fall she'd know, by Halloween. If she was still with him, they were going to have a huge party in the pumpkin fields, with hayrides and hot apple cider and ginger cookies.

"Even with the roses," Jane said, "you're still not sure?"

After dinner, Julie served iced mint tea and sherbet on the cottage porch, sewing while they talked. She was making a slipcover for her sofa. Sipping the sweet cool drink, two steps below the women, Jane wished they had the ginger cookies and hot apple cider Julie was planning for Halloween. June was cold here, as Jane had known her whole life.

Though she was a lawyer, Julie thought like an elementary school teacher. She always knew which holiday came next, and liked having something to look forward to. Jane and Mary assumed it was because her family came, three generations before, from the East. Most of the books Jane got from Amber had autumn foliage and winter snow.

Mary told Julie about Eli, how he lived in a garage apartment with a huge outside cage of birds.

"The main thing is," Julie said, "where do you want your life to be in three years?"

"I guess I'd like to feel settled with somebody and maybe even have another child."

"You do?" Jane said. "You want another child?"

Mary blushed. They spent so much time together, sometimes she almost forgot Jane was there. "I think I would. If everything was right. Don't forget you'll be getting older. You'll be in high school in a few years."

"If you guys ever let me go."

At that moment, Julie turned back into a lawyer. "And do you think Eli could give you that life?"

Mary shook her head, smiling, a meaningless smile like a caught fish. "No, I don't think so. No."

"See, that's what I learned about the man I was seeing before. And we don't have two years to figure things out."

"But Eli helps me. He really helps me see things."

That was true. Eli tried to give Mary confidence. Every time she had a new idea for a career, they stayed up late considering all the details. "I think this is going to be a really big deal," he'd say.

"Wait," Jane said. "Why don't you both have two years?"

"You know, I don't think I've ever been in love." Julie looked from one to the other, her face shining with an expression that was hard to decipher: bafflement, a little shame, the gift of a secret.

Mary held her knees and rocked a little.

"Is that so bad, though?" Jane said, from the steps below.

"I don't know," Julie whispered.

Then they both looked to Mary. For once, she was the one who had knowledge. "Oh, I don't know either," she said.

When they walked in the back door of the bungalow, Eli was sitting at the kitchen table eating ramen, rolling drumsticks on an overturned pan.

Then he started drumming on Jane's head.

"Eli, stop it—that hurts!" she screamed. It didn't hurt.

Julie planned a dinner party and invited someone named Bill for Mary to meet.

"Stop it with the lip, Mom. You're doing it again."

Children are like little police, Mary thought, sighing, used to it. They see everything wrong. All afternoon, she'd torn apart her closet. She took out one thing after another, tried it on, decided it looked terrible, and soon her wardrobe was heaped like a haystack on the bed. She was pacing the room when Jane returned from her lessons. "I'm just going to call and say I'm sick," her mother said.

Jane sat on the small corner where there weren't any clothes. "What about your gray?"

"That's not dressy enough."

Jane pushed herself up and ran to Julie's kitchen. Julie's theory about dressing was to wear one good thing, top or bottom, mixed with a tee shirt or jeans.

So Mary wore the long denim skirt and a white blouse, and brought chocolate fondue for dessert. Noah came to take Jane to the movies. She rode on his lap on the chair. That first year, when Owens was scarce, Noah often gave Jane rides on his chair. Once, in the rain, she'd held his umbrella up over both of them.

Later, Jane waited in the dark for her mother to come home. A bird had built its nest in the back of the kitchen, in the corner above the dryer, and Jane listened to its tiny ticking sounds.

"Well, what did you think?" she asked, when her mother came in.

Mary walked over to the drawer, took out two of her childhood birthday spoons and opened the fondue pot. "Want some? It was fun. A nice party. She had all different soups."

"Of Bill, I mean."

"He was an interesting person, but I didn't feel any sparks. Mmm, this is good. Should we sit on the porch? It's warm out still."

Jane hated sparks. She couldn't fight them. Invisible, they only kept her and her mother from what should've been their happiness. From the porch in the dark, they could see and hear people leaving the party.

Then the phone rang inside and Mary lunged, thinking it was Owens. But it was Thomas for Jane. Jane had started going steady with neighborhood boys. She waited, one leg bent up against a tree, outside the pink school at four o'clock. So far, she'd gone through three; one broke up with her and she'd broken up with the other two. They were all nice. She wasn't going to put up with much.

While she talked to Thomas, she made out the shapes of washed-out tin cans towering on the floor. Mary cut and punctured them to make mobiles. She had got the idea from children's snowflake decorations at the mountain camp, and thought she could sell them.

For weeks, they had been trying to reach Owens. Mary needed to ask him for more money. Jane wanted to talk to him too, about maybe going to school.

"What about Eli, Mom?" Jane asked when she went back to the porch. "Can Eli give us some?" Thomas couldn't. His allowance was only four dollars a week. They didn't say so out loud, but they each believed they might never see Owens again.

Mary flicked her wrist, as if to say, Oh, forget it. "He would if he could."

All her life before Alta, Jane had lived among the infirm. She'd stepped over drunks, shrugged at beggars, turning her pockets inside out in a shuffle-twirl of hapless apology. She knew the signs of drugs, in the walk, the eyes, the skin, as early as she recognized spiders and poison berries. And it was as if now, all of a sudden, she'd looked up and seen it was not like that here.

They sat in the dark, among the nutmeg smell of jasmine, eating the rich, still-warm chocolate from silver spoons. But now they didn't know if they could stay.

They waited on the steps a long time. Lawns unfurled, plush and even, in front of the small cottages and bungalows. But every fifth or sixth was a mansion built to the edge of the lot line. The neighborhood had gone up and the land was worth something, so even people with the small original houses felt pride of possession and planted flowering sages, begonias and roses in pots. The cars were washed and new, and the families tended to be young. In the morning, the sound of hammers rang up and down the street.

Fixing the car had cost four hundred dollars. Mary looked at the spoon. She imagined she could sell the silver in the wooden box, one fork at a time. She'd save the spoons for last. They agreed on that.

During the months he didn't call, Owens was not angry.

He was simply preoccupied at work. The new team was late and burning money every minute the clock ticked. When the idea of Jane and Mary rose to the surface of his attention at all, he felt a slight echo of their request, like a wince, caused less by them personally than by the notion that people saw him as someone illimitable in his resources and thus guilty. During this urgency at work, friendship fell away and Owens spoke only to the guys on the team and Olivia. He taped a message from his old friend Shep, regarding his daughter's confirmation at Saint Anselm's, to his computer screen until it was weeks past the event, and then he threw it away. It was easy simply to turn his concentration to the problems at hand and leave Jane and Mary on the bottom of the To Do list Kathleen supplied him with, fresh, every morning. Most days, directly above or below *Jane*, was *Call Mom and Dad.*

Along with his To Do list, Kathleen gave him a new stack of envelopes containing money. They kept coming in, and he figured he'd received more than three hundred envelopes so far. He now understood that the San Francisco hostess who'd introduced him to Albertine was the cause of this ludicrous bounty; it was her chain letter his address had been inadvertently linked to. A temporary secretary had mistakenly sent it when she found the letter in his out box under a party list. Now there was nothing to do to stop it. He made a point of keeping the five-dollar bills in his pockets and regularly handing them out to beggars. Eventually, though, he considered the money his own.

Finally, Owens left a message saying he would pick Jane up from her lessons.

She waited under a peach tree, knee bent, foot against the trunk. The late ripe peaches gave off a warm scent.

Across the street, a boy stood sweeping the sidewalk. "You go to Lindsey?" he called.

"No," she mumbled down to her shoes. She made herself not look up because she didn't want more questions about school. She heard his whinnying laugh, picked up a soft peach from the grass and tossed it. It fell wetly apart on the street before him.

Then Olivia was coming, smoking as she walked.

The boy whistled. "That your mom?"

"Hi, Jane," Olivia said. "Owens asked me to pick you up." She and Olivia both acted as if time started now and they weren't late. They never made excuses, never apologized. "I told him to meet us at Waves."

Waves was a converted cannery that rented hot tubs by the hour and served sushi in a square room; it was where Owens had taken Jane and Mary that first night. Olivia's school friend Karen worked there as a masseuse. It was midafternoon, between lunch and dinner, and the three of them sat at one of the wooden tables, drinking juice in the humid air. Karen's teeth were gray and overlapping, and she had a red-head's freckled skin that aged before it was old.

"No, it's terrible," Karen said. "No one would do that to a married couple."

"Are you getting married?" Jane asked, looking up.

Olivia straightened in her chair and sat with perfect posture. Karen sank closer to the table and leaned over, on her arms. "Does he say anything to you?" she whispered.

Jane heard Olivia kick Karen under the table.

"I don't know anything," Jane said. "Nobody tells me."

A frantic conversation went on between the two women's eyes.

"No, we're not getting married now," Olivia said, in a low voice, attempting authority.

Karen's face loomed towards the table. Scolded, she tucked her bottom lip under her overlapping teeth.

"But I had to tell him I'm not going to just stay in a hotel while he goes to a party. He can go without me. We'll take a trip together some other time." A few minutes later, Olivia excused herself and went to the bathroom, after a warning look at Karen.

"Do you like living near your father?" she asked Jane.

"I guess. I don't see him that much."

"Travels a lot, huh?" Karen looked over her shoulder to see that the coast was clear. "She wants to marry him, and sometimes he's good. Then he pulls a stunt like this."

Jane felt like telling all the things he'd done to them too, but Olivia made her cautious. "I know," was all she said.

Then Olivia slid back over the floor, fingertips in her jeans pockets. "Karen, you know his mom's experiencing some pain, and he wants to hire someone to give massage twice or three times a week."

"I could do that." She nodded solemnly.

That night, Owens took Olivia and Jane to some people's house for dinner, but they arrived an hour late. Everyone seemed to have been waiting, as if it were a surprise party, but they were all pretending not to. The hostess brought out fresh trays of untouched appetizers. Owens, for whom everything special was saved and around whom all this swirled, alone noticed nothing. Theo, the host, worked for Owens and knew about his eating, so his wife served a mostly vegetarian meal. Two little girls were led down from upstairs in their nightgowns, rubbing their eyes.

Owens walked out onto the backyard deck, his head up, sniffing. "Jasmine," he said, lifting the flower to show Jane. Theo stood in the corner, grilling salmon steaks.

They ate sitting on the carpeted floor. Olivia absentmindedly French-braided her own hair. She braided beautifully.

On the way home, Owens concluded, "Well, that was nice."

Olivia sat in the front seat, upright, not saying anything.

"So you didn't have a good time."

They rode home the rest of the way in silence, Owens driving grimly, carefully. They were long past the time of sharing mutual impressions, discovering, with pleasure, similar tastes and opinions.

"How much do you think salmon steaks cost?" he finally asked.

"I don't know." Olivia didn't eat fish. "A lot, I think."

"Well, figure in an average restaurant they're about eleven dollars, ten at the least? So wholesale must be about half, so what you pay in the grocery store'd be six, six-fifty a steak." He calculated the cost of the rest of the meal and determined that it must have been a strain. Theo's wife didn't work. "A guy like that, works as hard as he does, he ought to be able to serve salmon steaks if he wants to serve salmon steaks." Owens decided to give the guys a raise, even before Exodus made them rich.

Jane heard her mother yelling at Eli when she touched the door—it was a continuous sound, like a shell she wanted to set down and run away from, so she walked over to the cottage. Julie was on the telephone and motioned her in, and Jane looked around until she discovered a shelf of children's toys in the bedroom, a teddy bear and a stuffed goat. Jane thought they were probably from when Julie was little. She was excited at first, but it was all really too simple for her, the books just pictures, and she felt overgrown. Sometimes she wished she were younger.

"You've discovered my secret stash." Julie had a soft, pealing laugh. "I've started collecting."

Oh, I guess she really wants a kid. That had never occurred to Jane before. Her mom hadn't meant to get pregnant; and if it had been up to Owens, they wouldn't have kept her.

So this was how it began, what so many people had and she always wanted: before you are born, from the beginning and years earlier, you were already wanted. Jane thought of her mom having a kid and not going to college. She wouldn't want to do that. Sometimes when Jane started thinking like this, it got worse and worse and she had to bite her finger hard to stop.

Julie stirred water into a gingerbread mix while Jane helped cut stars out of gold foil to fold into Christmas tree ornaments. Julie pleated the centers.

"You should be the artist," Jane said, "and my mom should be the lawyer."

Julie told her she'd wanted to be a fashion designer in college but that she liked her job for now.

It was the way she was with time, Jane decided. She saw an order to it. The way God in the Bible divided life into days and nights at the beginning of the world, Julie saw shapes in weeks and months and seasons. Now she was a young woman, with her dating and parties. She'd already made a home of her cottage and was starting to collect toys. Pretty soon it was going to be time to get married and have a family, and Jane didn't doubt that she would. Later, it would be time for something else; Jane didn't even know what came after. Time didn't move that way for Jane and her mom. They were a jumbled mess. Jane had never had a steady bedtime. They both stumbled out in the morning, stunned and wet in the new light. When they ate a treat in the middle of the day or charged things they couldn't afford, her mother would say, "It's overdue for us. Remember what that palm reader told me? It's long overdue."

"Ready," Julie called from the stove, holding up a toothpick. "Do you want whipped cream?"

"Oh, yes, please," Jane said, sitting down as Julie sprayed on cream from a can.

Jane and her mother had good in their life too, though. They hardly ever ate things bad for you, but when they did, they whipped cream from scratch and flecked in vanilla bean. Mary could make time out of nothing at all; she could break open an hour when Jane felt bad enough, and they'd have a whole afternoon, eating in beautiful places, with a new ornament in Jane's hair. From a day like that, Jane still owned a long green sparkly glove. The time they made ice cream, with the teachers' crank machine, her mom had jogged to the store so they could have raw pecans on their hot fudge sundaes.

Julie lit one candle, and the light caught in the folds of the gold stars. "Jane, your dad asked me to have dinner. What would your mom think about that?"

"I don't think she'd like it." Julie had always been the one coaxing them out of his realm, making them see life in all the little houses. That she wanted in now made Jane dizzy to think of. So Owens could bend her too.

"Well, that's fair. I was thinking of asking him to the party. But I won't, then."

"I wish he could come to your party. Why can't they all just get along?" Jane said, thinking not only of Owens and her mom but of all the people she'd already left in her life. They hadn't even heard from Bixter since her operation. Jane had friends scattered all over the northern coast. "I wish we could all be in one room together for a holiday."

"That's called your wedding," Julie said. It was not Jane's energy or even her difference that attracted attention, she decided that night. Instead her quality of beseechment was so imperative that everywhere she and her mother lived, a small circle of people formed around them, each one believing it was her or his responsibility to help this one child on her way. "Nickel for your thoughts," Julie added.

"Oh, I was just thinking I wish I knew what my mother wants. I mean, now she's trying to be an artist, but sometimes she's different. I don't know what would be better."

"Well, maybe she wants to get married. I think that's what I want."

Jane said no and then stopped, hitting a wall. That was it. Mary wanted to be a wife. But whose? Owens'? She felt that idea dissolve like a sweet but not real.

Then they heard the bleat of a smoke alarm, and Jane knew it was theirs, hers. She ran across with her hands in her pockets, while Julie watched from the door. A fine soot of ash covered everything inside the bungalow, even Jane's stack of new paper, like a growth of hair. They'd left the kettle on for tea.

Jane flicked the light and saw the pile of unfolded laundry, the charred flaking kettle. They were arguing about who forgot.

"Why aren't you ever done?" Jane screamed, letting the back door bang, and she heard them fighting still.

Mary and Eli cleaned the rest of the night, and Jane begged her mother to stop. An hour later, Jane heard noises and got up.

Mary was leaning on the end of the broom. "Right now, there are so many things I can't do. But this I can, okay?"

Jane put her sour clothes back on then and began to help.

And then, in the middle of the night, Eli discovered the easy way was just to blow. The ash scattered like dandelion seed.

‹‹

Julie kept on with the pumpkin farmer. "He's just too good to let get away," she explained. She told Jane he was a wonderful dancer and somebody she could always trust, but Jane overheard her saying something to Mary about monkeys scratching each other's skulls.

One day, Olivia's cousin Huck called Mary and asked if she'd like to go hiking, and for once Mary decided to try it. Julie and Peter went too, so it was a double date, but Mary wasn't sure it was really a date or just friendship.

It was after ten o'clock when Jane heard her mother's key rattle the lock. "So how was it?"

Her mother stood in the kitchen, making hot water and lemon. "You want some? You should be asleep," she said, calm. "Well, he's a really nice person. We had a good time."

"Were there sparks?"

"I don't know. Not really, not like with Eli. But we'll see. I hardly know him. And I may never feel what I felt for Owens. I'm beginning to think that's really rare."

Peter Bigelow and Huck wanted to take Mary and Julie to Napa for the weekend.

"I'll go if you will," Julie said.

The Spanish Influence

❧❧❧❧❧❧

When Owens was invited to speak at a convention of educators, he took Jane along so they could visit the Mission San Juan Capistrano.

Owens had always admired the Spanish influence in California. He'd grown up around a thousand Spanish names without ever learning the language, yet was not immune to its music. He made a point of seeing all the missions, and Capistrano would complete this ambition. He wandered through it for an hour, admiring the calm austerity that suggested a remote permanence. The day was cold, with a fine rain, and nothing inside the building suggested that the life lived there had ever been opulent or plush. Furniture was rare and substantial, primarily oak: desks Owens could imagine writing on, tables he would want to eat on, hard beds.

"It's like your house," Jane said. "That's why you like it."

"Yeah, it kinda is. But simpler." Jane understood that simpler meant better.

Evidently, in the damp chapel, Indians had sung Gregorian chants. Owens loved these chants and collected their recordings. He clamped his earphones over Jane's head and played one of them on his Disc-man. It sounded rainy, like a huge, cold place.

All around the mission, as far as they could see, orchards swayed in the wind. The *padres* had grown oranges, lemons and olives.

"I wonder what California would be like if it had just been the Spaniards and then the Asians. If the—what did they call them?—the Okies and Pikers and Hoosiers never came." They were standing in the vineyard, under climbing roses.

"Course, that would leave you out," Jane reminded him.

"And you," he added.

But the next day, despite his attraction to the Spanish tradition, he had to say in his speech to nine hundred California teachers that he opposed bilingual education; to him this was no contradiction. He wanted every Californian child to speak English. "Why?" he asked rhetorically. "Because it's the language used in this country." His good coat collar brushed the bottom of his chin, and his hair whipped back from his forehead in the high wind.

"Your father looks dashing," Kathleen whispered.

"Because all over the world, it's the language that's the standard human tongue. If you're a biologist in Sweden, you write your scientific papers in English. If you're a computer scientist in Italy, you program in English. If you're a Russian doctor, chances are you already know English. And if you don't know it yet, you're learning."

"Why not both?" someone shouted from the audience.

"Because a lot of studies show that when you try to do that, it's the English that suffers. A lot of these kids are hearing Spanish at home. School's their only chance to learn to read and write in the language that'll help them succeed."

"Aren't the studies biased?" came a grumble from the side.

Owens stood at a podium in a decrepit football field, half a mile from the convention center, the teachers sitting on the edges of damp, peeling bleachers. He'd begun in the assigned auditorium, then persuaded the teachers to follow him outside. They'd murmured as they'd come into the billowing, watery, blue-and-white day, but most of them felt glad to be outside. Teachers are used to changing their day for weather.

"Even without any studies—let's say they don't exist—it makes common sense that it's harder to do two things well than it is to do just one. And here in California, in our public schools, we're not even doing one thing well yet!"

A young woman stepped up to the microphone. She had a wide face, dark skin and a particularly upright carriage. "Don't you think we're in danger of losing an entire culture if the language that contains it falls by the way?" She had her hands in the pockets of a green parka. I want one like that, Jane thought, with the strings.

Kathleen scribbled quickly on a note card and handed it to him. He gave it back, mumbling, "I know how to talk without subtitles." And then he spoke slowly, with care. "I think the best parts of a culture naturally last. For example, my parents come from the Midwest, where they eat a lot of pork. But when I became old enough to decide, I started eating rice and beans, which is not a part of what you would call my culture. I adopted it not because it's from this culture or that culture but because it's *good*.

"So I don't think we have to worry about preserving every little thing from each culture. It's like when your great-grandmother dies. Do you keep every button and figurine from her attic, or do you remember what you learned from her and make it part of yourself? The good things will stay because people want them.

"If your kid learns English, chances are he'll do well in school. If he does that, he's pretty sure of going to college or getting a good job. And don't you think, at that point, if he wants to learn the language of his grandparents, he can do that pretty easily?"

Tentative applause rose from spots in the audience, then sputtered out.

The young woman in the parka had not left the microphone. "What language did *your* grandparents speak, and did *you* learn it in college?"

"Well, that's kind of a hard question," Owens said, walking out in front of the podium, arms crossed over his chest, "because I dropped out of college after one semester and also because my mother died when I was born and I didn't know her parents. All I know about what they spoke is that one of them was Middle Eastern. And no, I didn't learn that language. And the one grandparent I knew didn't influence me much."

"But doesn't that prove my point?" the young woman asked. "Doesn't that make a case for the integrity of an indigenous culture?"

"Absolutely the opposite!" he exploded, head shaking. He addressed the young woman directly now, his arms moving. This was easy for him, Jane realized. In front of an audience of nine hundred, what her father was doing was flirting. "She didn't influence me because I didn't really care for her. People being related biologically is irrelevant. What matters is if you like 'em. Or even more important, if you respect them."

Kathleen fiddled with the recording equipment, gazing at the woman in the parka.

"What languages *did* you learn besides English?"

Jane felt pierced to the ground where she stood. She could tell it was going to sound bad here if he said just English. She wanted to give him her Spanish. She'd been teaching herself since she met the man from the post office picture, delivering Alta's milk. She tried to catch Owens' attention with a wave, so at least he could say his daughter had another language. But he didn't see her.

"Well, I know FORTRAN and BASIC and probably about forty other computer languages. Oh, and pig latin. I like to think I know not the language of my grandfather but the language of my grandsons and granddaughters."

Applause with a foam of laughter rolled through the crowd. Jane looked up at the sky, blue through the fronds of pine. Canary Island pine, Noah Kaskie had taught her. People carried seeds and cuttings from their homelands sewn in pockets, preserved in raw potatoes, and planted them here.

So he'd pulled it off again. It amazed Jane that though she'd felt a point in her heart like a splinter when he was on the verge of failing, now that he'd succeeded she was left feeling not victorious but chagrined.

Was he truly the most confident person in the world or, like her mother said, insecure?

In fact, Owens had not been invited to speak on bilingual education, pro or con. His assigned topic was science in the schools. But since Jane's arrival in Alta, Owens had become interested in education.

He wanted every child at large not only to eat but to eat well. This he considered to be no problem. Some of the cheapest food you could buy happened to be what he liked best and believed in. He went on to establish a campaign for California's fifty-eight county school districts to offer a free hot lunch daily, composed of beans, rice and one banana per pupil. He would donate the seed money himself, but the beauty of the idea was that beans and rice were cheaper than the junk kids ate now. After months of occasional meetings with his five political advisers and numerous phone calls, a bill had actually been drafted and put before the legislature. The rider Owens insisted on attaching called for the abolition of the milk subsidy, whereby children received a carton of milk, often chocolate, at ten o'clock in the morning for a nickel, which had once been Jane's only incentive to go to school.

As his five advisers predicted, this provoked a real controversy, during which three hundred holsteins were led into Genesis' parking lot by angry farmers and bellowed under the conference room's panoramic window.

"I just don't think cow's milk is very good for us," Owens shouted down, sticking his head out, over the sea of cattle and newspaper photographers. "We're not calves!"

And as he explained later, it wasn't the publicity that bothered him, the holsteins, or the three-inch headlines saying LET THEM EAT BEANS! He figured what was right was more important than what was popular and that popularity came at the end, not at the beginning, of honest work. But when he'd started visiting local schools, it occurred to him that there were problems greater than lunch. What seemed to him to work best was Huck's eighth-grade laboratory classroom, where children sprawled freely on carpeted floors and the teacher came over to supervise, one by one.

Owens believed his first priority, after Genesis, was public education. But he despaired of the cost of changing thousands of schools, already entrenched in miniature military regimes; he didn't have enough time, or even money. So he hired Henrik Henderson, who'd written the book that Huck's eighth-grade experiment was based on, to develop a pilot program. Within the year, Owens hoped, school principals up and down the state would be angling for subsidies to abolish order in the classrooms, free the wooden school desks from their regimental rows and scatter them in happier constellations.

He had hired a New York advertising firm to come up with a slogan to explain himself to the papers. He'd answered the questions himself too many times. *No, I'm not running for anything. I'm a businessman. I work for a company called Genesis, in Auburn, California, and I'm also a citizen. A concerned citizen.* The copywriters used his own words to produce a slogan, and his public service announcements began: "I don't have any degrees in education, I didn't finish college myself, but I've got eyes and they work and here's what I see."

"How many of you drive Ford Tauruses?" he asked the crowd. "You can't buy a car like that in the Soviet Union. Well, I'm asking you, where is the school that's the equivalent of the Ford Taurus? And the answer is, it doesn't exist because that car is the product of competition, and right now teachers' unions have a monopoly."

The teachers, whose salaries and vacations were negotiated by the union, began to stir. Teachers, in general, Jane noticed, were very well behaved.

Afterwards, a man who looked Mexican held out a wrinkled brown bag. "I wanted to show you," he said, extracting a book, itself enclosed in wax paper. It was a dictionary, in Spanish, with thousands of English words scribbled in pencil. "This was how my father taught himself English. It took him nine years to really know it."

Owens sat for the next twenty minutes, studying the English words written in soft, blurry pencil on the frail pages, translucent and flaking like insect wings.

"Well, you guys don't agree on anything," Jane said, sprawled on a large hotel bed. As Owens changed to jeans, turning into himself again, he'd asked her what she thought of the young woman in the parka. "Besides, if you're so interested in schools, how come I can't go?"

"I want to get one working first. But in about a year, you should be able to go." He sighed. "There's some journalist coming here. Oh, so tell me about your friend Julie. Is she really great?"

"I think so. She's really good at making—I don't know—occasions. If you have a talk with her, you feel like you've almost had a tea ceremony."

"Would you say she's neater than Olivia or not as neat?"

"I don't know. I can't compare."

"But if you had to, would you say she's as beautiful as Olivia, more beautiful than Olivia, or not as beautiful?"

"Maybe as beautiful."

"Really?" He raised an eyebrow.

"What do you enjoy?" the journalist asked. She had a pointed face and a very small body. More young than pretty, Owens decided. On the phone, she'd had an eager quality that reminded him of Albertine.

Jane sat in the corner at the desk, skimming the Gideons Bible. Their conversation all pertained to business and was dull. She kept thinking of what he'd said about being a college dropout. She didn't want to be that.

"I like doing things well. I like doing the things I have to do in my life well." At that moment, he was thinking of the small plastic bottles he'd bought with Jane from a mountaineering shop, to pack their Dr. Bronner's soap and conditioner in—it was a point of pride for him to pack neatly—but he talked only about scientific applications, how with the information known now the world could already be changed. Jane listened for a minute and then her attention waned. She was thinking, I would know my answer: wind cuffing her neck softly, like it did this morning in the early sun with the top down on their rental car.

"So you're not trying to discover the secret of life?" the journalist asked.

"The secret of life? The secret of life's already been found."

"Don't you worry about being too lucky?" She mentioned the king whose touch turned everything to gold. "Do you sometimes think the gods might be out to get you?"

Thinking of the five-dollar bills, he said, "Well, maybe that's where my girlfriend comes in," and then laughed.

"Is it true that you have political aspirations?"

"I like my job a lot. I can't think of any other job that would make me want to leave it."

"Really? You wouldn't, in a few years, say, consider running' for governor? Or something bigger?"

Owens smiled enigmatically. Then the journalist glanced at Jane and asked whether he would encourage young people to follow his example in having children out of wedlock.

"Just to be clear," he said, basketing his hands, "I'm not running for anything. And if I ever do, it won't be for canonization. I'd run for some office that's been held by men who might've done a great job for this country or a poor job but, without exception, men who've made mistakes. Whether they've acknowledged them or not. And I acknowledge my mistakes."

"Oh, great," Jane said when the avid young woman left. "It'll be on the six o'clock news that I'm a mistake."

The women in his life were not happy with Owens.

He was on television, answering a reporter's questions in a Martinez apple orchard that had once been owned by John Muir. In the bungalow, Jane and Mary were perched together on the old love seat Julie had lent them, while Owens lay on the floor watching, his face as blankly studious as if it were any other news. Every day now, the California Dairy Council published full-page attacks on him in the newspaper.

What was it exactly that Owens did? Jane often wondered and tried to figure out. Well, he started a company, he and Frank Wu together. They manufactured LCSF and that turned out to be really important. But why? Owens didn't even discover it. She asked Noah once what was the big deal and he said it was because they'd figured out how to put the protein into bacteria. They used to get insulin from pigs, he said, but people had immune reactions. They got human growth hormone—what they gave dwarfs—from cadavers, but it wasn't safe to isolate proteins that way. That's how Balanchine died, Noah said.

Most people knew only that Owens and Frank had started out in his parents' basement and ended up being millionaires. But sometimes Owens talked about changing the world. And they did, I guess, Jane thought; but doesn't everything, then, in a way? Like what Noah told her, which she'd never known: that broccoli hadn't existed, someone made it. Now millions of people, probably even in China, ate broccoli. That made a difference. And in the wintercamp she'd met the great-great-grandchildren of the man who'd invented the zipper lock. Peter's family was connected with Ex-Lax. Somebody invented paper towels and the toilet and self-defrosting freezers—which would be a miracle to her and her mom since they'd waited too long and now the freezer was solid ice. But all those people weren't on television. They weren't famous.

When the news turned to weather, Owens suggested they go to the burrito place. It was still light out, and as they walked, Jane's parents ganged up on her about makeup.

"You're just too young," her mother said. "Kids shouldn't think about these things."

"You know, Ingrid Bergman never wore makeup," Owens said. "Or Sophia Loren. Isabella Rossellini doesn't wear makeup, or just the slightest bit. And Olivia doesn't wear any at all. Yeah, the most beautiful women in the world don't wear makeup."

Kicking a pebble out of her sandal, Mary hated him. Without thinking, she rubbed at her eyes, which had a buff of dark-green shadow and itched. Besides, wasn't that Rossellini woman in the ads for some cosmetic?

"Well, I'm not even the most beautiful girl on our street, okay?" Jane sputtered as they entered Juan's Burritos. "And I think I look better in makeup."

"One of the things I really respect about Olivia is she doesn't care about her looks. She could go up to the city, you know, buy herself some good clothes, and she could probably end up in the south of France on some yacht." Owens raised his eyebrows, considering Olivia's prospects, then turned back to his menu.

Mary was thinking that Olivia didn't need city clothes. Her boyfriend was wealthier than most of those playboys in France. She was doing pretty well right here, with her jeans.

Just then, Olivia strode in, looking taller than usual. Her hair brushed her elbows, a living entity. She didn't even say hello, just stood looking at Owens as if nobody else were there.

"What did I do now?" he said.

"You didn't even call. I told Huck I couldn't eat with him because I wanted to wait to hear from you first. And you don't even think to include me. That's not what people who are involved do, Tom. That's not how people live together."

"I'm taking my daughter for a burrito because she was hungry."

Mary looked down at the table. What was she, a baby-sitter? No one counted her.

"I was not," Jane mumbled. "*You* were hungry."

"But you didn't think to call and see what my plans were." Olivia shook her hair and walked out. A minute later, he went out after her.

"I'm still hungry," Jane announced.

Mary and Jane sluffed up to the counter to order. They were paying anyway. Now that he was gone, Jane ordered beef. Mary sighed. "I think I'm going to stop eating red meat and see how I feel."

"Don't expect me to, just because you do," Jane said. "I like hamburgers."

By now Jane understood that Olivia was the most beautiful woman in Alta. She was famous, locally, as Noah was for being in a wheelchair. People she'd never met said "Hi, Olivia" when they passed, and she always said hullo back.

And she was even more beautiful than that. When he visited New York or Washington or Tokyo, Owens told Jane, he was invited to dinners with important people, men and, occasionally, a woman or two, who had accomplished something. He admired these women, he said, and Jane asked why he didn't fall in love with any of them, then. And he said they were generally too old to fall in love with. Once, though, in Paris, a perky millionairess his own age had asked for his hotel room number. "So why didn't you fall in love with *her?*" Jane asked.

Not answering, he explained that most of the women he met at these events were along only as accompaniments. Though as a rule they were more put together and done up, none of them was ever more beautiful than Olivia. Still, her accomplishments were of the passive variety, a matter of what she'd not done but easily could have. She probably could be on a yacht or some Greek island. She could definitely at least be in San Francisco, buying a new dress every day. But he only rarely gave her credit, from what Jane could tell. In his book, there were two kinds of people: those who do and those who don't.

Other people gave Olivia more credit than Owens did, Jane noticed, but that happened in couples a lot. In a town the size of Alta, it was pretty easy to be known for your hair and height. It seemed almost an accident, Olivia still being here. How many girls in America have the looks to be models and never try?

In the ledger of life, there was more than one method of calculation, Jane was figuring out. Whether you counted every success and ignored the failures, or subtracted the failures from the successes, made a difference. Olivia, like Jane's mom, was cautious: more afraid to do something wrong than not to do anything. Jane noticed that men talked about making a name for themselves and women worried about protecting their good name, as if women had only the one value they were born with and had to keep from tarnishing, while men were given blank slates, on which they could prove their worth. Jane didn't like thinking this. She already had bad grades from the mountain town school on her record. She wondered where the record was stored, if there was a place she could break into and burn it. She wanted to start out new here, blank at the little pink school. This time, she would make her record be perfect.

Olivia had her bike, so Owens couldn't catch up running. Half an hour later, he slanted across the lawn, yelling, "I just want you to be proud of me! That's why I do all this!"

"I'm *always* proud of you," she called, and he glimpsed her through the doorway. "But I'm not proud because you're on the news."

Owens lay down on the bare floor of his living room, and in a little while Olivia came in and sat beside him. He liked it here, with his head in her lap.

"I feel like I have a responsibility," he said softly.

"To whom?"

He shrugged. "Hey, I have an idea. Why don't we go out on the motorcycle?"

Then they were zooming through the hills, unsettling the natural calm. He took the back roads and ended up in Auburn, on his parents' street. He cut off the engine in the fragrant dark and they leaned against the bike, their feet on the wet lawn.

"See," he said, "sometimes a small life seems good to me. All these little houses."

"Who do you think is expecting you to do such great things?"

"Not them, that's for sure," he said, looking up to his parents' house, where all the lights inside were off.

Somehow for Mary it had all come down to fruit. Owens apparently bought Philippine mangoes and yellow blush cherries from Mount Shasta. He had fresh Medjool dates flown in from Indio, still on the branch. He bought the best berries, oversized, in season or out.

"I mean, wouldn't you think he'd want his daughter to eat the same as he does?"

All this made Julie uneasy. Julie was the person Mary railed to about Owens, but it seemed to her that Mary was hiding behind her daughter, as one would behind a mask. It was simpler to fight for the rights of a small person than to say, *I want those big strawberries for myself.* And Mary forgot she was talking to someone who ate the average Chiquita banana from the A & P for lunch and didn't feel deprived. But then Mary whipped her own cream as if it mattered, which Julie understood, on account of her not working. Even in their close friendship, the two women maintained a delicate system of balances.

"And how dare he mention the most beautiful women in the world and include Olivia but not Jane's own mother? How must that make Jane *feel*?" Mary asked, even though Jane was sitting right there with them.

It was as if she were afraid to say *me.* "I'd be offended," Julie said, "even if Jane wasn't along."

"Especially if he's counting people, not movie stars," Jane added.

Then Eli slouched in the back door, cupping a small bird in his hand. They all gathered around as he fed it with an eyedropper.

Mary stuttered with embarrassment, introducing Eli to Julie. Mary and Huck went out with Julie and Peter every weekend, but Eli still came most nights, after his band practice. He had to go home every morning to take care of his birds: baby quails he traded at the pet store for bird food, or baby mourning doves he released into the general sky. Peter and Julie were always telling her what a great guy Huck was. "Really, oh," Mary would answer.

Huck came wearing a sweater, his hair down wet from a shower, every Saturday night. "How're ya doin'," he'd say when Jane answered the door. "Fine," she always told him, and then he looked around the room as if he didn't know what else to ask, even though he was a teacher. He seemed relieved when her mom came in, and he rubbed his palms on the front of his pants. Mary liked it because she felt she was learning things on their dates. He was teaching her to play tennis, for example. And with Huck, her mother said, paying for things was never a problem. She'd leave the house with hardly any money.

Eli was bending over the bird, intent. He placed the soft, breathing ball into Julie's tentative hands. Mary looked to her friend shyly, as if to ask, *Now do you see?* He came to Mary like a boy with a broken kite for her to mend.

Julie sighed and excused herself, putting the bird into Mary's palm. Mary had agreed a hundred times that she should break up with Eli. I have to, she always said, I know I have to. And Julie had wanted to discuss the invitation she'd received that morning to Owens' birthday party. The truth was she wanted to go.

Dying Young

<del>◄◄ ◄◄ ◄◄ ◄◄</del>

On a hilltop, in a ballroom, Owens was throwing a thirtieth-birthday party for himself, Noah told Jane and Mary. Like many people, they had reason to be amused. Owens had frequently declared he would not live to see thirty.

"How do you know?" Noah had asked him, three years earlier.

"I just know," he'd said, tapping his breast pocket, "I know it right here."

Noah'd teased him. "Well, that rules out being president."

"Bet he didn't like that," Jane said.

His somberness had seemed almost touching to Noah that day, but then Owens added, "A lot of the best people die young. And a lot more should've. Like if I were Bob Dylan, I'd rather have died while I was still in love with Joan Baez, you know, and she was still beautiful."

"But he's not Dylan," Mary said, "and when he's thirty, he won't want to be dead either."

"And she is too still beautiful," Jane insisted. "We saw her, Noah. At the nursery. She was buying geraniums. Red ones."

And Mary was right: at the time of the party, they heard no more about the best people dying young.

Noah Kaskie wanted a date for the party. He wished his sister were around. He'd long known the advantages of having a pretty sister, and with her it would be fun. But she was in the Peace Corps now, in Togo, Africa, building latrines.

"Yup, the big three-oh," Owens said, slapping a hand on what was beginning to become a belly.

Noah and he were sitting at the Café Pantheon. A woman was reading at a table near them, a glass of wine in her left hand and a cup of coffee by her right. Though she was small, there was nothing girlish about her. She seemed entirely adult, alternating beverages, a pencil behind her right ear. Despite this activity, there was a neatness to her, as if her bookbag, by the leg of her chair, contained many compartments. Noah recognized her first by her trademark earrings, longer than her hair. He had never seen that before Louise. It seemed to defy everything he had absorbed from years of listening to his mother and sister: big earrings went with long hair, studs with short. This earring hung long and slender, a good inch below her white hair.

"That's my postdoc over there," he whispered. This was the first time he'd seen her outside the lab, and he'd noticed, not her beauty (he found her odd-looking), but her earring. And her self-administration.

"Why are we whispering," Owens whispered back. "Hey, have you ever thought of asking her out?"

"No, not really." Noah hadn't until just this minute. "And I can't. It'd be wrong."

"I bet she'd really like you," Owens said. "I've got an idea. You could go over and ask her if she'd like to come to my birthday party. That's not a date. It's a party."

She was biting her nails, as she often did in the lab. She somehow made this look intelligent, a purposeful woman's anxiety honed down to a delicate activity.

After Owens left, Noah did wheel over and invite Louise to the party, knowing full well she wouldn't go. So he was stunned when she said yes—a result that mildly thrilled but did not altogether please him.

He didn't have tenure. You couldn't *date* people in your lab. That was not only improper but probably illegal. For another thing, Rachel, the crystallographer from upstairs, had picked up the invitation from his desk and toyed with it. "Black tie," she'd said. "Sounds kind of fun." Kaskie most definitely did not own a tuxedo. The one suit Kaskie did own was dark, and several friends had suggested he could "probably get away with it." Or, Rachel explained seriously, he could rent evening clothes. But *Owens* in a tuxedo? He had never seen his friend in anything but jeans.

Olivia and Owens moved together in the twilight room. He stood at the dresser, picking out socks. The black garment bag with his tuxedo hung on the closet door. This reminded him of his parents dressing to go out on a Saturday night—the impending dread of the baby-sitter, hurried happy tension in the house while it was still light outside. His parents would drive away in the car his father most recently fixed, a long rose from the garden on the seat.

"Oh, no," Owens said. "I didn't invite Pony."

"Call her now," Olivia said.

He found his small book in his jeans pocket and sank to the futon to dial.

Her friends Karen and Dave weren't invited either. Olivia almost said something. Now she could get them added too, but Karen would refuse out of pride. She'd know other people had been invited before.

"Pony, hi," he said, standing in his underwear. He gave clear directions, not only to the hotel but where to park. "Just tell them your name when you go in."

His mother and dad wouldn't be there, though he wished again they would be. But his mother wanted to see the lilacs of her childhood one more time.

Olivia stood in the closet, putting on a black silk dress that seemed to Owens a little bit too shiny. But Olivia always looked worse dressed up, and he shook his head. He'd asked her to do one thing for this party, and that was to get something good to wear. She was tall, as tall as he was, and could look great in clothes. He should have bought her something.

Olivia lifted up the price tag from the sleeve and bit it off with her teeth. "I guess you don't like it," she said. Now she didn't want him to see how much it had cost.

Owens had not had money for very long, but he'd had it long enough so that things which had seemed nice before didn't seem nice at all now. Things to eat, things for the house, things to wear. If he had to characterize this quality of discrimination, he would have said he thought he had good taste. He would vehemently deny that this was connected with any notion of "class," a word he never used and that in fact gave him the creeps. It was nevertheless true that more details occupied his conscious life now than when he was twenty. Italian track lights, nurseries for old roses. He had even begun to notice doorknobs.

Even so, since he and Olivia would wear Levi's and tee shirts ninety-nine out of one hundred nights, it seemed to him that the hundredth should be wand-tipped.

But whatever Olivia was wearing, Owens took pleasure in his own clothes. He opened the drawer where he kept cufflinks. The iron studs were there, in a little box, with an old note from Olivia, a scrap of yellow paper that said *LOML.*

There was once when it was earlier, when Olivia was new to love and unafraid, drunk with the first arrogance of feeling, the conviction that all joy is matched and somehow protected. The LOML days: Love of My Life. Owens had come home late from work one night and found she'd safety-pinned that piece of paper to his pajamas.

On the way to the party, Owens slowed the car to show her the mansion where his biological mother had grown up. Eliot had found the address, reporting that the house had changed owners several times since then.

"Have you ever been inside?" Olivia asked. By then he had been a guest in many mansions.

"No, I never have. I have no idea who lives there."

His mother had been an only child. Her parents, who had retired to Arizona, were now dead. "They probably wanted their daughter to marry some rich guy and go out dancing every night." Owens laughed, hollowly but with a rind of bitterness, because fog was coming in and they were on their way to a party and they were rich.

Even as a child, Owens had considered birthdays a waste of time and bargained with his parents to give him the money instead. He turned off the ignition and waited before getting out. "I was just thinking there probably aren't many people my age who've never had a birthday party or a surprise party or, really, any kind of party. And now I'm wrecking my streak." He touched her hand. When they stepped out, the cool air uplifted their breath and the lit palace tilted vertical over them.

He'd spent some money and some time on this small attempt at happiness. He'd taken more than a day on the invitation list. Frank had not RSVPed.

Olivia smiled. "So here we are. Happy birthday."

The first people he saw in the ballroom were his two cooks, who were wearing what he recognized as his old clothes. Eliot Hanson was talking to Albertine. The guys from the team at work looked a lot different in formal clothes. Owens glanced at the band in the corner, the lit chandeliers, the high windows reflecting the winks of table candles, spots of flowers. The five bald men in tuxedoes sat huddled at one table. Nobody at Genesis went to many parties like this; that Owens knew for a fact. With one hand in their pockets, the other holding drinks, they looked even younger here, shier, but they were laughing. He smiled with a tender, custodial feeling. As the band started a hopping tune, he thought of Jane, jumping up and down the way she did with her legs straight, never bending her knees. It was a jump a woman would never do. She did it whenever she got something from luck: out of the blue, she called it. She had jumped when she saw the coat Noah had bought her. She thought her *out-of-the-blue* quotient was way below average. He wished she were here right now, but it was late already, who would take her home, people were drinking. No, he liked the thought of her safe in the bungalow. His cooks, Susan and Stephen, were talking now with the accountant, while Albertine's hands made excited rectangles. They were all having a good time. He felt glad, watching.

Noah Kaskie did not buy or rent a tuxedo. He hated anything to do with dressing rooms. His sister could sew, and most of his life she'd tailored down his clothes for him. But Michelle was in Africa, and he wasn't about to call his *mother*. So when he picked up Louise, he was wearing his one dark suit, which dated from a growth spurt not long after his bar mitzvah. She was waiting outside for him, in a small black dress that somehow made her limbs seem nicely joined. Although she still didn't seem beautiful, Noah liked to look at her. There was something coherent about her body.

But when they entered the party, it was immediately obvious that he was the only man in a suit. After twenty minutes he'd spotted two more, both sorry people, one a kid with acne and the other probably a caterer. Better to be wearing a jeans jacket, he thought, like the tall woman with cornrows who'd thrown one over a long white dress. He'd always thought he didn't need clothes, he was an academic scientist. Now he remembered what his sister said about having been a bridesmaid. "You get this awful little fuchsia dress you're too big for and you think, Well, she's my friend and I love her and of course I can wear this. But you forget you walk into a room full of other people, even interesting other people, and that's the only way they'll see you."

"Do you know many people here?" Louise asked him.

"Hardly anybody." He picked up their cards and vaguely scanned the crowded room for their table.

"Good. I like parties where I don't know anyone." She was always saying something that yanked him back for a double take.

Most people were standing and talking or wandering around, while waiters, also in dinner clothes, served champagne. Kaskie wanted to find his table, fast.

"Is something wrong?"

She always sounded ironic and possibly critical. "Nothing," he said. "Just a lot of butts in my face."

"Should I leave?"

"Oh, no. It's only—I'm one of the only men here who's not in a tuxedo."

She made a dismissive sound with her mouth. "People spend too much money on clothes," she said with authority.

If this is a date, Noah thought, it isn't going particularly well.

I'm flying back tomorrow, Albertine reminded herself, with another sip of wine. She was sitting at her assigned place, adding up the money it had cost to come and thinking, *I have so much to do.* The drudges in her class were probably working right now, up in their garrets, windows open, flute music ribboning through.

"You *have* to come," Owens had said on the telephone. But now that she was here, she wondered. She sat, chin on fist, talking amiably to the people on either side of her. To her left was a cute guy in a wheelchair, who ate everything with great relish; on her right was a man who seemed to be Owens' accountant. Olivia, whom Owens had described long-distance as not that serious, stood next to him on the dance floor, like a wife. What she was wearing, Albertine noticed with a pouting satisfaction, made her look clumsy. Big. Albertine sighed, accepting her fish from the young waiter, who was beginning to seem like the most interesting man here. The guy in the wheelchair had finished her soup, and she now handed him the plate of pasta directly. It wasn't just the money; it was the time: eleven hours, round trip, in the air. And the day lost to shopping with Ash. Albertine didn't just *hap*pen to have something in her closet suitable for spring black tie. Ash trooped her through the good stores, where they discovered they'd come a month and a half too late. The spring selection was all but gone. Finally, Ash plucked something off a small rack in Bergdorf's. "Show a little," he said, slapping Albertine's flat bust. The price was impossible, but Ash promised to take it back the day she got home. "They'll credit your card before you even get the bill. Just don't spill," he'd said. And now I owe him a favor, Albertine thought, some little gift. She sighed in the exhaustion of befriending the rich. Gifts from the rich were never free. But Albertine didn't seriously consider an alternative. She was a young woman perfectly adjusted to her society.

Just then, Owens lifted her hair off her neck. "I like your dress very much." He led her to the edge of the floor near the windows, where they danced. They kissed for a while—she didn't know how dark it was—and he was pulling her embarrassingly close.

Then a man with a clipboard tapped Owens' shoulder, and he said, "Oh, excuse me for a minute. I've got to get my sister in."

Albertine then had to make the painful walk all alone across the floor, as if this were a runway and everyone watching was deciding whether to clap or boo.

Owens had forgotten to put Pony's name on the list, and she'd been turned away at the door. But she kept telling them she was Colleen Owens, Pony, his own sister, and as a small group of waiters gathered, Eliot Hanson noticed and intervened.

"Help yourself to everything," Owens gestured, throwing an arm around her, once she was securely inside, realizing only at that moment that there would be no place set for her at any table.

"They told me I couldn't get in if I wasn't on the list. Hmph," she said, looking back over her shoulder.

He put her down in his own seat, next to Olivia.

As they passed her table, Julie whispered to Peter, "There he is. Should I go and introduce myself?" She had a mild voice with an easy laugh in it. She was often the first and the last one laughing.

"Man, it's incredible—the guy invites *you* and *they're* not even here."

Julie had come to the party just because she wanted to so much. She'd meant to explain to Mary ahead of time, but whenever she was about to bring it up, she lost her nerve. She thought that when she saw Mary and Jane here, they might assume Peter had somehow been invited. She made Peter promise to be mysterious. But it was even stranger now that they weren't here. Now, Julie thought, she could never tell them.

Intrigued by the idea of meeting Owens, she felt a little evil bringing Peter along on her adventure. If tonight did lead to something, she didn't see that Peter really had to know. Julie considered herself to be near the end of her dating years. It seemed appealing and somehow proportional now to date a famous man. It would be something to have done, to put in the box that was her youth, for her daughters to take out and examine, as they ransacked the dress-up trunk for her hats and gloves and fine pointed shoes. They would find an old magazine cover with Tom Owens' face on it.

"Guy wants to meet you something bad," Peter said. For him, too, there was something not altogether unpleasant in the famous man's enchantment with his girlfriend.

"Well, that wouldn't be too hard. He could come and introduce himself. I feel like someone at a Gatsby party."

"Albertine, hey, how're you doing," Peter said. "Julie, this is my cousin Al."

A narrow-shouldered girl in a sleek dress sat down, gracefully arranging her limbs. They talked, full of animation, and Julie saw Peter a little differently. She was uncomfortable here, but he eased back in his chair, looking straight at his cousin, talking about some old woman who'd taken care of them, whom they both called Tante Elise.

Without moving her head, Albertine kept track of Owens' movements, his arm around Olivia again. Oh, well, she thought, I've done it and he'll appreciate it and now it's over with. Too much of her life was a matter of getting things over with.

Olivia and her cousin were fighting in hushed voices, as they had a hundred times before.

"He invites her neighbor but not them?"

"Huck, it's his party. I can't help who he asks. He probably thought Jane's too young."

"Well, what about Mary?"

"They're not that close, Huck. Besides, most people don't invite their ex-girlfriends."

"I've met Julie and Peter a bunch of times with her; now what am I going to say?"

"I don't know. Say hello, I suppose."

Huck laughed in alarming spurts, so hard he began to choke and Olivia had to slap his back.

The tall woman with cornrows had shed her jeans jacket and was now hopping, slapping the dance floor. When she reeled past, she winked at Owens. She was a clarinetist. She'd played once on his bed, beautifully and nude.

A couple waited in line to talk to Owens. "Shep and Lamb," he cried, when the crowd cleared and they stepped up to say goodbye. Seeing them dancing together across the room had given a deep accent to his pleasure. They had to leave now, something about the baby-sitter, but they wanted to have him to dinner. Yes, of course he'd come, he said, bending down to kiss Lamb, whose gown had stars on it, like Merlin's.

"But before you leave," he said, "you've got to do one thing for me." Trailing behind them, he found the photographer sitting next to Noah, eating cake. He made the man stand up, napkin still in his collar, and take a picture of the three of them: Owens, Shep and Lamb.

Noah and Louise had discovered that the waiter controlled a great store of ice cream, which he now brought out in stemmed silver goblets. Noah was drinking his third glass of champagne.

"Are you an alcoholic?" Louise asked. Then, without waiting for his answer, she stood up, dropping her napkin. "Oh, I've got to go. It's already eleven. I've got to harvest the virgins." It was her damn flies again. Eight hours after the flies on a cross start to hatch, you had to take out the virgins so they wouldn't interbreed and spoil the whole batch. Flies were fast. They could go through as many generations in a month as mankind did since history began.

"So it's settled, then," Lamb said, her hands on Owens' hands. "You'll come for supper." He followed them into the elevator and through the lobby. He stood a second outside in the fine rain. His in-augural party was still going. Even from here, as he looked up at the arched windows, he could hear music and see dancers' shadows.

"Your parents weren't here, were they?" Lamb asked. "And what about Frank?"

He just shook his head. On the way back through the lobby, he ran into his sister, carrying a centerpiece of cut flowers that would be dead tomorrow. "You had a lot," she said, giggling nervously.

"So who was there at the party?" Jane asked.

"Well, I was there," Owens said, pulling a pillow from the couch down under his head. "A whole bunch of people I know. In fact, I've got a really cute picture of Olivia."

"It *is* a good picture," Mary said. Before the party, Olivia had complained to her about having to buy a new dress. She told Mary she was so nervous and busy right then that she just drove up to the city one morning and spent three hundred dollars on the first suitable thing she could find. She said she'd never spent that much before on anything for herself. "Not even a couch or an appliance."

"Who else was there?" Jane asked.

"Oh, lots of people. People you don't know. Remember Albertine Maguire, that friend I told you about? She flew in from Boston." He smiled a little, looking at the ceiling. "I asked my sixth-grade teacher, Mrs. Tine. She was there."

"You did?" Sixth grade was what she would be in now, Jane thought.

"Yeah, and we had a little toast for her and she seemed really happy. She was the first person who taught me how to think. Before that, I really didn't care about school."

Mary and Jane made a good audience for Owens. One with an open face, the other with a face held closed, they sat up straight in their chairs, rapt while he spoke from the floor.

"She was trying to get me to do my math. She said, 'I bet you could be really good at this if you tried.' And I said, 'Yeah, but why should I?' And she opened her purse and said, 'Because I'll give you five dollars if you get it all right.' Out of her own money. And so I did it, and that's when I started to get excited about math."

"Did she pay you again?"

"By the next time she didn't have to pay me. I was hooked."

"She gave you the five dollars," Jane said. "That's really good."

"Were your folks there?" Mary asked, as if calculating something. "At the party, I mean."

You can really tell when Mary's thinking, Owens mused. Her face is like an old computer, obvious and clanking.

"Oh, they were away. They went on a trip to Portland to see their relatives."

This didn't sound all on the up-and-up to Mary. Portland or no

Portland, Nora wouldn't miss his thirtieth-birthday party and being his mother there. Mary suspected he'd sent them on a trip and didn't tell them.

Jane pictured two old people standing with luggage at a brick train station. She'd never even met them. When would she ever get to? She intended to ask him, but she had to do it alone. Her mother was still mad at his parents.

"So," she said, "what did you do at the party?"

"Well, there was a dinner."

Mary and Jane looked at each other. They both wanted to know what was the menu.

"And there was champagne and all along people were dancing."

"Oh, they danced," Jane said.

"Many people, I would say most people, danced."

"And did you have a birthday cake?" Jane asked.

"You know, I forgot until you said that, but they did have a cake. I think Olivia and some of the goons at work planned that. It was pretty horrible, though, one of those fluffy gooey cakes. I didn't actually eat any."

"Mmm," Jane said. "That's the kind of cake I like." There was a long pause. When she said something he didn't approve of, he often pretended not to hear. Or else he'd raise his eyebrows and say, "You do? Really?" to give her a chance to improve her answer. But Jane only looked at her mother and then at him. "So how come you didn't invite us, if so many people were there?"

Mary wouldn't have asked, but she was waiting too to hear his excuse.

He looked at his child. "You're not old enough. It was an adult party. It went on late."

"What about my mom? She's a grown-up."

"She had to stay home and take care of you," was his quick answer.

Jane and her mother looked at each other, and Mary's mouth went crooked. He'd lied again or something like that, but neither of them said so.

"God, a ballroom. I've never seen a ballroom," Jane said, heaving back on the old sofa.

He grabbed her foot. "I'll take you to see one sometime."

Mary fell into activity the way she did when she was mad. She got up, followed the trail of mugs and glasses through the house and took them to the sink to be washed.

"All I'm ever gonna see is empty ballrooms after the party's over," Jane said.

As Jane followed her father to the car, she heard the radio switch on in the kitchen. Her mom listened to AM radio, American Top Forty, while she cleaned the house. A lot of the songs Jane knew by heart, the soothing up-and-down hills of ride. She heard her mother's voice lift to sing along and the shrill tune the pipe made with the water.

She slammed the car door hard from inside. When he turned on music it was classical. She knew classical was better; her mom did too, and whenever they put it on, they tried to pay attention. But tonight Jane didn't feel like learning anymore. She'd been learning for almost two years now, and she was tired.

Owens drove home, where Olivia might or might not be. They were fighting again. That morning, she was talking about moving out, getting her own place. As it was, she'd set up a room for herself at the opposite end of the house, half a mile away from him. "It'd be great if we walked in and Livia had supper ready," he said.

Jane could not even imagine that.

With one hand off the wheel, he slid a picture from his wallet. "I could do a lot worse," he said, shaking his head. "I'm pretty tired."

"From work?"

"No, from the party. Which kind of amazes me, I have to say. Before in my life, when I've been this tired, it's always been from work."

Jane thought it was fine to be tired from a party. A party was an accomplishment too.

"Or maybe love." He fell quiet then, as if into some strange, sad mood.

In the picture Owens had given her, Olivia looked beautiful. Jane mumbled that, thinking there was something tender in the way Olivia gazed up at him.

"And young," he said. "Sometimes I think, if this doesn't work out, she'll probably be the last woman I'll be with who's gone out with only a few guys. And you know, one of the things I respect most about Olivia is she cares about what's right. When she was thirteen, she just came home one day and said that she'd thought about it and she wasn't going to eat meat anymore." He looked at Jane purposefully, as if to say, *You're not thirteen yet. You still have time.*

Olivia was thirteen when her mother died, Jane remembered. She wanted to ask him, was being vegetarian before or after? But he didn't like to think about things like that. Also, she had the feeling he wouldn't know.

And he and Olivia fought even about food. On Tuesday, Olivia had brought home soda for Jane. "That's what she likes, Owens, and she's our guest."

"Next thing you know, people'll be roasting hogs on a spit in our kitchen."

"And what if they did, if they're our friends?"

"I'm not going to roast a pig," Jane said.

But Jane knew she was as vegetarian as he was, maybe more. He ate fish. Olivia really did it for the earth. She told Jane statistics about how much land it took to feed cows and grow grain, and how many people the grain fed, and what it meant for the rain forest. Jane forgot exactly how it worked, but she believed absolutely it was terrible and true.

Owens teased Olivia about leather shoes, which she wore only half the time.

"I could be a lot better, I know," she'd said, when he'd toed on her toe, pulled her close, and whispered, "Cowhide."

She'd gone on, "Let's really stop buying animal products and start washing out Baggies. I know these people . . ."

He had this look, like, Oh, God, this wasn't what I wanted to start. He'd been just teasing. And even though Jane believed Olivia, she liked leather shoes.

But when Owens loped through his door with Jane following, Olivia wasn't home. The house was dark and empty. He hulked in the kitchen and studied the note from the cooks, as if hoping for something from her. He played the white telephone answering machine, fast-forwarding through all the thank-yous for his party, slowing down to hear Albertine.

"To be perfectly frank, you had *quite* the crowd."

But nothing from Olivia. " 'Fixin's for burritos in the fridge,' " Owens read aloud, from Susan and Stephen's note. " 'Adzuki beans. Completely oil free. (Except the cheese.) There's also sour cream, if you feel like splurging.' You'd think they'd notice we never touch the cheese."

Their temptations didn't tempt him in the least, apparently. But they did tempt Jane.

He began to take glass bowls out of the refrigerator. White corn kernels, beans, basmati rice, sliced avocados and carrot salad. He grabbed a new package of lavash bread. "Oh, and they made fruit salad too." He inhaled; he was a vegetarian for *this*—the numb smell of raw food in his kitchen.

Jane really wanted some cheese, but she watched the refrigerator door suck closed. And she wanted to cook it all up in a fry pan the way her mom did and make it warm.

Once, he'd told her his vision of disgust: butter with crumbs and bits of jam on it. Butter under a clear butter dish, soft and shapeless, flecked, smeared. "Just butter. You know, in houses with big families." But she remembered and thought if she weren't there, he would have just said families. *Maybe his real disgust is us.*

It was strange: in her mother's bungalow, Jane always felt beautiful—she was, she knew that. But here, all that fell off like a joke and she was left with her plainness. It wasn't what they said but the way they forgot her.

Owens and Jane did what he did a lot of times when Olivia wasn't there: they ate standing in the kitchen and then climbed upstairs for the night. He inhabited his mansion as if it were a one-bedroom apartment. The two rooms he used were furnished with his needs, and the rest was pretty much empty. He meant to watch a movie tonight and narrowed it down to three, letting Jane pick; but when they were on his bed, he put in Olivia's commercial.

Olivia's whole family had lived off the royalties from this commercial, which ended with her face when she was only four years old. Jane bit her cheek. She was already so much older and hadn't done anything yet. Owens had tracked down the tape in the archives of a defunct advertising agency, kept it by his bed and played it when Olivia wasn't there. She couldn't stand to see it.

When Jane and her mom had gone to the flea market with Julie, Jane had spotted a canister with Olivia's childhood picture on it. She recognized it from the commercial. The man wanted eighteen dollars, even though it didn't have a lid. Just to say something, Jane had told Owens about the canister, and he kept asking if she knew the name of the person selling it. He wanted it so badly, she'd gone back three times with Julie. When they finally found the stand, the man said he'd sold it a long time ago. The commercial had been popular, he explained; lots of people remembered its telltale whistled song from childhood: *What do you want, when you've got to have something, and it's got to be a lot, and it's got to be sweet, and you've got to have it now?* The commercial showed sailors in sailor suits so dated they were eternal, and a boy and a blond girl skipping on a pier. It played for ten years and then for another five in the third world.

"It's really *good*," Owens said, as he always did. And again, he considered his own ad agency's work; he'd actually brought in the tape of this commercial when he hired them. (They'd listened politely and said it certainly was good for its time.)

That commercial earned Olivia a hundred thousand dollars. A hundred thousand 1960s dollars, he'd pointed out; more like a million now. But it was all long gone, on her mother's doctor bills. By the time Olivia was a teenager in Alta, she'd stacked pennies in little cardboard tubes to take in to the bank.

Since Jane heard that story, she'd watched the ground as she walked. But so far, she'd found only two pennies.

Looking at Olivia's four-year-old face, Jane could see why they picked her. The commercial ended with her big in black and white, her hair in sloppy pigtails, pulled back with rubber bands, her front teeth uneven stubs—an open face everyone could feel she once had.

When the phone rang, he caught it on the first ring. It was Olivia, calling from a party.

In his softest, most conspiratorial bedtime voice, he questioned her about the contents of the party, most of whom were from Alta High, where he hadn't gone. Even now, all these years later, Jane could tell

Olivia was still an Alta girl. It was one of the things she had. It meant a certain ease and dominance on the streets. However late it was on, say, a Saturday night, in the center of town, Owens and his friends still had had the long drive home to Auburn. Alta kids could just walk, picking their way through the dark, fragrant gardens.

That, he told Jane, was why he wanted her to live in Alta. But then why wouldn't he let her go to school?

"Is Karen there?" Owens said. "Could Karen give you a ride?"

Jane tapped him on the shoulder. "I can drive," she said.

He listened for a while, then shook his head. "I'll call Noah and he'll go over." Then he hung up. Owens lived twenty miles away in the woods, and Noah was probably within ten minutes of the party.

"He'll be sleeping," Jane said.

"Noah's a hip guy; lemme just call."

With Noah, Owens assumed a drowsy voice to imply that he was in bed. And it turned out Noah was too.

"Hey, you wanna do me a big favor? Olivia's in Alta at a party. With Alta High people. I thought you might have been there." Owens' voice lowered. "I think she's been drinking." He was like a father from long ago in a movie, who put his hand on your shoulder, telling you something hard. "Could you maybe go and pick her up?"

After Noah answered him, Owens' voice continued its soft drowse. "Well, what I'd really like you to do is pick her up and bring her here." He paused. "Oh, thanks a lot."

Jane could tell he meant it, but she'd heard him that way at his office too, when Owens made sure the other guys would work for another five hours while he went out to eat. She wished she could tell Noah, No, don't, stay in bed, but she wanted to see him too. It was late and she wanted to go home now. She thought when he came she'd run down and ask him for a ride.

"You should go to sleep," Owens told her.

Her futon was in the next room, and she pulled the down quilt over her, with her clothes still on. It was cold.

On the other side of the wall, Owens waited on clean sheets like a bride. Wind russed the trees. He was always pleased when something he arranged was in motion. He was waiting in a state of excitement, no longer even for Olivia, but for something large and momentous. A hawk flew from the native oak away into the mountains, a darker blot on darkness. Then he slid in the commercial again.

"What are you doing up?" Olivia said, pushing the hair back on Jane's head.

"I wanted to see Noah."

Olivia kissed them both in a hurry and ran upstairs to the bedroom, tripping.

Jane had the ring in her pocket. She had given it once already to Owens, right after she arrived, the day he came to pick her up. "What's this?" he'd said. "It's to prove I'm me," she told him. "You gave it to my mom once in a cherry pie." He looked at her blankly. "I did? Really? So why're you giving it back?" He left it on his dressertop, in an ashtray. She'd never seen him even look at it, and so tonight she took it. She wanted to give it to Noah, but all of a sudden she felt paralyzed. "Can you drive me home?" she blurted. She didn't know how to tell him.

"Did Owens say it was all right?"

"I didn't ask."

"It's not a good idea, Jane. We don't even know if your mom's home. It's her one night off, and she might have a date."

That gave her a bad feeling, the bungalow empty and dark.

Jane bounded back upstairs after watching Noah's van drive away. She knocked on their bedroom door to say good night again.

"You know, I never asked you," she said. "What did you get for your birthday?"

"Guy from work gave me a peacock. Maybe tomorrow morning we can find him. I think he might have flown away already." He shrugged.

"Where are all your presents?"

Olivia had a strange smile. "He left most of them at the hotel."

"You did? Can I have them?" She pictured a tile floor in the hotel, and a huge pile of presents wrapped with long ribbons.

"No, Jane, you can't," he said. "And it's time to go to bed."

"Do you know if my mom's at home?"

"I don't know, Jane. But it's late. Time for bed."

The ring hadn't worked. Maybe the canister would have. All this time, her mother had wanted to get into his world, which still seemed marked off with an invisible chalk line. She thought Jane was the magic word, the key. But Jane knew there was a further secret.

Going to sleep, she pretended she had gotten him the canister. She could have; she had the money in her box. She could have unwrapped the damp, soft bills and bought it. Maybe it was the present he would have kept.

Owens recognized the wine collapse of Olivia's body and the dryness in her mouth. Tonight she was floppy and sharp at the same time. She wanted to sit up straight and talk. And it was a loud, bright night outside, with a veined moon. The final proof of what different vegetarians they were was her drinking. He couldn't believe he was in love with a woman who drank and smoked.

"You're so beautiful," he whispered in her ear.

"In high school, when people complimented my appearance, I thought they were making fun of me."

"Why, Olivia?"

"My father was always very critical of us. Someone would say I was pretty, and he'd say, 'She's got too much hair on her arms.' Because he was an artist, maybe, he was always fussing with us, fixing us."

She had only one picture of her parents: a woodblock her mother had made, both of them young and straight-haired.

"Turn that off," she said suddenly, pointing. He'd fallen asleep with her four-year-old face frozen on the screen.

Olivia's great tragedy was her childhood. Her mother, as a girl in Sweden, cried herself to sleep every night in a green-and-ivory bed shaped like a boat. She had pimples and a round face. At fourteen, she vowed to herself and God from her small painted bed that if she ever had daughters who weren't beautiful, she would drown them at birth. She believed, at fourteen, in the mercy of this.

She had grown up to marry a long-faced, gray-toothed artist who believed she was beautiful. Perhaps he was the only person who had ever found her so, and she was, when she was able, grateful. Owens had studied her picture and saw little resemblance between the woman and Olivia, except the hair. But Olivia's father loved the slope of his wife's shoulders down from her neck. "This," he'd once said, running his knuckle-back down her spine, "is my favorite part of you." Olivia's mother had told her many times. "Can you imagine? A back." And Olivia, from the moment she could walk, was in her mother's eyes a rare beauty. "She is ordinary," her father insisted.

And eleven years later, her mother killed herself. Her father lived alone in the hotel where she'd died, in a room smelling of cigars and old laundry. Olivia sometimes saw him lurking in Mitch's bookstore. He always seemed startled to see her, then he slumped in disappointment. It was because of her hair. She had her mother's hair.

"I got some pictures of us today, from the party. We look like we're really in love."

Her body turned sharp in his arms. She never liked pictures of herself. "We still need to talk about the party."

"Hey," he said, "I've got an idea. Let's just forget the party and go back to being us."

Her head stilled for a moment. She closed her eyes, rolling in the ship-safety of drunkenness.

Her silk thing from the party hung in the closet; he could see it beyond the open door. It wavered a little in the night breeze.

He thought of something Noah Kaskie once told him: right now he was thirty and he wanted to live.

Mrs. Em Tine, six years retired and fifteen widowed, still woke on a school schedule. So she got up and started her day. She watered plants, paid the bills when there were any, and continued her correspondences. She exchanged letters regularly with two sisters she'd taught with in Auburn.

"Save a dance for me," he whispered in my ear. That was after the toast. He'd come and made me stand up and they all clapped. But he was busy, I suppose, with the young ones, and we didn't get our dance. That was too bad.

Mrs. Tine didn't write that she'd seen him necking with two different girls. She would have liked a chance to fox-trot, and to ask him which girl he liked the best. She had her own favorite—the thinner one, in the pink dress. She seemed more like Mrs. Tine's own daughters. The other one was just too beautiful.

She had taken the bus home yesterday. She didn't live in the valley anymore; it had become too expensive after Walter died. The night of the party, she'd stayed in that hotel. The two sisters had offered her a room in Alta, but they went to bed early and she didn't want to have to leave before all the others did. She'd asked the desk to be sure and deliver her present. He can always use another vase, even if they have one, she thought. Now she just hoped he got it. She expected she'd get a note in the mail any day now.

I didn't even have a chance to say goodbye. But guess what I did that night? I got myself a massage. Me! They had a card by the phone saying you could order a massage all night long and they send a person up. They ask you too if you have a preference, woman or man. And I said, definitely it would have to be a woman. She was a young girl, only twenty-five or twenty-six, but was she ever strong. It felt so good. All the way home on the bus, I just felt different.

And then the next morning, I was in the lobby and I ran into Hanson, the lawyer I told you about who found me and invited me and all, and he said, what was I doing there? And I told him the last bus left at nine so I'd stayed. And I said, wasn't it ever a nice hotel? But he said, no, he hadn't stayed, he'd just driven up to make sure everything was settled. I guess he'd arranged a lot of the party, and then when I went to check out, they told me my room and the massage and everything was all paid for. They wouldn't let me give them another cent. So I thought that was nice.

The European Way

❤❤❤❤❤❤❤

*O*wens liked to drive his car, and that is where he came up against civilization. They took away his license once, he told Jane, so he had to ride his bike to work for a month. And he often ran out of gas. Now this was somebody else's fault; ever since he'd had money he hired people to manage the material side of life, including filling up the car, but they sometimes screwed up. Before, when he'd shared a car with Frank, he admitted, it frequently ran out of gas.

Tonight the fuel needle was wavering below the quarter-tank mark. Susan and Stephen, his housekeepers, had gone to Bangkok and also planned to travel in Burma and the Philippines. Owens hadn't really thought about it until then, on the highway, and he didn't like the idea very much. He thought he could probably get to the city on a quarter tank. He tapped the dashboard. He knew his car pretty well. He thought it'd be close but he could do it.

There were people who didn't live like this, he realized, people who would certainly stop and fill up the tank, but those people wouldn't leave for a dinner in the city ten minutes before they were supposed to be there. It was a forty-minute drive, a half hour speeding. Those people wouldn't speed either.

He sighed. You could live like that. You could leave early, with plenty of time for gas and accidents and bathroom stops, but pretty soon that's what your day was: bathroom stops.

He knew a guy like that. Todd. He worked at home and couldn't concentrate until everything in his house was organized. He'd do the laundry, fold it and put it all away. He'd never sit down before three or four o'clock. He lived in a very neat house. Owens had to fire him, and eventually he'd got out of the business altogether. Probably for the best. He was talking about going back to school, to be a nurse. Owens gave him the advice he'd have given anybody: Figure out, if you were going to die in a year, what you would want to have done most. Make that one thing the first thing you do every day and leave the rest for later. Which in Owens' case was probably never. And if the rest never got done, he could live with it.

Later, Jane sighed, listening to her father talk like this. She knew she was part of the rest.

The thing about Genesis, it could take all he had. For a long time now, Owens had allowed himself one other thing in each day, and that was love or some idea of it. But when he found himself leaving work, he gave it, as if in appeasement, five minutes, ten minutes more. It was almost impossible to leave before dark. The office building was like a communal house, the refrigerator full of whatever the guys liked and Owens' juices, stereos were rigged into the walls. It felt good to be one of the gang staying late. When he left, he knew he was probably missing something better than what he was going to.

That was one reason he was chronically late. He also canceled. Owens' eyes for life were bigger than his stomach.

Tonight he was meeting Lita. In the middle of his birthday party, he'd suddenly remembered he'd forgotten to invite her. She was in Berkeley now, studying photography.

He'd met Lita when she was a schoolgirl living with her parents. She was sixteen, curly-haired, coming home every day on a dented school bus. One day when Owens came to see her father, she was raking leaves in her plaid school uniform, and he'd stopped to pick up chestnuts from the ground.

She had been a virgin and had some virginal ways. The three adults sat in triangular chairs drinking coffee, while she played on the floor, making towers with her little sister's blocks and then toppling them. Another afternoon, he caught her perfecting the outfit for a clothespin doll, and often he saw her bouncing a small brown ball.

But in her room, in the afternoon, she let him undress her on her own bed and lay there trembling, plump and expectant. She was rounder than he'd anticipated, her skin not smooth but marked with childhood cuts and bruises.

He began slowly, his own breath sucked in, a staticky blanket of air between his fingers and her nipples, but by the time he entered her, she was around him, tight and beating, her blood's noise ringing in his ears. Her chin puckered like a dry apricot, and she wailed something babyish and willful. Afterwards, he'd sat dressed, while she washed the blood from her belly in her bathroom. Sadness overtook him in this small, soft room full of dolls and paper cutouts. He wished he could restore her to her former girlishness, and when he said goodbye, he cupped her chin with a nostalgia.

But the next day, he discovered his damages sealed over by the night. She was the same again, buoyant as her dog, who leapt up against his thighs. Her playfulness returned entirely, and he came back every day, still ambitious to leave his mark.

They'd meet in the late afternoon, before her parents came home and expected her to set the table for supper. He returned to work a little after five, quieted, peaceful in the body, ready for a long night of toil and discovery. Sometimes, eating a sandwich at his desk at nine o'clock, tinkering over questions of science and business, he would look at the dark sky and remember that she was moving through her parents' house in knee socks, sliding on the thick wood planks, perhaps lying on her belly, doing her homework. A requiem would be playing on the stereo as her father read scientific journals, drinking his transparent grappa. At ten o'clock she would be asleep, in her small bed in the room that smelled of chalk.

No one ever knew. They had never attended a party together or had dinner with anyone except her parents, whom he'd always admired. Her father was a satisfied man. "I don't own the land," he used to say. "God owns the land and I'm just holding the lease." He had been part of the war effort that first purified and manufactured penicillin, "the most temperamental mold I ever knew." He called himself a prospector, panning not for gold but for microbes from the dirt. At that time, his company paid half the airfare of family vacations and handed out vials for samples. His name was on eighty-four patents, and he himself had been responsible for five best-selling drugs. And Lita was always there, coming home from school, her hair smelling of apples already on the ground.

Once, Owens had asked him, "Do you think I'll ever discover a drug?"

He'd closed his eyes and mused. "I think you'll discover something important when you're very young. But nothing you do after that will ever live up." In the last year, Owens had often considered this harsh prophecy.

He felt weakness in the gas pedal. Oops, very little left. There was no exit or gas station as far as he could see. He pumped gently, coaxing the car up the hill, then coasting down. He slid into the right lane, alive to every moment, still moving in the now slowed race with other cars. The commute became beautiful, cars small and rich-colored under the deep-blue sky, their headlights lanterns, until his power was gone and he could flap the accelerator panel loosely. He banked on the gravel, got out and crossed his arms. I'll forget this in a year, he promised himself, walking.

The gas station turned out not to be far, a mile and a half or maybe two. He called the restaurant from the pay phone on the lot. "Guess where I am?" he shouted. "I ran out of gas!" He heard sympathy on the other end of the line. Not Olivia; Olivia would not have been kind. "We all have to put gas in our cars, Owens," she'd said the last time. "Why is it so much harder for you?"

An old man stood by a truck, with a tall, pointed can of gas. Everything was battered: the truck, the chipped and peeling can. It felt good to let the man drive, the can banging in the back. As they neared the place where he'd stopped, Owens wished it weren't a sports car. But the man stood impassive, gassing the tank. Owens opened his wallet. "Don't you want to go back to the station and fill 'er up? This won't last you long." Cold wind, thick with fog, buffed Owens' neck. Gravel by the side of the road poked his soles. He felt rough and alive, and now he did have time.

When he walked into the soft world of the restaurant, Lita was returning from the rest room and swiveled involuntarily from being watched. He had to smile. She had her hair up in a bun and wore high heels, but she was still round at the middle.

Arms long over the table, he ordered for them both. Then he asked, genuinely curious, what she was doing with her life.

She answered him plainly, and as she described her classes, her semester in Paris, all she'd done in the two years since he'd seen her, he felt himself at a loss. He was so much older, but he'd missed all this; it was something he had not had. His eyes tightened and he was thinking he'd done what he had done because it was great, even crucial, and anyway, he'd been too poor to go to Paris. But it probably looked to Lita as if he was judging her, and she said, "You don't really respect me, do you, Owens?"

"Of course I do, Lita. A great deal."

"You know what I am for you?" she said. "I'm your mistress."

Then it was his turn to take offense. After he'd protested, claiming injury and showing it in his hard eyes, she slowed down to explain, taking his long hand in her round ones. "No, really. Listen to me. I just meant it as a matter of fact. We're not in each other's daily lives. And you come to me for sex and—"

"Not just for that, Lita—"

"For romance. I think day-to-day life changes love. It can't stay high, if you know what I mean. Little frictions develop. Do you ever notice the way people married a long time don't believe each other?"

"What do you mean?"

"If she says, You get more seasick in the cabin than on deck, he'll say, No, it's the opposite, and she'll say that whatever he thinks, it's a matter of proved fact. And unless there's a third person, they'll never get anywhere. If anyone in the world told my father a war just broke out he'd believe it, unless it was my mother. Then he'd say, 'Where'd you hear that?' "

"I suppose I know what you mean, yes."

"Or even understanding. I could always listen to your problems and you could to mine, because it didn't cost us. I think that's why affairs work in a way marriages can't. My father listened to his mistress when she spilled coffee on her baby so bad he'll have burn marks all his life, and he cried with her—with true deep sympathy, no hate in it. But her husband could only half listen to her, knowing it's his child."

"Your father had a mistress?"

"Uh-huh."

"Wow. I never knew that."

"For a long time."

"I always remember your parents together. But your dad's European. I guess there's a long tradition of that in Europe."

She laughed. "Try everywhere in the world."

She politely asked him about business. Who knows, he told her. NT12 was pretty amazing, but they were waiting on FDA. They had it but they were still having trouble making enough of it cheaply. And the rest of the company was getting pretty bureaucratic. Even Rooney, the guy he'd hired, was going corporate on him. "So we'll see," he said.

"You can do it," she claimed.

"I don't know. Did it once. We'll see if I can do it again."

He walked her to a battered Toyota—he'd never noticed her car before—and kissed her on the forehead, a father's kiss. Later, he told Jane he was thinking of buying Lita a new car.

It was Jane's Tuesday. After dinner, they took a walk down a dirt road. Split-rail fences lined a neighbor's horse pasture. Jane bent down to pick rotting apples out of the long grass and weeds to feed the horses. She was trying to find a good way to ask him about school. It was almost September again, and another year.

Owens asked her not to tell anyone about his dinner with Lita but said that he could trust her because she was blood.

A horse's soft black lips accepted her offering. "How old was she again when you were together?"

"She was pretty young. Sixteen."

Jane was almost twelve. "Was she in school?"

"She was in high school."

Jane was keeping track of Owens' girlfriends. "Does she know that I exist?" This was the same question she always asked.

Owens had to think for a minute. Lita had never heard about Jane. "You lived far away then," he said.

"Where were you when we lived in Larkspur?" she'd asked before, her eyebrows an accusation, or: "What about when we were in Mariposa?" They had lived, she and her mother, in thirteen places, and she wanted answers for them all.

The answer that always came to him was, "I was young. I was in my days."

A horse reared up and cantered across the field. She sighed. "Everyone gets to go to school but me."

"You'll go to high school too," he said. "So don't worry."

She looked up at his calmness. This was the first time he'd said that. "Oh, good."

They stood watching the horse and the mountains beyond. "It's really nice here." His profile tilted, as he breathed in. Then he shrugged, an apology in movement. "It was a love affair. Family didn't come into it."

At least now he'd said she was family.

The Hard Way

⊰⊰⊰⊰⊰

*N*oah worked underground, at a desk with a window at street level, and seeing legs all day had made him a connoisseur. He liked smaller legs, refinement. And those men's lace-up shoes women wore now with just bare legs were cute. The one thing Noah couldn't stand on a woman was cowboy boots.

He recognized Mary and Jane as they passed above, Jane's small hurrying steps to catch up, her mother's good legs, unshaved and unproud, slamming into downtrodden sandals. Jane's sneakers somehow stayed white and her turned-down socks perfectly even. He wondered where they were going, then Jane hurried into the lab, balancing a tall cake.

He was so happy somebody had remembered his birthday besides his family. And everyone in the lab, including Louise, would see. "Shouldn't you be in school?" he teased, then realized from her face that he'd said exactly the wrong thing.

"I don't go to school, Noah. I want to go, but they won't let me."

"I meant the good tutors. I hear you're halfway through *Middlemarch* with them."

Jane stamped her foot. "But I don't like *Middlemarch*. All I get to do is old. The old math. Old reading." As Jane set the tall cake on a counter, Mary whispered, "Is this an okay time?"

"Sure," he said. "We're just sitting around doing what we always do."

"So this is a lab." Jane tentatively walked towards a shelf of beakers, all containing transparent liquids. In addition to the standard laboratory benches, Noah's lab included a fish room and, now, the fly alcove.

Just then, Olivia rushed in and handed him a wrapped book. "This is from Huck too. He's in class."

Mary bent over the cake, inserting candles. Men and women younger than she was slowly neared, awkward with their hands free, unhinged from equipment. The lab people were waiting, looking at her, and she hadn't thought to bring forks. She didn't even have a match to light her candles.

"Can I borrow a light?" she said. A young woman with white hair lit one of her candles on a Bunsen burner, and Mary used it to light the others.

"Make a wish, Noah," Jane commanded. "A big one."

"Wonder what *he's* wishing for?" a lab woman said. Everyone laughed, as if they knew his wish.

"What?" Jane said.

"Results," the white-haired woman mouthed to her.

They sang "Happy Birthday" and he blew out all the candles. The woman with white hair handed around rough brown paper towels, and everyone stood eating the cake. It didn't seem much like a party, because people didn't know what to say to each other. Several of them asked Jane what grade she was in.

"I'd be in seventh," she mumbled, and that seemed to satisfy them.

For a while everyone was silent, eating the delicious cake. Mary and Jane and Noah each had two pieces. After the scientists finished, they went back to their benches and started working again.

"Noah." Jane touched his shoulder. "I want to tell you something."

Watching her daughter standing next to Noah's chair, whispering in his ear, Mary felt, as she often did, that she shouldn't be here. She had a vague suspicion that Noah tolerated her only to get to Jane. And while Jane had chattered happily as they baked, she didn't think about the cake one second before, not like Mary, pushing a metal grocery cart at ten at night to buy baking soda, and shaking the wildflowers dry. Sliced, the cake was beautiful, lapidary, flecked with confetti color.

Jane was asking Noah to talk to her father about school. It was as if she understood that he'd helped Owens over some crucial hurdle with her before, a hurdle Owens himself no longer remembered and certainly hadn't told her about. "Just try, okay?" she whispered. "I have a present for you. But don't tell my mom." She pressed the ring into his hand. "Look at it later."

Olivia stood reading the bulletin board, where Noah hung copies of articles from recent journals. "Noah, you never went to that place in New York, did you?"

"Nope. I'm staying here." He'd turned down two eastern job offers for no reason other than sanity. Things were set up enough for him here, and for his new ambition, beyond fish embryos or flies, it might help to stay put.

Olivia sighed. "I'm not going anywhere either, for a little while." They both knew that she was staying for Owens, who was to her what science was to Noah.

"I'll think about what you said," Noah told Jane as she left. By the time they were gone, everyone was working again. And it had been hardly an hour.

Science didn't seem like that much fun, Jane decided. They didn't even get to wear lab coats.

Noah worked the rest of the morning on his fish embryos.

On birthdays, it was hard not to think about where he was and how far he'd come or not. He tried to concentrate on signal transduction, pathways, discerning the moment the cells had started becoming a brain.

In his small way, Noah had had a success too, and he was acutely aware of it. His mutation had earned him a measure of fame and gotten him the job here. At that time, he was one of the promising young scientists people were watching. And he liked his mutation personally, not only for what it brought him but for its closeness to the real mystery of knowledge, which ran the fine edge between matter and soul. Science now, however basic, pitched itself into the soap operas of disease and cure. Because, of course, that's where the money was. But his success, however small, had not come easily. He'd worked relentlessly, morbidly. He believed he had to work harder than other people, and he figured that was okay, he could and would. But now he didn't want to lose what he'd gained, and at the same time he recognized an expansion in his sensibility, an openness to the things of leisure and even, after the black-tie night, to clothes.

In this way, he supposed, the plots of his and Owens' early careers were parallel, except, of course, that he still worried about money. Noah's great-great-grandfather Josiah had brought the bees to California; and though bees had populated western skies ever since and Noah's relatives considered honey to be a family contribution, the enterprise didn't make him rich. Josiah's brother came for the gold rush and never made his fortune either. There'd now been five generations of Kaskies who never got rich. Once, for a year, Noah's father had taken night classes in landscape architecture, with the hope of changing careers. But it was too much money and too much time, and he resigned himself. He'd worked all his life as an insurance salesman, never liking it, loosening his tie with a sharp gesture when he came in the door at suppertime. He left ties on doorknobs, on the stairway banister, all over the house.

Maybe he'd end up like them, Noah thought, resting his head on his arm, listening to his blood tick. He wasn't poor, but he wondered what he had to offer anybody. He'd been willing to throw his life away for the girl in college; she hadn't wanted it, and no one had come close since.

To make matters worse, while Kaskie plugged along every day, two of his friends had up and got results. Rachel had become out-and-out famous. Her molecule, HLA, turned out to be important for organ transplants, and if there was any fairness, she probably had a chance for the Nobel Prize. It depended on how much of a pig her adviser tried to be.

Noah's bench partner from graduate school, who was working on mice now at Caltech, had an article in this month's *Nature*. At noon,

Noah shut himself in his office and read it. When he finished, he threw up his arms and wheeled outside to announce to his students that the paper was brilliant, much better than what he was doing.

"You mean what we're doing," Louise said dryly. "Let me see." For once, he welcomed her skepticism and handed her the journal. Some days she looked quite plain to him, and other days, like today, she seemed almost beautiful. At least I've joined the world's problems, he thought.

She edged herself into Noah's office and closed the door. No other postdoc had ever done that; there was, after all, a meeting room. Since taking Louise to Owens' party, he was pretty sure the others in the lab assumed she was his favorite. They might even think they were having an affair. He wasn't sure how to stop it.

While Louise read, he decided to take a piece of cake upstairs to Rachel.

"Oh, *no!* I'm on a diet," Rachel protested, beginning to eat. "My one leg is as big as your waist."

Women, in Noah's experience, were relentlessly self-deprecating about their bodies. How do you think I feel? he was thinking.

"While you're here, let me get a curl." Rachel came down every week or so, to harvest his hair. She claimed its texture was perfect for seeding crystals. "What are you doing to celebrate your birthday?"

"Work, probably."

"You should go out. You look nice in your new clothes." But there was a plaintiveness in her voice.

She knows I took someone else to the party, he thought. And she was right about the clothes. He'd bought two new pairs of trousers, three shirts and the first tie he'd ever owned. Today he was wearing mostly black. Thank God for the goddamn Gap—you could buy the same thing in any size from baby to giant. When he thought his worst about what he looked like, he pictured some Vietnam guys, wobbling in their chairs. But now he tried to think of a baby in a stroller. Some you saw looked dirty, food all over them; others were like miniature adults.

Kaskie thought he might need a new apartment too. He had some money in the bank. He'd been saving vaguely for years, and all of a sudden, he decided it was for precisely this.

There were two messages on the machine in his office. The first was from Owens, who sounded happy. "I have Olivia here in my arms," he said, and Noah fast-forwarded.

"You don't know me, but I'm a friend of Julie Carradine's. I'm calling because I have a thirteen-week-old baby who's been diagnosed with Sillence Type Three O.I. And I was wondering if you might talk to me. My friends say it may help me to talk to somebody with O.I. who's having a"—she paused—"a happy life."

Noah jotted the woman's number in pencil. He didn't feel like calling her today but shoved the scrap of paper into his pants pocket. He was Type Four, but in the jumbled system of categories, that was better. And just being born had broken two of his ribs.

Louise walked in. "What's this?" she said, pushing a letter from his desk at him.

Noah was endlessly behind on mail, invitations and conferences. This was a job offer he had no intention of considering, and one of the many things he wanted to improve about himself was how long it took him to say no. "Oh, that's nothing real. Charlatans."

"Lot of money for charlatans."

"Charlatans are the only ones who have money."

"What is the Miami Project?"

"Oh, some kid, a quarterback on a football team." He didn't like talking about this with her and didn't realize until just now that there was a whole realm he talked about only with other disableds. "He was out playing one day and got a spinal cord injury. His father happened to be some millionaire, and on his deathbed he promised his son he'd make him walk again. So they have this big endowment and they hire all kinds of doctors and scientists, anybody whose stuff can be remotely construed as having anything to do with neural cells."

"So they want you for signal receptors."

"They want me because I'm a crip."

"Kind of a touching story, the father and son."

"It's pretty controversial. I don't consider it touching, actually. All this money just to make smoke, and meanwhile people wait ten or twenty years to walk again. There's better things to spend your time on."

"Was it ever a big deal for you to walk?"

"I used to try all the time. They had to strap me in chairs. I knocked out my four front baby teeth."

"How old were you?"

"One, two. Whenever you started walking. It's hard-wired into us, wanting to. I could never even stand for more than a second. I had too many fractures. But I liked the sensation, so I kept trying. Now I couldn't tell you what it feels like." But that was a lie. He did remember the teetering sensation, the breeze, the light fleeting moments before he fell again. It felt *natural,* the way being with the girl was in college. "For years, all I wanted was to walk. Now I'd trade it for knowing I could be a good—no, not just a good; walking's something—a great scientist."

"Just that?" She touched the point of his elbow. "Maybe that's the trade that's already been made for you."

"I've still got scars from trying." He thought to himself, And I'm one of the lucky ones. I don't have to shit in a bag.

The only real job he'd had before science was in the run-down place that put people into schools and jobs. People who worked there tended to be pretty impaired. The furniture was cheap and old, the walls scuffed with wheel marks. The paras hated the quads, the deaf hated the blind, and everyone disliked the DDs, who used to be called retarded. My agency days, Noah thought. I really should call them. He was a kind of hero at the center, but so was anyone with a halfway decent life.

And some of his friends there wouldn't think so well of his hidden hope to marry out. There was always one couple married, a polio and a para, with their own kids.

One Sunday afternoon, he'd made chili for everybody. They ate by the back of the building, where the tall tomato plants smelled like weeds along the railroad in the dusk. He felt close to the people there, but he was luckier. He was an O.I., osteogenesis imperfecta. He had sensation, a working bladder and bowels. He had a good family. He could choose. For most of them, this was the only choice. It was funny, this center for mainstreaming. A lot of the people inside didn't really believe in it, so they had their own everything. Dances for kids in chairs. Contests. Miss Wheelchair America. But Noah wanted to enter the regular contests. And win.

"Okay, this article your old friend wrote," Louise said. "I don't think it's so amazing. He's got a structure, but no one knows what the protein actually does. Did you read about about Bernie's flies? 'Cause I think we can make some interesting hybrids. I'll show you."

"Wait. I've already made a library. You have a probe. It's your job to find the one-in-a-million bacteria with the one plasmid I care about."

"Before I start entering the lottery, could you at least look at these mutations?"

After an hour studying Louise's hybrids, Noah felt optimistic. At the rate drosophila bred, they were bound to find at least the gene's neighborhood before Christmas.

"Yoo-hoo," Owens called into the lab.

Noah slapped at the fruit flies glittering at the edges of his curls—he'd have to live with them now—and decided to go for a walk with Owens.

Once outside, he asked how Exodus was doing. He was genuinely curious. According to a lab assistant whose cousin worked for Genesis, fresh juices were replaced every three days in the E Teams' refrigerators, and expensive sushi and pasta were delivered late every night. When they chipped in for pizza at midnight, Noah's students joked about defecting.

"I fired this guy," Owens said, "and now he's suing us for age discrimination. To tell the truth, until he served us papers, I'd never had any idea how old he was. But I've kind of always wanted to see a trial."

Noah laughed, remembering that Owens hadn't responded to the last three summonses he'd received for jury duty. Noah had once found them stacked on his kitchen counter; Owens had shrugged and claimed he was too busy. "How old is the guy?"

"He was forty-nine last year when he was fired, and now he's trying to say we're all young. That was true once," he said.

A yanking breath of cool air lured them to the open doors of the old church. Inside, girls were singing and playing hopscotch on the wide aisle. Jane was, at that very moment, bending to pick up the rock, but neither of them recognized her voice in the song, and they drifted down the street.

"You know," Owens said, "I've been thinking: Love is very rare. We might just get one or two shots in a life. And if you blow those, that's it."

Listening to Owens talk about love was easier today. Noah might not have a girlfriend, but it occurred to him that he had at least some talent for love. He was constant. The last time he'd seen the girl in college, she'd left his house in the rain, tying a silvery coat at her waist. Her perfection remained, like a small portrait inside a locket, and she had been gone now for a very long time. In a way, he couldn't blame Louise for not seeing him as sexual. The last thing he would fantasize about was a disabled person.

Owens looked at him intently. "I wonder if you and I will ever get married. That's the million-dollar question."

All of a sudden, Noah wanted to call the mother of the O.I. baby. He felt in his pocket for the number, but it wasn't there. His mother had always said she'd had to learn how to touch him. One of her first hugs had fractured him. He'd have to search his desk drawers.

By the time he returned, though, Louise had the architecture for the experiment lined up. She'd called the purchasing department to put a rush order in with Sigma, the Sears catalogue of small molecules, and he forgot all about the mother.

At seven, Rachel stopped down to see if she could take him out to dinner. She'd obviously gone to the rest room, brushed her hair and put on mascara. But Noah had to tell the truth, that he was expected at his parents' house for dinner and already late.

His sister was on the phone from Togo when he walked in. She told him about a guy she met there, bald with cancer, who'd put a personal ad in a Chicago newspaper. He had a girlfriend now, a blond actress.

Michelle was devoted to fun. It was her life's purpose and philosophy. For all of Noah's life, she'd been a counterpoint to his pains. As she traveled, he'd received postcards from the world's widest and most rapid rivers, from Andean ruins and the glacial plains of Alaska. At home, he followed her on expeditions to the artichoke capital of the world, on hikes in an off-road chair to see the desert bloom or the tree where monarch butterflies flock every August. He had, when he could, joined her Tuesday-night poker game. Michelle worked part time at clerical jobs she didn't care about to support her photography and her life of pleasure. Noah admired his sister and missed her acutely. But for him, fun could not bear so much intention; it had to be side-glanced, stolen from the edges of a life dedicated to more trust-worthy things.

That night, he opened a closet door in the kitchen and saw the scratch marks. *Michelle 1969* was scribbled at about three feet. *Michelle 1971*, six inches higher. The last mark was *1974*. There were no scratches with his name. His parents had painted the house since he and Michelle moved out, but they must have preserved this, as a me-mento. He'd never before thought of it that way—his and Michelle's childhoods being for them too.

His mother cooked him her best meal. He'd brought what was left of the cake, and only then did he imagine he should've brought Rachel or even Louise. But that would have got his mother too excited; she'd assume the best and start buying whomever little thoughtful gifts.

But then his mother and dad hadn't been in love when they married. They'd never seen any reason not to tell their children the truth. They went to the prom together one night. They hardly knew each other. And she got pregnant. "We came into love late," they always told him. "We did it the hard way."

Christmasing

⊰⊰⊰⊰⊰⊰⊰

*I*n November, Peter Bigelow called the bungalow from his farm in Half Moon Bay and asked if Mary and Jane would help him pick out Julie's birthday present. He drove them in his truck to a department store in the city.

They thought of a pair of boots, or maybe a purse: things they'd want themselves. Then Jane spotted the dress she'd always imagined—red, on a headless mannequin.

"Do you think she'd wear something like that?" Mary asked.

"Oh, yeah," Peter said. "She's gonna flip when she sees this." When he learned the price, he whistled and pulled out a silver money clip. Jane had never seen a money clip before.

"Will it last a long time?" Mary asked the saleswoman.

"Of course," she said. "It's a classic sheath."

"I see." Mary didn't know what that was. The fabric maybe.

After the saleswoman handed him the large gift-wrapped box, Peter said, "Let me take you two out for a restorative cup of hot chocolate."

They were on the top floor. On the way down, he bought them each a present—a hat that looked wonderful on Mary and flowered tights for Jane. Even though she never wore dresses, she had a pair of short pants that would let them show. In department stores, it seemed to Jane, the most expensive things were on the top, all the way down to food at the bottom.

They sat at a table on the first floor, sipping hot chocolate from a silver teapot and eating ginger cookies wantonly.

Then Peter said, "I'm gonna show you something." He took out a felt bag from his inside corduroy pocket. "I need some paper."

"I have construction paper," Mary offered, digging into her big purse.

On a blue sheet, he poured sparkly stones from the little bag.

"What is it?" Jane asked.

"Diamonds."

Neither of them had seen diamonds before, up close. Jane counted nine, all different shapes. When you looked, they were slightly different colors too.

"I asked my mother." Peter grabbed Mary's arm and stared at her, as if he were telling her something important. "This's how crazy I am. I told her I was getting close to proposing, so she gave me these. 'Maybe this'll help,' she said. 'They're all from women in the family, their engagement rings.'"

Jane wondered where all the rings were now—in some junk pile, empty of stones, in a dump? She thought of asking if she could have just the rings. She would find a stone, from the seashore or the ground, or wear them all together on a chain around her neck.

Thunder clapped outside now, with an answering peal of rain. This was the kind of day Jane always wanted, an afternoon that went on and on and no one left.

"Would you pick out a ring, or how would you do it?" Mary seemed timid, as if the proposal was something she hadn't considered.

"No. Julie would have to pick out her own," he said. "I thought I'd pour these out and let her see which ones she liked."

"More than one?" Jane said.

"As many as she wants." He smiled, but the smile cracked. "She's not ready, though." He stared up at Mary, and his neck seemed white and weak, like the tender inside stem of a weed. "What do you think, Mare?"

Mary and Jane glanced at each other. He was right. Yesterday morning, Julie had walked in when they were eating almond butter on toast. "I think Peter's getting close," she'd said.

"Huck wants me to go to New Orleans," Mary had said. "For Thanksgiving."

"That sounds like a proposal to me," Julie said.

"We're not nearly ready. I don't even know what would happen with me and Owens."

"What about Eli?" Jane said.

"I will if you will." Julie had laughed.

But today, under the sway of Peter's eyes and the sound of steady rain on the tall department store windows, they wanted Julie to be.

"I think if I asked her now," he said, "she'd run scared."

But he was the one who looked frightened. They drove all the way back in his truck in the rain, Peter humming a way that seemed binding. In the bungalow, Mary found the bag where she kept fabrics. Someday she meant to make a quilt for Jane. She held up a scrap of deep-blue velvet from the coat Noah Kaskie had once bought for her daughter, which she'd now grown out of.

"Here," she said. "You can use this instead of paper."

"I spread this cloth out and then pour 'em and say, 'Just pick out the ones you want, honey.' " He shook his head, looking at Jane. "Your mom and Julie, two peas in a pod."

That made them happy for a little while.

The teachers offered to take Jane when Mary went to New Orleans. "We'd be ever so glad to have her," Amber insisted, though both sisters felt dubious about the trip.

"I'm not even sure I'm going." Mary sighed.

"I can understand that," Ruby said.

"You don't *have* to go," Amber added.

Jane kicked her mother's leg under the table and held up a glass jar of preserved limes. The teachers' house no longer seemed like Christmas. "I'm not staying there," she declared when they left. "They fuss all the time. Just forget it. I'll ask Julie."

"I already thought of Julie, but Peter invited her to his family's ranch."

"Fine. I'll find a place myself."

The night before Mary left, she and Eli sat at the kitchen table, leaning down over Japanese teacups. In the cone of lamplight, their heads looked pretty and serious. The house was mostly dark and the heat was making funny noises. Jane ground her shoe on an anthill. Anthills had begun to rise in the corners.

Jane took her suitcase, and looked back at her mother and Eli, their hands in front of them on the table, then slipped out the front door. She didn't want to go to the teachers. She saw them so many hours every week. Time in their hotel-clean house moved so slowly that Amber seemed to release powder into the air whenever she moved. Jane had read in the newspaper about new math. There were probably new subjects—new reading, new science, new spelling, new history—and Jane was learning only the old.

She carried the suitcase, head down, to the first corner, then decided to go to Owens' house. Once she crossed the highway that separated Alta and Auburn from the hill towns, she'd be in the woods. She looked up at palms and eucalyptus, an occasional pine. Nothing here frightened her, and the air billowed warm.

One tree more, and the aunts must have arrived. She thought of the way Ruby drove, so slow it was dangerous, with Amber quibbling from the passenger seat. They would be wearing their going-out clothes. Once they got home, they'd want her to go to sleep even though it was a loud bright night and only eight o'clock. They would want to begin the long business of undressing and putting away. Ruby, the younger and the one Jane minded less, ate a bowl of cereal in the kitchen every night before bed. For a second, Jane longed to be in that chalky kitchen, eating the milk-wet Rice Krispies and wondering what novel written by a long-ago Englishwoman Amber had left where the sheet folded down like a turned-back page on the bed.

But she wasn't there. Amber and Ruby would've talked Mary into calling the police. They would all be looking for her; maybe they'd drive by soon, any minute. She had to cross the highway; she imagined the long roaring. After that, it was slow uphill, pines and easy. She slid down the embankment, her hands grabbing weeds and her feet at cutting angles. She was almost on all fours, dirty. This highway was Owens' favorite, clean and black. Cars came few but fast, streaking, and Jane made a run for it to the center, then she panicked, startled in a daze of headlights, the traffic pouring the other way, big halos. She had no idea if the drivers could see her. She panted, shivering, but then she remembered from further than she could place or catalogue a highway animal, something small and ruminant, a skunk or a raccoon, and went for it, abandoning caution, her chest in front of her, hair falling out of its rubber band, and on the other side she tasted the sweet night air like happiness, the sharp inhale of mint.

From here she walked through waist-high weeds and wild fennel onto streets that led by the yards and corrals of millionaires. Dense horses moved through the grayey dark, rustling weeds and scattering insects. Occasionally, far back, she could see a light. Now she was close, and she slowed, hoping he'd be home.

After she passed through the crumbling stone gate it was still a long way, but the noises seemed owned and safe, his. The road was lined on both sides by feathery pines, and then it was there, the old mansion, and she knew from the two cars that he was home. She went in through the unlocked front door.

Owens was standing in the kitchen, testing a noodle on a chopstick. "Jane! You okay?"

She nodded, and he invited her to sit down and eat. He ladled out noodles and cut an avocado on top of hers while she explained.

"My mom's going to New Orleans with Huck and I didn't want to stay with the teachers."

"What does Eli say about all this?"

"He's not happy. But Julie told my mom to say there are two states of being at their age, and that's married or single."

Owens looked at Jane, genuinely intrigued. "I don't believe that at all. I'd be really upset if Olivia took off on a trip with some other guy."

"So's Eli."

"Wow," he said, eating with his chopsticks. "Well, I better call Mare and tell her you're here."

Everything at his house was for health. It didn't taste good. At the end you felt both full and hungry, as if the one part of food that binds and makes it a meal, the oil maybe, that was what was missing.

Lying on the futon in her cold room, trying to sleep, she remembered her mother at the wintercamp once handing her a hot yam in a rag, the melting gold inside. Sweet the way burnt things are.

In the morning, Owens asked if she wanted to come with him to the office or stay home. Jane wanted to be here, alone. After she heard his car drive away, she loosened in the house. This was where she'd come that first day, when it looked strange, like a dilapidated castle. She hadn't gone inside. She'd knocked with the knocker on the huge front door. Even if they'd been home, they never would have heard. If she'd only pressed the latch down, she could have walked right in. She was two years younger then and different, a girl who'd lived most of her life in communes. She hadn't imagined for a second that people who lived in a place like this would ever leave it open. When no one answered, she'd turned back to the overgrown garden and pressed herself into the dirt, a hand under her cheek, to fall asleep.

In all this time she'd never been alone here. She tried to see what could have been if she'd been different that first day, not expecting big doors always to be locked.

She was still disappointed: old curtains no one had ever cleaned or taken down; a vase without flowers. The mansion had twenty-nine rooms, but only a few were livable. The parlor had a magnificent piano, which no one knew how to play. She sat down on the polished bench, surprised again that her fingers could coax no music. On either side of a man-sized fireplace stood speakers taller than she was. Twelve chairs waited in the dining room around the table.

She raced upstairs to where Owens lived. There, alone in his bathroom, she opened a cupboard and discovered a warehouse. There were duplicates and triplicates of things, more, still in boxes. She counted fifteen identical full bottles of a shampoo she'd never heard of, geranium, with the price tags still on, thirteen dollars. Then there were soaps and toothpaste, twenty stacked. He had ten toothbrushes never opened. "It was always here," she said to herself again and again, as if her mother's life and hers had been a cruel game, an obstacle course set by an unkind laughing god that made their suffering not noble but embarrassing. It was always here, what they'd wanted and gone without. She would never completely forgive herself for not pushing that heavy door open the first day and coming inside.

She didn't know until she found the treasure that she'd been on a hunt. She ended up in the storage room downstairs, where she'd been once before, with her mother. Posters, plaques, magazines, boxes and boxes of Genesis mementos, were scattered around among old skis and a parked motorcycle. Mary had told Owens he should file the stuff for posterity, not that she and Jane kept such good track of their own lives. Owens had looked up. He'd been digging pictures out of piles for more than an hour. "It's probably better if all this gets destroyed in a fire or something. You shouldn't live with this stuff." He was sometimes wise about himself. But what he said was better than he was.

She sat down and read about him; there were letters from presidents and photographs with kings, but she was looking for something else. And there it was, amidst his papers and an architectural model of Katsura on the cluttered Ping-Pong table: the pictures her mother had sent. *Jane, first grade, age six.* On one her mom had handwritten, *So maybe we haven't done such a bad job after all.* Jane fingered through the room until she'd seen all the evidence of herself, and then she fell fast asleep on the floor.

The phone woke her. Before they lived in Alta, they'd leave messages for him that bore no relation to answers, like letters in bottles thrown to the sea. They always spoke to secretaries or into his machine. Jane now understood there were phones he answered all along, but they had never had the right number.

The number they always had still worked: it belonged to the white answering machine in the kitchen. But he'd explained: too many people knew it. So he let the machine answer, and every week or so he played the messages. He got new numbers, gave them to three or five people, used them until they too became cluttered, but for some reason he kept the old ones too. Perhaps out of some sense of the miraculous in his character, he wanted to be able to be found. He wanted someone—not them, obviously—to reach him.

Jane wondered, as she touched the machine where they'd left all their hopeful complaining messages for so many years, who the person was he was waiting for, the one he would have called back. She played the button: whoever called had left no message.

Jane tried to make sense of the ramshackle kitchen in order to prepare dinner, but she couldn't find basic things like milk. Then Owens walked in, saying, "Hey, I thought we could call your friend—what's her name, Julie?—and maybe go skating."

Jane called her, hoping she'd say no. But she sounded happy to be asked.

"What about Peter?" Jane asked.

She laughed. "I'm too old to go steady."

Before long, she came through the kitchen door, carrying a pair of old-fashioned roller skates. Owens had bought Rollerblades for himself and Jane several months before.

Roller-skating was in fact the last thing Julie felt like doing. She still had on a suit from work, and her ankles had always been wobbly, but she was curious about Owens. Tonight, up close, he seemed both smaller and more handsome than he had at his party. This made her fingers fumble with her laces.

Owens led the way, and to Julie's surprise he wasn't a very good skater. His long arms flailed as he turned and yelled, "There's some downhill here, but after that it's flat for miles."

Julie's legs spread wider and wider as she sped down. At the bottom, Owens grabbed her and spun her until they both slowed. Julie felt a wet patch on her neck. Had he kissed her? She twirled around once more, as if she could catch sight of a ghost, then looked ahead as Jane bombed down like a skier.

They emerged in old Alta, where the quiet streets were empty and smooth.

Owens yanked a handful of plant from someone's yard and held it near Julie. "Lavender," he said, as if it were a gift.

I like him, she thought, with a feeling of alarm.

Sprinklers raked back and forth over the lawns, and night blooms opened their fragrance; here they entered a room of jasmine, then a scarf of oregano passed over their faces. Julie's ankles tilted in, and she wondered how much longer this would go on. But it was easier here, on the flat. She'd already decided she couldn't skate all the way back. Maybe he could pick her up in the car. Far away, the bells of the old church began their evening call.

They passed a park, where a Little League game moved slowly on the lighted diamond. Owens twirled to a stop, his arms above his head in an unintentional parody of figure skating, and Julie slowed by grabbing the wire fence, burning her fingers. Children's uniforms glowed bright in the dusk. "This is nice," Owens said. He seemed to be waiting for her to talk. This was a date that was overdue, and she felt nervous and excited. "So what is it exactly that you do all day?" he asked. Perhaps for him it was an ordinary evening and he was bored.

She laughed amiably. "Well, I'm a litigator in a small firm that does everything from white-collar crime to antitrust—"

He looked at her intently. "Do you love being a lawyer? Would you say it's a *passion?*"

He said the word so carefully it made her want to laugh. This, Julie understood, was her chance: he was waiting for her to prove she was interesting. But she detested making speeches about herself. Most of her life, she'd conducted herself in a quiet, diligent way that encouraged others to speak on her behalf. Her grades in elementary school, the names of her college and law school, *her record,* and, even now, working where she worked—that was enough for most people. But Owens didn't seem to recognize her credentials, so she smiled and fumbled on. "Well, I don't know if I'd call it a passion. I don't consider it an art or a vocation, but it *is* exciting. And trial work is very . . . dramatic. Years of somebody's life are at stake. So I don't know if I'll do it forever, but for now I like it a lot."

Just then Jane swung back, colliding into him, huffing. "This girl I know from the park? Mona? She's up there getting her ears pierced at Woolworth's tonight for a dollar. Only a dollar! And her parents say she can wear studs to school." She used every opportunity she could to say the word *school.*

"Well, she's pretty lucky to have those parents. 'Cause you're stuck with us, and you're going to have to wait."

"For school too or just to get my ears pierced?"

"Ears pierced," he said quietly. The neighborhood was falling into darkness now, and a concentration of birds called from the trees above. They skated toward the center of town, Owens detouring briefly to a bank parking lot, where the blacktop was smooth.

I really, really like him, Julie said to herself, with an excitement that was not unlike fear. *Maybe this is what it is.* She thought of the small bird Eli had placed in her hand; she'd felt its heartbeat, racing in terror, through its whole body. That was how she was now. And she knew that what she'd said about herself didn't sound very good. Had it been the talent portion of the Miss America Contest, she'd have been knocked out of the finals. *If you're going to have a job, you might as well sound enthusiastic about it.* That was something her aunt Amber would say. But her job, she thought to herself in a harsh inner argument, was mostly a foil, much as accomplishments in music or handiwork "finished" a young woman a century ago. These were the years before family—which Julie fully expected to be the great work and devotion of her life. But it would be impossible for a woman of Julie's time and background not to have a career in her twenties. To wait overtly for a proposal, with a flimsy job or no work at all, would have made her seem undesirable or even desperate. So young women entered law or medical or business school, only to someday drop those hard-won skills and titles once they became, not wives, but mothers. Julie had no doubt that this was true. This is how we—in our time—meet our husbands, on the way to something else. Her only mistake was letting the edges and incongruity show. The problem was that she found it all mildly funny, and Julie knew this meant she was ready to quit.

"We used to live here," Jane said as they passed their first apartment in Alta, but no one stopped or said anything.

She just skated by the garage apartment, with its huge wire aviary, where Eli lived, without telling. Then she wanted to go into the post office: the tiled floors were the best surface for skates.

"You hurry up," Owens said. "We'll wait outside."

As he said that, Julie knew, all of a sudden, that he would kiss her.

The high-ceilinged long pavilion echoed every time Jane's wheels passed over a tile bump. The barred windows were closed for the night, but the chandeliers were on and the doors open, in case residents came to open their own boxes or to slip mail into slots in the wall. Jane slowed, as she did every time, at the gallery of criminals. He wasn't there, of course. She'd long ago stopped associating that narrow face with Owens, but she still looked for the young man in the picture, who every year came closer to her own age.

Together again, they skated down the main street, past the stores and little restaurants. Julie felt a warmth in her chest as she looked over at him. He smiled and shrugged. Kissing him had been so easy, as if it was something she'd always known how to do.

"Noah!" Jane shrieked. They'd almost passed, but Jane sensed him there. The world always seemed toy when she ran into someone by chance. For so many years of her life, no matter how much they'd thought of him, Owens had never materialized.

"Here you are," Owens said, putting a hand on Noah's shoulder.

Noah and Louise had been talking for the first time about romance, a subject that made Noah excited and happy. After chatting for half an hour about drosophila, Louise had told him about Andy Ruff, who seemed to be dumping her. This is my chance, Noah thought, and that's all anybody gets. The last thing he wanted now was company, but Owens was straddling a chair. He signaled the waitress, then ordered four large orange juices to start with. Noah, who'd intended to pay for Louise's dinner, winced.

"So how's science?" Owens asked after introducing Julie.

"I don't know; we haven't seen too much of it lately."

"You're a scientist too?" Jane said to Louise. "But don't you work for him in his lab?"

"Jane," Julie said.

Louise launched into a detailed explanation of the hierarchy in science, explaining precisely how far behind Noah she was.

Noah looked around the humming room. I'm in love with Louise, he thought, but that's no problem yet.

"But just 'cause you're younger," Jane said. "Not 'cause you're a woman."

This introduced another long disquisition, because in fact Louise was not younger.

"She won't admit it," Noah interjected, "but she's better than me."

Owens was less than fascinated with the problems of women in science, and he began a second conversation with Noah, about his cooks. "We haven't said so explicitly, but I think this'll be a chance for us all to reevaluate if we want to keep working together."

"I think they want to stay working with you," Jane said, popping up from her conversation and then returning to it. Jane often talked to Susan and Stephen in the kitchen when Owens was late.

Noah was seething. First Owens barged into his quiet supper with Louise, and now he was trying to engage the whole table in a discussion of his small domestic problem. It was as if Noah had brought up the subject of lab storage and told them all about his weeklong struggle to decide whether to buy neat metal cabinets or just scavenge cardboard boxes from liquor stores.

"And the few of them there were worked in their husbands' labs," Louise added.

"How long are they gone for?" Julie asked idly. She was following both conversations, finding little to add to either. No one answered her, and as she watched Owens talking animatedly with his friend, she suddenly understood he hadn't really liked her. She could almost hear him telling Jane, "She's not that pretty." Fine. For all his success, he didn't seem particularly nice. He could have found something polite to say about her measly job, which she didn't care about so much anyway, she realized, as she listened to this woman go on and on about biology.

Julie actually liked Louise, her intense narrow shoulders and exotic face. Once in a while, a woman like her would come along, who, having become something, would wish to stay it, probably even as a wife and mother. But not me, Julie thought. Maybe if I were a designer or an illustrator. But not a lawyer. And I'm glad she's not my mother. It's a shame, Julie thought, and not for the first time, that all the people who really wanted traditional marriages couldn't just raise their hands.

"I think Kaskie here's a really great scientist," Owens said.

"Me too," Jane chimed in.

Noah smiled. It was Owens' nature to believe that any artist he liked was a great artist and that Kaskie himself was a genius in science, when what, really, were the chances of that for any of them? Just this once, it didn't matter to Noah whether he was or wasn't one of the elect. Within his small circle of friendship, in this soft winter evening air, he was honored, his efforts acknowledged. Louise laughed next to him. He felt a lessening of pressure, the happiness of reprieve. "Tell it to the cells," Noah said, and laughed.

Eventually, the moment he'd been dreading for the past hour arrived: the bill came. Noah had intended to take Louise to supper, and of course he didn't mind buying a sandwich for Jane. The friend—Julie—had considerately ordered only a hot chocolate. The question was, what about Owens, who'd had a total of six large orange juices and two dinners, each of which he'd picked at? Noah knew, as the waitress was writing, that Owens would probably offer to pay. But if Noah let him, he wouldn't be taking Louise out. And Owens himself probably deserved to be treated once in a while, even if he never understood how unusual it was to order six large orange juices.

"You know, I'm not sure I can make it back on skates," Julie said, not caring what Owens thought of her. Her ankle hurt, and a half hour earlier, in a calculation much quicker than she was aware of, she'd decided he was no longer worth discomfort.

"Oh, there's a back way," Owens said winningly. "We don't have to go up that hill."

But she was already unlacing her skates. If there was a back path, she was thinking, why didn't you take us there in the first place?

"I can drive you in the van," Noah said. He noticed some friction between them and wondered, for the first time, whose friend she was. She seemed pretty, though too thin. But almost instantly, Noah assessed Louise's view of her—*off the map, she doesn't count*—and accepted it. Years afterwards, he would think back to that moment of easy judgment.

Owens slid his hand over the bill.

"No, this one's on me," Noah said, putting down his credit card.

◄◄

"You know, I'm wondering," Owens said, after Noah had dropped the three of them off at his house. "I'm not sure Mary'd like the idea of us all skating tonight. Maybe we shouldn't mention it."

"Not say we went skating?" Jane asked.

"Well, you can say we went skating, but maybe don't mention that we all did."

Julie stood next to her car, holding her keys. I get it, she thought. He has no intention of seeing me again, so it's not worth riling Mary up. "That's fine. I won't say anything," she said, getting in her car and slamming the door. And in the course of that one evening, Julie changed. She would no longer say with perfect sincerity that she'd never been in love. From then on, she spoke of "that kind of love" as something dangerous and immature. She called Peter when she got home, and they talked for an hour and a half.

Jane walked through the empty house in silence. She wasn't used to keeping secrets from her mother.

"Jane, wake up—it's me. Come on, get dressed. Eli's waiting in the car." Her mother's face was alive and hard, leaning over the futon. She wasn't supposed to be back from New Orleans yet. She had finally had her own adventure. It was all her, she was the center now, in the middle of the night.

"Mary?" Owens' voice stopped them, halfway down the hall. "Everything all right?"

"Thanks, Owens, for taking her." His voice, Mary remembered, had often been kind.

Eli sat with the motor running, like a getaway. No one talked as he drove the dark roads home. They told Jane to get into bed, but she couldn't sleep and she shuffled into the kitchen. "What are you talking about?"

"Jane, this isn't for you, this is for grown-ups. Go to sleep. It's past your bedtime."

"Then why'd you wake me up in the middle of the night!" All of a sudden, she was supposed to have a bedtime.

"I wanted you home, that's all."

And Jane was glad to be back in the bungalow. She always sneezed in Owens' mansion, up and down in her jacket, the way dogs shake. She wiped her nose with the back of her hand and hoped he didn't notice.

So many times, the night rinsed her mother back to what Jane knew.

Owens gave Jane a camera for Christmas. It was the same thing he gave Olivia. He gave Mary perfume, which was what he'd given her the year before.

Julie and Peter drove to his family's ranch, two hours east. When she called on Christmas morning, Julie said they had artichoke and almond orchards. "Well, we're engaged, but we're not telling anyone yet," she said to Mary and Jane, who had their faces pressed together near the receiver. "Any news on your end?"

"Oh, no." Julie still didn't know that Mary had left Huck in a French Quarter hotel room and come home early.

"Well, hurry up," Julie said. "I will if you will." She laughed.

Mary and Jane had known beforehand it was going to happen. They had even helped, with the blue velvet from Jane's coat. But still, when they hung up the phone, they didn't know what to do the rest of the day. Eli slacked around. Mary suggested they go to a movie.

A week later, they were at Julie's cottage. She'd found little tin charms in Chinatown, and they helped her hang them on ribbons all over. It was going to be a New Year's scavenger party, and at the end, you'd string them together for bracelets.

While they were making dinner, Jane slipped into the bathroom. Sitting there among plaid towels and a plaid shower curtain, she overheard them talking.

"I don't know if I'll keep it," Mary said softly.

"Whose?" Jane yelled out, over the flushing, before she even thought it.

"What are you talking about, honey?"

"Whose baby?" She was winging it, guessing, being smart-alecky, with every sureness she wasn't right.

"Well, Eli's, of course."

"Why of course? You went to New Orleans with Huck." Jane was stunned. She'd said the most shocking thing she could imagine, now it was true, and she was the one who was shocked.

"Honey, that didn't really work out."

The way her mouth went, with the lip, Jane wasn't sure she believed her.

"I guess the question is, you've done it this way already," Julie said. "Do you want to repeat yourself or do something different this time?"

Mary sighed. "I'd like to try it the right way once, being married and having enough money."

"You deserve that," Julie said, her hand flat, at a sharp angle. Sometimes Jane could see her being a lawyer.

Eli was waiting on their porch. The bungalow glowed from inside. He'd put lightbulbs in all the lamps and swept the anthills from the corners. When they came in, he put his palm over Mary's belly, and then Jane understood: he wanted her to know. As far as he was concerned, this was her sister or brother and they were going to be a family now.

It seemed almost nice that night. Eli had stopped at her grandmother's old bakery and brought them each a dessert. Years later, Jane would remember that as part of the problem, those little pretty fancy pieces of pastry. That night, her mother wanted the whole cake, big and decorated, even if there were only three of them and it would be a waste.

It didn't help that the ring Eli stuck on top of Mary's nasturtium poppy tart, her favorite, looked more like one of Julie's Chinatown charms that there were a hundred of than anything meant and precious. He'd gotten it out of a bubble gum machine. He seemed sheepish saying that, not like himself, then admitted he'd put in nineteen quarters. Jane knew that a year before, her mother would have loved it. She and Eli didn't want to live the way their parents did, they used to tell her. But Mary and Jane weren't hungry, even though he'd remembered their favorites.

"Eat some dessert," her mother ordered, as Jane's fork dallied and scrolled. Eli stood up and shut the back door. "He brought it," Mary whispered. Just then, Jane realized what was horrible: it was all up to her.

Afterwards, people would always tell her it had not been. Because of her age and all. She was the daughter only. She knew the decision should never have been hers to make at twelve, but it was. Nobody ever judged her, but she did, gravely. And it was something she would struggle with for a very long time.

Owens didn't know. He lived high up and far away those years, like a rumored emperor. He didn't know what they were really like. Eli did know, and he understood that she'd been the one. Ever after, he looked at her as if he'd been harmed.

When Jane finally made the decision, she was alone in the bungalow, doing laundry and trying to clean up. They'd been to Julie's cottage, which was becoming Julie and Peter's, and which more and more put them in a bad mood. The work they had to do at home was infinite. Every little drawer you opened had a whole new universe of mess.

Jane worked furiously. Julie had them over for celebrations, and her house always stayed perfect, while theirs was in the perpetual process of becoming.

"Do you want a little brother?" her mother asked, walking into the kitchen.

On her knees, Jane was scrubbing the tiles, one by one. "You don't know it's a brother."

"I kind of sense it. Do you ever feel like that, like you can't really know but you do?"

"No, I don't, really. And I don't especially want a brother or sister. I feel like we should get our lives the way we want them first. I think if you and Eli have a baby, we'll never catch up and be on time." She plunged her arm into the bucket of suds water.

Jane didn't fully mean what she said, but her mother didn't question. The next day, they went together in Eli's car. The clinic was like any clinic, with stupid cat posters on the wall. Jane sat in the waiting room while her mother and Eli went inside. Eli looked in the toilet bowl and said it was a boy.

"You shouldn't have looked," Jane said.

"We're Christmasing tonight," Julie said, laughing into the phone, a year later. Mary softly complained about how much she still had to do, and Julie said it was the same with her. "It's not easy to make cards and

get presents for everyone and deck a tree and bake and still have a job,"
she said. This was a fragile and unconvincing point of connection.
They were not in the same situation anymore, if they ever were, and
all they could find in common was being behind on Christmas. Mary
and Jane even doubted that Julie was really behind. They believed that
whatever it was Julie decided to do, she knew how to do it. Mary and
Jane didn't send cards. And Mary didn't have a job. The parties, the
wedding, Julie just did it all and never seemed flustered. She'd be the
same way with her baby. Jane could never imagine herself or her mom
like that.

The only thing that flustered Julie was easy for them. She didn't
know how to really want things, or want them badly enough.

She did want some things, Jane remembered, to be fair. She was so
glad when she found out from the test her baby was a girl. Jane
couldn't understand that, honestly: how you could be so sure you
wanted a girl. Jane would want a boy; she couldn't even say why.
There are too many reasons to be a boy to know which is first.

Mary and Eli broke up, stayed apart for a long time and then drifted
together again, but not as much as they once were. Mary never did
have another child.

And the rest of her life, Jane knew: I could have had a brother.

Cherries

⋖⋖ ⋖⋖ ⋖⋖ ⋖⋖

*E*veryone seemed to know what wasn't true. Friday night at eight o'clock, under a transparent sky, Owens had his hand on his key in the parking lot when a guy from the south building speared by in Rollerblades and stopped still, tall in the dark and neon. The sleeves of his tee shirt billowed back, winglike. "I'm sorry to hear about your mom," he said.

"Don't be," Owens answered. "She's not dead yet."

"They were saying she was sick." He had light-red hair and freckles, and there was something phosphorescent about his skin. He wavered on his skates, huge like a defective angel.

"Yeah, she is. But I think she's going to get better."

"Well, God bless her," he said, wheeling quickly, turning his whole self on the skates, that big galumphing guy talking about blessings.

Some of the things Owens knew best he could never explain. He could fix a machine, especially a machine he used every day. And he believed he could cure his own ills. He understood his body the same way he tapped those machines. When his stomach swelled at the top, bunched just under his rib cage, he knew what would cure him was fruit. Because he could, when he needed to, tamper or trick a machine to work one more time or coax his body to mend itself, he believed fundamentally, and no matter what she said, that his mother need not die.

It was almost June and there were cherries. All along 580 East, there were fields and fields of dark double Bings, some yellow with a blush of red, dotted faintly. Queen Annes, Rainiers, Jubilees. He wanted her to fast. But if she couldn't do that, she could eat cherries.

At the farm stands, cherries came cold, opaque with condensation, under burlap. Like most kids who grew up anywhere near the Great Valley, he had picked when he was a boy. Fifty cents a bushel, when money mattered. He would see her tomorrow. He'd get up at five or six, take the motorcycle and bring the cherries back to her by noon.

But Saturday he woke late, at eleven, caught in sticky sunlight. He would've enjoyed the bike ride—it was a dry, clear day—but anyway there was a place here, and he drove with the car top down. The stand had Bings and Rainiers, two sizes. He asked how much it was for all the big ones.

"More in back. Many as you want."

He had to know how much for them all.

Nine ninety-nine a pound, that was high; on 580 they'd be less than half, maybe a third. He'd grown up waiting for the fruit prices to come down. His family could never afford the first strawberries or white anything—albino nectarines, Babcock peaches. Now he bought the best fruit, regardless. This is what he felt most from his money.

A one-hundred-dollar bill for the farmer's cherries, and the full bags collapsed into a torso on the passenger seat, almost touching him. They made sifting noises as he drove. From anywhere he ever was, he knew his way back to the house. In different layers of sleep, when everything stretched to become unrecognizable, the house endured. In one dream it was white, older, alone on a low dark span of land, with lighted windows and round, old-fashioned furniture, but he knew it was the house. He was running, being chased; if he could only get to the porch she would open the door and let him in.

Right after the war, a developer called Handelman made this neighborhood and named it for himself, Handelman Hills. He put up cheap houses for families first starting out. Sometimes Owens drove through the small streets just for the smell. Smoke from burning leaves curled through the air, grass released the aroma of tart earth as the sprinklers sissed evenly back and forth, back and forth. They were beautiful, simple houses.

Before Handelman, the hillsides were covered with bare weeds and scattered oaks and alders. Long ago there had been a Spanish world, shepherds in slow migrations. Even before that, Indians lived on roots from this ground. The streets now alternated between Spanish names and those of Handelman's relatives back in Ohio. Nothing remained of the Indians except stray arrowheads boys of Owens' generation dug out of the dirt. No one remembered much past the last conquest.

When he turned up into the driveway, a sprinkler beaded the lawn next door, the fan of water turning itself inside out.

"Yoo-hoo," he called, slanting in.

She sat at the kitchen table and he joined her, hoisting three huge bags. His dad was out back. The kitchen looked the same as ever, clean-countered, but now it carried a slight lace of rot and the firmer smell of medicine.

"I've got something for you," he said, eyes serious. "I brought some cherries. I think what you need to do is purge your system. You need to just eat cherries, and nothing else, for three or four days. I think that's what's going to cure you."

"You got so many. Put them in the fridge so they'll keep," she said. "And take some home. We'll never eat all those."

He poured some into a blue bowl on the table between them and got out a smaller plate for pits. He stuffed the other bags in all the empty places of the refrigerator. He stood eating handfuls, as she took them one at a time.

"Shouldn't we wash them first?" she said, frowning as if she'd done something wrong.

"Forget about it," he said with his mouth full. "They're organic."

"Don't help with the dirt," his dad said, clumping in.

"How're you feeling?" Owens asked.

"Good today. Today I'm good," she said. "Last night I slept."

His eyebrows were so you couldn't say no to him. She ate the cherry meat delicately, around in a strip the way children eat apples, because they are told.

"How are you? How is the business?" She always called it "the business."

"Everything at Genesis is pretty great." This was not altogether true. Outside, light faltered over the close-cut yard.

His dad came in again, this time carrying carrots, dirt still attached, in a sheet of newspaper. "We read in the paper about the stock split." He nodded once. Approval.

"Yeah, so you know what that means. You guys are rich! You should take a trip or buy yourself a new car."

They heard the electric clock move. He understood too late that was the wrong thing to say.

His dad said, "We don't want to go anywhere."

"But we enjoyed the trips we did take. Especially the one to London. With you and Olivia." His mother picked up the pendant around her neck and let it drop back. "How is she?"

He sighed. "How is Olivia? That's an excellent question. I'm not sure I know the answer to that, Mom."

"Well, you see her, don't you?" His dad stood cleaning the carrots at the sink. In his huge hands, the small white roots looked delicate, like nerves.

"If you don't know," she said, "I don't know who does."

"She calls here," his dad said. "Comes up to see her."

"And the past few times, she brought a friend along and the friend gave me a massage! That was real, real nice."

"Karen. Yeah, I knew that."

"Say, tell me, did you pay her something? Because we tried and she wouldn't take a dime."

"Oh, yeah, don't worry about that."

"Did you pay her or not?"

"Yeah, sure, I'll pay her. But that's not the point. She's a friend of Olivia's and mine, and she wants to come. She liked you a lot, Mom."

"Oh, and I like her too. Very much."

"You know, with Olivia, sometimes I get the feeling that when I'm old, I may look back and think, I really blew it, because she could have been the love of my life. But we'll have just missed. Because we can't really get along."

Nora leaned in. "What do you fight over?"

"It's not that."

She pulled back again, neck retracted.

"I'll remember this really beautiful girl I was with for a while in my twenties."

"You going to marry her?" his dad's gruff voice came. "You're thirty-one."

"I don't know. I don't know if she'd marry me. Sometimes I worry about what'll happen to her if we don't stay together. I feel like in five years, I could be driving out to Napa to visit her in the hospital."

His dad made a noise with his mouth. "Olivia's not crazy."

"She kinda is, Dad. You don't know her that well. She's got a lot of problems."

"No crazier'n you are."

"I remember hearing the mom did that," Nora said quietly. "And the dad, isn't he sick too?"

"Yeah, her dad's got cancer. But he smokes." Owens shrugged. "She does too."

"So she hasn't had it easy."

"No. But I wish she'd do more to help herself. Like quit smoking."

"Such a pretty girl. And a nice girl too."

When he was a boy, Nora thought, they'd looked so much alike that people in stores often remarked on the resemblance. She'd been pleased, extra pleased, but why? It didn't amount to much at all. He always knew—they'd told him right away when he was old enough to understand—so what did it matter what people said who didn't know them?

"Cherries are the best fruit," Owens said. He rolled the stones around in his mouth, then spit them out into a brown bag he took from under the sink. Nora ate one by one, cleaning the pit thoroughly, then taking it out with her red-tinged fingers and setting it on the plate. They'd always had cherries here, every year, from the first of their marriage.

"Say, if you do want to marry her, I'll give you my ring." Nora took the slender ring off her finger and offered it to her son.

"Naw," he said, looking elsewhere, out the window over the sink into the yard.

"You put that back on your finger, Nora," his father ordered. "You keep your ring. She's always giving away too much."

"I don't know what'll happen. I suspect we won't be married. But that we'll never really forget each other."

"Why do you think you don't get along?"

Arthur Owens had to leave the room. He couldn't stand the way she got with him.

Owens took another handful of cherries. "I wonder if some people are the same and see to a very deep true part of each other. But maybe those people can't have a kind of everyday life where you eat breakfast and go to movies and raise a family and have it be kind of nice." His head came up, as it often did with a new idea. "Did you have a great love in your life?"

"Well, your dad is for me."

"But there wasn't ever anybody else, before Dad?"

"Nobody special. Now they seem like—oh, I don't know—maybe people in a book I read. I can't even remember the names. Your father and I, we had our whole lives." She gripped the arms of her chair to steady herself.

"What do you think I should do with Olivia?"

Owens' gaze was straight on her; it felt like a mercy of sun. She wanted that to last. It was all at once what she'd wanted, and it was almost too much. What should he do? She truly did not know. And she was tired. She felt grateful, all of a sudden, for her Arthur. There had been thousands and thousands of days, plain little notes he'd left, his five o'clock phone calls, the way he turned at night and made one noise that let her sleeping body know he wanted sideways now with her arm around his belly and her foot between his calves. There was that and head on chest.

But her boy was nothing like that. "Try to get along better," was all she could think. "Because love is really your day-to-day life. With your family."

If she'd said, "Marry her," Owens fully believed he would. He was a young man who rarely granted anyone power over him. But he also knew his mother well enough to understand that she would go to the edge but not over the cliff, not for this. She liked Olivia but was never truly comfortable with her. Like most mothers, she wished for a young woman more like herself.

"Say, have you talked to Colleen at all?"

"Pony? No. Why?"

"Call her once, Tom. She's your sister, and she hasn't always got it so easy either. Maybe she can help you talk out some of these things."

"Mom, I don't know how to say this, but Pony and I don't really get along."

"Well, try a little. You always played so nice when you were children. You have to work at things sometimes. You don't get along with Olivia, you don't get along with Pony. Maybe you have to put a little more in."

"We just don't have much in common."

"Maybe you can help *her*, then. Just until she's back on her feet."

At first the cherries tasted only like themselves. Now, after an hour of eating, they acquired a brown tinge, a maturity, like tea. They had not really played so nice, though Nora had tried for years to make them do that. She remembered Colleen sitting hunched at the edge of the lawn, patiently looking for a four-leaf clover. She picked a regular one and twirled the frail stem around and around as if it might have more. Then he walked beside her, reached down and picked a four-leaf from right next to her knee.

"I found one," he said, running to her, the mother, carrying it like a flag. And Colleen ran up too, clutching the bottom of her skirt. She had loved the little girl because she clung like that. And Colleen always got less from everyone else. I had her by me, day and night, when she was a baby, Nora thought, even in the hospital. She needed me. He never did like that. A few times, always in private, she never even told Art, she took him to the bedroom, closed the shade and tried to let him suck. She didn't have milk, of course. And he wouldn't suck. He cried and looked away. Later, Colleen sucked for almost a year.

"Be good to your sister. Do it for me." For Pony, Nora could go all the way and ask.

They sat a moment, hearing nothing but the dull sound of the refrigerator. They were still eating, but by now the fruit was rote in their mouths.

"I think you should really eat just these cherries, nothing else until they're gone. Just cherries and water. And when you eat them all, call me and I'll bring some more. You might start feeling a lot better in a few days." He talked with the indifferent authority of a doctor.

"So what do you think you'll do about Olivia?"

He shook his head. "I want her to be proud of me."

"I'm proud of you," Nora said. Her tooth hit a liquid and sweet cherry.

"I know."

"Promise me you'll look out for Colleen. Just try a little." She took his arm. "Won't you give that to me?"

"Mom, we're really different. We've never been close."

Arthur stepped into the room. "Just leave him be, Nora. What's his promise worth anyway if he don't want to give it?"

Owens was talking on the phone, feet up, when Eliot Hanson walked in. Owens did not consider the entry of another person a reason to truncate what he was doing.

A large book of black-and-white photographs devoted to North America's national parks lay on one of the tabletops. While they waited, most of Owens' employees pretended to occupy themselves with this book. But Eliot carried a novel with him at all times and easily sank into a chair, returning to it.

A half hour later, Owens hung up. Even then he didn't immediately turn to his guest. This behavior didn't upset Eliot Hanson in the least. Nine-tenths of insult is surprise, and he billed in quarter-hour increments. He'd worked for Owens a long time and he was well paid.

"Hi, Eliot," Owens said at last, while typing on his keyboard. "What can I do for you?"

Eliot stood up and closed the door. "I came to talk about your real mother."

"Biologic—" Owens started, then bit his lip. "Yes. Did you find anything?"

"Do you have a little while? I've got quite a bit of information. There's also a story about how I met the doctor who delivered you. He was retired and living with his wife in Santa Rosa. And I called—"

"Listen, Eliot, since I asked you to do this for me, my mom's gotten sick. And here at work, you know, things are tough. So I just don't have a lot of energy to give this right now."

"I'm sorry to hear about your mom," Eliot said. From what he'd heard, Owens often did this: assigned a project and then, when people came in to report, acted as if they were nagging him. But Eliot had become involved with this particular project. "Well, what do you say— shall we drop it for now?"

Owens knew little about his biological mother. But one of her wishes had become abiding policy in his childhood: she had insisted that Arthur send him to college. She had demanded this, merciless, regardless of means. And Arthur capitulated, promising away vacations and household margin, nights out at supper clubs with his friends. All the years of Owens' childhood, Arthur and Nora kept up a college fund for him and, in fairness, also for Pony. Christmas gifts from relatives and understanding friends came in the form of cash contributions. And when the time came, he went for a semester and dropped out with great relish. He wasn't going to let a woman he never knew determine his life.

"No, no, I don't think you should drop it. I'll tell you what: I'd like you to just keep it for me. Sometime I'll want to know all this stuff, but I don't want to hear about it right now."

What was he like before?

For Olivia, during the years which were and always would be the time of her great love, that was the constant question. Was he always the same?

The only people who'd known him before were his family. His father had opinions; his father could say, but he wouldn't. "Stubborn," was all he offered. "Still is."

Pony wasn't close enough to know much, but she said he studied magic. "I can make you go away," he'd warned her. Apparently, for a month Owens went around measuring things between his thumb and first finger. "You're as big as this; I can measure you. You fit into my eye, so you're not very big." He claimed to have made a horse disappear.

"I think he believed it himself," his mother said, shaking her head. Nora's illness provided Olivia with an opportunity she'd wanted—to prove herself entirely good. She went up after her shift at the hospital, in the late afternoon. Twice a week, she brought along Karen Croen, whom Owens had hired to give his mother massages. Karen was a person whom mothers always liked. "Just a nice, nice girl," Olivia's own mother had said.

Olivia stayed in the room, setting flowers in a clear glass jar on the dresser, and listened to Nora's confessions while Karen worked.

"I just felt like having a roll," Nora apologized, the day after Owens brought the cherries. Nora had always loved sugar. The three women were eating doughnuts off little plates, enjoying the soft, powdery food of convalescence. Olivia had been a committed vegan for ten years longer than Owens, but with his mother she would gladly eat a doughnut. Olivia liked these afternoons. The time passed slowly, and his mother and dad were easier to talk to than he was. Olivia left these visits happy and relieved; she went to Owens with a gift-feeling of kindness. She believed he was simpler than she'd once thought and that things were going to be better.

Nora could never help but talk.

"He wasn't very babyish-looking. He was always just different, he had the darker eyes. A lot of babies have blue and then they get dark. But he was what he was right from the start. Or at least when I met him, anyway. I wasn't the least bit ready. I didn't even know how to hold a baby.

"He was a good boy. Very pacific. When he cried, those eyebrows would make a real V, and he'd stare up at me like he knew everything and I was wrong.

"To tell the truth, he scared me a little. Sometimes I thought he was judging me and I wasn't coming out too good. And the once or twice I had to let him wait, when I finally came he was different. He'd look past me, far away, as if he couldn't stand my sight.

"You know, I think I was afraid to love him. I was afraid her parents would come and take him away."

"Could they have done that?" Olivia asked.

"The way the law was then, it had more to do with the mother, and they were the mother's parents. And they never wanted her to marry Tom's dad. They were a doctor family. Art wanted to hire a lawyer and so we did. But that first year was hard. They were difficult people, always pestering the social worker. I suppose they were upset. She was their only child. But they weren't happy with us, even after we signed saying we'd send him to college. We made up a budget to show them just how we could afford to save so much every week to put him through. After the judge gave us custody, they moved away. I think it was to Arizona. The first couple of years, he always got a birthday card with a check. But then we stopped hearing.

"They had me scared, though. That first year, maybe I didn't pick him up enough. Sometimes I think I let him cry in his crib when I really should've held him."

Nora gave the girls cherries to take home with them. Bag after bag of Owens' cherries were rotting in the refrigerator.

Once they left, Arthur scolded her. "I don't see how that's anybody's business."

"I didn't even know until I said it. I didn't know that's what I thought."

Years earlier, in their beginning, Owens and Olivia lay side by side in front of the Copper King's huge stone fireplace. Olivia made the fire. Birch logs popped and cracked, spitting lines of sparks. Olivia understood fire, blew on it, tented the logs to coax a vertical lick of flame. She'd been a Girl Scout. Owens was twenty-seven and already one of the five hundred richest men in the country, and that night they were alone in the huge unlocked house.

In a slow voice, he told her that he felt *grateful* to Nora, letting silence around the word batten it. "She took me in when I had no place to go."

A traveler with no money and no shoes. No crib for a bed, the evil innkeepers. As if all he'd needed was a room. "You were just a little baby," Olivia said. "Who took care of you the first eight months?"

"Some neighbor woman," he shrugged. "I don't remember her."

"Do you know anything about your real mother?"

"Well, I've always thought of my mother as my real mother. But I don't know much about my biological mother, no. She was some college girl." He pictured her holding books against her sweater, wearing college shoes, tie-ups with those liver-colored soles.

Olivia, who'd never gone to college, felt ashamed. She could've gone somehow, but she hadn't wanted to put herself forward that way. And Owens sort of blamed her. His memories of his own three months already seemed important. He felt attracted to college girls, their intentness, heads of clean hair bent over long library tables. Later, he would want to give Olivia college. But she would be too proud. That was the problem with people around Owens. They got stubborn, feeling they had to keep something indefinable yet essential about themselves. Olivia didn't think the people who went to college were any better than she was. And so to enter a classroom and be behind them was more than she could bear. She was behind them every day in other, more obvious ways at the hospital, but that she could live with and had lived with for a long time.

Olivia had her arms around her shins. Her knee, through the hole in her jeans, was warm from the fire. She didn't want to tell about her family yet: she thought if she did he'd think less of her.

He told her that once it had snowed in Auburn. He was the first one up. He recognized a strange silence in the house. "The world is never that quiet," he said. And then he saw it out the window, white flakes filling the air. The snow apparently had no density or speed; pieces lofted down aimlessly, never in the shortest distance between sky and ground. The large flakes resembled pieces of bread. He'd put clothes on over his pajamas and stepped outside. He ran out again across lawns, bounding up shallow porch steps and ringing doorbells. Once he heard fumbling footsteps begin somewhere in a house, he was off and running to the next porch. "Nobody knew it was me. By noon it was all gone."

When she went to temp at Genesis, inoculating for Indonesian flu, Karen and Huck had said, "Do you think you'll see that guy?"

She shrugged. "If he needs a flu shot."

Owens never took patent medicines, and in the realm of vitamins he believed only in metals, particularly zinc. But he did accept a vaccine from Olivia, and a week later she was on his floor. She slept with him the first night, easily. She was a girl with no mother.

"What's he like?" Karen asked. She and Huck had read about him, so they both had questions and opinions.

In a blind way she didn't fully understand, Olivia resented people's interest. Perhaps because she intuited the other topic of conversation that surrounded him, though never within his hearing: the matter of whom he would marry.

Too many people speculated about Owens. The cooks, Jane and her mother, even the man who managed his money—they all gossiped. Rumor had it that two unauthorized biographies were being written about him. Reputable newspapers like the *Bee* and the *Mercury News* reported not only the glitches in Exodus and the controversy of his rice-and-beans school lunches but also his romantic whereabouts and the prices of his real estate transactions. Last year, a gossip columnist had suggested a secret engagement between Olivia and Owens. A different columnist described Olivia only as a "leggy blonde" along at the opening night of the opera.

Olivia stood in the room he'd grown up in, with an armload of warm-smell wash. She wished she'd known Owens as the little boy who slept in this bed and sat at this small desk. With Owens, it was easy to assume there was one clear line that divided his life. Olivia folded the laundry while Karen worked on Nora, who was talking. She liked to talk about her children's childhoods.

"Once, when the kids were young," she said, "we took them to see the circus. He wanted to watch the magician. But Pony wanted trapeze. Dad flipped a coin, and so we bought tickets for the Hall of Trapeze. We thought Pony was probably too young to get the gist of the magic tricks anyway. And while we were in with the trapeze, Owens had to go number one. So his dad sent him out to the fields. And then, after a while, I said, 'Gee, shouldn't he be back? He's been gone a long time.' Pony was unwinding her cotton candy, peeling it like an orange. 'I betcha he's in that tent,' I said.

"Dad told me, 'Damned if I know how he got in with what he's got in his pocket.'

"But we bought tickets for the magic show then, and there Owens was on the stage, in front of a big crowd, his face the way it used to be when he was mad about something, his eyebrows pressed together in a V. 'Just lift your foot,' he was saying, 'and if there isn't a silver dollar under the sole of your shoe, then you have nothing to be frightened of.'

"I felt real sorry for that magic man. He looked like a nice man, too. And that can't be an easy way to make a living. He was wearing a robe that was dirty at the wrists, and I could see he was trembling. 'Get down here, Thomas Rudolf Owens,' Dad called.

"But that crowd was on his side and he knew it. They were hooting, 'Lift your foot! Lift your foot!' Then the magic man looked down at him and said, 'Better watch out, little boy, or I'll make you disappear!'

"And Owens crossed his arms and stood there like a statue. Well, you know it too, he can get that way. 'Go ahead and do it,' he said. He'd been threatening to make Pony disappear all those years; he knew how hard it was to do. And that shut the crowd up. There was a real hush, everybody waiting.

" 'Do it!' another kid called, from way in the back.

" 'Make me disappear,' Owens ordered.

"Then the magic man's face turned upside down almost. In the tent before, that Hall of Trapeze, we'd been watching acrobatics. This magic man had a big face and it seemed like it did three flips and then he ran off the stage, his regular shoes showing through the flap of his gown. A band picked up then, I suppose to keep everybody from looking. And a midget came out, in a tuxedo and tails, real swell, and he had a saw he held up for everybody to see. But Owens reached down, stood on top of a box up there, used for God knows what, and so he was taller than the midget. He must have been eight or nine then. And he held up his hand in the air and waved it for everybody to see: and sure enough, there was the silver dollar.

"The people moved back and forth, and you could hear their candy wrappers twisting. The midget was saying he would saw his wife in half. An announcer said, 'Ladies and gentlemen, from far away

Lemuria, we introduce Lady Helena,' and a spotlight came around this little-bitty woman, she was about three feet tall, but real pretty.

"And Owens did a trick of his own," Nora concluded. "While everybody was watching that Lady Helena being sawed, he pocketed the silver dollar."

Olivia nodded. She'd been present before at his unmaskings.

When they walked out to their cars, Olivia tried to pay Karen. Owens had asked Karen to give his mother massages, and she kept it up twice a week. He might remember to pay her sometime, but for now Olivia would tide her friend over. Olivia was different with money since she'd been with Owens. In a funny way, he was expensive. It had to do with people's feelings. Promises and offers he forgot, or wishes, Olivia made good on. She earned a decent salary, and she could do this. She'd stopped saving. She'd waited before and saved for the time when she'd come into the importance of life. And she believed that was now.

It was still light out, but it was suppertime in this neighborhood, when men came home who worked at jobs by the hour. Karen had eaten at this time most of her life. Olivia had always eaten late.

"Here," she said, wadding a roll of money in her palm and slipping it into Karen's.

"Oh, no you don't." Karen jammed it down Olivia's open collar.

"Come on," Olivia said, chasing after her friend around the yard.

They'd been athletic girls, and the run felt good. They kept on long after either one particularly remembered the money, and it felt enlivening to tackle, with their blood beating quickly in their wrists, smelling the clean numb smell of earth.

"Please," Olivia said, her hand on her friend's cheek. "You never let me do anything for you." They had been friends for over fifteen years already, and Karen was always the good one, glad to help. Olivia's own mother had always thought Karen had a better heart.

That night, Olivia asked Owens if he still had the silver dollar. She was a little afraid to ask. Sometimes he didn't like to know people talked about him.

"What silver dollar?"

"The silver dollar that was under the magician's shoe."

"Oh, that. She told you that? It was really pretty great. The guy went tearing out and tripped on his dress, just about fell flat on his face. No, I don't have it anymore. I kept it a long time and then I spent it."

"Do you remember what on?"

"What are you guys talking about?" Jane asked. They were doing it again. "Who's *she?*"

"Yeah, I remember. I spent that silver dollar on my first date with a girl. I took Laurie Gallioto out for a Coca-Cola."

"A Coke cost a dollar?" Jane asked.

"I was speaking"—his mouth contracted in a small smile—"figuratively."

"And was it worth it?" Olivia said.

His smile moved through the full sequence of memory. "Yeah, it was," he said. "She was the first girl I really kissed. You know that lake up from my parents' house? I kissed her in front of that lake one night, right after supper."

Jane could tell he was remembering kissing Laurie Gallioto and thinking that nothing else since had been quite like it.

Olivia shook her head. He was always like this. For her, nothing in her life mattered, until him. Later that night, tucking Jane in, she explained. "*She* is his mom."

"Yeah, but by the time he and my mom decide to introduce us," Jane said, "she'll be dead, and then I'll never know my grandmother."

Olivia repeated the story of the magician, as best she remembered.

"My dad was taller than the midget?"

"Well, maybe he was standing on something."

Jane was thinking of him being taller than the midget when he was younger than she was now. He kept telling her she took after him, that she'd have a growth spurt soon. She worried that she might be a dwarf, then thought of Noah and felt guilty. "When you go again to see her," she whispered, "can I come?"

"You have to ask him."

"He'll say no. Just take me along, I won't tell."

Owens didn't excel in the usual places children distinguish themselves. He wasn't good in school or sports, and when the teachers received the state test scores every year, they called Nora in to tell her he was underachieving.

"We thought he'd be better in school. His grandparents expected him to be a college professor, or a doctor, even. So we tried to get him to bring his grades up. But he didn't care. When the teacher asked him a question he didn't know, he wasn't the least bit ashamed.

"He'd come in and watch while I fixed dinner. When I asked if he'd done his homework, he'd just smile his goofy smile and say, 'You know, that water'll boil faster if you put the lid on.' I said I could manage supper myself, so why didn't he see about his homework so his father'd get a good report card this time. And he'd say, 'Seriously, do you know why water boils?'"

Frank Wu came to visit on a Thursday. Olivia had never met Frank before, and she wondered if he'd come when he knew Owens would be at work. Olivia cleaned out the refrigerator while he talked to Nora in the living room.

Owens had told her about Frank. They were both on the night shift at Valley Electronics, and Frank was way ahead of everyone else. They started at nine and he'd have all his work done by ten-thirty. His mom packed great Chinese dinners, which he'd share with Owens. He was in graduate school then but already talking about quitting. Until Owens talked him out of it, he thought he wanted to go work for Ford. He used to fix cars in high school. He had all kinds of pencil sketches he sent off to the Ford Motor Company, Detroit, Michigan. "They were too stupid to even steal them," Owens had said.

The man had a high voice and a cascading giggle. "I'm frittering my life away, Nora."

Olivia had all the vegetables in plastic bags and the jars out on the counter. The last of the cherries had rotted. The shelves smelled faintly of pills as she lifted them out to wash.

"Don't blame him," Nora said about something. "I probably didn't teach him right."

Frank and Owens had paid Pony fifty cents an hour, and on Saturdays, Frank's four cousins, shy elementary school girls in pink dresses, worked for free. Three years after that, they made fifty men million-aires, all under the age of thirty. Frank bought houses for twenty rela-tives. Now he lived up in Berkeley, wandering in and out of classes. Owens thought he was studying arcane dialects of Chinese. They were not in touch. Owens had told her he was kind of mad at Frank for checking out. He had hired thirty-two Wus. Owens walked into the mailroom one day and found twenty-five men squatting with covered teacups, planning a union. "I had to choose," Owens said. "It was Genesis or Frank's uncles."

Frank's grandfather left too. He was the second Wu to come to Cal-ifornia and had lived all his life in a Chinatown residence hotel. His fa-ther had laid ties on the Central Pacific Railroad.

"No, Frank, listen to me. He didn't have any use for ours either."

The refrigerator began to hum again, covering their voices. When Frank came to say goodbye, he shook Olivia's hand.

"We'd love to see you sometime," she said. "Just sit across a table and have some supper."

"That Frank gave me blood," Nora said an hour later, while Olivia sat at the kitchen table, giving her a manicure.

Olivia had never had her own mother to herself like this.

Olivia wasn't the first girl to come to Nora's kitchen, bearing flowers stemmed in wet paper towel and tinfoil, carrying a washed-out jar, wanting to know about Owens. It had started already when he was in high school. At seventeen, Mary di Natali had come as a girl goes to a mother superior, asking to be let in.

Other girls arrived too over the years. Nora didn't mind much. Each of them was polite, acknowledging Nora's position. It was these girls, she knew, who remembered her birthday and coaxed him to be-have like a son. Every one of them nudged his generosity. Nora ap-preciated those girls. But she understood that Olivia was the last. She hoped, for this reason, he'd marry her. Olivia would be the last to know his mother.

On a day that felt like the culmination of a long job together, Nora told Olivia and Karen the story of the chicken.

Owens had had a chicken.

"I don't know anymore how he got it," she said. "I s'pose some-body gave it to him around Easter, and this one just didn't die. It started out a baby chick and grew up into a chicken."

"Them next door had coops," Arthur added. He was at home, ready to put in his two cents. "The older boy sold eggs on the paper route."

"And everywhere Owens went," his wife continued, "that chicken went too. That chicken loved him. They were together probably a year, he and that chicken. At night, the chicken slept next to his bed. And when he went around the neighborhood, he shoved that chicken in an old yellow coffee can and stuck it on his wagon."

Arthur laughed, or coughed. "That was the year we put in them sliding glass doors."

Nora looked up at him. "And was that ever a lot of work. But they didn't have screens, so we were always telling Tommy to close the door behind him. You know, the bugs got in. And one day I was in the kitchen and I saw him going out the back door, that chicken following behind his legs, and he closed the door and cut the head right off his chicken. I ran and scooped it up in my apron because I was so afraid of him seeing at that age. But he kept on walking into the yard. He never turned back and looked, and he never asked about that chicken again."

"Never once asked," Arthur added.

Arthur and Olivia were drinking coffee that day. Nora couldn't stand the taste anymore; no matter what they did, it was bitter to her. But she still loved the smell.

The three of them sat for a long time looking out the sliding glass doors. A spring wind blew iris heads and papery poppies.

Nora whispered, "Besides Pony, you're the nicest girl I know."

Olivia felt a grin growing on her face: the happiness that makes everything want to end. Nora liked her better than Karen.

Finally, bracing herself, Olivia asked Nora if she thought Owens loved her.

"I don't know," Arthur said, turning around, his lips tight and eyes alive. Olivia had believed the two things at once for so long that she recognized a clear truth: what that meant, not to know—but then Nora touched her arm. "He does; I can tell. A mother knows."

Jane sat at the little desk and then lay on the small bed. It was a boy's bed, decorated with cowboys. I wish we could take it home, she thought. A bedroom set was one of the things she'd never had.

Olivia had brought her along, but only as a helper. She hadn't told Nora who she was. Earlier, Jane had heated Karen's oil, and now she sat in his old bedroom, folding the laundry, making the socks into balls. But she wanted to be with them, to look at her grandmother. I'd tell her myself, she thought, just whisper it. Really, Jane was afraid to tell. She wanted her grandmother to take her hand and say, "I know you. I know who you are."

When she finished the laundry, she snuck out into the hall. Arthur and Nora were putting the dry dishes away in the kitchen.

"What are you doing," Arthur said, "telling her what you don't even believe yourself?"

Nora sighed. "Give him the benefit."

Olivia stepped out of the bathroom and ran up to Jane in the hall. "I almost forgot about you."

When Nora thanked Olivia for bringing her little helper, she didn't really look at Jane. And Jane knew that was her one chance. In bed that night, she wondered if his real mother would have recognized her.

Once, Karen made a silly hopeful mistake. They'd gone out to a movie—Karen, Dave, Olivia, Owens, Noah, Huck and some other people they knew then. And in the gravel parking lot, Owens had thrown his head back and laughed at a joke Karen made. His hand accidentally touched her arm, and she felt rough prickles. Even though Owens was with Olivia and she was with Dave, Karen felt he'd noticed her and esteemed her.

Of course, she had interpreted too much. Only a woman unused to love would rely on such small gestures, having no experience of the persistence of seduction, its unmistakable character. But Olivia was new to Owens and he was generous with love, giving off parts of it, like sparks from a torch. One of those burns fell on Karen.

After the movie, they'd all gone out for ice cream. The group clustered in chairs at the front of the small parlor, then Karen slipped outside with the key to the bathroom in the alley. From there, she overheard laughter in the parking lot.

"But she seems really *old.*"

Karen felt, with horror, that Owens was talking about her. She pressed against the dark wall and waited for the terror to unwind.

"No she doesn't. We're the same age; she's two months younger," Olivia answered. "She's pretty, I think."

"Really? I don't think she's at all attractive."

Karen stiffened, going back into the noisy shop. She could not let them see that she knew. She still needed a bathroom.

Early on a hot Sunday morning, Owens was packing. He poured his shampoo into one of the small plastic bottles made for hikers. He had the perfect garment bag—so thin it held only one suit. He packed shoes, socks, underwear, three new white shirts, still folded in their plastic, and four ties. At the top, he put his CD player and headphones. He would fly in jeans.

Then the phone rang, and it was over.

His father's voice was low and slow. "About nine-thirty, nine-thirty-five," he said. "You go ahead and tell Olivia. I've got to call Pony."

The first call he made was not to Olivia but to his secretary, Kathleen, who was out running, her husband said. She needed to call the White House and cancel.

He'd been wearing a tee shirt, but now he changed because he didn't know what would be necessary. On the winding road, two girls on horseback blocked the way. He waited for them to steer the animals across. One of the girls reined the huge beast harshly; its astonishing head tried to rove and circle, skimming the sky. It was an ordinary, glittering, California summer day, light falling through the trees. The girls' bare legs were white and thin, draped over horses.

You died on a day that was for no one else different. Girls woke up and pulled on shorts to ride.

He thought of Hirohito's funeral, the thousands of umbrellas. Churchill's. You had to hope for a day commensurate, or maybe not. Maybe it was best that those who grieve grieve alone—or not grieve but go on with their lives so the faint trace would rise up unbidden through their years like the scent of long-fallen apples.

Boys ran and then slammed into the lake, at the end of the day when there was wind, the sun a last twist on the surface. In the water were pockets of warm you found and lost again. When they climbed out, they wore only tee shirts and it was cold down the hill, his jaw and teeth chattering. Running, he tore at leaves to slow him. Trees on the hills where they lived were not old then. Handelman had planted them.

A hundred times she'd waited inside the kitchen door and, after his streak of cold collided into her open wingspan, cocooned him in towel.

Every day and every night he knew her. The way on the bottoms of her shoes it was lighter for her five toes and heel, like an animal's footprint. A dry rag always hung over the sink spout.

"Last educational degree?" the young woman requested.

"What does it matter?" Owens said.

"We need it for the certificate."

"She finished high school." Arthur said this as an accomplishment; he himself hadn't. "And then she took college courses from time to time, at night." He opened a folder in which he'd brought her diploma, encased in tissue and cardboard.

Owens thought of his stacks of magazines, plaques, commendations, and vowed to go home and throw it all out.

Then the woman led him and his father to a vast room where they displayed the caskets. They were extremely ugly, Owens noticed. Several seemed to be made of brushed metal. The wooden ones were polished, with satin interiors. And they were all incredibly expensive. Owens stopped before a particularly egregious example. "Why would people buy something like this?"

The young woman shrugged. This unnatural patience seemed to be part of her job. "A lot of people choose them," she said, "for the hardware."

His father stood before each one, holding his hands together, as the woman explained the special features. He finally settled on the least bad box, made of pine. It was also the least expensive.

"Don't you think we should just go home," Owens asked, "and make one ourselves?"

"We can buy this for her," his father said, and Owens let him pay.

Silvery olives and low fruit trees hummed in the distance. "You see this," Owens said. "Auburn was all like this once."

"When we were young," Mary added. She alone wasn't dressed in black. Eli wouldn't come. She'd tried to keep Jane still during the ceremony, but now she was cartwheeling over the smooth lawn.

"Yeah," he said. "I wonder how long this'll stay here."

"Forever," Mary said. "It's a cemetery."

"Just think a minute. There aren't any cemeteries in San Francisco anymore. Or new ones in Manhattan. It'll stay here until the land gets too valuable, then they'll plow under and start building." He stood in his best black suit, one pant leg dragging on the grass. "And that's probably all right. They should stick around for a couple generations, as long as people who remember them are alive, and after that it doesn't really matter."

Mary stood with her keys in her hand. Owens hadn't invited her to whatever was after, but neither had he asked her not to come. "I'm leaving," she said. "Should I take Jane, or do you want her?"

The cut-glass dish was divided in two: bright-yellow mustard on one side, mayonnaise on the other. "That's just like her," Owens said. To Jane's surprise, he joined the small line around the table and made himself a Swiss cheese sandwich.

She wandered to the den, where pictures of her father from magazines and newspapers covered the walls. A picture of him and a young Chinese man getting a trophy hung next to the trophy itself. On the other side was a citation naming Colleen Owens the Most Valued Employee of Red Owl Grocery.

Owens kept ending up next to his sister, and every time, they hugged sideways. He seemed oddly deferential to many of the people here, a way Jane had never seen him be. And right now, she missed her mother. Since Christmas, Mary always seemed to fall into a bad mood when Owens took Jane off without her.

Jane followed him down to the basement. "Look at this," he said, once he noticed her. "This is my dad's workbench. This was the spot he made for me." A three-foot rectangle at the end, painted orange.

"What are these?" Jane said, pointing at a bulletin board with forty or fifty small snapshots, each of a different car.

"Oh, those are all the cars he worked on. He used to ask the people if, once he fixed it, he could use it one night to take his wife out. So a lot of Saturday nights they'd drive off in some Cadillac or Lincoln he'd just fixed, all waxed and polished. He'd go to the backyard and clip a rose and put it next to her on the seat. He's a pretty romantic guy."

Then Owens moved to a slim bureau of drawers, running his hands over the top. "He made this."

Jane had to go to the bathroom, so she ran back up. It was locked and she waited, and a minute later, a woman came out.

"You're Jane, aren't you?"

"Yes. I remember you. You're Pony."

"I thought you were." The woman's hand fluttered. "I feel like we're related somehow."

"You're my aunt."

Pony giggled. "I guess I am, even if we don't know each other that well."

Stepping inside the bathroom, Jane gazed into the mirror. People were always telling her she looked like him, so of course he was her father. Pony hadn't said that, though, and Jane could see why. His sister had the same black eyes and looked much more like him than she did.

Olivia stood in her stocking feet, scraping plates for the dishwasher. She looked out the window at red bush tips and thought: Nora died believing her son was invincible. She would never see him falter or fail. That was true of her own mother too. She'd believed bitterly that all the world's gems were waiting in a basket for Olivia.

"Shep and I went to high school together," Owens was explaining to a group at large. "Are you around to just have dinner sometime?"

"Anytime," Shep said. "We'd love to." He took out a pen from his shirt pocket and painstakingly wrote out three numbers on a piece of paper. "In fact, we're having some of the old gang over two weeks from Friday."

Jane took note of the date, writing it down on her palm the way she'd seen her father do.

Olivia walked with Karen up the path to the small lake where Owens and his friends had swum as boys. They stood at the top and looked down. When they went back, Karen would get in her car and drive home to make Dave dinner.

Olivia again tried to pay her, and Karen again refused. There was love between the two women, but also grit. Karen couldn't completely forgive her friend for choosing a man who didn't value her. Their lots in life were different because of one simple enormous thing.

When she went down, Olivia ran zigzag, arms out to the sides, holding her high heels.

Karen walked slowly, with a stick, taking a long time.

They all had their seat belts on when Owens got out of the car and said, "I need to go in and talk to my sister a minute."

Olivia sighed. She had to think of a gift for Karen, some luxury. In the warm car, she taught Jane how to French braid. They took turns doing each other's hair while they waited.

"Hon?" Owens said when he came back to the car. "I think we should check in on Pony every week or so. Make sure I do that, okay?"

He had never promised, but now, they understood, he would take care of Pony for the rest of her life.

Owens' bag was already packed for the red-eye to Washington, D.C. But at home, he took his clothes off and changed into jeans, then burned his old papers and awards in a fire he built outside in a can.

◄◄

"I never did get paid for that," Karen Croen would say, later, to other people. But she was glad to have done it, for Olivia and for Nora. Still, he'd hired her without ever paying, and that was the truth, a monument standing somewhere in the world.

What was he like before?

Karen Croen knew. He was the same and always would be.

Matisse

◄ı ◄ı ◄ı ◄ı ◄ı

*F*or the first time he could remember, Owens planned a summer day in the city without business. There was a traveling exhibit at the art museum he wanted to see. As an afterthought, he asked Noah Kaskie to come along.

Years before, Owens had become rich on paper. The money was in stocks and in a bank, generating interest but still, strictly speaking, on paper. The first purchase he made, long before the house or the cars, after only a gift to his parents, was a painting. He wanted to buy a Matisse. Through Alta's one museum, he obtained the name of a woman in the city. Wearing black eyeglasses, she led him through numerous galleries.

At the time, Owens was quiet during discussions about art, hampered by a sense of what he hadn't studied. But he knew what he knew, and he'd always loved Matisse.

The woman, Celeste, spoke to him about investing in the young, the importance of getting in on the ground floor. "Of course, you know about that," she said.

"You don't understand," he told her. "I don't want to invest. I ven want to collect. I want to buy a Matisse. Just one. That's all."

Okay," the woman agreed, gamely. "We can work on that."

For the next year, she sent Polaroids to Auburn of drawings, paper cutouts and paintings in upcoming auctions or vulnerable private collections. Whenever Owens could, he found and studied larger reproductions in books. Finally, he saw the painting: a woman on a balcony. Waiting, but settled too strongly in life to be much changed by whatever it was she was waiting for. He bought it from a family in Cincinnati.

The painting arrived on a bright autumn day. He still drove the old beat-up car that rattled and needed a new muffler. He unpacked the painting alone, loosening the nails from the crate with the claw of a hammer. The crate was better made than most of his furniture.

He hung the picture in the rented house, drilling a hole for a Molly bolt. Celeste told him the frame had been purchased at a flea market by Matisse himself and had been overpainted by the artist.

But this purchase—made from a singular act of love—did not make Owens happy.

The first disaster occurred when a housekeeper cleaned the frame with Lemon Pledge. He ranted all night at his girlfriend at the time, the clarinetist, tormenting her until dawn. Then he paced the empty house until nine o'clock, when Celeste told him what to do. He spent the next hour buying soft toothbrushes. Celeste Federal Expressed some restorative wax.

"Are you insured?" she asked, when Owens insisted on having her home number to spare himself another night of misery.

He wasn't and could not be, because he lived in an old unlocked house and refused to put in alarms.

After he'd moved into the Copper King's mansion, he woke up one morning hearing sounds in the living room, raced downstairs and saw it was still there, the house quiet, in long laps of light. As he fell asleep that night, he told Olivia he felt frightened because there was only one.

"It's more important than we are," she said. "That's kind of comforting."

"Well, it sure is more durable."

In the end, he could not stand to live with something that would outlast him. It was too much custodial responsibility, he decided. He gave the painting away and did not love it any less for his inability to tend to it; if anything, his respect for it grew. Celeste had assisted with the bequest. And later on, she called him when the Cincinnati family visited California. They were delighted to have their treasure settled into a museum. Friends of theirs had given a dinner party to introduce Owens, and it was there that he'd met Celeste's daughter, Albertine.

After that, he bought things to enjoy. He bought the first of the beautiful fast cars. Though perfect, it could be replaced. "There is a mold, and the Italians aren't breaking it," he liked to say. Eventually, he wanted to buy art again but this time as a collector. He bought photographs and Japanese prints. He didn't want to own anything there was only one of.

Noah did not find Owens' invitation to the Matisse show simple. He too had a strange relationship to art. His close sister was a photographer, and at the age of forty, after years of working in a bank, his mother had begun to paint landscapes in the garage. During the early sixties, she had been able to supplement the family income by designing paint-by-numbers kits. It was an unremarked disappointment in Noah's life that he hadn't turned out to be "artistic." He had liked to draw, and his mother often took both her children out sketching. He understood, even as a fourteen-year-old boy, that he didn't have the energy to sustain two pursuits. It was a calculated choice, and what swung him was that science seemed easier. He figured if he succeeded at whatever he did, he'd have a better chance of getting married. "Hmph," he said, remembering and feeling cheated. Science wasn't so easy.

Noah's work was not going well. The way he saw it, he was now failing with both fish and flies, and he felt reluctant to leave the lab. He was generally nervous. When Rachel came for some of his hair, she told him the immunologist upstairs would have to quit her project because someone at Harvard stole her knockout. Noah's mutation had

ıshed for four years now. It was only a matter of time before
e got the gene.

me evening maybe," he told Owens. "We'd have to wait in line
et tickets now. The crowds are huge." Noah thought that should
it. Owens wouldn't put up with crowds, unless they'd come to lis-
en to him. And for some illogical reason, Noah could stand missing
the show if Owens didn't go either.

Owens called back an hour later to say that an art dealer friend
could get them in on Wednesday at noon, when the museum was
closed.

To be with the paintings alone in an empty museum was something
Noah had always wanted to do. In his chair, his view blocked by
crowds, he hardly ever could see anything. But somehow Owens'
offer put him in a cranky mood. In fact, no gift from Owens ever
seemed whole. Was it Owens' inability to give right, or his own to receive? Or was it only that Owens had so much that all his generosity
seemed easy and slight? And should the weight of a gift be judged by
the giver or the receiver?

Noah really wanted to be in the museum alone. Then he figured out
what it was that bothered him. Noon. Had the art dealer said noon on
Wednesday, or was that the time Owens wanted and demanded, without considering Noah's schedule? Take it or leave it: that was the offer.

Still, Noah didn't know anyone else who could get him into the museum alone. There was no way he was going to say no. At least he'd
drive up in his van by himself.

When Noah arrived at the museum, it was apparent that Owens had
made a mistake. The museum was indeed open to the public, and the
public was here in full color.

"I'm Celeste," a woman said, bending down to touch his wrist.
"And you're the scientist." Owens must have told her he was in a
chair. She had blunt blond hair that tapped her chin and bright-orange
stockings, striking on a woman of fifty. Noah had noted from his window that good legs didn't age. She had on a gorgeous raincoat, loose,
with folds.

Owens arrived fifteen minutes late. By then, Celeste had run into three people she knew.

Noah decided, uncharacteristically, to rent the headset tour.

A classful of parochial school children in brown-and-white uniforms filled the first room of the exhibition.

"Not bad," Owens said, looking at an early still life.

"I'd buy it if I saw it in a flea market," Celeste said, laughing.

Noah went slowly, listening to the tape's long explanations and reading the paragraphs stenciled on the wall.

"I don't really like this Fauvist stuff," Celeste said, drifting to the center.

Owens loped back to Noah. "I don't think it's his best work, but he's pretty great."

"I can't stand seeing pictures with so many people around," Celeste said.

"You know that Matisse I bought that's in the museum now?" Owens said. "For example, I think that's much more beautiful than these." Owens often went to see his painting. Twice, he'd been there when groups of schoolchildren like this one trooped through. "I should set up a little fund for buses to take underprivileged kids to see it." Sometimes, when everyone seemed mad at him and his life was crossed with complication and dismay, he remembered the painting in the museum. That was at least one thing he had done in his life. He thought, for a moment, it was how a woman might feel when she left behind a child; he hoped his mother had felt this way about him. He wished she could have known that he would be all right. I'll ask Eliot about her again sometime, he told himself.

Celeste met them at the threshold of the next gallery, fingering her scarf. "I'm going. I'm getting frazzled. Too many people."

Noah half expected Owens to defect too, but he stayed. He ranged ahead and then fell back, and the two men found each other in the final room, with paper cutouts. It had taken stamina to finish, but before leaving the galleries they lingered before huge photographs of Matisse as an old man in beach hotels, drawing from his bed, with a charcoal pencil attached to the tip of a pointer.

"That's probably when it gets really happy," Noah said.

They waited in line for their coats, behind the uniformed children. The teacher used a whistle to get their attention.

"This make you think of Jane?" Noah said.

Owens smiled. "I sure hate uniforms. And that whistle. As if they're circus animals."

Moist winds skirted up outside, and it felt good to sit amidst the taller, milling crowd.

"I'm glad we saw that," Noah said. "I'm glad we stayed." All his impatience with Owens was rinsed away by the lifetime of a man's work. Noah felt that he would never regret this life of trying, whether he succeeded or failed, because there was no other life.

"I am too," Owens said.

"People and all."

"People and all."

They were middle-class kids, Noah thought, for whom the public parks and museums were built. Maybe the Celestes of the world lost out when private collections were ceded to museums, but for Noah and Owens it was all gain. He'd read articles about the decline of quality, articles with titles like "The Cost of Progress," which pitted poor workmanship against the proliferation of state colleges and penicillin. Noah generally hated the rich on principle. But today he exempted Owens. Even if his work at the lab amounted to nothing, Owens respected him and shared his awe and reverence for biology. In a way they'd never talked about, Owens seemed to comprehend his bravery. No matter what, Noah still would have had afternoons like this, when he felt he knew how to live.

"She's pretty East Coast, Celeste, even though she's here," Owens said, standing in the rain. Noah handed up his umbrella, and Owens held it over them both.

"Do you ever doubt what you do?" Noah asked.

"You mean, do I wish I were an artist?" That wasn't what Noah meant, but Owens continued after a brief pause. "I feel like what I do is the place where art and science intersect. Maybe we are artists, Noah, but we're expressing our art in different ways."

"I think it's a one-way analogy. Artists aren't comparing themselves to us."

"You never know," Owens said.

Noah was thinking about what could be owned. What mattered most—knowledge, paintings, children—should never be owned. Could only be destroyed by owning.

"Do you know a really good restaurant around here that would make steamed vegetables?"

"No, on both counts," Noah said.

"Let's just go to Stars."

"We can take the van."

Owens lifted his hand for a taxi. "It's raining."

Noah hefted himself into the cab's back seat, folding his chair for Owens to put in front. He had something to talk about, and he didn't know how to start. Jane wanted to go to school. She was sick of the tutors and wanted to be with other kids. How hard could that be to understand? But a lot of things that seemed totally normal in any other context were difficult to talk about with Owens. He kept his own rules, irrelevant to the general referendum. Weird, Noah thought again to himself, that the guy thinks of politics. For Jane, Noah had gone to see the old ladies. He'd expected a delicate conversation, but halfway in, Ruby said, "We couldn't agree with you more. A girl her age needs society." He decided to wait until they arrived at the restaurant to bring up the subject. It took them a good ten minutes to be settled at a table; in the rain, Noah had to get into his chair again, then there were four steps and no one to help Owens carry him. Once inside, the restaurant table banged Noah's knees. Many people were afraid to eat meat in front of Owens, but Noah ordered a two-pound steak and a Scotch. Owens just raised his eyebrows.

"How's your schools program going?" Noah asked.

"Well, the dairy lobby's calmed down some. I really have to make the time and look into it. I've been pretty busy with Exodus."

"You should take Jane," Noah said.

"What, for a consumer's perspective?"

"She wants to go to school. I'm sure it's really just kids she misses. Parties and all that."

Their food came, and Owens was silent. Noah started sawing his steak.

"You really like that stuff?" Owens said.

"Mmhmm."

"Why?"

"Tastes good," Noah said. When you disagreed with Owens, he'd sort of leave you where you were and go off. He was still sitting with Noah, but his eyes weren't there. They followed different women as they treaded vertically through the room.

"I know Jane'd like to attend school," he finally said. "There's no question there. And she will, eventually. But"—he paused—"you'll find if you're ever a parent—and I think you probably will be, Noah—there's a lot of things kids want that aren't good for them."

"But school? You went. I went."

"Yeah, that's her argument too. But we went because we didn't have a choice. It wasn't necessarily the best thing for us."

"She doesn't have a choice either. And she's isolated. She needs other kids."

"I agree that Jane should have friends. And I've actually been giving that a lot of thought. An old friend of mine has a daughter. And I'm going to take Jane over to their house for dinner."

"You really won't send her to school?"

"I will when I find the right school. But for now, she's doing great with the tutors. She's a great kid." He shrugged. "It's not broken."

"Well, you're her dad," Noah said, understanding that this time he'd failed.

"I don't know. I guess I'm beginning to think I'm different from other people."

"We all do."

"But I really am."

"No, that's what I mean. You are."

"Much as I love Olivia—and I love her a lot—I feel I have a responsibility to people at Exodus." He sounded tired. "My parents, when they began to understand I was different, they never tried to stop me. And I guess that's what family means to me. Do you ever feel like that? That you sacrifice for what you do, and you might even have to ask a loved one to sacrifice too?"

"I think you're more confident than I am."

"But you know you're a good scientist."

"I know I have something inside, but I'm not sure I can get it out." There, he'd admitted it. It was so hard to say those things to Owens. "I'll never have the kind of confidence you do. I didn't have the life for it."

Owens looked down, perplexed. "Have you met anyone?"

"Not really."

"Come on, Noah. I tell you everything. Do you like somebody?"

"It's unrequited."

"So who is it? Come on, I'll never meet her anyway."

"Well, you have met her. It's Louise."

"Really? With the . . ." His hand moved near his head, then he yanked it down. "Oh, I bet she really likes you."

Because of her hair, he meant. Owens figured she couldn't do better. *Better than me.* "She doesn't. I'm quite sure." Noah cut one last piece of steak and began to chew it.

The waiter came and lifted Owens' plate away. Noah motioned with his knife to indicate he was still eating. Then he looked at Owens. "Have you ever fallen in love with a woman who didn't go for you?"

The question was a little mean, but Owens didn't seem to get it. "Let me see," he said, sincerely scanning the ranks. "No, I don't think so. I've been . . . fortunate with women."

"You've been fortunate in general," Noah said.

"Well, we need some luck for Exodus now."

That was true, and Noah knew it. Everyone knew Exodus was in trouble.

Owens loped to his car, the jangly colored lights of Chinatown smearing on the dark rain-slicked street. He'd had Noah's taxi leave him off, and the wind was riling his hair. *He's probably wondering how I can be in love with a woman who has gray hair, and thinking he could never be,* Noah imagined, watching the meter, as the taxi sped to the van. Owens, typical of a rich person, had paid for dinner and was letting him pick up the cab. Noah was sure, in Owens' mind, the generosity was all his. But the meter showed eighteen dollars already, and if Noah'd had his way they would have gone for pizza and eighteen dollars would have covered them both. . . . And she was not gray, she was silver. Her skin was a pale white with pink in it. Her teeth were perfect, like even white corn.

Back in Alta, Owens drove directly to the bungalow. When he'd called for his messages from the restaurant, there were two from Mary, both urgent.

It was about Jane. Some social worker in a pink suit and purse had come knocking on the bungalow door in the rain. Apparently, Jane had cried to the old-lady tutors. They'd called the Social Services Department and had a long and spirited discussion with the caseworker who'd answered the phone. "We're right in the middle," they kept saying. And so maybe it was time for Jane to go to school.

Mary had been glad to have an emergency to call him about.

Jane was already asleep. On her bedroom door, she had a drawing with the caption *Jane's DNA*. In a balloon, it said, "I hate pictures of myself."

"Aw," Owens said. "That's really nice."

"It is." Mary sighed. "He gave her a microscope set too."

Owens thought it was good that Jane knew someone like Noah. How many kids knew a scientist?

Mary made tea, and for once things seemed easy between them. A candle was burning, and she'd washed her hair. Something in his manner gave her permission to laugh.

She was thirty now, he was thinking to himself, and had pretty much lost her looks. Women seemed to him to have a half-life of about twenty-eight years. After that, they became something else. Mothers maybe.

"I saw Noah today. You know, I get the feeling he's a virgin."

"Did he tell you that?"

"No, but it's the kind of thing men can tell with each other." He lifted his eyebrows the way he always did when he was asking for something, and he looked straight at her for the first time in years.

She glanced down and giggled. It felt good to be seen.

"Some woman could do a really great thing just sleeping with him once. Just think what you'd be giving him."

Then the upper lip that had so pliantly spread in laughter became tight and uneven. "Stop trying to pimp me, you monster," she snarled. "Fuck him yourself"—words so ugly that Owens stood up, lifting his palms, backing off, saying, "Okay, okay. I just thought you could do a really good turn, that's all."

Money

⊰⊰ ⊰⊰ ⊰⊰ ⊰⊰ ⊰⊰

*J*ane played the white answering machine in Owens'
kitchen, to which she and her mother had once entrusted so many important messages. Bob Shepard had left a halting invitation about some
people coming over for dinner. Jane reminded Owens that at the funeral he'd said he would go. Owens accepted with enthusiasm and
marked the date clearly on his calendar. He also put a reminder into his
computer. Owens had missed enough appointments in his life to
doubt his ability to remember.

The address still belonged to the small white bungalow with a
cedar that grew up on both sides of the bay window and a
Japanese maple that towered over the back. He didn't re-
the maple, but it must have always been there. He pulled into
only ten minutes late and walked in with his hand on the
neck.

ed to be the only one of the old friends still single, and
quiet, sitting in what he didn't recognize was the best
Olivia had come. They were fighting again.

aughter, Minna, who was a few years older than

214

Jane, stood tall now, regal. Her long hair swung as she offered hors d'oeuvres. He hadn't seen her in years. Jane chatted with her happily, saying she wanted to take dancing lessons *too,* if her mom and dad would only *let* her.

It was new for Jane to try and talk about not going to school, a topic so embarrassing she usually avoided it. But these people knew Owens, and he was right here. So when Minna asked, she said she had tutors because her parents didn't believe in schools. What was strange was that this girl didn't sound surprised. She didn't like school that much anyway; she was blasé, complaining. And though Jane was fascinated by everything to do with school, with this girl she pretended not to care.

It was a nice house, small, the kind Owens and most of his friends had grown up in. He liked watching the women. There was something about people your own age. Tonight, Jane could tell, he felt acutely lonely for love.

"That's some Japanese maple you have," he said to Shep's wife, Anna. They used to call her Lamb. She was delivering tiny glasses of sherry. "No, thanks, for me. Can I go out back for a look?"

He followed her through the living room into the neat full kitchen and stood at the back door, next to the washer-dryer. The tree seemed to capture and hold wind. The leaves turned themselves over perfectly horizontally, in a way peculiar to Japanese maples. "That must be fifty years old."

"I expect so," she said, by his shoulder. "We've been here eleven now. I often stand right there and do the ironing before anyone is up. That's the only time it's quiet."

He looked at her, surprised, but she flustered under his scrutiny, wiping her hands on an apron.

She had him carry a large casserole to the round dining table. Neither the dining room nor the table could contain them all, so they'd set out rolled cloth napkins with silverware. It was pasta, Owens was relieved to see, pesto, and a big salad. Fruit for dessert; he'd spied it in the refrigerator. He became enthusiastic, as he always did when people ate the right kind of food.

When he'd made his plate he took it to an ottoman, next to Jane, who was stretched out on the floor. A wife he hadn't met before had taken the chair he'd been sitting in. This is really nice, he thought. He shook his head, mad at Olivia.

Joe and the wife in the chair were having an animated discussion about an upcoming election. "Who are you voting for?" the wife asked Owens suddenly.

He smiled haplessly. "I never vote."

"You're Mary's daughter." Shep sat down next to Jane. "I remember your mother, but I don't know if she'd remember me. Tell her the Shep says hello."

Jane wasn't sure she'd really tell her. Lately, her mother had been in a bad mood about Owens.

Anna was carrying in a basket of hot bread. "And your grandma baked our wedding cake," she called over her shoulder. "It was a real small one. When I picked it up, I remember, she only charged me two dollars."

None of them had such great careers. Bob Shepard did some kind of accounting and commuted every day on the underground train. All three guys had been in on the beginning of Genesis, and Anna had been Owens' first secretary. Joe became a poor people's lawyer; you had to respect that. Todd had traveled and done all kinds of jobs, and now he was studying to be a nurse. Two of the women had part-time jobs, but you could tell they were pretty much mothers now. This was going home, even more than his parents' house. People his age who weren't in biochemistry anymore. And these weren't the people who'd made their money and got out. They never stayed long enough. Shep had had stock options, the works. But Anna had Minna, and she didn't want the hours. If he'd only given it one more year. Owens had begged him at the time, warning him that he'd be sorry. Owens had Jane, but she was off in the mountains and he hadn't even touched her yet. All he had was the picture. Shep wouldn't look at Owens when he resigned, head down, mumbling something about responsibilities.

At the very beginning, when Genesis was only an idea, Shep had asked him to be Minna's godfather. He'd been late, of course, and they had to hold up the ceremony for him. The church was empty and cold, and when they poured water over the baby's forehead she cried furiously and they couldn't get her to stop. The memory was somehow disagreeable.

The wife in the chair had a wide face, shaped like the blade of a shovel. She didn't have children. Anna was asking about her work. That was like the old Lamb. It turned out the woman worked remotely in biotech, on the esoteric side, freelance.

"And are you working on any particular project?" Anna asked.

"Well, it's hard now," the woman said, glancing at Owens.

"Really? Why?" he asked. He couldn't help it. Exodus was having troubles, but the biotech industry overall had had its best quarter ever.

"Well, money's tight, so it's hard. And I was asked to do two projects this year I wouldn't put my name to."

What is her name? Jane wondered. "Wait," she said. "I don't understand."

"That would be selling out," she told Jane pointedly, so Owens bent down and whispered in his daughter's ear, "We can watch a movie when we get home."

"Oh, I don't really much believe in the notion of selling out," Anna said. "Everyone does the best they can."

In the corner, Joe and Todd talked about cars. Todd apparently drove a truck, with four-wheel drive. "I got the chassis fixed. That hurt. I put four hundred dollars in it."

Owens concentrated on eating from his plate. Good pesto, at least. Too much salt.

Diane, Joe's wife, had a nice rising laugh. "We bought another Impala. We don't love it, it's not our identity, it's just a means of transportation."

Jane looked around, suddenly self-conscious.

"If we had the money," the woman who didn't want to sell out was saying.

Was Jane just picking things, sensitive, or were they talking only about money? She had noticed that Owens didn't talk about money. He never brought it up, except in global or at least national terms, or abstractly, to theorize about some business.

As much as was possible, he lived a life without money. He hired a man he never saw to pay his bills, and when he ran out of cash, Eliot had it delivered to him in a plain brown envelope carried by a bonded messenger. Owens kept one credit card in a thin wallet. But he liked to forget about petty systems of barter altogether, and ordinary conversations about the price of things caused him the pain some people felt listening to fingernails on a blackboard. He never discussed his own expenses, probably due to an embarrassment of scale. If someone else brought up a matter of finance and in particular the question of *Can I afford this?* or *Should I stretch to do it?* Owens just sat there and continued to do whatever he was doing, as if he hadn't heard. This could be maddening to people close to him. Jane remembered the night he wouldn't lend them a car. It was true: he didn't need to finagle and struggle and plot over money, but *they did.* And sacrifice, allowance and judgment in spending formed not only drama and suspense but also structure in most people's lives.

"I don't see any point in getting another used car," Diane said. "Wait till you can get new."

"We bought a new car—a red one—and I just love it," Anna exclaimed. "Ever since Nancy Drew, I always wanted a red roadster."

Everything she said made Owens smile.

Listening to the conversation about cars, Minna said, "Doesn't everyone hate the rich?"

Owens looked up again, pleased. Her parents had never told her.

"I don't hate the rich!" Anna declared, her voice ringing with ardor. "I've always envied them!"

Her daughter, unflappable, just shrugged. She had an unusually erect back.

Jane bit the inside of her mouth. She remembered his celebratory glee over his coupon. It had come to Theo in the mail, addressed to "Resident." He'd brandished the paper, told them each about it three or four times, then given it to the waiter with a flourishing triumph. He'd only once wanted to be included in the game.

As they went on about money in the small living room, Owens felt there was nothing he could say, short of opening his wallet. And there had been times, at the beginning, when he'd done that and only made things worse. He sensed they were obliquely asking him for the gift that would make them resent him if he gave it, and also that they were blaming him for the absence of those worries.

Jane knew from the other side that it was true, people did both. What was worse, they probably couldn't help it. She and her mother had felt those things towards him too.

A stunning thing had happened when he was young. He had tried for it, having some inkling of its magnitude, but there had been months, too, of closed-door failure. But then they'd tripped over a protein that saved hundreds of thousands of lives. He had been trying to make a way out of what he'd known, for himself and for Frank. All of a sudden, he missed Frank.

It was easiest to talk to Anna. She was standing in the dining room, ladling pasta, and he went over for seconds. "This is really good. How do you make it?"

"Oh, I suppose the usual. Basil, pine nuts, cheese, butter, a little salt."

Jane looked at Owens, waiting. He never touched butter. To her relief, he laughed. "You're kidding me."

"I don't think I am. Did I leave out something? Oh, well, of course the spaghetti."

"You don't really put butter in pesto."

"Not much, but I think this recipe did call for a little bit."

"You're not serious," he said. His plate was already down, set on the table.

"Are you allergic or—"

"His tongue swells up and turns black," Jane said. "No, I'm just joking."

"I just don't like to eat butter. But no big deal," he said, his chin high, eyes roving; he was ready to leave.

The woman in the chair stood up and told Todd it was time to go. He stuck his hand out to say goodbye to Owens. "Say, I'm really sorry about your ma."

On the other side of the small room, a dress came up in conversation, how it was made on a covered wagon and first worn in a field wedding during the overland crossing. Bob took it down from where they kept it, on the top shelf over the refrigerator, opened it to a Christmas of tissue, and then Minna ran up to her room to try it on. It was her great-great-grandmother's wedding dress, and Jane wanted to see.

Arrayed over footstools, couches and chairs, everyone was eating dessert. Owens loved the fruit salad—there was nothing in it but fruit—and was still eating after everyone stopped. When he took his plate to the kitchen, he stood alone, looking at the Japanese maple, while Anna busied herself at the sink. She was a calm, patient woman, who always seemed to have time. She opened the refrigerator, and in the weak light he saw the chain letter on the door, the same one he got. He almost laughed. "You got this too!"

"Oh, yes, isn't it silly? Shep's against it, doesn't believe in them, but I don't see any harm. I sent a few copies out just to our neighbors and some other mothers. A couple teachers. I say it's like buying a lottery ticket. I haven't seen any return yet, and it's been, oh, more than two months, but I've already gotten my five dollars' worth of fun."

Could they have been on his list? he wondered as she was talking. Then he realized his temporary secretary had sent copies to everyone on his party list. Anna had gotten the thing from him. And without intending to, he'd already made a small fortune from it. He felt in his jeans pockets, where he had several five-dollar bills that had arrived in the last week or two.

When he went to the bathroom, he slipped a fresh bill between two magazines.

After a half hour of hooks and eyes, Minna stood there entranced, barefoot, her hair up, holding the full of the skirt in one hand.

"Minna, you're beautiful," Bob Shepard said, his eyes humble.

She was a beauty now or almost, Owens thought, but the dress seemed so poor and fragile, the old muslin tearing, and it was their treasure. The bustle was made from a flour sack, and you could see the blue markings. Then they showed the picture of Lamb, thin in that same dress, not on her wedding day but before, standing on a porch with her sisters. She and Bob had stood in city hall after their blood test, a nothing wedding, cake for two, he in work clothes and she in a brown dress for the ceremony, but it had lasted now fourteen years. Anna sewed, and she talked about fixing the dress for Minna's wedding someday, and Owens wanted to say he'd buy her a new, great dress, but then thought how that would sound and would make him feel even more separate, so he kept still.

In the album, Jane saw a picture of her father a way she'd never seen him, with long hair and a beard. "That's when they went public," Shep said sheepishly. Owens knew he hadn't been there; they'd cut the picture out of a magazine. All Owens' victories were in their scrapbook. "And that's Minna's christening. Your dad was Minna's godfather."

In the bask of attention, Minna twirled.

"Do you ever see Frank anymore?" Anna asked.

"Not too much," Owens said.

"We saw him once, quite a while ago now," Anna said, "and he was still studying, carrying a stack of books. You know, I called him for tonight, but from what I gathered, he's in China."

Frank had always talked about going to China. There was no reason now for him not to.

"That must be something for him," she continued. "All those relatives he's never met, who don't speak a word of English."

Owens grinned. "He'll probably want to bring them all back and give 'em jobs."

"Remember that uncle?" Shep turned from the bookshelf, where he was reaching down another album. "Man, oh, man. Guy's a loser."

"I've been meaning to tell you," Anna said, "our school has two little Owenses this year, in the kindergarten. I think parents are naming their sons after you."

Jane stood staring at Minna in the dress. "It's beautiful," she said to Minna.

Owens whispered in her ear, so close she felt the moistness: "When you get married, I'll buy you a beautiful dress too." But she pulled away. Jane had two friends so far in Alta, but they weren't like this.

Then, thumping back in her nightgown and slippers, a child again, Minna danced with her father, covering the kitchen floor with waltzes and jitterbugs, bumping into cupboards, the stove. Jane grabbed

Owens, who danced in his way, awkward and gawky, but glamorous to his daughter, counting the steps. "Dad, listen. Step-slide-step, step-slide-step, step . . ." Anna hummed the music under their laughter.

After midnight, the fog came up from the bay, obscuring the Japanese maple, then revealing its ghost form, as thinner rags blew past. The house was the only one still lit. Owens sat in his new low car, feeling for the headlight switch. He'd had the car a few days, but he hadn't driven it at night yet. And though he'd had three cars just like it, he couldn't work the switch. Looking at the small street, he remembered a night when Minna ran prancing in a white nightgown down the stairs, younger than Jane was when he first saw her. He hadn't had Jane near him then; those years were lost, forever. She lay sleeping in the passenger seat, with her feet propped up on the dashboard, and he reached to touch her sleeping head, her jeans-protected knee.

Then the light went out inside, leaving only the porch lamp. It reminded him of instruments being packed in their cases and carried away, when a few minutes earlier, they'd been inside the orchestra, the clanking, jangling, warm aroma of home. The cedar that framed their bay window hadn't always; Shep had trained it to rise in two spires. And they didn't even own the house. They rented.

Then Anna stepped onto the porch in a long robe, with a hand on her forehead.

He stood up out of the car. "I can't get the lights to work." Why'd I bring it? he thought. The car was black and gleaming, small, extraordinary. He wanted, all of a sudden, something less conspicuous and hoped he'd remember this in the morning.

Then she was beside him, her large feet bare, her hair braid down, whispering buoyantly, "I think I know." She reached in through the open window, her cheek so close the hairs of his Saturday beard felt her; she found a knob and pulled, illuminating the world. "Mine had the same, our old one," she said, breathless, then stopped, embarrassed by the comparison. But her dented tin can did have the same latch. "One of those little ironies of life," she called and was off, a tall swoop archangel, her braid swinging across her back.

And he wondered for a moment, looking into the rearview mirror at his own face, which looked to him not handsome but goofy. Who are you to be speeding away from all this, off into nothing?

That night, Jane was still small enough that he could carry her to the bungalow and hand her, knees jointed over arm, still sleeping, to her mother.

Parking

⊰⊱⊰⊱⊰⊱⊰⊱

Owens had never declared or claimed his parking spot. "I believe in democracy," he told Jane. But she could tell he thought he earned it, just by the hours he put in, the late nights and early mornings his car waited there, alone in the autumn moonlight and the cloud-luff sky.

He'd used the parking space in all his years with Genesis. Even when he traveled, it was always left open. Now that he worked most of the day in the Exodus building, he still parked in his spot and sprinted over.

Today, though, his space was taken. Furthermore, it was Rooney, not some stranger who didn't know. Owens instantly recognized the car, because it was identical to his own. When Rooney had first driven it to work, Owens approved, almost. He'd done some research and concluded that if you wanted a sports car, this was the best. But he now wondered if Rooney'd discovered this for himself, or if he'd just gone in and said he wanted one like Owens'.

Things with Rooney weren't what they had been. He'd had to have talks with him too many times lately, and in the last month they'd more or less agreed to disagree. When Owens parked and got out, he saw *G. J. Rooney, President* painted on the curb. Rooney's car was sealed and locked. Most likely he used the car alarm.

Owens had heard that back East, where Rooney came from, hundreds of CEOs had their parking spots painted with their names, like plaques on auditorium seats, and that sometimes it was even a negotiating point in contracts. But he'd never wanted Genesis to be like that. So far, Owens didn't have anything named after him, although a week earlier he'd sent away five hundred dollars to a horticultural laboratory that would hybridize a rose named Olivia. He'd ordered fourteen Olivia bushes to plant in his garden. When he told Jane about this, she wished he'd ordered roses named Jane.

People deserve to own what they use, he said. Everyone in the company knew where he parked, and a few hundred people, maybe a thousand, unconsciously glanced at the spot when they entered and exited, to see that Owens was there. Owens stooped down to the curb. The paint was dry and *G. J. Rooney* was the only name there. If he'd put Owens' name somewhere, Owens probably would've railed and had it painted over immediately, but this, in its way, was even worse. He ran up the stairs two at a time, his heart going like something hitting inside a paper bag. From all the hours, he felt more at home here than home.

First generation builds, second enjoys, third destroys. That triangle jingled. Jane was his second generation. But the way Rooney saw it, Exodus was; and with its expensive fruit juice and the lavish ad campaign, Rooney thought they were enjoying, all right. Rooney was nothing if not prudent.

Through the glass wall, Owens saw him stretching, hands on back hiphandles, teeth clenched. Full suit and tie every day. Owens told him from the beginning this was a place he could wear jeans, though Rooney always got a straight slight smile when he said that.

For a long time, years, Owens had an impermeable protection. He tested the limits, dared fate, told more and more audacious things to reporters, missed appointments, canceled, let his temper flare. And nothing happened. He appeared on more magazine covers. In negotiations, he went for the high fair price and stayed firm; more than once he'd walked away. His stamina outlasted others'. The stock rose. Genesis had been rising, and so was he. But now, all of a sudden, it seemed he'd turned a corner. The Exodus guys had created something amazing, but no one could use it yet.

Owens sat down in Rooney's office. "Hey, we need to talk."

"All right, Tom." The space between Rooney's teeth showed not a smile but forbearance of pained anxiety. He reminded Owens of his father's mother, an old woman who looked out the window and wanted to be left alone. He'd always tried to make her laugh.

Owens scanned the desk, picked up a memo. Rooney stayed standing, hands still on his hips. "What can I do for you?"

"See, the way this is written reminds me of corporate BS," Owens said, slapping the page down. "Like Detroit, threatening people. Remember: *they* want to be more like *us.*"

"CFO made a study of our one-day-air bills, Tom. They're forty-five percent over any other company, including the big Swiss boys. Same thing with long distance, prime time *and* international."

"Okay, so maybe we have to cut back. But there's a better way to say it. See, this just isn't what I ever wanted to do. I didn't want a company where people who do great work have to worry about these little things. I didn't want people afraid of getting caught. I happen to believe that impairs creative thinking."

"Tom, we don't need to be paying for everybody's Christmas packages flying Federal Express. There is such a thing as a post office!"

"I just think if you start having all these rules, people cheat. The smart people find ways around them. I would."

"Not everyone's you, Tom. We're not monitoring your phones. You can send all the Christmas presents you like, for Christ's sake. We're talking about a company of over a thousand people."

Owens shook his head. "That's not my point at all. As it happens, I actually don't give Christmas presents."

"Tom, let's talk about next quarter's budget. I don't much believe in pyrotechnics."

They talked for a good half hour, without convincing each other of anything.

"I think I've learned in my ten years here that it pays to do things right," Owens said, "even if the bill's higher at the end. You know, you have to spend some to make money."

"You yourself are proof against that!" Rooney exploded. He then explained what he thought was a reasonable proportion: most capital outlay to Genesis, which was still supporting the whole show.

"You really don't understand," Owens almost whispered. "Exodus is awesome. In five years, millions of people all over the world will be relying on our drugs. Rooney, this is what's going to make our name. And you know I love Genesis." He walked to the far end of the office and put his hands on the wooden molecular model of their first, best-selling compound, LCSF. "I manufactured it. It makes stem cells, precursor cells. It helps people live after chemo. But NT12 is a cure."

The phone rang and Rooney spoke into the speaker. "He's here, Kathleen. Go ahead."

"I wanted to remind him they're expecting him in fifteen minutes at Jane's school."

There was a lot more to be said. But so far he and Rooney agreed on exactly nothing. And this was Jane's first month of school.

Second generation, Owens mumbled, swinging into his convertible, glancing at Rooney's tight car, barely used and scratchless.

Owens had gone through three of these cars, all the same model and all black. He'd run one into a live oak the week before the public offering, and he'd banged the back of the next right before he'd introduced his rice-and-beans bill in the legislature. Now, every time Owens tried something big, he expected to crack up a car. That put him at a rate of one every three or four years. He planned not to use the new one the month before his Berkeley speech.

Once cracked up, he determined, they were never the same again. The only way to console himself for the damage was to order a new one. To spend money replacing something he already had bothered him, but then he forgot about it. "Just as long as you don't buy any more date farms," Eliot said. "Talk to me before you do anything like that."

He didn't give up the first car and still drove it a good deal of the time. He kept one perfect and used the other to park at the airport. By now he'd learned to forgive himself such extravagance and to allow for a certain amount of loss. He understood there were elements of destruction in his personality that he could not expunge.

Second generation. There were signs everywhere that he was beginning to lose. His luck had turned, but he'd give it a run for its money. Because unlike a lot of people as smart as he was, Owens knew he knew how to work.

A bumper sticker swam up in front of him. MEDICINE WILL CURE DEATH AND GOVERNMENT WILL REPEAL TAXES BEFORE TOM OWENS FAILS. Somebody on the team had designed yellow letters on black, like a bumblebee. The type was gorgeous. For labels, he'd learned a lot about type.

To make a bad day perfect, Owens had a fight with Mary outside the school.

"I think this is a school for little geniuses," Mary blurted, tripping on her high heel. At the meeting, the teacher had told them nothing good. Jane was, she said, "a little butterfly," excessively concerned with her social life.

"Cricket more like," Mary whispered into her lap, because Jane's voice veered high and screechy.

> *Step on a crack*
> *Break your mother's back.*
> *Step on a line*
> *Break her spine.*

Mary listened to girls' incessant chanting, up and down, on the sidewalk, almost at the end of the jump rope years. Now, since she had been in school, boys called at night on the telephone, a gulp in their voice, saying, "Jane there?" Their impudence rendered Mary helpless, not indignant, and she soundlessly whispered, "I'll get her."

Her friends, the teacher said, were not the serious students. They were children from troubled homes. Just today she'd discovered a balled pair of stockings and long earrings in Jane's locker. She handed the contraband over to Mary.

"Like that Madeleine," Owens added, continuing the conversation outside, "without the last name." Madeleine had a last name—the way Jane did, from her mother—but she didn't use it. "And the other one, what's her name?"

"Johanna." Mary sighed. She'd never liked her own last name. "I suppose it's natural. We're not the most normal family either. I never had friends from good homes."

"What you did, Mary, is not the point. None of this is the point."

"Well, what do you think the point is?"

"Jane's gotta work harder, that's all. I'll talk to her," he said, as if that finished it.

"Well, she's waiting. She's making muffins to bring you."

It was Tuesday. He'd forgotten all about it. "I'm gonna have to do another night."

"I told you a week ago, Owens. I can't tonight."

"Okay. I'll get her, then we'll go to the office. I'll set her up at a desk."

"But she has to be in bed by ten. She's a kid, Owens."

All these years outside the school system, Jane had been perfect, a rare something. Here, in school, she went unrecognized. The teacher hadn't said anything, as other people did always, about how Jane was special. Mary was used to uncertainty about herself. But for Jane to be unexceptional, even to this one big-hipped teacher, tilted the whole world.

Jane strapped on her seat belt without being asked, balancing the cardboard box of still-warm muffins on her knees. She was glad they were going to his office: she'd made too many for just the two of them. The muffins released a faint sweetness into the car.

"Now, do you think your muffins'll be enough for dinner?"

"Muffins are enough for me," she said.

In a way she never was with her mother, Jane felt confidence in his driving, even when he sped. They made up the road, gliding through dark, in no place, really, but together.

He'd told her about the parking spot and his argument with Rooney, and now was talking about gears and transmissions. He liked to explain machines and chemical reactions and weather, what made fog, how precipitation began. She tried to be alert because he'd often stop and quiz her, make her tell it back in her own words. She didn't yet understand this was a quality he reserved only for her and that made up a great portion of what he understood to be paternity.

Jane enjoyed these rides, the sound of road air humming up from the floor, night all around them, and she always regretted the minute they touched ground. He waited too, and they both stared ahead at the dark buildings—ordinary office buildings, rented, like others along this highway. Someday, he told her, they'd build. Genesis should have its own buildings, with land around. He envisioned it as a college campus.

He'd had architects out from New York trudging these hills, jackets slung over their shoulders, getting mud on their wingtip shoes. The problem they couldn't divine was where to put it. Owens loved this highway and remained loyal to it; he'd lived and worked off it for years, he wasn't going to move to El Camino, even though a fleet of historians reported that it was the original El Camino Real that ran through California all the way to Mexico. He figured it had changed a lot since then.

They parked in the slot that now said *G. J. Rooney*. Jane took small fast steps to keep up, across the wide lot. Owens sighed. "Olivia could be more a part of my life here. I told her at the beginning, we could set up a little office for her and by now everybody'd know her."

Walking her child's mincing double steps, Jane tried to be what Olivia wouldn't. Tonight she'd baked thirty-six muffins, with oat flour, bran, molasses and bananas. She'd tried to copy a muffin from a place Owens liked, called Mae's, but her efforts were doomed because she listened so carefully to her father that she was limited herself to ingredients he approved of. And Owens, like many people, enjoyed some foods in total ignorance of their composition.

Jane liked going to her father's office. She didn't mind hanging around, waiting. She would have liked a little desk set up there for her.

She couldn't start her homework yet. She'd been banished to the microscope room to study, but every time she opened the book it went dull on her, like a pill without water, so she searched the desk drawers and found bags of trail mix, and in the file cabinet a smelly pair of high-tops. An electric guitar leaned in the corner. She would do just one more thing and then her homework. She took out her postcard from Noah.

Today I heard a boy whine, "What do I need a penny for?"

"They say when you find a penny it's good luck." This wasn't his mom but some baby-sitter. She looked young and bored.

"But I don't need luck."

"It's nice to have, just you keep it, someday you may need it, everybody does."

"I don't like this penny, it's not shiny."

"Give it to me, then," the baby-sitter finally said.

He said no.

Remember, Jane: never give away your luck.

Noah asked her to write him back, and Jane meant to do that and her homework, but she didn't have nice writing paper or an envelope or a stamp. There were so many things she always meant to do.

At midnight, her father had finally come to tell her it was time to go home. She still hadn't done her homework, but now it was too late to try. She sat on a couch, her knees hooked over the old arm, while he went over just one more thing. Her muffins lay ravaged on the table. Jane craved another one, the banana melt with oats, but he was talking, and to get it she'd have to walk across the room, and everyone would see.

Owens was his best now, half sitting, talking to guys who trusted him. "We don't really have much time. We have a deadline, and people are going to be making judgments about us. But what they don't understand is that that's not at all what it's about. What I saw Rich doing down there in his corner or the tests Henry's going to do just before the sun comes up tomorrow, this is what we're here for. So in another way that's not exactly logical, we have a lot of time—all the time we need to go into each one of these problems to the bottom. The worst thing we could possibly do now is pull back. We can't afford interruptions. Because as you all know, it's not hard when time is smooth. When there are no days and nights or Tuesdays and Fridays and there's only the clock of the work. I've been on two projects like this, and I can tell you we're going to do more now, in these eight days, than we've done in the past year. We weren't far enough *in* before."

Jane pulled her knees closer, her tongue touching skin through the jeans hole. She tried to apply what he was saying. But there was no work yet she did. When her mind wandered, it entered lush scenes of reunion with all the people she'd known in her life, watching her receive an award. . . .

"We got to stay healthy," he said. "That's crucial now."

Rich stood hunched. He was tall and embarrassed of his height. "Shit," he said. "My family's coming in two days."

Jane looked around the room at the guys so familiar to her father. He'd given her a book about the Manhattan Project and said it was a lot like here. But in the book, the men wore shirts and ties, suit pants, hard shoes. Like Owens, they had faces like fine dogs. But these guys were wilder. Henry's hair frizzed out five inches, and everybody except Rich wore running shoes. Rich was the one good thing from his semester at Harvard, Owens had said—his professor, who'd come for a year to help him out (as Owens put it) and to secure his children's inheritance (as Rich explained it to Jane). Owens said he thought all the guys were nice-looking. He could probably hardly see them anymore, the way he had at first or the way strangers might. It occurred to Jane that this transformation could happen to women too, if he knew them this well. But he never would.

In the beginning, he had hired the people he knew. They smoked dope together and hiked the Grand Canyon. But now he interviewed at graduate schools all over the country. He lectured at these schools and drew audiences of more than a thousand. They offered him large fees for appearances, fees he always donated to their scholarship funds. Young guys like Henry, he said, were as different from Owens at that age as they could be. But he no longer worried, as he once had, that he'd be unable to love his own children because they would be so different from himself. Jane was just glad he'd changed his mind.

"You're right," Rich mumbled. "I gotta know you're right. I just don't know what to do with my folks."

"Well, these are tough choices. And I'd have to say, your folks, much as you love them, might just have to wait till after D day. We've got to find that one step further in purification so whatever protease is eating it up, can't anymore. I mean, this is the way I look at it. There are people I'd love to see for dinner and go to their house and meet their kid—no, I really would. There's introductions I'd give, keynote addresses, I'd go to birthday parties, baptisms, the works, I'd meet every one of these women people promise to introduce me to. These people are fine, there's nothing wrong with them, I like them, I'd learn from them, I'd do ten lectures and I'd have dinner with your parents, Rich—if I weren't going to die." He swiveled in his chair. "Come to think of it, even as it is, I'd still love to meet your parents. But after we're done with this. Same goes for meeting women. So keep those names."

The guys started making jokes now, about vitamins and what to eat for energy.

"Pills," Henry said. "Many, many pills."

"Oh, and one last thing before I leave, guys."

Rich was pacing, head curled down, feeding himself raisins from his hand.

"I've got good news for the night owls. I know you all like juice and you like it fresh as possible. And the same is true for Mae's muffins. And so I've arranged with both companies to deliver starting this morning at five, every day between now and D Day."

Sounds of gratitude were emitted in the room.

"And even better," Rich said, "tonight we have Jane's muffins."

Jane put her head down in the bask-wash of happiness. Her mom understood the secret of muffins: it was the baking powder. People let their baking powder go old. They bought new baking powder every time, even though it maddened Mary to throw out the red cans nine-tenths full.

"Well, I've had Jane's muffins," Owens said, stilling his head as if he were considering an important judgment. "And they've got a lot of love in them, but overall, I think Mae's are better."

Rich exploded. "Don't you see, Owens? Having love in them *makes* them better."

"It's okay," Jane said. Rich looked at her, shaking his head, as if he was thinking she was a year, maybe more, away from enlightenment. She shrugged. "My identity's not in my muffins."

"Well, guys, I've got to get Jane home to bed," Owens said. "See you in the morning."

Jane had been thinking of a way to take some muffins home, at least two for breakfast. But now that he'd said Mae's were better, she felt ashamed to care. She wanted one for herself, but she couldn't get it without him seeing.

On the way downstairs, he said, "Listen, I want to talk to you. This is your first month of school, and as you know, I had some doubts. And a lot of what I was worried about is coming true."

The teacher conference, he meant. She started sinking. She knew she hadn't done her homework, but she thought it was possible the teacher would say she was excellent anyway and give her a star.

"I want you to stop socializing and think of yourself as a nun on a retreat. No telephone. I think you should try to work a whole lot. Not just homework. I'd do that first, get it out of the way, and when that's done, then go a lot deeper into the subjects by yourself."

"But a lot of times it isn't that interesting. And I don't know why I can't talk to my friends."

"Sometimes we need to make our days very simple. Like now, I see the guys at work, I see Olivia, and I see you."

"And my mom."

"And your mother, but mostly just when I pick you up. There're people I really like, and if I think about it, I miss them. But sometimes things require more than you can give if you're leading this full-fledged social life. Now, when you're older you can decide whether you want to devote your life to a vocation or be some little social butterfly. But right now I'm your parent, and it's my job to teach you. And I'd like you to gain some experience of solitude."

"Did my mom seem okay this afternoon?"

"Yeah, I guess so. Why?" He laughed. "As okay as she ever does."

She sighed. "I'll try." When he put it that way, how could she say no? Plus he wasn't around enough to really tell. She could probably still talk to Madeleine and Johanna.

She knew that for him, there was never a month or a day or a year when the answer came back, *Yes, you did the greatest thing,* because at exactly the moment it was done, his eyes opened and he saw how much else in the world was going on at the same time. Now he still worked the extra hour—against weather, movies, picnics, browsing, being bored on the phone and dangling so it went on longer, against life, really—to prove to himself he could do it again.

"I've got more work to do when we get home. That Berkeley speech is in seven weeks."

He was sensitive about his education, she could tell. Maybe he wished he'd stayed in college longer. He did a lot of speeches at big industry conventions, when he was introducing new products; and at universities, he talked about Genesis.

But she knew the Berkeley speech was different. He told her Henry James had spoken in the same lecture series and the guy who found the shape of DNA. She had a feeling this was not for Genesis. This was for him.

"There's those people we went to see that time, over across the bay," she said, pointing to an old picture in the foyer.

"Aw, Shep and Lamb. They look really young, don't they? And there's Frank." He sounded fond, as if he wished he could see them all. But Jane suspected he could, if he just called them. Maybe not Frank.

Jane remembered that evening at Minna's house, months before, and she thought about why movie stars married movie stars and why, most often, the rich marry the rich. When she and her mother delivered the tuition check to her school, the administrator had talked, as people often did, about whom Owens would marry. "My sources say it won't be the one he's with now," she said. Later in the conversation, she'd said it might be easier for Owens if he found someone who already had money.

Although she was pretending to read a brochure on the table, Jane had almost burst out and asked why. It seemed the opposite. If one person had money and the other needed it, you'd think the one person would be grateful and the other would be glad to be of help. She had been thinking about that *why* ever since.

Jane remembered Minna's family again. "Do you think the reason you're not better friends is they're jealous of you?"

"No, I don't think so."

"I think they are. Because you're rich and you have good clothes and a good car and everything. And their house was pretty small; they just had one bathroom."

"You know, I've found in my life that it doesn't really matter how many bathrooms you have. What matters is what you're doing all day. And I think Shep probably admires a lot of what we're doing, and once in a while he might feel a little pang, but I wouldn't say he was jealous. I don't think people are jealous of things that are really great."

"Oh, I do," Jane said. But in time, over the years, she changed her mind. She would put it another way. People didn't envy those far above themselves. They envied their best friend or their sister, somebody they thought was just a little better, a person they felt, with a bit of luck, they could be. Probably for Bob Shepard and the people at dinner that night, Owens didn't get thrown into the comparison at all. He wasn't close enough. Minna's parents seemed to like her father, but she could tell they weren't that interested in what he did. They had their own pursuits, their books and the way they kept their house, their daughter's wedding dress in a box over the refrigerator.

The only people who really resent him, Jane decided, are us.

Who Will Be Queen?

‹‹‹‹‹‹‹‹‹‹

Owens would look back on 1989 as the year he did one thing right: He bought the house on Mayberry Drive that later became his first home.

One of Owens' qualities was loyalty. No matter how many appointments he missed or phone messages he didn't return, he nonetheless considered his friends his friends. He generally blamed lapses on himself.

This loyalty extended even to objects. He had never yet sold or junked a car; when he purchased the new house, he kept the Copper King's palace. He'd bought the estate for the land, to tear down the mansion and build a small wooden house, and he still intended to do that someday. In the meantime, he'd lend it to a friend, maybe Kaskie, who could improve the garden.

The purchase of the house was unusual, for the sellers had not known it was for sale.

Owens had decided it was time to move to Alta. He walked through the quiet streets many evenings, until he settled on the best house. Then he knocked on the front door and made an offer, before he saw the inside. The owners had always felt a secret immodest pride in their home, and even with an offer that doubled what they deemed possible, it was three days before they accepted his bid, and then only with the stipulation of a substantial nonrefundable deposit. Owens had the reputation of an impetuous young man. Eliot Hanson quickly delivered the check.

When Olivia found out, she hit the roof. And their fight did not remain private. Guarded as he was about gossip, Owens nonetheless told quite a few people about their daily ins and outs. Olivia was so volatile that he often needed to unburden himself, and the prospect of having to catch someone up on the events of even a week when he needed comfort and buoying was exhausting. He kept a number of confidants up-to-date.

Of the people in this circle, Mary and Jane craved information most acutely; they felt it influenced their future, though it was not at all clear how. A rare alertness organized Mary's features whenever Owens complained about Olivia. Since they'd come to Alta, Jane and Mary had heard all about Owens' problems with Olivia, and Olivia had heard all about his problems with them. Over the past year, the triangle had finally closed, as triangles will, and Olivia and Mary and Jane now confided in each other about their frustrations with him. They talked about him like a difficult boss.

As she sat reading in her small apartment, Olivia noticed Owens' car outside. They had not spoken for three days, although separately each of them talked of little else. Olivia had moved into an apartment in the back of an Alta house. Two chairs and a shelf of books furnished the living room. She'd hung the one woodblock print she had of her parents together, when they were her age. Only the futon and a stack of books that worked as her night table fit in the bedroom. She knew Owens loved her here in this house even more than in his own. She was supposed to be different, not like Mary, haggling for appliances. And she hadn't wanted those things at first, but now she wasn't sure.

She worked in a hospital. She read European novels. She'd renounced meat at thirteen. At one time, books and vegetarianism and nursing together had formed a particular kind of life, which was also expressed by letting her hair grow under her arms. Now it was hard to tell who she really was. And when what she was coincided with what he wanted her to be, she felt suspicious of herself. . . .

He would have to come here, that was for sure. Since she'd moved out of the Copper King's mansion, she'd never gone back once. Susan and Stephen, as much as he, were the reason she'd left. Living with them had not worked. For one thing, Olivia's housekeeping standards were high, from working in a hospital, and she didn't believe they tried very hard. She found herself in the lonely mansion on her hands and knees, scrubbing the floor of the kitchen and the one bathroom they used. Olivia did this every week for the past year, never telling anyone; but on the fifty-third week, she left.

She blamed the cooks for the proclivity he would never allow in her: they were bewitched by his things. One night, when he was in Asia, she came home and found them lying on his bed, watching a movie on the big TV. They had their own television in the backhouse. She knew because he'd given it to them for Christmas. They'd had a fight over whether to sign it just "Owens" or "Owens and Olivia." In the end, Owens had put both their names, but they thanked only him anyway.

"He said we could use his when he wasn't here," Stephen said, when Olivia walked in and stared. Susan didn't even lift her head, and they didn't leave until the movie was over. But it was her room too, the only place she belonged in that odd house.

He gave them a monthly household allowance that was more than they could easily spend, making every shopping trip an exhilaration. They had to look for things to buy. And the line between his and theirs blurred, because most of the time he wasn't home to eat the food they'd prepared. But they were. Every month they spent it all. As Owens didn't use the cappuccino maker or the new flour mill, Olivia couldn't help but think they'd bought for themselves. Olivia had no allowance and paid for her groceries with her own money.

The cooks made no pretense of working for the two of them. When Owens was in town, dinner waited in the refrigerator, fresh and sealed with clear plastic. They took the uneaten food back to their house in the morning, after he left for work. But when he was away for a few days, they cleaned out the refrigerator and brought the appliances to their own kitchen. Twice, they'd taken her food by mistake.

It is common knowledge that among the minions of a rich young man, a favorite topic of conversation is the question of who will be his wife. And Susan and Stephen had bet against Olivia. She was just the leggy blonde he was using. This is how, to her horror, she believed they saw her, and she hated them for it.

She had fuel behind that fury: it was an insult she'd been fighting all her life.

Olivia was riding her bike in the warehouse district when she saw Owens' car again. The door slammed and he hauled out two enormous garbage bags and threw them over his shoulder like a Santa.

She stopped her bike with her shoes. "What're you doing?"

He sighed and then came back up with a very wide smile. There were things in his life he didn't like to admit, but the relief of her was, she already knew them. "I'm throwing out my old clothes. The Goodwill box."

"I'll help you." She laid her bike on the ground and picked up a bag. Moments like this, it was a matter of honor that she was exactly his height. "You can't get Susan and Stephen to do this?"

"Well, that's what I always used to do. But the problem was, they'd go through it all. I got sick of seeing my old clothes on everybody around there. My suits on Stephen, Susan wearing my shirts; the gardener had some too, I think. I'm pretty sure the scarecrow's wearing my jeans. So I hauled these out myself."

After they hurled the bags into a receptacle, he said, "Wanna get a cup of coffee?"

"I can make tea."

She rode her bike, and he beat her there. She found him flipping through the pages of a mail order catalogue. The ceilings were so low that Owens looked like a grown man sitting in a dollhouse. "These are nice," he said, showing her a picture of Christmas tree balls. "We should get some. For the new house, if we go ahead and move in. You know, I was thinking about maybe telling Susan and Stephen it's time to part ways."

"You could get a European housekeeper who'd do things you couldn't even think of."

"See, a lot of people have servants," he said. "And I don't want servants. And I have to say that with Susan and Stephen, I never felt I had servants."

Olivia restrained a snicker. He had parasites. No wonder he didn't feel he had servants. In fact, Susan and Stephen were from rich families. Owens attracted kids like them, at work too, who felt devoted to him in a way they could not be to their own prosperous fathers.

"There are two problems," he went on, authoritatively. "One, I need someone to deal with my laundry."

"That's not hard." Olivia shrugged. "You just have to have a lot of socks and underwear. If you have a washer-dryer, you can do it while you're doing other things." Since she'd moved, Olivia did her wash in a public laundromat.

"Oh, I'm not worried about jeans and tee shirts. I can do that myself, that's no problem." Owens avowed this carelessly, although in fact it had been nearly a decade since he'd washed his own clothes. "It's business stuff. I spend a lot of money on suits, and there's only that one dry cleaner that doesn't ruin them."

"Are you sure there's nowhere closer?"

He sighed. "I don't really see them much, but I have some rich friends. I guess I could call up and say, 'Celeste, you know those four-thousand-dollar dresses you buy—now, you don't just throw them in the wash machine, do you? I didn't think you did.' "

So this is what they talk about, Jane thought with amazement. She was listening underneath Olivia's open screenless window. She'd seen his car and followed it, running. So many times she and her mother had wanted in, and maybe all that was going on was this. She couldn't quite admit to herself yet that she was bored. Instead she felt a craving she knew no name for, akin to hunger.

"I always thought we could have managed by ourselves," Olivia whispered. "And, in your new house, you should set up a room for Jane."

There. That was something that fit, like a food. Jane loved hearing her own name in their privacy. But that was all. She waited a long time, and it didn't happen again.

Olivia often made ardent pleas on behalf of Jane and of Owens' sister, Pony. This was something so ingrained in their life together that Olivia fell into a beseeching tone automatically, without even thinking whether or not she truly meant what she was saying. Tonight she felt a twinge: Does the slipper fit, or am I pushing my foot in?

Olivia wasn't the only person who found herself urging his generosity. He heard these same speeches from his father. Almost everyone agreed that Owens should be more generous with somebody else.

"I like this place," Owens said, looking around the tiny apartment. When she'd moved out, she did it exactly as he imagined a beautiful young woman would when she was mad at her boyfriend. She'd put up bamboo blinds and rice-paper lampshades. Her bike rested against the outside wall. No other girlfriend had inspired his enchantment. He'd been tempted to tell most of them what to do, even as they walked out on him.

He moved to the futon, lay down and crossed his arms under his head. "You know, I saw some really nice chairs yesterday. I'll show you. I'm thinking of buying some things for our new house."

"Don't," she said.

"Aw, come on, it's our first house together."

"But we don't need to buy things. That's not what matters. I don't care about chairs," she said, in an impassioned voice, not because she felt this so strongly but because her renunciation was a familiar step in their dialogue of forgiveness. She didn't *know* if she cared about chairs or Christmas tree balls. She didn't think so. But recently she'd come to understand that she wanted some of the normal things too.

"He tells the same story over and over again." More than anyone, Mary had an unquestioned faith in his brilliance, so his lapses left her incredulous.

"Have you heard about the five guys begging him to run?" Olivia was at the bungalow because she and Owens had made up again and she regretted some confidences she'd exchanged during the days she'd been angry.

"Yes! He told us two or three times—"

Jane skidded into the kitchen from behind the door. She couldn't help it. "Oh, I *know*. Like I told him, you should really go and taste the rice and beans yourself, just a surprise visit, and then you could find out why people are complaining. And the next day he said he would, like it was his idea."

Olivia smiled. "I like it that he forgets. I don't have to have new things to tell him every night."

Jane was sent back to her room. Both women felt uneasy talking in front of her about her father. But once she was gone, they didn't know where to begin again. Interruptions were not easy between them. Although their talks sometimes reached a pitch of confessional intensity, they were still not, in the usual sense, friends. Their relationship lacked ease and laziness. Mary's full kitchen was wide and windowed, and she moved through the dim room with an air of propriety, making her tea with dried lemon peel and cinnamon. She had a certain standing as the mother of his child. The apartment Olivia rented was smaller than this one room. But she knew what no one else did. "He's going to fire Susan and Stephen," she blurted, even though she'd vowed not to confide in Mary.

Mary's eyes fell open so wide that her long forehead seemed stretched. She was calculating whether this would make things worse for her and Jane. When something threatening occurred to Mary, she became very still. Owens interpreted this as stupidity. She slowly poured hot water into a glass pot warming over a candle. Unable to come to any conclusion, she stalled and asked, "Why? Isn't he happy with them?"

"No. And I don't think they're so great either." However wary she now felt, Olivia couldn't resist a conversation about Susan and Stephen. They had humiliated her, and it was a matter of some importance that they go. "They could do a lot more. They take care of him, but they don't pay attention to anyone else. Like when Jane comes over, they could give her clean towels. Just little things to make people feel at home."

Mary herself had never felt at home in Owens' house, but she hadn't considered that a possibility. "No, you're right. They're a little cold."

"I don't think they're such great cooks either."

"No. No, they could be much better." Mary laughed. "I even think we do better here. He should maybe get an older woman, who could really make a home. We could even use her. That way, if she made a nice meal every night, it'd get eaten, now that the new house is so close." She giggled, a first foot in, planning. "I'd even bring our laundry."

Olivia controlled her voice. "I don't think he's planning on having servants."

"He needs somebody, though. Susan and Stephen do a lot, and like you said, it still never feels like a home. Between all he wants done and then what Jane needs too, the way he is, he has to have help."

Olivia's eyes closed. It was always the same. She was an adjunct. "But, Mary, if he did hire someone—and I'm not saying he will—I'd supervise the person. I'd be mistress of the house." There. She'd said it.

It took Mary a moment to absorb that she was out again. Then her tone became the one she used with Owens. "I just thought if Jane needed something."

"Well, that would be fine. I'm just saying . . ."

But Mary's forehead stretched again, that same uncomprehending look. Maybe he's right after all, Olivia decided. Maybe she is dumb.

Owens didn't hide his chagrin when he discovered that the beans in the Alameda County School District had been fatted with lard. He was sitting on a small plastic cafeteria chair, holding a forkful in front of him. "What's in this?" he asked.

The principal rubbed his hands together. "It's beans and rice."

"No it's not. There's something else in here. Some grease. See this yellow stuff?"

Jane, who was along, was thinking whatever it was made it taste good. She was eating fast, because she knew she'd have to stop when the ingredient was announced.

"Could you find out what this is? I'd really like to know."

Lunch capped off a bad morning. Owens had been visiting a school funded by his open-classroom initiative.

Desks and pupils faced every which way—forty, fifty or perhaps more in one classroom. It was difficult to count because many of the students were in constant motion. Who knew? Certainly not the teacher, who looked cowed and meek, slump-necked, handing out pencils with an infinite slowness and asking the students to share. Then it became clear that there weren't enough pencils to go around.

Owens had three pens on him. "Here," he said, donating them.

Children erupted from their seats to a stinging hive around him until two boys hit their heads together with a loud *thwock* and three children emerged victorious. Then, almost immediately, the rupture closed, the pens were owned and forgotten, and the class roared on in its manifold disorder.

This teacher seemed lacking in any aggressive virtues. She had no visible pep, limited imagination and even, it occurred to Owens, insufficient wind power. But what she did possess was infinite patience, which was either what they needed more than anything or the worst possible obstacle to their progress.

"I'd get those desks back in rows," Owens volunteered to the principal.

Owens was still persuading Olivia to move into the new house with him, but he found the challenge enlivening. The romance of pursuit and his own talent for recruitment contributed to a vague restlessness when they saw each other every night. When Olivia described her argument with Mary, he had to smile: two women quarreling over who would use the maid, like children fighting for the rule of an imagined kingdom. Who would be queen? The easiest solution, he thought, was not to hire anybody. He considered himself a Solomonic mediator, but that drove Olivia crazy, his regarding her as only one party of a dispute, with no special connection to him.

"Ah, the women in my life," he said, with lifted eyebrows and a merriness in his voice. "I'm going to tell Susan and Stephen this week."

This soothed her, but not completely. She couldn't say why, even to herself.

"I mean, I'm not mad," she said. "I think of Mary as a fragile flower. I like her."

Olivia learned certain words from reading. She didn't look them up in the dictionary, although she underlined in books, intending to go back later. But eventually she apprehended the meaning, if she found a word enough times. And sometimes with the new word came an idea, a tint of life. She'd discovered that it didn't work to try and please him; it made things worse. The more *insouciant* I am, she thought, the happier he is.

This was a lesson almost any mother of a certain generation would have taught her daughter, from the playpen on. But Olivia had had an unusual mother, who believed her daughter's beauty was so extraordinary that she took a small, mean pleasure in depriving her of some of the common tools.

"You think this is nice?" Owens asked.

"Oh, I think it's beautiful," the clerk declared.

He turned the ring, studying it, and then shook his head. "Because I don't think it's very nice at all. I want something simple. But because I'm probably going to get married only once in my life, the stone should be . . . special." He was speaking very slowly, as if he considered it a distinct possibility that the woman was an imbecile.

"Did you ask her and she said yes?" Jane whispered. They'd driven all the way to the city, but he hadn't told her anything.

"No, and that's why you can't say anything. I'm thinking about it."

"And you're getting the ring first?"

"If we find something really great."

But they didn't. The woman led them to a private room in the back of the store, where a man showed them several stones Owens considered too large, too yellow, or not the right shape. Owens wrote down his number, and the man promised to search.

When they emerged, the streetlamps were coming on and people on the sidewalks seemed to be hurrying. Jane would have liked to stop. *A restorative cup of hot chocolate,* Peter Bigelow had said the time he bought Julie the dress—the kind of thing he would probably do only once in his life, her mother said—and that was what made the day beautiful. He'd bought them both gifts that afternoon, but the day was a gift too. They wandered through the streets, in and out of stores, with a sense that something momentous had already happened. They stopped and looked up at the sky. Peter's eyes seemed gelatine and far-holding. It was the first time Jane had seen a strong man frightened. She had hoped someday she would marry a man like Peter.

But she also admired her father's stern profile, his long fingers, as he examined the fine rings. She wanted to marry someone a little like Owens too.

Driving, he seemed preoccupied again. Jane wished they'd found a ring and bought it: maybe that would have made the difference.

"Want to see the house?" Owens asked Noah Kaskie, who was waiting on Mayberry Drive when they returned, half an hour late.

"Sure. I want the full tour."

Once inside, Owens moved on his hands and knees to show his friend the method of hand-planing the floor planks. "In Japan, they have this incredibly smooth wood that feels really good when you walk barefoot. And it's all just hand-planed wood with no finish."

"Not even wax or polyurethane?"

"Nothing. So we can have a shoeless house."

Noah reached down a hand to feel. He was self-conscious about his wheels. It had been over a week since he'd hosed them off. He'd have to clean them with a rag whenever he came here.

Of course, finding Japanese hand planers wasn't easy, but that was precisely the kind of challenge Owens excelled in. He contacted sixty-two men—in Japan, the United States and Canada—before he located the right one. He'd done it all from his telephone.

Noah looked around the empty rooms, impressed but not particularly envious, even though it was so far beyond his present and even eventual means that he didn't like to think about it. To him it wasn't beautiful. If he were buying a big house, he'd pick something more classic. Brick or stone around a courtyard; one story, of course. He'd want a dining room and a pantry and broom closets, plus lots of little bedrooms for children.

Noah's mother had often gone to garden shows, to see the insides of

rich women's houses. She and her friends had not returned home de-
feated; they came back like divers with one tip minted from the deep.
They too would use paper narcissi as centerpieces!

They were standing by the fireplace when Noah saw the tracks his
wheels had left on this soft wood.

"I think Olivia and I should either break up or get married," Owens
said all of a sudden, staring at his friend with a peculiar intensity. The
fireplace waited, impeccably clean. "You know what I did this afternoon? I went shopping for a ring. A ring can definitely be had. But do
you know how you'd propose?"

"There's no one to propose to."

"But how do you think you'll do it, when the time comes?"

"I don't know. I guess I'd wait for a moment when we both were
happy. When you can't stop laughing. I'd ask then."

Owens carried Noah upstairs to see the bedrooms. "I was thinking
of taking her to this little restaurant where I know the cook, and I'd
ask her to make us a soufflé—like a fresh raspberry soufflé—and have
her bake the ring into that. What do you think?"

"Memorable," Kaskie said. "A little messy."

"I know. I thought of that." Owens proceeded to outline his various plans; each one involved the ring being hidden in a beverage or a
portion of food.

Cracker Jack prize, Noah thought. Not a question for her to answer, but a treat. Noah had never considered purchasing a ring. Now
he wondered if he should've bought some jewelry for the girl in college. Women liked those things. But he couldn't stop thinking about
the scuff marks downstairs. Would Owens have to get the workman
back to fix it? Noah wanted to write a check then and there. But how
much would it cost? Would they have to fly the hand planer from
Japan or Canada? "So Olivia's definitely moving in, then?"

"I think so. We had a little fight about it," Owens added, forgetting
he'd already told Kaskie. "You know, I wish Olivia would *do* something with her life. Like, say we had a couple kids and she wasn't that
happy with the schools. And so she started her own school, and then,
after it'd been going a little while, she decided to go out into the busi-

ness community and raise money so poor kids could go too. I think that'd be really great."

He doesn't love her enough, Noah thought, wishing she were there. He could tell her about the wheel tracks.

A small futon with twisted sheets lay in a corner. "I slept here last night," Owens said. "It was great. In the morning, some kids were sort of yelling on their way to school."

The bathroom was strange. Owens had spent days combing the world for Japanese hand planers, but he could live with chartreuse tile? He'd already set his toothbrush on the lip of the sink. Kaskie recognized that they had the same razor. "Oh, you've got that too," he said, seizing on this commonality after an hour-long discussion about home renovation to which he had nothing to contribute.

"It's great. I threw out my electric. Where'd you hear about it?"

"Remember my friend who was sequencing the enzyme? Rachel?"

"A woman. Really?" Owens raised his eyebrows.

"I guess she uses it for . . . you know. Actually, come to think of it, I'm not sure she shaves. Her legs maybe." Noah tried to remember Rachel's legs. She usually wore pants.

"Is Rachel the woman . . . ?" Owens got a faraway, indulgent smile. "She doesn't shave?"

"Not underarms, I guess. I don't know," Kaskie blundered. He hoped he wasn't compromising his friend.

"I would've guessed she was a shaver. She struck me as being very East Coast."

"She's about five minutes away," Noah said, "from a Nobel Prize."

Every minute he didn't bring up the black lines was a moment gone. Noah remembered his grandmother reading to his sister and him when they were young, a book about manners. If you break something in a house where you're the guest, go immediately and tell the hostess. And Noah understood that if he didn't say anything and they left the house, they both would know and it would be a problem between them. But he didn't want to tell.

Stalling, Noah picked up the small instrument. "Feels good in the hand." With old razors, he'd habitually nicked himself.

"Yeah, their stock shot way up." Owens sighed. "And it should; it's a good product." This was true word of mouth—an idea Owens had never thought about while his first product was selling wildly and had learned to monitor only this second time around.

If worst came to worst, he could pay for the ads himself. But that wouldn't look good if it got out. Maybe Rooney was right. Maybe you couldn't buy word of mouth. Yet he didn't doubt the worth of Exodus, and these oppositions disturbed him. He rubbed his eyebrows. "But you like the place?" he asked.

After a thorough tour, Noah felt satisfied that Owens didn't own a house he could love. For that he was both grateful and relieved, and more ebullient praising it than he could've been if he'd found it truly beautiful. "It's making me think I should move," he said finally. "Owens, look. I made marks on your new floor, and I'm sorry. What can I do?"

"Oh, I don't care about that, Noah."

"Yes you do. You paid a lot of money to get it right. Let me fix it."

Owens shrugged. "You get it as beautiful as you can, and then you live in it. This counts as living in it. I'll mop up later. Let's take a walk."

Ribbons of jasmine seemed to float among the woodsmoke. They kept walking, each believing that whatever was wrong with their lives, it was never this place. They might be random specks of matter, but in this they were fortunate—they were born to a place that would never grow old, that voyage could not daunt or diminish.

"Do you think everyone feels this way about where they grew up?" Noah asked.

"Yeah, a little," Owens said. "But this is different. It really is better here."

The place had its own grandeur, the dark mountains like a proud woman with her shoulders thrown back. It was more than their love for it.

As they entered town, Kaskie felt in his pocket and fingered the worn bills. This time, he could treat. "Should we stop for a coffee?"

Owens patted his stomach. "I'm getting a little fat. Let's look in there instead."

Kaskie reluctantly crossed the street and entered the bike store. Owens bought a new kind of roller skate and Kaskie allowed himself to be talked into a set of wide off-road wheels. Just when Kaskie had a twenty in his pocket, Owens had done it again. Kaskie had to borrow cash.

Jane was sitting on the curb when they returned, eating her own scab. "I forgot my key to my mom's," she announced, "and it's locked." While they were walking, she'd picked out the room she wanted in the new house: the one next to Owens'. She'd tried it, lying down on the bare floor.

"I'll drive you there and we'll find a way to break in."

Before they left, Noah wrote out a check to Owens for the wheels.

"Don't give me that. Come here, let me show you something." Owens opened the passenger door of his car and reached in to open the glove compartment. "There must be ninety checks in there. See, I don't cash them."

"Why not?" Jane said, incredulous.

"Too much time. Not worth all the bookkeeping."

Noah laid his check on top of the car. "Well, cash this one." This whole scene embarrassed him. When he subtracted the amount of the check from his register, he had a hundred seventy dollars left. He would count the money gone, and if the check wasn't returned in his next statement, he'd give Owens cash.

Jane opened and closed the glove compartment as Owens drove her home. Among the checks she found five dollar bills and a crumpled piece of paper with "Bob Shepard" written on it, and three phone numbers, one marked *office,* one marked *home,* one marked *mom's place.*

"You know, I actually do have a ring," Owens said. "If you look in the back left corner, under those checks, you'll see a little box. My mom left it to me in her will. I thought she was buried with it, but a few months ago my dad gave me this and said she wanted me to have it."

Jane opened the box and there it was, what they'd been looking for all day. She slipped it on her finger, and it fit.

"Let's see. I think that's nicer than all the ones we saw today."

Jane agreed.

"I'd have to have it made bigger. It's too small for her."

Jane slid the ring off and replaced it in the box. "Can I have some of those checks?"

"No, you may not," he said.

"Why not?"

"Because they're not yours."

"They're yours but you don't want them."

"That's right. They're mine but I don't want them. That doesn't make them yours."

The child at that time was worth more than one million dollars. Eliot Hanson had pointed out the need for arrangements. And of course that made sense, in case something happened to Owens. And so his compromise in the awkward matter of his love, which was at odds with his values, was to leave her money in the material world, on paper, but at the same time to let her think she'd get nothing and would have to work for a living, the way he had.

"You have so much, but you won't give anything away even if you don't need it."

He looked at her as if examining an odd, perhaps alien, creature. "I give things away."

"Like what?"

"Well, Noah's van, for example. I bought him that."

"I didn't know that," Jane said, biting at the skin on her knuckle. "What made you?"

"I was driving along one day—he didn't see me—and I watched him getting on a bus."

Noah came to the conclusion he always eventually arrived at after an episode of envy: the only thing to do was work harder. He decided he didn't know enough, a conviction he had periodically. This time, it was history. He sent away for a twelve-volume history of the world.

Noah had attended ordinary public school. His fifth-grade teacher had told everyone in the class to make a taped-together banner showing two centuries of births and deaths and discoveries, connected with dots. Noah was so late with it that the teacher called his mother. She helped him with the time line, pointing with her fingernail on the kitchen table; he remembered her standing there watching while he drew and marked, reading passages aloud from the *World Book.*

He turned it in the next day, folded like a fan. The teacher made two students hold the ends of Noah's time line, saying it was the best one and probably deserved an A, the only A, except that it had been turned in three weeks late. His feeling of glory lasted less than a minute, pride turning to shame. His time line had been marked D in red.

Now he wanted to paint a time line on a wall in his lab. "I don't know what was being written in Asia at the time of Shakespeare," Noah told his graduate students, "or anything about Africa when Darwin sailed in the *Beagle.* Or during the Russian Revolution, what exactly was happening in Latin America? And what was going on in the rest of the world besides Holland during the seventeenth century? Everything I know is scattershot. So I'm going to draw the basic outline, and I'd like you guys, whenever you learn something, to just mark it down so we can all benefit."

"Do you want vaccines and elements?" Louise asked. "That kind of detail?" Louise was now developing mutants that could be neighbors to their mutant. She was also sick and occasionally crying. She and Andy Ruff had broken up for good. She'd moved a sleeping bag, an electric kettle and a suitcase of clothes into the lab.

Noah started reading his history of the world while they waited for data. He jotted notes, making his students anxious with all those little scraps of incidental knowledge he intended to place on one clear line.

"After all," he said, "who ever heard of an uneducated Jew?"

"You're not," Louise said, passing with slides to show him.

"I know little bits of things, but I don't have the and-thens." The only museum in Alta showed Indian pottery and the baby teeth of the founders' children. And Owens' Matisse.

He painted the actual line in the middle of the night, while Louise slept on the couch. He'd bought twenty markers in five different colors. Reds would be political upheavals, revolutions, the deaths of presidents and kings. Blues were cultural events, books, paintings, symphonies. Yellows were scientific advances, and greens were births and deaths of famous people. Purple he'd bought just for Louise, for minor details.

⊷

That night, Owens told Kathleen how depressed he was about the razor and its word of mouth.

"But people are talking about NT12 that way too," she claimed. "They really are."

He had always had sales. Sales he'd taken for granted, expected, almost scorned. They were shooting for something higher. Now he found himself in the odd position of working day and night, begging for something he'd said and believed he didn't care about.

Popularity, gem of carelessness. Perhaps impossible to will back.

It occurred to Owens that he avoided sharing his doubts with Olivia, for fear of the smile that was an I-told-you-so and an unspoken sympathy for the other side. Kathleen's enthusiasm was unalloyed. But he didn't quite believe in it.

He had known when Genesis was rising; he could feel its ascent within him.

The only way he knew how to fight was with grim work. Few people could outlast Owens' will.

Shoes

<><><><><><>

*J*ane grew up believing her father could have been governor if she hadn't stolen his shoes.

There were things about him that only certain people knew. Susan and Stephen knew because they had to replace his dry-cleaned clothes in his closets. His girlfriends knew, and there had been two between Mary and Olivia. Each of these women had been awarded a small house through a lawyer, involving papers they signed after the breakup, promising never to tell his secrets. Both women later married, and Jane liked knowing that deep in the night in their beds in those smaller-than-his houses, his secrets were being whispered, slowly disseminating into the world.

Girlfriends came, were romanced, and went, each taking with her some stern compensation—property—and a set of the chin, to be carried the rest of her life, when she would be wiser, grimmer, less young.

But Jane knew his secrets too, and for nothing. One of his peculiarities was the shoe room. His feet were unusually long and quadruple narrow, and his arches rose too high. He usually had his shoes made for him. But if he found a pair that fit, he'd order ten or twenty extra. There was a room full of just the shoe boxes. This was the kind of detail he intended to keep out of the papers, but he told Jane because it was a pleasure to show his overall good sense and economy.

Jane did what she did before the Berkeley speech because she knew about the shoes.

The night before, they'd eaten dinner at his dining room table. He'd opened a bottle of wine he hadn't liked and then another one, which he said was extremely fine. He let her try a sip.

"Children in Europe drink wine," he said, then put his glass down. "This wine is thirty years old. But this table is almost four hundred years old. This table was around during Shakespeare's lifetime."

"Yeah, but Shakespeare wouldn't have had a table like this," Jane said. "Shakespeare wasn't rich."

"No, he wasn't rich. But this wasn't a rich person's table. It's a very simple table, and that's why I like it. It could've been in Shakespeare's parents' kitchen."

"I guess so. But in Shakespeare's time there were probably rich people who had tables from somebody else's kitchen hundreds of years before that, and Shakespeare probably had a table just like the one my mom and I have, that came from the same place everyone else's did."

"You're right, Jane," Olivia said.

Owens lowered his head. "What is this—Jump on Dad Day?" Nobody said anything for a few minutes, then he asked, "Do you know who William Faulkner is?"

"No." Jane wished she did. She almost said yes, but then he'd ask who, and she had no idea.

"He was a very great American author. And he told his daughter, once, probably when she was being a brat, 'Who remembers Shakespeare's daughter?' "

"Who says you're Shakespeare?" Jane said. "Maybe you're Shakespeare's father."

Olivia laughed.

"What?" His face opened, perplexed; he truly did not get the joke.

"Never mind."

He told them about vintages then, and the vintage of the year Jane was born was no good or at least not anything special. Nineteen sixty, on the other hand, Olivia's year, was awesome.

Then it was morning, and Jane ran downstairs, squeezed oranges and put on oatmeal. But Owens said he was fasting.

He was driving up to Berkeley himself, in his low-to-the-ground car. She was scheduled to take the bus with everyone else. When Olivia had offered to drive, he said he wanted them on the bus. Olivia hadn't even slept there. "I can't afford to have a fight," he said. "And given our odds, the chances of that happening are pretty good." The bus would leave the Exodus parking lot at nine sharp. The cooks were going to drive her there.

"I'm ready," she said. "I could come with you."

"I think I need to be alone this morning."

She just wanted to be with him in the car, pushing that lever to make the seat tilt back. She would've been quiet and left him alone. She always had.

The sky this morning was a pale blue, steady as far as you could see, with bulky white clouds. The columns of neat trimmed palms and shaggy sycamores already cast pure navy shadows. He stood outside the house like a traveler, holding his suit bag and his shoes.

"Good luck today," she said.

"Yeah," he said, looking out at the distant mountains. At moments that seemed important, he believed there was something to be learned from nature. He stood there trying to be humble. A plain moth fluttered near his hair.

"Come up on stage after and find me."

In his dressing room, Kathleen poured fresh pomegranate juice. She was tall and ready-handed, and in the last two weeks Owens had found it very hard to keep from comparing her to Olivia.

Though she was twenty-six, a college graduate and married, Kathleen seemed to him unspeakably innocent. He was pretty sure she'd slept only with the one guy. From the wedding picture on her desk, he guessed there was fondness but no great passion. Her husband had a mustache and the beginnings of a belly, a salesman kind of guy.

She took his bag and hung the garments up, smoothing the good fabrics with the flat of her hands a little longer than for the clothes, then set the shoes on the closet floor.

Where was Olivia, he wondered. She could be here this morning with juice.

The bus hadn't left at nine sharp. The driver had a list, and quite a few people were not there yet. So the bus waited in the empty parking lot. Exodus was closed for the day, because everyone was going to be in the audience. They'd hired temps to answer phones. Down the road, at Genesis, spangles of light twisted off the tops of cars. For everyone else, it was a plain Wednesday.

Jane stood on the blacktop, one shoe scratching an itch. It was strange to be out of school at this hour. This was the first day she'd missed since she started. In the mountains, she'd been absent all the time for no reason at all, but down here she wanted her attendance record to be perfect. Still, Owens had told her this was important, and his father and his sister were already on the bus, facing forward.

Just then, Owens' father unfolded out of the door. He seemed like a sheriff, very tall, his mouth crossed with lines. He had on an open-collar shirt, like the boys at school wore. All the men up in the mountains had dressed like him, but Jane wasn't used to that anymore.

"What do you think about Olivia?" he said.

"Maybe she decided to drive."

"Told me we were leaving at nine and she'd be here. But it's nine-thirty! I don't know what to do and neither does the bus driver. Man's got a job. I don't blame him."

"I could call, I guess." A pay phone wavered at the end of the lot. The diagonal walk in early heat seemed like wading in clothes through water. Jane understood she could save Olivia, but she didn't want to. If she did, no one would remember, but if she didn't, would they count it and blame her? Jane's fingers punched the numbers. Maybe Olivia was already driving, but Jane knew she wasn't. Jane could leave her in the warm silence and change the day and ever after.

" 'Lo." Olivia's voice curved, hollow with sleep.

"Aren't you coming?"

"Oh, my God. Thank God you called, Jane. Just go on without me. I have to take a shower. I'll drive up."

"Did you get a new dress?" Jane had heard Owens say she'd better buy one.

"New enough. What are you wearing, Jane?"

"My uniform."

Jane's mom had a new dress, but not for today. They'd bought it together to cheer her up. It had cost ninety-four dollars. She was meeting Jane there. She had an appointment with her orthodontist this morning, and if she canceled she'd have to wait another six weeks. She was in a hurry to get her teeth straight and on with her life.

The bus still arrived forty-five minutes early, the way Owens liked his plans to work. And when Olivia raced in through the backstage entrance—her deep smile bordering on apology—he threw his arm around her all the same. He whispered that there were seats saved for family in the first three rows.

Everyone wanted Jane, and there was a fuss over whom she sat next to. Olivia scootched her hand open and closed and then talked with her chin down, her voice slurring all motherly. And then her grandfather strode over and whispered, "She wants to sit down front, we got a place."

One place, Mary noted; he has his nerve. "I think I'll keep her here by me," she said. When she was pregnant, he'd told people she was the town pump. And now he wanted her daughter for the front row.

Jane was the only child here. People nudged to point her out. Now she wanted to hold her mother's hand because of what she'd done.

She'd done it fast, and it had come to her like an inspiration. Olivia had waved and asked if she wanted to see Owens. And she'd said yes and not turned back to her mother, who felt looked at without her.

There was a door and a man in a uniform. For a second, Jane thought of her mother, the two of them standing holding hands before a closed door. But with Olivia, she went right through to the other side. People she'd seen at his office walked around holding clipboards.

In his dressing room, her father had seemed calm. He was wearing suit pants and a white shirt, no tie or jacket. He hugged Jane without looking at her, then wandered out to the hallway. Jane realized her mother was right about Owens, his faults and his talents: both were true, just outsized. He was like Mount Rushmore, so big.

But he was too big. Jane wanted to be felt, like putting a pin in a huge balloon.

The room was quiet, except for the noise of Kathleen peeing. Jane's eyes hit the shoes with their cedar shoe trees. She picked them up and hid them behind some boxes in the closet. Then she went out into the hall, near her father. It seemed maybe nothing had really happened. His hand drifted idly to her hair.

Kathleen waited at the door of the dressing room, as if she were not allowed out. Her face was all on him, alive. If his head made the slightest turn towards her, everything opened. She had freckles across the bridge of her nose and on her arms. Jane imagined her in a clean kitchen, holding a bowl of cupcake frosting and stirring.

Owens had told Jane that on a business trip to Washington, D.C., they stayed up until four in the morning, talking on the steps of the Lincoln Memorial.

"Talking about what?" she'd asked.

"Oh, I don't know," he'd said. "About God and what we owe America." Then he admitted they'd made out, and it was some of the most exciting kissing he'd done in years.

"But she's married!"

"I know. That's why I'd rather you didn't tell anybody. I don't think she's too happy in her marriage, though."

"Who do you love more—Kathleen or Olivia?"

He didn't seem pressed to decide.

Then it was time for the speech, and nothing happened. Jane believed and didn't believe it was because of his shoes.

Waves of tiny noises rippled through the crowd. Jane knew she wasn't supposed to talk to the men crouching with cameras. Even the balconies were full. "Why do you think they're late?" she whispered.

"He's always late," Mary said. "He's always been."

"You can tell this is important just from the place." The ceilings went so high. The seats were wood and rich, soft velvet.

"They probably just rented it," Mary said. "But colleges are beautiful. Maybe he'll have this for you when you get married."

Jane knew he wouldn't. For a wedding he'd want someplace small. Or that cold, bare, rainy mission he liked.

As the minutes passed, Jane got worse and worse. It was becoming irrecoverable, like in a dream, and now there was nothing she could do but clutch the armrests on her chair and wait. They would leave soon, all these people, and he would have missed his best chance because of her.

Then, just like that, her father came out in a spotlight, his same hulking walk, and everyone stood clapping. She felt the warm relief on her chest: you couldn't harm him if you tried.

But there were some other black shoes on his feet.

"Hello. My name is Tom Owens, and I didn't go to any school to be governor."

The crowd was suddenly loud, and Jane and Mary popped up cheering, as if they'd been suppressed under lids all this time.

"I believe there are two kinds of human endeavor in this world that have produced great results. One is collective effort, and that's the way of working I know best. And the other is the individual achievement of poets and artists."

Jane knew the secret. Her father was going to work around to him at the end. She'd been there when he'd first read about him in the newspaper. Today he was going to say, "One morning I was reading the newspaper with my daughter, and I read a story about a man in a country which has been engaged in a tragic civil war. And this man lived in the oldest city in his country. And at a time when most everybody who possibly could was getting out, this man made no plans to move from his apartment. But every day, around dusk, he walked into one of the main squares of his city and sang for an hour until it was dark, with artillery shells exploding all around him. And he's here today to sing for us."

But when it happened, he'd changed his speech and didn't mention having a daughter at all. And for the first time ever that she knew, he was making a bad speech. All her life, Jane had learned to count on few things from her father, but one of them was charisma; she'd never considered that he could fail to mesmerize. It was an absolute she'd had to live with, and now that it was slipping, she felt frightened of so much.

He was reading from notes, as if he didn't want to let himself be himself.

There was a quality in people that lived beneath the surface and only sometimes sparkled up, which she could not match with a word. "Terror" was only approximate. But Jane was keen to those glints and shards—which showed themselves not so much in the face as in movement—because she believed she could help. "You shouldn't worry about that *at all*, Mom," she'd whisper, slipping a hand into hers. She had divined this in everyone except Owens. And now, as she watched him speak, it occurred to her that because he didn't feel it, she felt it for him.

Years before, he'd started out quick and smart with journalists. He said he'd seen his words twisted into helixes he didn't recognize. So maybe he was trying to rein himself in. This speech, he'd told her, was a personal honor—not just a platform to evangelize for Exodus or run for political office. He'd already given four gubernatorial speeches, and the men who wanted him to run had scheduled a fund-raiser at the Bohemian Club's Russian River retreat. But he intended to use this podium for none of that. He had aims he could hardly put into the right words, he'd told her.

But he was going on too long; even Jane could tell that. He was talking about education, pointing to an elaborate chart he drew on a blackboard. In secret, she had been going to the Alta public library and studying him. Articles she'd read had accused him of rhetoric, hyperbole, an absence of facts; on the front of a newspaper's Sunday magazine, someone had called him the ultimate salesman. But Jane knew he wasn't that. So today he was giving facts and differentials and equations. He kept his own levity about the stupefying idiocy of the system from rising up into words.

Or maybe it wasn't the journalists. Maybe it was here. Jane knew the places her parents lied. And the one they had in common was college. They both said college didn't matter, but even when they said the word, they sounded wistful. Maybe he thought this was the one thing better than he was.

Then somebody in the audience went out the back, letting the door slam. The noise rang through the auditorium as Owens continued on about his plan to issue vouchers to every parent of a school-age child. Then, before the echo of the noise finally ended, someone dropped his keys. Jane watched with alarm as heads turned, searching for the sound. People fidgeted in their seats. Then coins dropped somewhere else further back. By now it must have been on purpose. People were dropping money: not all at once, but one at a time, the silvery sound falling from different parts of the audience; as soon as one dimmed and there was only memory ringing in the air, another began. Owens riffled through his pages. She knew he saw the patches of movement, but he had many pages more to go. This had never happened to him before. What he did then was almost preordained. His father, who looked like a sheriff, sat in the front row, perfectly right-angled. Owens read every line on every page.

In the end there was booming applause, but of a nature that seemed too exuberant for even Owens to find flattering. The next day, he would ask Kathleen to cancel all his speaking engagements for the rest of his life. He'd decided it was time to stay home.

Now cameras popped white lights as Jane ran to the lip of the stage and shimmied up. Everyone came: Olivia, Mary, his father and sister, people he knew but she didn't. Kathleen stood near the curtain, still offstage. Owens picked Jane up. She whispered, "I wish I was wearing a dress."

"I'll get you one," he promised. "You're old enough now."

But before they left, he said, "Could I please see Olivia and Jane for a second?"

Now it was going to happen, she could tell, just when she'd almost got away. She followed him, walking with her arms at her sides.

In the dressing room, he said, "Now all three of you are here. One of you took my shoes, and I want to know who did it."

"Not me," Jane said first.

Kathleen shook her head, looking grave.

"Well, I tend to believe Kathleen, because she's the one who thought of spray-painting my running shoes. I started late because we were waiting for them to dry."

Olivia smiled weirdly, looking at him from the side. "I didn't hide your shoes, Tom."

"So nobody put my shoes in this closet? Kathleen found them."

Jane sat on her hands, bouncing a little.

"Nobody." He sighed. "Well, I've got to get ready for interviews. I guess it'll have to remain one of life's little mysteries. Another one."

"I didn't do it, Tom," Olivia blurted, turning so her hair whipped behind her.

Kathleen, in white jeans and white sneakers, stayed in the dressing room, neatening. She seemed to have an instinct for order.

Outside, a journalist had found Mary and followed her, clipboard in hand, to the car. As she bent over to unlock her door, Mary felt the woman staring at her womb. The journalist looked at her frankly, with curiosity and no apparent kindness, as if Mary were a used mine. Mary was sure the journalist was a woman who had never been pregnant. "Jane's very pretty," the woman said. "Takes after her father. Does she mind being illegitimate?"

"I beg your pardon?" Mary's eyes dropped open as if she'd been stunned into pure incomprehension.

"I mean, does that even pertain in this day and age? Does she think of herself as a—I don't know—a bastard or . . ."

Mary's jaw went uneven. She wished Owens would pay for the operation to fix it.

"Get in the car, Jane," she ordered gruffly, as Jane came up, out of breath from running. "Lock your door."

They were sealed in the car then, but the journalist stood her ground. "Wait. I mean, we're on *your* side. We're sympathetic to Jane."

Driving fast, Mary pinched her thigh so it stung. She'd lived in a plain cabin at the wintercamp, with nothing. To them that bare cabin, the dirt and poverty, would be what she was, what she should be.

"Stop it with the lip," Jane said.

That night, Olivia came to the bungalow, carrying a bottle of champagne and a huge bouquet of sunflowers. Mary had made corn muffins. They sat on the floor and watched news on all the stations, but his speech didn't show up anywhere. It was as if it hadn't happened.

They all felt a little happy. Other places, far away, in the towers where broadcasts were decided, there were worlds where he wasn't so big.

After the press conference, Kathleen waited in the dressing room with pomegranate juice and his clothes all packed. He wanted to change into jeans for the drive back, and he did right there. Then they made love, for the first time, on the single cot. He asked her if he was only the second man in her life, and she told him he was. She cried a little while it was happening, her voice sounding to him almost unbearably lonely in its smallness and embarrassment. Afterwards, he began to talk about his disappointments in Olivia. She confessed that she too felt misgivings, though maybe it was her own fault; there was some way in which she and her husband didn't have the kind of talks she'd hoped for when she was a girl, reading books about life. She could have said more and more—the thread, once pulled, ready to unravel— but he stood up sighing and said, "I should really get going." He kissed her forehead. "Thank you."

And then he was gone and she was still there, in the university dressing room, with her clothes back on, perfectly straight. All her life, people had appreciated Kathleen's neatness.

Years later, long after Owens stopped talking about being governor, he would tell his daughter that some redheads have freckles everywhere on their bodies, and he would mention Kathleen's name to prove that a woman's hair does not always match her head. Jane asked where Kathleen was now. But by then she had long since left both Genesis and her husband, and Owens hadn't heard anything from her in years.

Jane never found out if Owens knew she was the one who did it.

Two Rings

+<+ +<+ +<+

*I*t is a little-acknowledged truth that in couples, the person only slightly less virtuous or slightly less flawed loses all credit or blame for that virtue or flaw, eclipsed by the other's greater valence.

Karen and Huck would have been surprised to learn that Owens thought of Olivia as punctual. The two sat at a table outside Café Pantheon, waiting for her. Olivia, for all her railing about Owens, was often late herself.

"It's really not our business," Karen said.

"See, I'd want you guys to tell me. Promise you will if it ever happens."

"Huck, you're a devil."

"Karen, is there something you know about me already?"

"*No,* Huck. Nothing. But you're just taking this woman's word for it."

"I'm telling you, Jessica wouldn't lie. She's a very sweet person, and she was hurt. Even now she says she's not ready to be with another guy."

"Sounds like a line to me."

"I know, I know. But I'd want to be her friend anyway. And she had no idea Olivia even existed. He was talking as if this was some really serious thing. Once, he brought *Jane* with him, carrying flowers."

"That's really . . ." Karen shook her head as if no word could express her disgust. "So then what happened?"

"After a week or so he freaked out. And she never heard from him again. I don't know, I think we owe it to Olivia."

"None of our business, Huck."

Just then Olivia whizzed by on her bike, calling "hey" over her shoulder.

Karen hissed. "Don't say anything. Promise you'll shut up."

"All right," Huck said, folding his big hands. He squirmed in his seat. It was painful for Huck to keep secrets, and the Michaelises were a secretive family. Since Gunther, Olivia and Nicholas Michaelis moved in with him and his father, when he was a boy, Huck had become excitable and antsy.

Olivia strode over, wearing the jeans she always wore, cloth Chinese slippers and earrings Owens had given her from the Italian Renaissance. The earrings were clear blue, with filigreed gold workings. Their fragile ornateness was set into relief by Olivia's long straight hair.

"You smell good," Huck said.

She shrugged. "Shampoo maybe."

The two cousins talked, as they always did, about their fathers. Gunther Michaelis had become more reclusive, leaving the hotel only once a week. When Olivia had gone by to clean up on Friday and tried to empty the ashtrays, he'd barked, "Leave that be." He'd mimicked and scolded, calling her "little nurse."

Huck shook his head. Otto, his father, a community college professor, whose zeal for petite undergraduates remained undiminished at seventy, was having trouble with his eyes. "I don't know what I'll do if he can't drive." Huck kept his head down and toyed with the salt and pepper shakers. He was a large, thick man, and both his cousins were slender, fine.

"Is something the matter?" Olivia asked.

"No." He shoved his chair back and offered to get them all coffee. "Three blacks?" Their usuals.

"I'll have warm milk with honey," Olivia said.

"Warm milk?"

She put a hand on her stomach. "I might be pregnant."

Huck sat back down, took a sip of water, choked and had to be hit. Karen slapped him hard on the back.

"I haven't told Tom yet," Olivia said. "Just something funny's going on in there. A little fizz."

"But you might be, really?"

"Well, yes, Huck, it's a possibility. I'd like to have a baby someday."

"Olivia, I've got to tell you . . ." His hand was on her arm already. "Now, this is bad—"

Karen groaned and crossed her arms on the table and rested her head inside them as Huck hurtled into his story. Olivia interrupted, sounding cool and rational, to demand dates and names. Karen, waiting for this to end, felt her own breath wet the top of her arm. She should have known there was no stopping him. Asking Huck to keep a secret was asking him to swallow a piece of metal. Huck had taken Olivia's hands now, and she was asking if she could meet the woman. Karen couldn't stand it anymore. She went to get the drinks.

Huck felt a great unburdening, a loosening in his chest.

That night, Jane and Owens waited at the restaurant. "I'm a little worried," Owens said. "Olivia's never late."

When she arrived, Jane was talking and noticed her only because Owens was watching something, rapt. Because he generally appeared last, he rarely beheld the spectacle of Olivia's entrance. She possessed two striking physical features: her verticality and her hair. She was an absolute blonde, a color so rare it lent the expectation of beauty. Olivia's mother had had the same hair. Perhaps it was the daily falling "oh" she saw on faces when she turned around that made her appearance painful to her. She'd not lived long enough to go gray.

Olivia slid into her chair, crossing her arms. "I know about Jessica, Tom."

"Jessica who?" Owens said.

"I don't see why you had to drag Jane into it. You could carry your own flowers."

"I don't know what you're talking about."

"You do too," Jane said.

Owens sighed, then stood up enough to reach his keys from his pocket. "Jane, do me a favor. Go out and wait in the car a minute. I need to talk to Olivia alone."

A table had never looked so sumptuous, light hiding in the folds of the cloth, the earthen pitcher releasing tiny beads of water, a candle flame, its blue stamen and the rich, thick yellow. Ice tinkled, somewhere.

Olivia was reaching slowly under the curtains of her hair, to unlatch the earrings. She laid them on Owens' bare white plate.

Jane walked in a straight line, hands at her sides.

"Guilt jewels," was the last thing she heard.

She tried to companion herself with a song, but she couldn't re-member many words. Girls at school knew whole lyrics, the ones with older sisters or brothers.

Keys were unnecessary. The door was open. She locked it, though, from inside. The car was cold. The restaurant door opened, closed, but they didn't come out. On the far corner was an empty phone booth. Quarters lay on the carpeted car floor. She could go and call her mom. Her mom would come. But would they get mad then? Maybe they'd run out any minute, beckoning her to her steaming dinner. She couldn't decide. She waited, picking at a scab. It was a yellow one, old, too tough to be good. The good ones were thick and black-red.

Owens had no idea that she knew how to drive. He'd never believed her. He thought Mary had driven her here and then gone back, or else got someone to give Jane a ride. Why the truck remained, if Mary had gone back, didn't seem to intrigue him at all, or the mystery of the driver.

Jane hadn't had the opportunity to drive again since that night years before. She still wanted to talk about it, but her mother wanted to for-get. Mary considered Jane's voyage the greatest blot on her otherwise clear-souled motherhood. She now told Jane she'd learn to drive at the regular age, like everybody else.

Jane put the keys in the ignition, and the motor caught. Figuring out how to adjust the seat took a long time, but with the push of a button Jane accomplished what her mother had taken months to contrive, with sewn-in telephone books and screwed-on blocks of wood so her legs could reach the gas and clutch and brake. She sat ready then, strapped in, but she couldn't find the lights. She gave up and decided to go in the dark.

He loved this car. The fear of what he'd do terrified and thrilled her, but as soon as she was out onto the wide dark street, she knew that if anything went wrong she'd just keep driving. The steering wheel felt tight, but a little touch to the gas, and the car sped out. She didn't know where to go. He would still come back out for her, probably. And he'd see the spot where the car had been.

Then, on the sidewalk, she saw two girls she knew from school, taking fast little steps on both sides of a man who must have been their father. She felt like ducking but sped up instead. It wasn't like that first day. Now she knew people here.

She coasted back slowly, around the block. The restaurant door was still shut. She parked not where the car had been but on the opposite side of the street, going the other way.

Olivia knew he considered it unseemly: her wish to hand herself up to him, a pale translucent liquid in a glass jar. In Olivia's early love for Owens, everything seemed touched. She'd tried, for the sake of his judgment, to keep at least an appearance of interest in her life. But the same quality of erasure that made him queasy and slightly irritable during the day called up his most desperate cries at night. She gave herself to him entirely, and he accepted the enormity of her gift. Her pitched upper arms felt thin, grasping. She wore herself out against him, like the thinnest fabric, until she was raw.

Now, for a long time, it had been different. She was less young. She still felt the urge to pour herself into a small jar and hand it up to him, but he did not feel the same way.

Olivia scratched like a detective, trying to amass evidence of some evil. Jessica was proof. Having the material exhibit of what she'd suspected, she was relieved of a long haunting. It wasn't just me, she said to herself. She felt frantic and somehow excited. *Now we're finally getting somewhere.*

Owens admitted his wrong and apologized. He attempted to convince her one more time to try. "We're not kids anymore. We shouldn't be living like this." When he looked at her, he saw lines at the corners of her eyes. For the first time, he understood how you could love a woman as she grew old.

But Olivia reared up. The power of beauty could equal the power of power. It was in her, something she had and counted on. She felt rage and bearing, dignity. She could walk.

"Livia, let's move into the new place and start over."

She knew he believed he was her last best chance. But who could say whether fortune was more lasting than beauty? One was made of harder substance, but if she couldn't hold him, perhaps she would undo him first.

She stood up and pushed her chair back.

He pulled her hand down again. "Don't, Olivia. Forgive me. Try."

The most profound and also the kindest feeling they had for each other was pity. Each felt the other had lost, early on, the gift that allows most people, some of the time, to know happiness.

They touched with the tips of their fingers, but she refused to take his earrings again.

Jane at last got to eat. Owens ordered double portions for the table, not only entrées but appetizers, side dishes and dessert. Jane held the big spoon with her right hand and pushed vegetables onto it with her left. Her chin tilted down close to the plate. Occasionally, she looked up from eating. Olivia spooned beautifully.

When they left, Jane watched Owens find the car, then look at the spot across the street. He rubbed his eyebrows, as if he were counting animals in a procession no one else could see.

Olivia was a reader, and though Owens was impressed and consoled by the paperback European novels she carried around, it nonetheless made her hard to live with. At night, she liked to read in bed. He wanted them to talk or lie in the dark with the windows open and maybe a candle on, looking up at the sky. Her lamp wiped out the stars.

Also, he wanted to watch movies on TV. He liked it that she read, but he wished she could do it some other time of day. He thought she should be a teacher, like her cousin.

But Olivia was out of sorts when she wasn't reading a book, and she favored the great accounts of evil. In the beginning, Owens felt humbled when she read aloud stories of prisoners in gulags, Jews and Gypsies in camps, American Indians dying of European diseases. She deliberately sought out books about the worst extremities of humanity, it seemed, and more and more he was beginning to suspect that she identified the kapos and conquistadores with him. This bothered him.

"Comere," he said, standing at the open door to the patio. His bare foot rocked an anthill. "Before I can Susan and Stephen, I should get them to do something about all these weeds. And there's a beehive over there."

Outside, on the terrace, amidst the dark-blue night, Olivia stood by herself, hands jammed in her pockets. "Are you changing your mind," she asked him, staring. "Do you think Jane is yours now?"

She asked him again later, in bed. He turned over, holding a fist of covers, and closed his eyes against her reading lamp.

Love was strange, lying in bed with a man every night. She had no doubt that he would soon find himself in difficult conditions at work. He would be capable of great sacrifice and personal deprivation, somehow gathering his power. He would survive.

Her father once said, "I wish to perish in the first wave," when she'd asked why he wasn't building a bomb shelter, when all the other men were.

Owens was not like her father, and Olivia loved her father. But she remembered that all his life and even now, the man lying next to her with his eyes closed, a good day's exertion on his features, did not live in the regular outside world. Where he lived, the fundamental question was and always would be survival. Which was perhaps the greatest force of her attraction to him, the drive surpassing even desire; or perhaps that was desire, because her sympathies were always, would always be, with the weaker side. "Let me perish in the first wave," her father had said, in his light way, years before when the world was younger and bomb shelter building seemed preventative, almost optimistic in its carpentry. Now the first wave had perished and she had accidentally survived, a little dazed, wondering not how she had managed but for what, exactly, in a world so tilted and maimed.

She tented her book and pranced to the bathroom. Olivia was not generally a prancer, but his floor was cold, the bathroom down a long hall. They'd slept on this futon in this house hundreds of nights, but Olivia still felt shy going to the bathroom. She closed the door now, with her bare foot, and in the white cold room, she liked to imagine she was alone and he couldn't hear her. She couldn't have explained this furtive fastidiousness. Olivia wasn't squeamish. She worked in a hospital, after all. But she was conscious of the fragility of Owens' romance. The movies he liked and the stories he favored all involved heroes and heroines who were grand and clean.

Once, after making love in the middle of the day, he put on new underwear, and as he snapped the elastic, she could tell the clean dry cloth made him feel safe, like the last of his mother.

Huck waited while Olivia peed into a small plastic vial. The walls of her apartment were so flimsy he heard the water splashing and her nervous laughter over it. At her tiny kitchen table they administered the blue powder that came with the kit, using tweezers. Nothing made Huck so buoyant as helping Olivia.

Together they stared at the vial. It was turning deep blue. Huck got up to rub her shoulders. The kit said even faint blue was an indication.

She felt something then, strange in her belly, connected by a hairline to her jaw, which made her queasy, quick to gag.

"You can't tell anybody, Huck," she said. He was massaging her back, and she curled her shoulders, because he was coming too close to her sides. "And remember, Huck, you promised never to tell anybody about that other thing."

Years earlier, practically in childhood, Olivia and Huck had once been in a bed and taken their clothes off. The memory was something that still agitated Olivia. She believed she had benefited from her unusual childhood, except for that one night. Olivia had begged Huck to keep it secret, and to the best of her knowledge he had. But it worried her: she knew it was something Owens would not easily abide. She'd had to ask Huck again, although she hated to bring it up at all, because even talking about it seemed to include them in a primitive intimacy.

Huck knelt in front of her, hands on her knees. "Of course I wouldn't, Livia."

Even now, Olivia didn't know why she'd done it. He'd wanted to. They had been living together, she and Huck and her brother, Nicholas. They had been young and very poor, and she was their wealth.

Huck did remember that night, but not the way she assumed. He remembered bumbling, touching her mildly, trying to make her feel good. He revered Olivia and always felt a little guilty for the relief he gained when she was suffering; only when he was performing some service for her did he feel worthy of her company at all.

"He says he loves me more than anything else in the world, and then he leaves me alone in the car. He wouldn't leave a bag of money alone, but he left me in an unlocked car." Jane had delivered this little speech several times already when she repeated it for Julie and Peter. They were sitting around the remains of dinner at the table Julie had bought years before at the flea market.

"He left you for how long?" Peter asked.

The truth was Jane didn't know. She'd said forty-five minutes when her mother first asked, and now she tried not to think about it.

"That's terrible," Julie said.

Peter shook his head, arms crossed. "Like a kid, your dad."

"I don't know if I should even let him take her without me," Mary said.

Jane had enjoyed the meal when Owens finally came to get her. He'd hugged her to his side and they'd laughed, even Olivia. But when she came home and told her mother, she didn't ever get to that part. Her mother got too angry. As Jane was talking now, she remembered the glove compartment: he did leave money in his car.

"He just doesn't *get* it," Mary said.

Jane hadn't spoken to Owens since he'd had that fight on the phone with her mother, insisting it was fifteen minutes, not forty-five. "I believe my daughter over you, for God's sake!" she'd screamed, and then hung up.

"What if you made sure she had a quarter for a phone every time she went out with him, so between you and us, somebody could pick her up."

"She's a kid, Peter; she's not supposed to have to do that." Mary spit this out with such venom that Peter skidded his chair back.

"I still don't see what the harm would be in getting a solid child-support agreement," Julie said. "I mean, he's not giving you a *gift* every month, Mary. That's money you've earned."

"There's more than child support, though," Mary said. "There's a lot that's Owens and Mary, not just Owens and Jane."

Julie had heard this before. It seemed important to Mary to convince people that Owens cared for her. Only occasionally she slipped off the belief, when jagged facts made it impossible to sustain. Mary worried what would become of them if he ran for president and moved to Washington. She thought he could rig anything, even elections. It never occurred to her that he too might have silly hopes a sturdy woman would laugh off. You couldn't conduct a conversation of an hour's length with her without his name coming up. Whether he was God or the devil, he was never very far away.

"Peter's right," Jane said. "I'll call next time, so let's talk about something else."

She realized, with shame, that she and her mother used to build huge constructions in the air to convince people he was the monster. She couldn't possibly admit that she loved him. She understood, now, that all the years they'd talked about him later into the night, making him worse and worse, it had been a kind of love, and either one of them would have turned if he'd picked her. And Owens had picked Jane.

Olivia wanted to get married. All of a sudden, she knew that. Karen Croen had been urging her to for years, and now the idea pressed on her intermittently through the day. Emptying a bedpan, hosing it with the rubber shower end, she gagged and rested her forehead against the cool industrial tile. She imagined cleaning a kitchen in a house that was hers. Regardless of what he thought of her for it, she wanted some of the regular things.

That night, they drove up to the city for a big dinner. She wore the dress he'd once criticized but now seemed fond of; as they were dressing, he played with the sash. She was seated next to one of the five men in suits, Jane on her other side. Owens had invited Jane along, and here she was wearing jeans at a black-tie dinner.

"Here's looking at you, kid," one of the five men said to Olivia, with an expression of approval. In return, she lifted her water glass. Later, in the middle of dinner, he leaned over and whispered, "You want him to marry you, we'll get him to. Don't you worry about that. Course he will, darling. He knows what's good for him, especially when I tell him. It's good as done."

Jane watched while Olivia stalled, her hair falling over her face. Her hair is so pretty, Jane thought, a color almost not any color.

"Okay." Olivia smiled. "I do."

Jane knew Olivia must have wanted it a lot, to say that with her there, because she could tell her mother. She understood, better than her mother or Olivia, that the two women were not really friends.

Driving back on the wide, empty highway, Owens told Olivia about these men who long before had offered to wage his campaign. "How's she doing back there?" he asked.

"Fast asleep," Olivia said.

"She's so pretty," he said in a burst. "If I were a guy that age, I'd really go for her."

Olivia felt a pang. He'd said nothing at all about her tonight. But that was the way he was; he made the women in his life jealous of each other. And she wondered, as they drove in the dark, what if Jane had been a less attractive child? She was bright and pretty and a lot like him. An asset, easy to claim. But if she'd been ugly or disabled? Then suddenly, Olivia wondered if their own child could be.

Jane did tell her mother when she got home. Mary wished she could remember the bald man's name. They both felt amazed that there was someone above Owens who could make him behave.

＊

Huck ran into Mary di Natali at the Harvest Mall, walking with her head bent, examining a small slip of paper. He tapped her shoulder, then gave her a sideways hug. They walked together as she continued to study the slip, and then she blurted, "I knew it. He didn't give me the thirty percent off. Oh, excuse me, I've got to go back. This was supposed to be on sale."

For no reason, except that she was upset, Huck followed along. They hadn't seen each other since the November night in a New Orleans hotel room when, sitting cross-legged on the bed, she'd told him she wasn't attracted to him and he'd given her money for a taxi to the airport. He was surprised to discover that now, more than a year later, he felt no anger towards her. As always, he wanted to help, to prop her up, to convince her she was just as good as the others. He ended up on the fifth floor of a department store, in the ladies' coat section. Mary approached the desk with her head lowered but with a tone of such bitter grievance that Huck put his large hand on her shoulder and spoke himself. "Excuse me, but I'm afraid we thought this coat was on sale. . . ."

The young man behind the desk, politely relieved, spoke only to Huck.

Mary took the raincoat out of the bag to try it on again. While most people's concern went to Jane, Huck had always felt a particular sympathy for Mary. She tied the belt and turned around. The coat didn't flatter her; its color tinged her complexion green, and she looked shapeless.

Huck scratched his head. Jane, dressed by Mary, had always looked very snappy, so why couldn't she pick the right things for herself? He immediately pitied her predicament.

"Oh, Mary," he burst out, spotting a yellow slicker hanging on display. "Why don't you try that one? The color's so nice. Let me find it in your size."

The yellow coat looked a hundred times better. Her complexion returned. The coat latched with metal buckles, but somehow you could sense Mary's delicacy inside it.

"You like it?" Mary said, then sighed. "Oh, this one's not on sale."

"I'll buy it for you," Huck said, his arms shooting out in exuberance, forgetting for the moment that—given what Olivia told him—Mary lived on more money than he and all the other teachers he knew.

The salesman confirmed the superiority of the coat and began the paperwork of exchange. They settled that Huck would pay the difference.

Mary decided to wear the coat, and she liked it better every time they passed a mirror. Huck felt delighted to see her sneaking looks. He didn't think of her as someone who looked in mirrors. On the escalator going down, she began to tell him about her grievance with Olivia, not just Owens, for leaving Jane in the car.

"Oh, Mary, don't be mad at her for that. That was a terrible night, and it was all my fault. See, I'd told her about an affair Owens had had that she didn't know about, and it was the same day she thought she might be pregnant." The minute Huck said that, his hand on Mary's shoulder, he remembered he'd promised not to tell anyone. Oh, well, he quickly allowed, that had been the lesser secret. The other he would never tell.

But Mary pounced on the information. "She's having a *baby*?"

"Mary, I really shouldn't have told you. It's a secret, kind of, so don't say anything. I just didn't want you to be mad at her."

"But I'm glad I know. I should know. If he has another child, that'll affect Jane."

"Please, Mary, promise you won't say anything." He turned around backwards on the escalator, hands out, beseeching.

"I have to go, Huck." She ran out at the bottom of the escalator. The pain returned, her sacrifice. And she'd given away hers for him.

When Huck arrived at the bungalow, Jane was already sobbing on the floor. Mary was in her room with the door closed. He tried to talk to Jane, but she just hid her face in her arms, and thinking a woman might be able to help, he called Olivia. She sighed, not even sounding surprised, and said she'd be right over. And then there was nothing to do but pace and wait. Suddenly, Mary emerged from her doorway, looking blank and angry.

"Surely—oh, please don't cry. . . . Mary, it's not what you think."

She ignored him and sat down by Jane. Huck had rarely felt so helpless. He offered to take them all for ice cream, and no one even answered his suggestion.

Then Olivia came, and Huck stood back. Jane was still on the floor, with Olivia kneeling in front of her, saying, "A lot of times, I'm jealous of you. Because you're blood."

Olivia drove up to the old Copper King's mansion and waited for Owens in bed. Now she had to tell him. He'd always been bothered by her lack of virginity. He counted back the number of men who'd "been" with her. When he'd asked about her ex-boyfriends, his mouth went a certain way. She lied a little. He thought there were four.

Olivia needed a moment of stillness to remember she hadn't done anything wrong. It had been her youth, and the men she'd slept with she'd loved or thought she loved. Owens' idea of goodness was so fragile it could be corrupted by something as natural as breeze.

It's a small thing I do, she thought, not even nurse, but he really did save lives. Owens was always trying to get her to admit the enormity of it. And though Olivia would've liked them to be even, he had done that one great thing.

To say that Olivia was a nurse's aide was true and missed the point. She was not like Owens. For Olivia, there was such a thing as a job. She made decent money and had for some years now. She believed this marked her as an adult, distinct from, say, Mary, who enchanted her as a watercolor might.

Olivia told Owens when he came in and knelt on the futon. He suggested they take sweatshirts and get in the car and drive. There were things she knew in him that no one else knew. She slept in the back seat while he drove, but when he stopped at Buck Meadows, she got up and helped pitch the tent, and they laughed all night. They woke up early, drenched from the damp ground and aching.

"I was thinking we should go away," he said. "Live on the banks of the Ganges and think about God all day."

"Don't ever forget you were like this," she begged, taking his hand.

Then she gulped. "Why don't you give it all away? I promise you won't be sorry."

"I don't think I can. I mean, who am I going to give it to?"

"The poor."

"Which poor? It's not enough to go around. So the question is, are you just going to be cavalier about it or are you going to really do your homework? It's like business. You want the most bang for your buck."

"Okay. So do your homework, then."

"My homework would take years, though. I don't know anything about charities. Most of what I know is what you and everybody else know, and that's that they don't work very well or the world wouldn't be what it is. I always figured the best thing to do is just park it someplace and then take ten years and decide."

"It'll never be just us, will it?"

He took her chin and turned it to the sky. That was Wednesday.

On Saturday, they went to the city to look in stores for ancient carpets and tables like the ones Franciscan brothers had used. Before and after work, Owens drove to the new house. Nights, they slept in the Copper King's mansion, Olivia tucked under his arm, watching silvery miniatures of Ingrid Bergman falling in love.

It was hard for Owens to believe that a woman like Bergman was not alive and young, somewhere. When he read in a magazine on Monday that she had a daughter attending graduate school in New York City, he idly dialed the number of some advertising men he knew in Manhattan, who offered to make inquiries. He was listed in that same magazine as one of America's twelve most eligible bachelors. Kathleen had brought it in. He carried it around with him and on Tuesday presented it to Olivia as a kind of gift.

That afternoon, Owens had a reaction akin to waking up. The man from the jewelry store left two messages about stones transferred from a large safe in Texas. Every hour now, he felt pressure from Rooney. He had no time to plan a wedding, and that was exactly the kind of thing Olivia couldn't do right. He'd thought of the chapel Saint Francis built in Assisi, or, right here, Alta's first church. In the middle pencil tray of his desk drawer at work, he kept the slender ring that had been his mother's.

He needed two quarters, maybe three. Tomorrow he had to fire his chief crystallographer, which was going to be hard because Theo had been with him since the beginning. But Exodus had to come first.

That night he confessed to Olivia. "A lot of people are depending on me. They've got families. And for us, too, maybe we should get our house in order and then, in a year or so . . . I don't know, I've just been getting kind of sick whenever I think of it."

He made all his claims on behalf of others. It wouldn't be fair to them. He was always a we, even without her. And her needs were only for herself.

On Friday, Olivia went to the doctor's office and had an abortion. She told Owens that night, after it was done. When he understood what had happened, he began a long, slow sinking, nothing at all like the freedom he'd imagined, the freedom he thought he'd had before.

Olivia and Owens would never fully understand the end of that mutual week-long dream, because Gunther Michaelis got sick again four days later. This time was the real time, according to his doctor; the tumor was most likely inoperable, and in a typical storm of perversity the old man had refused all treatment and was simply preparing himself to die. Olivia's brother, in New Orleans, spent the day making and canceling plane reservations, deliberating and then apologizing too long.

For the first time ever, Olivia asked Owens for money, and he gave it to her with relief. She moved Gunther Michaelis out of his hotel, into a furnished two-bedroom apartment, where she and Huck camped out, to accompany him in his final days. The dinette looked out on the public garden Noah's father had made.

Olivia cooked for them all. Every night, she made her father meat, because he liked it. They pooled their finances and every supper became a feast, with roasts and chops, potatoes, a dessert. The main thing Olivia ate during this time was rice. She'd boil a pot of white rice and eat it with cinnamon-sugar and milk, the way her mother had fixed it.

Owens visited, but he was clearly a stranger in this apartment, where the floors were strewn with flannel shirts and books he'd never heard of. Olivia's father had never liked Owens and made no effort to hide it. "When did I ever say I liked you?" he asked, the third night there, and then looked blankly up at him like an owl.

Her father's illness was a marathon Olivia had nothing to compare to. Huck had written a master's thesis and that, like this, had been a period when time ceased to be marked by the conventions of weeks and hours but moved rather by internal measure, broken only with the repeated interruptions of meals and sleep. Olivia and Huck went through work by rote, watching the clock. Neither of them had a job that matched the intensity of life in the apartment, where everything was rented.

Gunther had few possessions. He'd lived for years in a small room with a kitchenette in the Presidente Hotel. But he now made an elaborate ritual of distributing what remained.

Otto Lark drove up the fifth night in his rickety convertible. The two men laughed and drank in the bedroom, speaking the faraway language their children never learned. As men, their lives had been as different as two lives that started from the same point could be. At twenty they had both been handsome, at least as they remembered themselves, and full of expectation. Otto loved literature and hoped to be a poet, and Gunther intended to paint; neither became what he loved. Otto spent years chasing the fleeting happiness he had known in his youth, with flat-chested women in his classes every semester. Gunther loved direly and only once. His wife had stolen his ability to paint when she'd stunned him with her greater talent. After she took her life, there had been nothing left to give him pleasure. But the two men sang songs from their youth, and before he went, Otto danced around the small living room with Olivia.

"I promised him you'd come over to eat once a week," Otto said. "Because I'll be the only one you have. Your mother was such a woman. He never got over her."

"She's a lot like her mother, don't you think, Dad?" Huck said.

Otto looked at Olivia sharply, as if for the first time. "I don't see it."

Olivia's brother, Nicholas, was always far. For three years now, he'd lived away from their family and not come home. For him especially, Olivia thought, their father was dying too soon. His father's decline had snatched away Nicholas' anger and left him mute. In only one year, Olivia thought, he could have come back as a man, with something of his own.

Near the end, Olivia had thanked Nora for letting her come, because she'd never had a chance to nurse her own mother. Nora had told her she would love her whatever she did and to go out and try to find a nice life for herself, one where she felt comfortable. The last time Olivia saw her was a cool, sunny day, and Nora wanted to sit outside. Olivia helped her sit down on the cement step, slipping a blanket under her loose buttocks. A watery wind bent the long grasses.

"He's my son," Nora had said, "but if he's not good to you, you go find somebody who is, who makes you feel real nice. Because you're a good girl, a good, good girl."

The first Sunday Owens came to the apartment, he found Olivia roasting prime rib. He drove to the bungalow, where Mary gave him leftovers.

"How's Olivia?" she asked.

"Well, you know her dad's sick."

"But she's not sick at all?"

"Oh, no, she's fine."

"God, I was so sick. I threw up almost every day."

Owens looked at her sternly. "You know we're not having the baby."

"No," Jane said.

"How would we know?" Mary asked, her eyes closing.

"I thought I told you," he said.

Jane pushed up in a jerk. She ran to her room and slammed the door.

"Why are we always the last to know? Doesn't your own daughter matter?"

"Leave me alone," Jane shouted through the door. She could hear the siss of shoe soles on the sidewalk. I am the one child, she thought, out of three who could have been. She remembered the long-ago picture of the man she thought was her father. She was almost as old now as him.

That night, Gunther Michaelis called Olivia and Huck to his bedroom and made his request, breaking into wicked fits of laughter. He relished outwitting the young doctor. His plan was to die when he wanted to die, not to wait one minute longer. "I've got the pills," he announced with glee, sweeping the plastic canister from under his pillow and brandishing it before their astonished faces. "I stole them."

Of course this was not all. He wanted them to help. Olivia and Huck tried to talk him out of it, but it was no use. His only interest at this late moment seemed to be in thwarting the doctor, fixed in his mind as a stand-in for the forces arrayed against him. One night, he repeated, they were to help him. Not yet, but soon. They would read the poetry of Rainer Maria Rilke, they would tell each other the burdens of their souls, then they would say goodbye and "put me to sleep," he said. "I want Nicholas here too."

And so Olivia and Huck and later Nicholas entered into another secret, a secret greater than any they'd known so far. Also, what they planned to do was at this time illegal in the state of California and punishable by law.

The next morning, Olivia sat at the kitchen table eating muesli, her mother's recipe, with lemon and oats, and fresh fruit chopped into it. Her mother bought good food, Olivia thought with consolation, even when they were poor. She took joy in it. Olivia was reading the newspaper.

"I heard you up," her father said. Disheveled by sleep, his curly hair stood straight. His face seemed even longer than usual, and his front tooth that was gray, overlapping the other, made him look almost tender. For the thousandth time in her life, Olivia was fooled.

"Sit down," she said, giving him her chair. "Eat my breakfast."

He sat and ate obediently.

"I made it like mom," she said.

The electric clock in this kitchen that had nothing to do with them hummed.

"Go ahead and marry him, then. You'll be rich, if he'll have you. Maybe you're just the one he wants to play with. If he thinks he's too young for a family."

Olivia's mind swept in great arcs for ways he could have known—the pads she'd bled into she'd carefully taken out to the garbage cans behind the building—until she realized with a stop that it was Huck. Of course Huck had told.

"I've got something to give you from your mother. It's nothing like what he can give if he wants you. You don't have his earrings anymore, I see."

"They're at home," Olivia lied.

More than anything Owens could give, Olivia wanted the earrings her mother had worn every day, or the bracelet she'd saved for special nights. Her usually guarded heart leapt ahead to gratitude, and she fell on his neck, kissing him.

"Get off me and let me eat my breakfast." That was like him and didn't bother her.

She sat for a moment on her hands, waiting with the happiness we feel when anticipation is accompanied by certainty. They were opals, both the earrings and the bracelet, its special little chain underneath to make sure something so precious could never be lost. Her mother had been buried with her ring, as Gunther had insisted, so she would always be claimed.

"Here," he said gruffly, "open your hand. She wanted me to buy this for you before you were even born." His fingers pushed something into her palm. It was a child's ring, gold, like the one her mother still wore, with a small opal in its center. "If you ever have a girl," he said, shrugged once, and then continued eating.

Olivia had a premonition that her brother wouldn't come to the funeral and that she would have to help him live with that.

But he came now. And then it was inevitable that Huck felt left out, as he always had. Nicholas and Olivia got tired of telling him he was no intrusion, that they wanted him there, but they began to feel that his constant need for reassurance really was an intrusion.

Their father changed every day, sometimes between morning and evening. One of his last possessions was a pair of pipes, fitted in a latched case, he'd been given by his grandfather when he went to university in Stockholm. One night, he slept with them, guarding them jealously, saying he couldn't decide yet to whom he'd present them. Nicholas very badly wanted the pipes, but he wasn't about to say anything. The next morning, the old man asked Olivia to take them away.

"Have you decided who you'd like me to give them to?"

"Throw them out, for all I care. It's no concern of mine."

Olivia offered the pipes to Nicholas, but he declined. With a stepchild's greed, Huck gladly accepted, justifying himself with the idea that he would save them and someday give them to Nick.

That night, there was a rasp on the door. It was Melinda, Nicholas' high school girlfriend, who'd continued to sleep with his shirt every night long after they broke up, and whom he scorned. She'd evidently heard Nicholas was back in town, and she brought a cobbler she'd baked, with peaches, blueberries and figs, the tin loaf pan warm through the towel. Olivia thanked her, taking it. Her hands were long and white; she'd baked with hope. And Nicholas ate it. They all did, on Gunther Michaelis' bed, after she left.

The third Sunday, Gunther Michaelis demanded a party. It was a clear summer night, typical of Alta in August, and Olivia and Huck reluctantly turned their thoughts outside the apartment and called the people they knew by rote to be their friends, although they hadn't seen them or truly thought about them for what seemed like such a long time. Nicholas, in his own mumbled gesture, went to the store and bought a fifty-dollar bottle of brandy.

Karen Croen came with Dave and offered Gunther a massage. He allowed her his shoulders while he sat in the recliner Nicholas and Huck had carried outside. Uncle Otto and Owens busied themselves making a fire. Jane and Mary brought Amber and Ruby, who knew Gunther from the bookstore. Melinda came with two pies, which

Nicholas tasted and complimented, but not within her hearing. Noah came to his father's garden, for an hour from the lab, where he and Louise were keeping vigil. Gunther had given him an extravagant gift that he still had, and he could recall Olivia's envy. It was an antique paint-by-numbers set depicting a horse in a field. In those years, her father called Noah "little gnome" and told everyone that he would be an artist. His own children's lives, he said, were too soft. Noah never completed painting in the little puzzle shapes, but his sister had, and the set gave his mother the idea that she could earn money from painting, even from a small California town. She wrote to the Canadian address on the inside of the thirty-year-old box and found her employment for the next eleven years.

Owens' father and sister hauled in a bushel basket of apricots. When each person arrived bearing perishable gifts, Olivia felt an unaccountable, immense gratitude. As if what she'd ever done in her life was productive only in luring one more person here to honor him. She counted numbers and felt satisfied with each new friend. They left the door of the apartment open so they could hear the telephone, and three people called.

By the end, forty-five people stood around the fire, singing songs and eating the homemade delicacies, and not one of them, even those who knew Gunther, came because of him.

Owens remained from first to last, making himself useful. Olivia seemed impassive, and he didn't want to disturb her facade. In her proximity to death, she too seemed to be living on a different plane. But they needed to talk.

He told Mary he'd wished a hundred times in the past weeks that he and Olivia still had the baby. What if Olivia hadn't been so swift to act on his passing doubt? The next day might have found him given to settlement. He confessed he often caught himself forgetting, swimming in the full daydream.

"A long time after this is over," he finally whispered to Olivia, "I hope we can go back to where we were and think of fixing up our house and starting a family."

"But it's your house," she said. "It's not our house." Her eyes were big, and she stared into the dwindling fire.

He took her hand and pushed on his mother's ring, which he'd had enlarged.

She wasn't used to wearing rings. The small, sharp stone hurt the fingers on either side.

The next day, Gunther Michaelis decided it was time. They read poetry about angels and he said goodbye first to Huck, thanking him, in a formal manner, for gracing his broken but beautiful family. "We shall always be indebted to you for your gravity and humor," he said, "qualities we don't organically abound in." Then he called his children to his sides. "I loved you both," he said quickly, "but forget about me." They stayed on his bed, each tucked under an arm that stayed warm for a long time after his breathing stopped, until they had cramps and shooting pains in their knees and Olivia's foot fell asleep.

Then they turned on all the lights in the house and worked in a frenzy. It was the last day of the month, and Gunther had decided he didn't want them to pay another rent. They had to clean everything out and be ready to give the apartment back by the morning. Huck took the towels and sheets to an all-night laundry. Olivia collected the food in the house and drove it to a shelter, where she left it outside the front door. Ants would almost surely get it by dawn. But it was too late to ring doorbells.

Later, she dallied in the living room. Boxes lined the wall; most everything was done. She'd swept the kitchen and cleaned the outside of the stove. She knew she should call Owens, but didn't. Why not let him sleep. She didn't feel like talking. She wasn't upset but flat, and it seemed to her everything now could easily wait until morning.

In her back pocket, she found a folded-up article he'd given her that listed him as one of America's top twelve bachelors. He had handed her the article with a gleam of humor and even a shy promise that he was hers now, no longer eligible; but at this moment it annoyed her. Her parents were both dead, and there would be no record, not even an obituary in the Alta *Sentinel*. Owens was a man whose name and picture already belonged to the kind of immortality offered by the printed page. Thousands of words in magazines had been devoted to him, he already occupied a place in several encyclopedias, and people whose names were printed in books seemed to exist differently in life.

Perhaps that night even Olivia felt a need as intense as that for love or creation, for at least a small fraction of immortality.

She tore into the first box of books. At the bottom she found the red Webster's Ninth Collegiate Dictionary. With trembling fingers, she searched the Biography section in the back. There was only one Owen, and that was Wilfred. She sank down against the hard wall, relieved to find Owens' name absent. She knew it was the dictionary he considered to be standard.

With that one small consolation, she felt she could now fall asleep.

Election

❧ ❧ ❧ ❧ ❧ ❧

*F*our years earlier, Owens had gone away for a weekend alone. He'd driven eight hours into the mountains and slept in a sleeping bag all night. He'd said he was going to figure out what would be harder than what he'd already done. He wasn't shooting for what they said about him anymore, he told Jane; he'd slipped free of that and was doing this for himself. He said he just wanted to keep interested. And up there, he'd decided to run for governor. He'd announced his intention to the men who promised to organize his campaign.

But the four years had not proceeded as Owens planned. And Jane understood that it was one thing not to care what "they" said about you when it was adulation; it was another altogether to ignore daily newspaper columns cataloguing your failures.

So now, as Owens drove to the hotel where he and his advisers would decide over breakfast whether to announce his candidacy, Jane interpreted his silence as dejection. He left his new house fully intending to say no; he told her that. A lot had apparently changed since his first heady days of conference calls, when the five men broke in on each other like a team of acrobats pyramiding. Things with Rooney had gone badly. And Rooney worked. Every day, Owens said, he felt Rooney's activity like the unpleasant buzz of a persistent, elusive fly. Olivia wasn't the same either, but Jane didn't know how that figured in.

Still, before he dropped her off at school, he described rooms he'd seen on a private tour of the White House, as if they might live there one day. Jane knew that to his way of thinking there was no contradiction between this and his current abstention. He didn't vote because right now, he said, there wasn't anyone really good to vote for. If and when there was, he would.

Jane understood his dread. No one likes to tell people who believe in you that you're quitting. He hadn't talked to the five men for a while, except the one guy who'd told him to marry Olivia. "She's ready," that guy had said. "Don't let her get away." Owens only smiled. He thought the guy had a crush on her.

Owens had the sort of imagination that precluded lapses of reality. Jane suspected it would be hard for him to imagine a love affair with a woman who'd been married before or had another man's child. And when he stopped at her school and she got out of the car, Jane understood that after this morning the White House would be harder to conjure.

He entered the hotel ready to resist their entreaties and promise that a time would come later for public life. He'd never considered himself a businessman, really. What he thought he was had been less clear, and different on different days: some days a scientist, others a teacher, most days more of an artist.

"I remember when you were a poet," Mary had said the night before. "I liked you best then."

"Maybe I still am a poet, but I'm just expressing myself in different ways."

"Poets write poetry," Jane had yelled from the bathroom, where she was fastening a brown bow to her hair.

He'd always told people he wasn't a businessman. It's easier to teach science nerds about business, he'd said, than it is to teach businessmen our philosophy. Now, walking through the opulent hallway to the conference room, he suddenly wanted nothing more than to be a businessman and a good one.

The five men were sitting, but he remained upright. "I think I probably owe you guys an apology," he started. "Because I'm going to have to say no this time around." And as he enumerated his binding responsibilities, they broke in and finished his sentences for him. *Of course* Genesis needed him now. "First things first." "Family time." "Too long a commute to Sacramento." They urged him to sit down.

No, he thought, in point of fact the capital wasn't far. He could drive it in three hours. Or he could get a private plane: a small gray one with rounded wings against the pale-blue Central Valley sky. As a boy he'd loved *Sky King,* a TV show about a rancher who flew his own plane.

"Time's not ripe," said the one who'd told him to marry Olivia.

That was it, Owens understood. They didn't want him now.

"Perfectly all right. Give you two time to put your house in order. Maybe have yourself a wedding. Baby or two."

For no reason at all, Owens picked up a doughnut and examined it. He hadn't eaten a doughnut in maybe twenty years. He bit into the soft, powdered-sugar bag and his teeth cringed at the chemical jelly.

When he pulled into the Genesis parking lot, the whole place was overrun by workmen. A kid with a whistle and an orange vest, with no shirt underneath, pointed him to the detour. Owens thought of just bumping over the embankment and driving on down to the E Building, but first he wanted to know what they were doing. Probably some routine retarring, but he hadn't noticed any cracks. He opened the window. "Hey, what's going on?"

"Hello, Mr. Owens," the kid said. "Painting. It'll all be done by tomorrow."

"Painting what?

"Lines for parking spaces. We got a chart with everybody's name on it."

Owens waited in his car for the worst, drumming his long fingers on the dash. The kid was running to get the chart.

He sat after he'd found his own name and slot, studying the pattern.

His stall was as far as it could possibly be from the main building, in a lot marked K. It would be a long walk just to the E Building. To get to Genesis, he could gather at a hub where a jitney shuttled back and forth every seven minutes during morning and evening hours.

"You always wanted to be treated like the masses. So I put you in a lot with two hundred people. What's the problem? Now you want to start living like an executive?" That's what Rooney would say. Instead of bumping over the divider and demanding to see Rooney, he backed up quietly and drove to the E Building, aware that this decision was a retreat.

"I just feel like playing hooky," he said to Olivia later on the phone. All day he'd had the tempting urge. He sat with his feet up, fretted a piece of string, thinking of the new house. Today they were repairing the deck. It had been very hard to match the old wood. Owens tried to track down the people whose house it had been, but they'd taken off for a trip around the world, and a month of faxes had not yet turned them up. And then yesterday Mary and one of her weird friends came by, and Amber said she remembered when the house was built. Owens asked if she knew what made the wood that nice color. She said, "Of course I do. They used beeswax, is what they used." He tried heating beeswax in a kitchen pot—and sure enough, it worked. Mary felt so excited she'd been able to give him something.

"I hope when it's done," he whispered into the phone, "you'll move there with me." Olivia was quiet these days, always smiling as if she knew some bad truth behind and at the bottom of it all. She'd moved back to the place she hated and spent hours after work roaming through the crumbling mansion. Owens had long since fired Susan and Stephen, but now that they were gone she'd stopped cleaning.

The five men in suits, he'd decided, were only five men. Besides, he'd seen them in grass skirts and muumuus at the Bohemian Club. He could run; not now maybe, but someday. Who needed so-called professionals? They were all Rooneys, watching the weather. He'd never lived his life the straight way, so why should he trust them now?

"I'd rather teach our guys about politics," he explained to Olivia, "than try to make politicians honest."

For a long time now, she'd realized that when he thought his own thoughts, he was practicing for saying them in public.

Olivia, Mary and Jane met Owens in the new house at five o'clock that afternoon to see the finished floors. The hand planing had taken eight months to complete, and Owens made them all take off their shoes. "See, we'll have a little rack built to put shoes on when you come in."

"Will you get slippers to offer people, like in Japan?" Olivia asked.

"No, they can just stay in their socks. Or walk barefoot. Oil from feet is what's really good for floors."

As she untied her laces, Mary felt again she shouldn't be here. Late-afternoon light seemed thrown from buckets into the beautiful, empty rooms.

Owens squatted to glide his hands on the planks. "Feel this." He grabbed Jane's ankle. "Hey, maybe by the time I run for something, you'll be old enough to vote for me."

"Yeah, but how do you know I will?" She ran in her socks, slid. She did it again, then screamed. "Ouch!"

Jane had the first splinter.

"Oh, that's not good," Owens said, frowning. "But I suppose we're not going to be running through here."

He patiently explained everything they'd done, every architectural decision, while Mary massaged her daughter's foot. That splinter would have to come out.

It was "we" again, Olivia thought, listening to him, he and God knows who else. In one place, "they" had raised the overhang of a door to make it symmetrical with another door.

Mary's hands jammed in her pockets as her head curled down. She was thinking how the bungalow could be better, but it couldn't; it was too full of junk, and it didn't get light like this, never. Then, as she followed into the next room, a cry jumped out of her. She too had a splinter.

"Oh, this is seriously not good," Owens said. "I've got to get them back here."

She glared at him for not asking how her foot was or Jane's. All he cared about was his damn floors.

But what he read in her blank stare was incomprehension. She probably did too many drugs in the mountains, he was thinking.

Upstairs, it happened to Olivia. "Whoops!" she said. "Join the club." Then she sat down and pulled her sock off, holding her foot in her hand.

Owens bent over her where she sat cross-legged. "Aw, let me kiss it. Are you okay? Really?" he said in a baby voice, while Mary and Jane just stood staring.

"I'm fine," Olivia said. "But I don't know about your floors."

Then they took turns, one at a time, in the large tiled bathroom, where Owens worked under a bare light with a needle, removing the splinters from each foot.

He sang, "We're here in the middle of winter, and each woman in my life has a splinter."

Owens had said so many times she would be the first female president that Jane decided to run for president of her freshman class. She understood, as he never truly had, that elections were popularity contests.

One afternoon, in the midst of her campaign, Jane visited Julie and the baby. Julie's maternity leave had just run out, and she'd decided to take the year off to be with Coco. The baby let Jane pick her up and clutched her shoulder with tiny hands.

Julie ran to get the Halloween costumes. She'd already bought outfits for this year and next, although the baby was not yet walking. This year's was a bumblebee made of yellow and black felt, with silk silver wings stretched over coat hangers. Next year's was a tinfoil robot. "Some mother must have made these by hand for her children. Peter's great-aunt took me to this incredible shop."

"But what about the other children? That's the only thing I wonder."

"What other children?"

"The children, I mean, not Coco, who don't have a great mom like you who finds them the best Halloween costumes."

"You can have a perfectly happy childhood without homemade Halloween costumes. Coco doesn't know the difference. This is for me, really, and for Peter."

"Oh, I know that. I never had great Halloween costumes either. One year, I was night, and I just rubbed myself all over with coals. And after we moved here we went to the dimestore and bought the ones in packages. Once, I was a fairy princess, all icy blue and glittery. But I mean, what if you stay home and do everything for Coco, like my mom did for me? What about all the other people you might have helped?"

"I had to think about that a lot," Julie said. "And you may decide differently, but I figure there are plenty of people who can do my job. I think I can make more of a difference raising one or two children—"

"See, I bet there's something I could do that would help everyone, whether they had a lucky start and good parents or not."

"Maybe you can."

"I know." Jane pulled her feet up under her on the sofa. She did think there was something like that she could do, but she didn't know what.

"I thought that when I was your age too. I remember in college I wanted to have a baby, but there were lots of things I thought I'd do first. Like win the Nobel Prize and get a Rhodes Scholarship and write a novel and, oh, solve hunger in New York City." She was laughing, a kind, hulling laugh. "And each year that goes by, you cross off one. Okay, well, maybe not the Nobel Prize. And the next year, maybe not a Rhodes Scholarship. You finally think, Well, I *can* have a baby."

"Yeah," Jane said, fingering her teacup.

Julie reverberated her lips against the baby's belly. "And it's not that you can't work. Most women do now. I'm lucky not to have to. You might just find you don't want to, that it's not the most important thing anymore. And being a mom—it's the hardest job I ever had." She understood that Jane was judging her harshly: everyone knows teenagers are the world's absolutists. Julie would have judged herself as harshly ten years earlier, or even five. But most of adult life, though quite enjoyable and full of rich satisfactions, would've sounded unbearable to her then. Not long ago, she'd had a wonderful conversation with Mary, and they'd decided that every girl imagines she'll be rich by the time she's the age they were now. What was impossible in advance was to fully account for pleasure. If she'd known in college that she would marry a man who didn't read treatises or swoon all night, she would have cried out words like "compromise" and "settling." But Peter was dear to her. She loved the happiness that leapt over his face, and she smarted when he felt slighted, then contrived to find ways to comfort him.

And Jane was lucky. Jane was bright and, like herself, beautiful. Coco might not have those endowments. Who knew what she would become? She might need more.

Jane idly patted the baby's warm back. She was promising herself not to forget what she wanted now.

Julie stood up to take back her daughter. She planned to move them into the kitchen and start on Peter's supper while they talked. Despite her allowance of understanding, it was unpleasant to watch a child, particularly this one, with her advantages, vowing ardently not to become you.

Julie hoped Jane would lose her election. She was becoming too much like her father.

"Politics'd be worse," Owens said to Kathleen. "Railroads and airports. Beaches. Highways."

"Libraries are cutting their hours," Kathleen added.

"Yeah, the libraries are all broke." The chronic problem that plagued Owens now was one he'd never in his adult life suffered—how to pay the bill. The operating costs of Exodus represented the first bill he'd ever encountered that he couldn't easily pay with his own money.

It was late at night, and he sat at his desk answering E-mail. Ten minutes before, he'd picked up the phone and called the marketing manager. Under everything he said and inside silence was the bad fact: Exodus, good as it was, was running out of money.

Rooney had completed his parking stalls. He'd assigned administrators—who traveled and were never there anyway—the wall that abutted the main building, where Owens' car had always rested like a ship's mascot.

"It's pretty clear to me now," he said, "they're trying to get rid of me."

Even Kathleen didn't disagree.

Owens hadn't once taken the jitney. He walked. Kathleen believed he'd decided not to let Rooney win over trivia. "To care too much about something stolen is to care about ownership at all," he'd once said. He wouldn't let these small intended indignities matter, she thought; he would keep his mind on what was important, on what was great.

Lately, he'd taken to getting in his car after midnight and moving it to his old spot, empty then, abandoned on all sides.

OWENS OUT! the headlines said, in forty-eight-point type, taking up a fifth of the page.

Julie, up at six with Coco, was the first to see. She allowed herself to read the article in full leisure, savoring a cup of coffee with sugar and real cream. She wanted to ask Mary over for tea, to talk about it, but she would wait. Mary didn't always read the papers, and Julie didn't want to be the one to tell her.

Jane found out at school. "Your dad got fired," a boy said.

"I was just there where he works last week." Or was it two weeks, even three?

"That's what today's paper said. On the front page."

"Oh, I didn't know," she had to say.

That evening, Mary and Jane drove out to buy the newspaper. They read the story carefully, but afterwards they still didn't know what it meant. "He's still got a job there," Mary said tentatively. "Here it says he does, but it sounds like there's somebody over him, so he's not the boss. That's just not like him."

They wondered if it was the man who said he could make Owens marry Olivia, if that man would now be his boss.

They called Owens that night, their heads touching, mouths close to the phone, but his machine was on and he didn't return their message. They called all the other numbers and still got nowhere, which made them feel back where they'd started.

Kathleen found him hunched over his desk, scanning prints by a famous photographer he'd hired to document Exodus from its beginning. And with the exception of one retreat, when the famous photographer canceled and Owens hired Kaskie's sister at the last minute, most of the landmarks were represented here in silvery black and white. When they came to Michelle Kaskie's pictures, he said, "Her bill was so low, I pinned it on the bulletin board." But her photographs were oddly apt. They weren't as polished as the others, and people hadn't liked the pictures of themselves—maybe, Kathleen thought, because they looked so exactly like them.

He stacked up the dull, beautiful black-and-whites of the team, the automated factory on its first day of operations, the intricate assembly line, every element picked by him, even the corrugated floor. "Maybe it was all better before," he said.

There were no good pictures of Genesis' early days. Just snapshots, Polaroids with cluttered backgrounds and thumbs over the lens. Lamb and Shep, probably Frank's uncles, the ones who didn't stick around for long, had the real documents in their photo albums, mementos of their youth. "And maybe that's the way it should be," Owens said. "Legwork for some historian." But he'd tried to keep the scraps and pieces of Exodus together, to make one clear book to hand on. And the documents were here, ordered and elegant. Yet this time, maybe no one would want them.

Kathleen supposed he'd have to leave. To imagine staying was unthinkable, but so, at the moment, was doing anything. What happened had been happening slowly for a long time, over a year now. Owens had been staving it off, working days and nights against this, and now he had lost and what he felt most was exhaustion, a temporary relief he was afraid to wake up from.

He called Olivia and asked her to meet him. They'd get a room somewhere. He couldn't go home because they'd all call there, the reporters; and even if they didn't answer the phones, enough people knew where he lived.

"Mary and Jane called," Olivia said. "They're worried about you."

"We'll call later. I can't think about them right now. Just meet me at—"

"My car's in the shop again."

"Oh, Olivia."

"That's okay. I'll take a taxi."

They arranged to meet in the small hotel where her mother had died and her father had lived. Olivia would check them in. Once in the room, they found their way quickly to the bed. She was all he'd ever wanted then, and he marveled for a moment at how he could have doubted her. He'd asked testing questions a thousand times. He'd once asked if she'd vote for him for president, and her pause before answering told him no. Now her face showed that she already had. She had voted for him with her life.

"Olivia," he called, when she went to the bathroom. She was too far away.

It was still a bright, dusty afternoon outside, but he felt like nothing but sleep. The cool anonymous sheets seemed clean and tended. Olivia closed the venetian blinds, and they gladly gave up the day.

Lab Nights

⊰⊱⊰⊱⊰⊱⊰⊱

*N*oah was worried about his hair: his one bounty. His mother had run her hands through it. His sister was jealous. His hair was what he liked about his looks, and now he was beginning to lose it. In his comb, he found a delicate weave. This morning, he lifted out a small web from the bath drain. He always cleaned the drain and remembered to put down toilet seats even though he lived alone: habits from having an older sister. When Rachel came to clip his curls for seeding crystals, he almost asked her to switch to unwaxed dental floss. In graduate school, he'd once heard of someone using cat whiskers.

In the closet Noah had allotted for her fruit flies, Louise showed him her hybrid mutants. Then they went to the microscope. When he lifted his head up from the lens an hour later, his neck ached but he felt convinced. There were enough eyeless flies with his mutation to establish the genes right next door to his gene. If he was right, they were only three or four months away from finding it.

"So what do you think?" Louise wore jeans and high heels. Noah had never seen, much less been attracted to, a woman wearing high heels in a lab.

"I think I want to marry you," he said.

Just then—as she had all her life, at the worst possible moment—Noah's grandmother appeared. Entering the lab with her walker, she was dressed in a royal-blue suit with matching shoes and purse, and a scarf that seemed to be a catalogue of butterflies. The old woman shook with the precise, limited range of certain birds. Noah loved to watch her smile accommodate the involuntary motion.

"I have a granddaughter your age," the old woman said, when Noah introduced her to Louise.

The old woman took every opportunity to inquire about Michelle. "Ask her yourself, Gramma," Noah said more than once, and his favorite answer was: "It's not so easy to get ahold of her in *Africa*."

Her head swung wider, as the interview went on. The point of the visit finally came out. She wanted both grandchildren present for her ninetieth birthday, in January. Noah's job was to get his sister home, and he promised he'd try.

As she left, she touched his stubbled chin and said, "Ouch."

"Oh, she doesn't like me very much," he explained to Louise, later. "Or maybe she does now. But she always preferred my sister. Michelle looks a little like her. When Michelle went to college in New York, my grandmother told her, 'If you go to live back East, you'll make friends back East. And then pretty soon you'll fall in love there in the East, and it'll end up with you marrying an easterner, and you'll live there and never come back.' " He smiled, then shook his head. "But when I was little, she wanted them to put me in a special school in Vermont. She had the brochure with all the prices. She blamed my dad for keeping me home."

"And you've forgiven her?"

"Now she's worse with Michelle. I'm doing what I'm supposed to. I have a job. But Michelle's running around the world barely making a living, with no husband and no children."

"And that's okay with you, to be approved of like that?"

"I take it how I can get it." Noah shrugged. "I love her."

Now, in the vicinity of their gene, Noah and Louise worked with pieces of DNA from a normal fly and from their mutant. They would sequence it by hand.

During lunch, Noah quickly wheeled across campus to see a doctor he'd just called, to find out if he could have children. The fee was eighty dollars; he'd asked on the phone. As in many waiting rooms, Noah suspected the ruffled magazines were read at home, spilled on by many messy children, and only then brought here. Asleep on a plaid sofa, a pregnant woman was sucking her thumb.

A nurse took him to a small room, where she handed him a paper cup. He gingerly touched a worn magazine, very different from the ones outside. The frilled fingered pages made the women seem somehow out of date. He wondered if the nurse was waiting by the door, and if he was in any way being timed. He tried to imagine himself with Louise, as he often had while falling asleep at night; and though he'd invented more than twenty scenes, complete with dialogue, of nights they found themselves alone in the lab, he couldn't conjure the actual moment of touch. For this he had to imagine other people. Not himself. He imagined Louise with Andy Ruff.

After Noah had been shown to his office, the bearded doctor asked, "How long have you been trying?"

"Oh, I'm not trying yet. But I hope to. And I want to know. Being in a chair and all, it seems the least you could tell a person. If I can't."

"Mr. Kaskie, as I'm sure you know, your disease does not express itself in infertility. Your kid's chances of being affected are about fifty-fifty. So if you are infertile, it would be a coincidence."

Noah's own doctor had never talked to him about this or anything like it. Noah felt the burden of a long and seldom-looked-at fear slowly lifting.

"But I still want to know for sure. To me that's worth the lab fee."

He and Louise would be in the lab all the time now, for at least a month or six weeks. Working this way was oddly relaxing. Since they were always here, they never had to hurry. He loved working while she slept in the next room.

How much more do we have to do on fish after the flies? Noah wondered. Of course, like every scientist, he wanted to get the results out for publication. He had to, if he was going to have a career.

It was August now, and everything was ripe: the corn had a deep scent, and for dinner tonight, he and Louise and the Danish postdoc ate ten newly picked ears. Noah loved corn, especially white corn, fresh and tangled with translucent silk. Near where he grew up, there were miles of corn. He ate it raw, right off the cob. He took Louise to those fields just after the sun went down, and they filled a brown paper bag. He showed her how to cook it in the lab, for only a minute at a high boil. Noah could do these things with her, things there'd never been time for with the girl in college. He made up a greater part of the composition of their friendship; with the girl in college, he was hardly in it at all. Perhaps for that reason, it was harder to feel in love with Louise every minute. He kept slipping in and out of the spell.

At two in the morning, Louise shuffled into his office. "You know what I'm afraid of?" she said, flopping into the old chair. She smelled of fish viscera and fixative, as she usually did these days. "I don't want to be one of those women scientists who are forty and living alone. Maybe having a sperm-bank kid. And then, every once in a while, they have an affair and suffer." She shivered. "I want to get married. Have a normal life."

"Then you will," Noah said, "if you want to. But not with guys like Andy Ruff."

Louise folded her arms. "I would never marry him."

Wind and rain of eucalyptus buttons drew their attention to the window. That night, it seemed to Noah he loved this life more than she did. He imagined he would attend her wedding years from now, after she left science, and that by then it would seem beautiful to her, children growing up haphazardly in labs with takeout cartons, knowing the periodic table like an alphabet.

"What do we have to eat?" She wandered over the kitchenette, bending down to check the cabinets. "Want a Pop-Tart?"

"Sure."

His eyes sketched across the lab, at the work, building like an abstract city, at different benches. Cell archaeology. Archaeology of a past that was still alive. Someday all this would be known. A billion nucleotides were in a fish, and nobody knew the sequence. Bacteria— *E. coli*—had just been sequenced, but they had only a million—a difference of three zeros, and in science, three zeros probably equaled about fifteen years. "Do you sometimes wonder how far it'll go in our lifetime? What we'll get to see and what we'll miss?"

"Yeah. Who was it who said, 'Biologists don't have their bomb yet'? And still no cure for the common cold."

"Not to mention leukemia or hay fever."

"Hey, Noah, can I ask you something?"

"Sure." Did his heart beat this loudly all the time; and if so, why didn't he hear it?

"How're you going to sign this paper?"

"Me first, you second. Then Arne."

"Mmn. Okay." She had a swallowing look of pleasure, studying the toaster oven. "No, I'm sorry to ask, but I think you have to, if you're a woman. Look at Rosalyn Franklin."

"What about her?"

"Well, they stole her data. It's clear Watson had her X-ray photographs. She was dead by the time they got the prize. I was just checking. I wanted to be in the top three."

Only three scientists can share the Nobel Prize. Noah felt miffed. "I think we're getting a little ahead of ourselves here. And I'm offended you think I'd steal your data and not credit you. Franklin's pretty much acknowledged for her work. Nobody thinks of her as some bimbo. Not that you *could.*"

"But if she was prettier you could believe she'd done nothing?"

"I'm not saying that."

"You know," she said, "I always wanted to ask you why you didn't stay in Matt's lab." She handed him the warm crumbling tart in a napkin. "Here."

"My wheels were always crushing bugs in Boston. I had to wash the treads every couple hours." He shrugged. "Then it got to be winter, and I was cold. These tiny little balls of snow were blowing up my sleeves. And I'm not a good shopper. My sister used to sew; she'd buy me things and tailor them. I'm asymmetrical, like Mondrian. You know he used to trim his mustache an inch longer on one side to even out his face?

"So anyway, I went to this department store. The third floor was all coats, and for a while I just rode between aisles, smelling. Sleeves brushed my cheek. There was every kind of wool. 'I need a coat,' I said, and that's how I met Maria. She was a sales clerk. I really liked this cape, but she said, 'No. Not for you. You have to be tall to wear that.' And she was too short herself. But we finally settled on a gray coat. All told, I spent about six times what I expected."

"But then you never expect to spend anything."

"I know, thanks. And when the tailor took my jacket away, Maria rubbed my shoulders. I admired her for that. In retail, it's probably smart to find a way to touch people. People don't get touched enough."

Noah blushed. He was saying too much. He also remembered the woman who'd washed his hair when he'd had it cut the last time; rubbing her knuckles into his scalp, she told him he had beautiful curls. Those touches, which seemed to open the body to caving sparks, did they sound dirty out loud—like an old man copping feels off sleeping girls?

"So did you ever see Maria again?"

"No. I was lucky. When I picked up the coat, they told me she'd quit. I didn't even know her last name. If she'd stayed, I'd probably still be back East. Deep in debt."

It was so easy to talk. He wondered if this was what it was. Maybe one person couldn't feel this without the other. There was nothing else he'd rather be doing.

"What time is it?" she said. "We better get to the isotopes."

As she bent over her two-by-four dish, which held ninety-six small wells, he asked what he'd wanted to know for a long time. "Louise, what color was your hair?"

"Blond," she said, then sighed. "It's such a hard time to be young. The way we get together and break up wouldn't ever have happened to our parents."

She probably wore her hair long too, Noah thought. Maybe she wrapped a bracelet of it around her wrist. Michelle had done that when she was a girl. "I don't think it's such a bad time for me," he said.

"For me either, I guess. For women. But it'll probably be a lot better for our children. They'll pity us the way we pity our parents. Still, I envy their romance. I think they had the last of that."

"My grandparents had a grander youth than my parents. But I still believe in love."

"I don't. Once you tear away all the stage curtains, I'm not sure what you're left with."

"You're left with Andy Ruff."

Noah rolled home fast down the smooth center of the road because it was four-thirty in the morning and there were no cars. It was over. They had the markers for their gene. Whatever it was, whatever it did, it was theirs. More would become evident soon.

The light was on in Olivia's rented apartment across from Kaskie Square, so Noah tapped on the window with his knuckles.

Slumped over the table, Olivia stuck out her hand for him to see the ring. So many men had been in love with Olivia. He and Huck and her father and probably many others had wondered how far it would go, and now it was done.

Noah had thought about going down the aisle with Olivia, everyone looking on. His chair and her long tall dress with a train, a congregation of cypress, at the front altar a lurching pine. He touched his head, the spot where less hair seemed to be. He'd have to buy a new white shirt for the wedding. A person in a chair, more than anyone, should probably take pains to appear clean. In that way, he thought, my lot is similar to a fat person's.

But Noah knew he wasn't especially careful. For days on end, he forgot altogether and, like today, was a mess. He hadn't shaved—his grandmother had noticed—and his lap was full of crumbs from the Pop-Tart he'd eaten three hours earlier.

And now Olivia was once and for all marrying Owens.

It was the fifth straight week Noah and Louise had lived in the lab, running their experiments all night. They had been finishing, it seemed, for months now. There were no more brilliant flashes, only small steps, changing one of a hundred factors fractionally. Still, the fish embryos were finally telling their secrets.

At four in the afternoon, Noah received a call on his office line. It was autumn, Nobel season, and here and at Harvard and Caltech and MIT, all the full professors were racing to their answering machines every hour. Last year, Noah's ridicule of his senior colleagues was fierce. Now, because for the first time they had results, he viewed it as part of the human comedy.

"You can have all the kids you want." It was the doctor. "Like I told you you would be, you're fine."

Nothing changed, not even Noah's expression. He felt his good news most just by holding still, keeping on with his work in the normal way.

He went to the microscopes to see how Frank was doing with the slides he was making of double-mutant flies. It was strange to have Frank around again, this man who for so long had been a parable. When they were in graduate school together, Frank worked graveyard at the company where he'd met Owens. Then he quit school to make money for his family, and of course he made plenty at Genesis. But that was years before, and now Frank was back to biology, an unpaid researcher in Noah's lab, with a good temper and no seeming regrets.

For no reason then, looking at the slides, Noah thought again of the woman with the O.I. baby. That paper with her number kept getting lost and turning up again. For over two years now, Noah had been meaning to call her. Today he would, but where was that little paper? He'd seen it last near the centrifuge. He left Frank to his meticulous work and rolled over, but he couldn't find it.

The child would be about three years old, with no help from him. Noah had already failed them. He didn't even know if it was a boy or a girl. When I was that age, Noah thought, I'd had ten fractures. His father had made him a four-caster scooter, around that time. He'd become too heavy for his mother to carry. The child would have bruises, certainly. Noah had never seen himself as a baby: there were no pictures. Michelle started taking pictures of him when he was seven and she had her first Brownie camera. He wanted to see the child.

He had to find the mother's number. He could call her friend Julie Carradine and ask.

After midnight, when he finally got home, Louise was waiting outside his door. "Forgot my key," she said.

Since they'd been working around the clock, she sometimes slept in his apartment. He had two single beds, each against a wall, from the last time he'd fractured an arm and needed an attendant. He asked her to turn around and face the wall while he maneuvered into bed.

"You don't really seem like a Californian," she said.

"I'm a Jew," he said, surprising himself.

"I know," she whispered, still facing the wall. "Ready?"

"Yes."

They talked in the dark. She was used to him and he was used to her, so they never worried anymore what they would talk about, and their conversation had momentum.

She told him a long story about a dog she had in high school, and how her mother had thrown a rock at another dog to protect hers.

Why is she telling me this? Noah wondered.

"Do you have to marry someone Jewish?"

"I'd want to," he said, without knowing why. His grandmother maybe. "But I probably won't." Marry at all, is what he meant, but was she asking if he'd consider her? He was probably imagining it.

They didn't say good night. There was a pause, then Louise fell asleep. After a while he heard her deep regular breaths. She made a sound when she slept, a very fine whine.

Noah couldn't sleep. He heard the occasional traffic outside. His life was hurtling forward too fast, like a whirling ride he'd gone on once as a child in his chair, with the wheels locked, hanging on to the back of a huge metal teacup. They were getting very near to their gene's structure, and Louise and he were having these talks. He wanted to skid his hands on the wheels to slow it all down.

He slept with his chair so he could touch it. He thought of the small picture of Louise's father on her lab bench, his uneven shoes.

Now he wished he'd said it didn't matter to him if his wife was Jewish.

In the morning, he got up first so she wouldn't see, then wheeled to the bathroom. He liked thinking that she'd wake to the sounds of water in a bath. Noah had some ideas about how to live, and he could appreciate increments. His family had never been like that. They had to have it all perfect, or the rest was wrecked.

Noah's favorite part of the day was his bath. He loved to sink down so all but his head was underwater. Sometimes, when work was yielding, he seemed to swing from pleasure to pleasure, and this was the first one. He had always loved water. He somehow had to tell Louise he could have children, but that there was a chance . . .

In the bathtub, holding up a small mirror, he shaved. He blew steam onto the glass and made thumbprints. His hair was wet, the uncurled ringlets falling below his shoulders.

The apartment was perfectly quiet. But he hefted himself out. She'd be up soon. He sat a moment in his chair, bare legs out in front of him: maybe six inches less didn't matter. Then he put on socks and shoes. He never wanted her to see his feet. His shoes were unmarred, like a baby's, decorative.

"Morning," she finally called, then ran in a dredge of energy to the bathroom, to brush her teeth and wash her face. She was wearing a man's watch. Her wrists and ankles, though no other part of her, were extremely thin.

He sat stirring the oatmeal as coffee brewed. Here at home he had enough pots to do both at once.

For the first time, they went to work together. He felt extremely self-conscious. This was the worst of everything, in a way. Not sleeping together but looking as if you were. She was his postdoc. And he didn't have tenure—oh, God. He decided to take the elevator up to Rachel's lab. They couldn't walk in together at eight in the morning.

Louise said, matter-of-factly, "I saw a guy in a wheelchair doing wheelies and turning around in the air." The way you'd mention, *One of my best friends is Jewish.*

He didn't say anything, and they entered the campus. Louise was taking small fast steps, half running to keep up. He was wheeling faster and faster ahead of her. "Can you do that?" she called after him.

"I don't do tricks. Don't dance. Don't play basketball."

"In other words, you don't do anything you're not the best at."

"How do you know I'm not the best dancer? Actually, I'm going to a dance in December." This was true. His yearly duty. He volunteered at the annual oxymoron, the Wheelchair Prom, for teenagers at the center.

He wheeled over to the elevator. "I'll be down in half an hour."

Noah picked up and put down the phone a dozen times that day. He'd found the slip of paper in a pants pocket and wanted to call the woman with the baby. But a man answered every time, and he hung up. For some reason, he wanted to talk to her alone.

That Tuesday evening, at nine o'clock, holding the X-ray film up to the light, and after finally deciphering the sequence, Noah saw the ladders. They were unmistakable and beautiful. It was their gene.

He looked again. Then Louise looked and the Dane looked and Frank looked and his two graduate students looked too. It was there.

"Let's get out of here," Frank said, and everyone left to get a drink. Noah didn't want to. There were a thousand things to do. But it wasn't even that. He just wanted to be in the lab. To keep still.

After Frank left, Noah took over the slide-making. In an hour, the two grad students came back to their benches, along with Louise, who offered to help. Noah didn't mind doing it himself. He'd always had good hands.

But at midnight he knocked the nail polish they used for mounting off the arm of his chair. Oh, shit. The bottle spilled out empty; he rolled over to the cabinet but couldn't find another. Everyone but Louise was gone for the night, and she was asleep on the couch. She'd probably be touchy if he woke her up to get nail polish. "Just because I'm a woman," she'd say. "I don't wear it either." And she didn't. She chewed her nails down so the cuticles puffed.

He wheeled out to a 7-Eleven across the highway, open all night. Clear Base Extra Strength was what he needed.

The 7-Eleven's selection was limited. He didn't see any clear. Not to mention base extra strength. He was willing, this once, to switch brands.

"Excuse me," he said to the acned boy behind the counter. "I need some Clear Base Extra Strength nail polish. Not for me, obviously."

"Hey, whatever. But we just got what's there. They lock up the storage room at night."

The closest thing was a palish pink. This was the kind of thing that drove him crazy. How could he send in slides tinged pink? On the other hand, what did it matter? He couldn't wait around all night to get the right shade of fly mount. It had taken him years to find this gene, and it would be just his luck to be beaten out now that he finally had data.

He bought the small bottle of polish and, finishing the mounts back at the lab, he thought of the mother with the baby. He could send her the article, if they took it, as some sort of apology. These past two years I've been busy with . . . flies. He lifted a hand to the ends of his curls. Louise's damn flies loved his hair. Maybe they were expertly sawing it off.

Later, Louise yawned and stumbled over. He explained about the pink polish.

"Oh, you should've told me. I've probably got some at home."

He looked up at her, surprised. There were sides to women, all of them, he would never understand. "Too late now," was all he said.

The next day, he brought a bottle of French champagne to the lab, with a warm peach pie he'd made with brown eggs and honey. In Kaskie's family, all pies were made with honey.

Noah wrung his hands, showing the chairman around his lab. If he had his way, his lab would run forever, always working and never watched. I did my best, he wanted to be able to say. I did what I could do.

He wished he knew specifically why his gene was important. All of a sudden, he thought of all the labs on higher floors. He always got basement rooms or first floor for his labs and classrooms, as if there were no such thing as an elevator. He wished he had a lab with a view. He always wanted one more thing than he had.

An hour later, he'd forgotten about the window. The chairman had slapped his back and called him "old boy." Noah suspected he'd forgotten his name. The chairman was now back at his desk, writing letters to the journals to send with the abstract. Maybe they'd have a chance at *Science* or *Cell* or *Nature*. Rachel had already come down to report. "He was *majorly* stunned," she said.

After today it wouldn't be them alone anymore. Louise was already receding, as uncharacteristically humble as a regular graduate student. The department chairman hadn't said anything to her.

He remembered the full smell that came in the van's windows as he and Louise drove up through the hills on a summer night. This great romantic time in Noah's life was over now perhaps.

Everyone in the building would be coming by to see. Secretly, Noah felt he had things others didn't. He went through his desk. There was the scrap of paper with the number. It felt better just to have it. He put it in his pocket.

In April, two weeks after the acceptance from *Nature,* Noah's chair got a flat tire on his way to the gym, and he didn't have his tool kit. It was four o'clock in the afternoon, and he was stuck in front of a clothing store, whose large window caught him like a mirror. He looked at himself as if opening an envelope: against all odds, maybe it would be a gift. He'd gotten used to being lucky, but what he saw was the first bad thought. So this is really it, all I am. It was over before I was born, in a whim-crack of biology. Scuff marks on a white wall. He touched the top of his head, where his hair was thinning.

A rasp on the pavement, and it was Jane, walking fast. She took her sleeve to wipe his eyes. "What is it, Noah?"

"I'm losing my hair."

She ran her left hand through it as his mother had, but even his mother had often seemed distracted. "You've still got a lot left." She touched his shins with her shoe. "That's what you mind, isn't it? Yours are just smaller."

"And crooked."

"My feet are flat," she said.

"I don't even want to tell you about my feet."

She squatted down and held on to the arms of his chair. "You know what? You should let me take a picture of you. I can make you look great."

"Not with a camera you can't. My sister tried for years." Like FDR, he liked no photograph of himself that showed the chair. All the pictures he kept were from the chest up. Certain girls in school had liked him for his face; one had told him he had beautiful tragic eyes. But Michelle did photograph his chairs, all but the first. And he loved those photographs, cherished them. The second chair she'd done in black and white, empty on the pavement with all its nicks and dents. But he was thinking now about that first wheelchair, which was thrown away long ago. *I learned how to love by loving a thing.*

Noah was okay now. He felt like a bird after a ruffled squawk. He sighed. "I got a flat tire and I don't have a spare. Can you push me down to the bike store?"

"Sure." Jane pushed him slowly, a little fearful. For all the time she'd known him, he never liked to be pushed, ever. She'd asked him years before, when they first met, and those were the only times he'd sounded mean.

"My problem's a woman. Do you think a woman could see me as a man?"

"You are a man," she said.

"I know," he said, suddenly wanting to change the subject. "How's your dad?"

"Well, I'm afraid to go in his house, he has it so perfect. The walls are all smooth. And the *floors.* I got a bad splinter and I had to have a tetanus shot."

"There's a reason people use polyurethane," Noah said.

"Yeah, and when I have an apartment, I'm going to use it a lot." Jane handed him a homemade campaign button: JANE FOR JUSTICE. PRESIDENT. Her election was in a week.

She waited in the bike shop while Noah helped the repairman fix his tire. "Where were you going anyway?"

"Oh, I was on my way to the gym. You want to hitch a ride?"

Jane had always loved to ride on the chair, but he hadn't asked her in years, not since she was a small girl. And she never asked, because she thought she might have got too heavy. But riding now, she remembered the old sensation: Noah really did have a different life. You're lower, and you always have the sound of wheels. She closed her eyes, hearing that sound again, as if she were inside a flock of birds and hearing the strenuous work of flying.

His gym was like nothing she had ever seen. She was fifteen years old and frankly embarrassed. A blush rose to her face, and she couldn't think of what to do with her hands. All over the walls were blowups of big men and women with huge muscles posing in tiny underwear. And that wasn't the worst part. Men and a few women with muscles like that were actually here, wearing shorts and thong tee shirts, grunting and making horrible noises with machines.

"Do you come here a lot, Noah?" she asked.

"Not for a while. I've been working too hard. But it beats physical therapy."

"Aren't you scared?" she whispered.

He laughed. "They're sweethearts," he said. "Up you go now, so I can exercise." He rolled to what looked like a torture machine, swung out of his chair, wriggled onto the bench and began to engage with the hanging silver balls in a series of sit-ups.

Noah didn't see Jane again for two months. One morning in June, he opened the door for the newspaper and there it was, in four-inch type. His first thought was, They didn't call me.

He felt something like fear growing as he read the article. He couldn't imagine Owens without an office and a staff—he was a lone man always backed by a chorus. He was Chaplin, Busby Berkeley. He was the only famous person Noah knew.

Before he finished reading, Noah tried to call. Four numbers, and none of them worked. He felt like a stranger. Owens had always been able to slip into the anonymity of the rich or famous, either or both, whenever he wanted to, but this time he'd taken Olivia with him through that wall, into the other, unreachable world. Why this now for Olivia? Her time for peace had never once yet come.

Noah called Jane. He learned that she'd won her school election and that Owens now saw almost no one, so everyone in his life had begun to see more of one another. Olivia stood by as his nurse, giving reports from the front door of his new house. Only Jane slipped in and out freely. More than a handful of adults checked in with her daily, for information. Not one believed it was fair. He deserved many scoldings from them, but not this, not taking Genesis away. Genesis was what he had been good to. And Jane came to love him as she'd imagined loving the young criminal, with a regular care bent towards protection.

"I tell him, 'You've got to eat, Owens,' but he won't, Noah. He'll only eat asparagus."

Listening to her, Noah remembered a wager he'd once made with her father. Owens bet she'd get married, have a kid before she was twenty and not go to college. Noah said graduate school, the works. Jane was probably ten at the time. Typical of Owens, he'd bet dinner anywhere in the world, winner's choice. Noah knew he'd win, though by then Owens would have forgotten and collecting would be out of the question. But as she went on about her father now, Noah thought, She'll just be a mother, like them all. Her spirit as a child had promised more.

Noah arranged to meet with Jane and Mary after his workout.

When he emerged from the gym, wet and re-dressed, he bought a coffee to take to work. He opened the lid to his cappuccino, blew on it, waiting for the girl he saw every Tuesday. And here she was, in a pink coat today. She had those polio crutches and she swung quickly between them, then sat down with a hard fall, into her car.

Then a woman in a suit passed Noah fast, thighs flashing, and dropped a quarter in his cup. The liquid splashed up, and Noah was so startled that he threw it at her, coffee arching towards her legs, probably staining her stockings.

"Two-dollar-fifty cappuccino," he yelled.

"You little monk," she yelled back. Pretty women, he thought, can sometimes just change.

At that moment, he understood something. He had found his gene, which had meant more to him than anything, but he had also failed an unknown child.

Voting

⫷ ⫷ ⫷ ⫷ ⫷

*T*he first visitor Owens accepted after his father, who came
with a bushel of apples, was Frank. When Olivia walked in from work
one day at the end of summer, she heard laughter on the other side of
the house: Frank's high giggle and the lower bell of Owens.

Frank had just knocked on the door. It had never occurred to him
that Owens would not let him in. Owens might have admitted others
too but everyone else felt hesitant to presume sufficient intimacy.
Whether Owens himself cultivated this quality of reserve or his
money and fame created its aura without his consent, no one knew for
sure.

Although Frank believed that Owens had betrayed him, he had
never been able to hate Owens, because they'd grown up together.
Owens was foreign-looking too, but his mother had made birthday
cupcakes for the class with tiny paper flags attached to toothpicks.
Frank had always loved Owens' mother. Other boys copied the way
Owens' jeans fell to his hips and his hair was disheveled. Frank
had looked too neat, as if his mother had zipped the zipper all the
way up.

Owens had given Frank his first car and actually taught him to drive. They drove with the windows down and the music blaring— Owens had stapled speakers to the back seats. Owens knew where to pick apples. He had a strange combination of drive and calm, like an old-fashioned man in the movies. Frank was more variable, high-strung. Without doing anything in particular, Frank stayed clean. Once, driving, Owens lifted his eyebrows. "Hey, if it doesn't work," he said, looking over at Frank, "we're having a good time. What have we got to lose?"

"Years," Frank said, his hand dragging out the window.

"Worst-case scenario, this doesn't work? They'll take us back at our jobs."

"But people are waiting."

"You're only young once."

"They already were. And *they* helped their parents."

"You don't owe them that, Frank, even if you think you do. This is a gamble. Who knows? Maybe you'll be able to pay back big." They waited a minute, listening to Buddy Holly, who was already dead, on the radio. Owens loved those girl songs. Frank's sister had also died, five years before, but Owens called up something high and light in him. His face filled, round as a berry.

"Hey, tell you what." Owens swerved the truck into a field he knew where they could steal peaches easy. "If we fail and have to go back to work, I'll give you the money you would've made in the time we take off."

Frank didn't answer. The offer was too generous to be fair, but he wanted it anyway; he needed insurance more than fairness. They never mentioned this conversation again, though both young men considered the promise binding. Even now Frank didn't doubt that Owens would have kept his word. That was why today he was here.

"Tell me something," Owens had said on the plane home from their first trip to Asia. "Chinese women are much more beautiful than Japanese, aren't they?"

Frank blushed. "I can't say that. I'm Chinese. Some Chinese women are beautiful, some aren't. Same everywhere."

"No, seriously." Owens partitioned the air with his hands—as he had, tall and American, to the men at the corporation; looking at Owens, they'd seen every American millionaire they'd ever watched slide down his own banister in the movies. "I've been doing a study. Chinese women are more delicate. Their necks are longer."

"Maybe taller," was all Frank would say.

"Your sister was probably really beautiful."

Frank looked out the window, down at the clouds. "I don't like to talk about her like that."

"If she'd lived," Owens said suddenly, "I bet I would have married her."

When Owens' mother became sick, Frank had given blood. Owens had tried too, but his blood type was rare and incompatible.

"I read a lot, I watch movies. I sit in the garden." Owens raised his eyebrows. "It's pretty nice."

He cooked during this period, and he was in a cauliflower stage. For six weeks, he'd made cauliflower every evening. He sent Olivia to the market for the firm white heads. They went through more than thirty a week. Because he never left the house, he had to entrust these orders for basic needs to Olivia and Jane.

For tonight's dinner, he steamed the cauliflower lightly so that the small pieces became faintly green and transparent. He served it in a large bowl, and they ate sitting outside in the yard.

"Taste how sweet," he said to Frank, by way of encouragement.

Olivia ate deftly with wooden chopsticks.

"It's great," Jane said loudly, making Frank unaccountably sad.

"I've got to go," Frank finally said, rubbing his stomach. "I could use a hamburger."

They all laughed as if this were uncannily funny, though Frank meant it.

As he walked Frank out, Owens said, "I know I probably did a lot of things wrong. I could've been wiser about people."

Frank mumbled, "We were young."

Owens hung his hands on the fence. A moon had risen up over the huge live oak. "Believe it or not, we still are."

⊷

The next day, Mary and Jane found Owens in his bed with the shades down, watching a movie at four in the afternoon. They stood waiting for his attention, as he still stared at miniature lovers on the screen. "I need new clothes for school," Jane finally said.

"And we need a new dishwasher," Mary added, "and I'd like to see a therapist."

He finally turned to them. "Is that all you want from me, is my money?"

"No, not *all*," Jane said.

He sighed, touching up the volume. "Oh, look at this—she was so great."

They hadn't come only to ask for money. They had other problems too, the worst kind, because they were problems between themselves. Though the old habit of asking him for money provoked his exhausted response, at least this was a dismissal they were used to, and was often followed by his relenting. The few times they'd asked for his help with a more ineffable, recondite problem, he had done something frightening. He made it disappear, but only for him.

Tiny violins played, and the beautiful actress reappeared in a new dress on Owens' TV.

Jane's jeans were clean and pressed, and she was wearing lip gloss. She didn't like the way Owens lay around all afternoon. Despite the cauliflower, he was getting fat. He didn't shave anymore either. "You promised I could get a dress," she said. "I want a dress and highlights." She enjoyed having both parents look at her.

"Maybe we'll shave your head," he said. "That's what I'm going to do when I start going bald. I already shaved my head once, and people said it looked rather nice. So maybe we'll just be a shaved-headed family."

Mary's hands clasped. Was he including her? For a moment, she wanted to shave her head too. She lifted her daughter's hair up off her neck, where she had two moles. When Jane was a baby, Mary had often traced those moles, thinking that a man who loved her would know them as her markings. "She's got a beautiful-shaped head," Mary said.

Owens didn't answer.

"Jane is an unusually good-looking child. You know that, don't you?"

Owens gave a crooked half-smile. "I don't think that's particularly important. And anyway, Mary, she's not you."

Olivia entered the house, banging a door, and they could hear the whirring of her bicycle wheels.

"How did you get the floors to stop having splinters?" Mary asked.

"They had to be sanded by hand," Olivia said.

"I thought they were already."

"No," Olivia said, head down. "I mean between each board."

Mary laughed softly. At least Olivia knew to be embarrassed. Somebody's father spent days on his knees, sanding the cracks with a nail file. Of course, he was probably well paid. Mary walked through the house as if it were a museum and they were paying guests. Fireplaces in many rooms waited, the grates clean and unused.

There were small sharp moments that stayed with Mary and made her want to wince and stop remembering: Owens' long, flat hand on her head when he was telling her no—that meant something she felt but couldn't say. The hours before Jane was born, when she looked out the hospital window and saw a landscape so clear. The night she'd given him her virginity—and they both knew that was what it was, her gift to him, so much so that he'd asked if she was sure. Other people, she understood, did not save these shards; they felt the cut and denied them, breaking the truth to fit their stories.

He doesn't love you, her friend Bixter told her, no matter what he says. Mary let both truths fight each other until she buckled. She buckled and then she sent Jane away.

Walking home, they had another fight. Jane was going to have a party and invite her whole class. The question was where. For the first time, she thought she might have a choice.

"Go to his house, then!" Mary shouted. "I hope your friends like cauliflower!"

Owens had once said, "She'll come to me in the end." And Mary had been counting. Sometimes she realized she'd had her time to love her daughter, to touch her, and now it was over. She'd had that time and she missed it, Mommymommymommy always ringing unfinished in her ears.

Jane did want the party at Owens' house. She could tell that other kids, and their parents too, were curious about his investment in her.

When Mary had left her alone in the playpen for the first time, Jane cried before her mother reached the door, but Mary went through it. She waited on the other side until she heard quiet, and then she left. She got used to it, and being away began to seem normal, each day a little longer or farther. She didn't worry, when she had to run to the drugstore or even out to see a friend for an hour, although Jane's round face seemed to look at her strangely when she came back. But it was like money in a meter: if you didn't get a ticket, you were all right.

Mary thought it was probably something all mothers did. She prided herself on safety, checking the stove knobs and locking the door twice. Once, though, in the mountain camp, the women were showing their breasts, comparing their shape after childbirth, and Mary told about leaving Jane alone, just trying to be a part of things, and they all looked at her as if she was dangerous.

By the time they reached the bungalow, they had to call him. Owens stood listening, holding the telephone six inches away. Since Jane's arrival in Alta, he'd occasionally imagined that she would someday want to live with him. He'd even talked to Olivia about it, and they'd had a little fight. He'd said he would come home for dinner every night. "For her you'd do that," Olivia said. "But what about for me all these years?" She understood that of course children come first, but she never had when she was a child. Who would ever make up for that now? She was always afraid of seeming selfish. "I'd have to change my life," he'd concluded then, "but I can do it." And now his life had changed. He was always home for dinner.

While Jane walked over, Olivia dug pillows and a down comforter out of the closet, Owens trailing behind. "Maybe I'll start a school," he said. "Right here in the yard."

Jane walked in at the back door, carrying her school clothes tied in a bandanna on the end of a stick. Olivia hauled a lamp downstairs, and it was already late by the time her makeshift bed was ready.

Jane talked excitedly. "And so she *didn't* want me to have—"

"Did you bring your schoolbooks?" Owens asked.

Olivia would have liked to make Ovaltine, the warm drink she remembered from nights in her childhood, and then sit up talking at the end of Jane's bed.

"I'm not speaking to her, even if—"

"You have to talk to her. She's your mom. And it's time for us all to be in bed." They followed his order, feeling both deprived of something rare and wonderful, and safe.

The next morning, Owens was awakened by footsteps. Mary rushed in, flushed, and searched the empty rooms. Jane jumped into her arms and there they stood, the mother holding the eighty-five-pound child, when Owens and Olivia ran in.

"She's my daughter and I want her," Mary said, with both apology and accusation in her voice.

Owens did a double take, gaping at them in his underwear. He felt ashamed of his plans the night before. He'd actually stayed up another three hours, revising his curriculum. He didn't dare let himself love her completely, because Mary could always take her away.

After school a few weeks later, Jane found her father in the garage, occupying himself with his woodwork. He made simple, symmetrical birdhouses out of birch. Seven were already complete, on the floor.

"When I was about your age," he said, "I began to figure things out about myself."

She stood watching him work the lathe. "You studied magic, I remember."

"Yeah, I did. I wanted to bring things back to life. But that didn't really work. It was mostly card tricks, so I quit."

"Did you ever learn to do anything great before you quit?"

"Well, once I made a horse disappear." He looked intently at the wood.

"How did you do that?" she asked quietly, as if she were sneaking up on a bird.

His face broke into a shaking giggle, then he turned to tickle her.

"Are you really giving away your cars?" she asked, when she could talk again.

"Yes."

"Can I have one, then?"

"No."

"How come?"

"That's kind of a long story."

"I have time," she said. And for the first time since she'd known him, so did he.

Although he didn't leave the house, Owens kept up with the world by reading newspapers. In many ways, he felt better informed than he ever had been. With his daughter, he discovered the pleasures of general conversation. Of course, reading daily about his own crisis—by now relegated to small items in the business section—had made him briefly skeptical of the press. But while he plainly saw that the reporting about himself was false, and knew these same journalists covered other stories, he somehow found it difficult to remember that the news he was reading might be distorted or even untrue, just as it's easy for most people to happily trade gossip though they become frantic and horrified to discover rumors about themselves.

Tonight would be the last of the season's cauliflower, Owens thought, then he started to explain the history of the Ford Motor Company to his daughter. He had a working knowledge of the industries that had built the country and of the men who made those industries. He understood Ford's passion for order and why he wanted all cars to be black. Owens too liked a symmetrical world. He patiently explained why uniformity helped the middle-class buyer. "If it's all one color, then parts can be mass produced and interchanged!" he exclaimed in the dim garage, tools from his father hanging on the walls.

"But people want car colors they like," Jane said. "Didn't he think of that?"

Ford's downfall, he explained, was to impose his superior vision on the people. Indeed, she was right: Americans wanted color, and that's how the General Motors Corporation was born.

"But you still haven't said why I can't have one, if you're giving them away."

"You're fifteen. You can't even get your license till next year."

"You could save one for me."

"Most teenage fatalities are from kids cracking up cars."

"But I wouldn't. I'm careful."

He shook his head. "Anyway, Ford didn't even see that Hitler was crazy. I don't know how he could fall for that."

"I can see how," Jane piped up. "The teacher said he made the trains run on time. That's the same as making everybody have black cars when they want other colors."

Owens disagreed: trains could run on time, he believed, without cruelty or repression. He argued eloquently, but he'd already decided to call Eliot Hanson to change the order for the new car he planned to surprise Olivia with, from black to deep green. Privately, he believed his daughter·was living on a higher moral plane. Owens understood that he'd made mistakes and was now in the long rest-of-his-life, living with them.

"Maybe time will tell," he mused, "and we were all just wrong."

Jane heard him express sentiments like this frequently, now that he had time to think. She wasn't sure it was the best thing for him.

Jane was in the kitchen that day when Owens played his messages back. The white answering machine and its attendant number had somehow been moved from the Copper King's mansion to the new house on Mayberry Drive. One person who certainly wasn't reluctant to call was Albertine Maguire, who had just flown in for a week's vacation. She clearly expected her presence to delight people; besides, she had the socialite's instinct to speak directly to a friend who'd been in the news. That impulse would have made Owens shudder, had he known, but in fact there was nothing malicious in Albertine's intentions. She gladly would've heard, and then repeated thirty times, his version of what had happened. That others should not speak of his tragedy at all, as he wished, was to Albertine a ridiculous impossibility. But they had kissed once on a dance floor, and it would have been equally unthinkable for her to believe anything but what was most kind.

"I'd like to meet her," Jane said, after Albertine's long message was finished.

"Be my guest."

He had no idea that Jane would take him literally. But she called and made arrangements to meet the next day at four o'clock, in the tea salon of the Palace Hotel.

Jane had already calculated the years Albertine had occupied her father's life. "Did you ever know I existed?" she asked this woman she had never seen before.

They were in a room with white tablecloths and flowers on every table. Jane wore her first pair of high heels and her mother's stockings on legs she did not yet shave. She appreciated the water glasses clinking with ice, the smell of bread roaming from the kitchen.

"Believe it or not, I think I saw a picture of you once, when you were younger."

Jane bit her lip, remembering her mother in line at the post office, sending Owens her report cards, curls of her hair and those little cutout pictures. *Jane's first grade.*

"But I didn't know who you were."

"Oh. Not that I was his daughter."

Albertine had long since sealed Owens away in the crowded chamber of memory she reserved for her own haphazard youth. She was taking these things out carefully, trying to give the girl what she could. She liked Jane's frank tenderness, in which there was something of Owens too. Maybe she'd been wrong about him, then. Albertine had been crushed more than once, and had a deepened, broken smile. But Owens was someone who had pursued her across the continent with full gallantry. She'd never had the misfortune of falling in love with him.

She tried to decide whether to tell. Albertine noticed—as she sipped her tea and Jane dunked cube after cube of sugar into her own, not with the small silver tongs but with her fingers—that the girl bit her nails. Until three years earlier, Albertine had done the same thing. Then she'd quit, and just this week she'd treated herself to a French manicure, knowing her mother would lift up her hands to check when she came home.

Two men had tricked their way into her heart, Albertine told Jane, but her father had been kind and foolish, pursuing her with ingenuity. Albertine had wanted to be a journalist. Since then she had worked several jobs and was now trying to become a writer. "And so your father, impressive as he is, wasn't really in my sphere. I was more enamored with the young novelists. Who, believe me, are bad news anyway."

"You weren't in love with him?" Jane's face opened. This was the first time in her life she'd encountered the possibility of Owens' rejection.

"Once upon a time he was in my room and we were in bed together." Albertine looked up in alarm. She'd never spoken to anyone about being in bed with his or her father.

Jane felt embarrassed too.

"Something terrible happened to me a long time ago. Well, I can tell you. I was raped by a boss—a much older man. I'd told Owens about that, and the next morning he said he was sick, and it was like I'd never told him. I'm sure now he doesn't even remember."

"Oh, he's like that. He forgets."

There. Now Albertine had told this girl what she'd once given her father rashly and then had the good fortune to take back. She forgave him. Her confidence had been in error, and they stood now where they always should have been.

Jane sputtered. "I just can't believe you were never in love with him."

"I just wasn't."

"Well, you better not tell him. Because he thinks you were. Desperately."

Their two heads fell close together, as they laughed in a way that seemed hysterical and exhilarating.

When they walked out, Jane remembered this was the same hotel where Owens had left all his birthday presents—vases, clothes, a live peacock. Jane wondered if the presents were still here somewhere, their ribbons dusty, the peacock in a pen in back.

When Albertine asked Jane if she'd ever met Noah Kaskie, Jane said they were very good friends. "You know him too?"

"No, but I sat next to him at your father's party. And just the other week, I read about his discovery in the paper."

Jane stared at Albertine as if through an open door, where she was discovering new and unsuspected life in alleys behind what she'd always known. Today she was first considering that a woman might not love her father. And that same woman deemed Noah famous.

When Jane came home, her mother was lying on the floor, having tea with Bixter, who'd come in on the Greyhound bus. Her one eye went off to the left and the other other stayed still, always.

Jane was weighing this life in the bungalow against his. For the first time, she knew she could live with Owens, and this ticked in her like a small, safe bomb. She either noticed things more at home or they bothered her more. Bixter offered to read her palm, and Jane said no, thank you, she had homework.

Her mother followed her into her room. "She took care of you when you were a little girl, and now you don't have time for an old lady to read your fortune?"

Home was home. Jane sighed, then returned to the living room and stuck out her arm. It seemed darker in the house now than it was outside. A candle wobbled in a dish.

"You have healing," the woman said. "It's undeniable."

"What does that mean, exactly?"

"It's just a fact. You could be a prophet."

"Uh-uh, I don't think so." Jane had known too many mystics before she was ten years old. It didn't strike her as a very secure life. "I want to be a politician," she declared. Still, without knowing it, she saved the folding mysteries from her childhood, like faint flowers inside unreadable books she would later take out and try to smell.

Bixter wanted to see the desert, so they left in the car at dawn and drove for hours. Eli drove, Jane routing them on the map, and suspected misturns all the while. She and Bixter sat in the back and did the hand song:

> *The spades say tulips together,*
> *twilight forever,*
> *bring back my love again.*

> *What is the sto-o-o-ory*
> *of all the flow-ow-ow-owers?*
> *They tell my sto-o-o-ory—*
> *my story of love from me to you.*

Although neither Bixter nor Jane had yet experienced it, love formed the majority of their interest. Years earlier, they'd camped in the Mariposa Mines and read letters scrawled on the cave walls by the forty-niners. *Was it worth it?* someone had written.

They parked the car deep in the desert next to mud flats, and the next day they wore no clothes. No one else was around, no life for miles; they were absolutely alone. "What would happen if robbers came and attacked us?" Jane said. "We couldn't call the police, that's for sure."

"Never call police," Bixter muttered, in mud up to her shoulders.

They sat under stars in the warm springs. Mary and Eli turned on the car's headlights and radio, then put on clothes and danced in the high beams, tripping on the uneven earth. Sitting cross-legged in the warm mud, Jane wondered if her mother knew a happiness in love Jane would never find because she was so different from her mother.

Eli hummed along with the music, and Mary's long dress frilled at the ankles. Jane thought of Eli's birds and her mother's homemade cookies. She picked a scab from the outside of her knee and touched the smooth place underneath.

She couldn't move to Owens' house, though. This disorganized life, with extra people around, was her life too. But she wanted something. Then she hit on it: she wanted to have his name. Mary wouldn't mind. She'd never liked her own name.

A month later, at the ceremony, Owens lit candles. He'd sent for a form at the County Clerk's Office and had a special wooden pen for them to sign with.

"Your declaration of dependence," he said, lips diamonded, eyebrows raised.

The next evening, Jane ran through the house to Owens' bed, where he was watching a movie. "You really have to help my mom. She left this note. I think she's getting on the train."

The note said: *I'm going north to find Bixter. You don't need me anymore.*

"We better go find her, then."

He walked with her to the gate and, for the first time in months, stepped outside. He smiled to see his town, the same one-story roofs the height of the trees. It was a lambent, early-autumn evening. He drove them down the slow, leafy streets, looking for a walker.

"There she is," he said. "I'm glad to see her."

"I know."

"Maybe I should get out. I'll follow, but maybe she'd listen to you more."

Jane drove the car, opening the window to her mother. "Hey, want a ride?"

Mary walked on resolutely, with old shoes and a tight ponytail, her fists clenched. The light seemed dusty and bright, the houses fake. Time beat in blood pulses. "Oh. No." Her mouth winced, then more walking—to the train, Jane figured.

"Mom. Come on." Jane had to drive slowly. Owens' car was big and heavy, and she was being extra careful.

"You're fine. Look at you. You're in good here. That's for sure."

"Isn't that what you wanted?"

"I guess it is. I just always thought we'd be together. But you don't need me now."

"Please stop so we can talk."

"Do me one favor. Leave me be, Jane."

Her mother walked firmly, a crumpled brown paper bag in her hand. Jane sat in the car and watched as, minutes later, her father sprinted and overtook her mother, touching her shoulder. There was still sumac down by the railroad tracks from summer. They stood together for a while, her head down, one foot pawing the ground, and then he brought her back to where Jane had stopped the car.

Now her mother was laughing, hands in her pockets, and he said they'd all go to dinner. Some long fight seemed over.

Now that he's seen me like this, Mary thought, it's really done.

The next day was the election. Jane told Owens at dinner that Alta's per capita voting record was one of the lowest in the state, as if this were somehow his fault. He'd thought of running for governor but lived in a town that hardly voted. He didn't vote himself. "I just might this time," he said.

His polling place was a YMCA, and Owens was the first person of the day to cast a ballot. The machines were old and enormous, with mechanisms little more complicated than an abacus or a rudimentary can opener.

"Now what?" he asked, sticking his head out of the curtains.

"Pull the lever back again if you want it to register, mister."

He liked the grind of the lever and the small tick of registration, like a coin dropping into a large empty jar.

Now, what makes him come out and vote? Owens wondered, as a man limped up in a walker. There seemed to be several gardeners, one of whom actually carried a hoe. A fat woman had her hair in pink foam curlers. Owens was amazed at the variety of humanity that took time from their day to perform this minute act that couldn't in any direct way benefit them. He wanted to glean from this tattered parade how it was they came to believe. By the end of an hour, he still couldn't understand even the scornful radicals, waiting to pencil in an unknown name, but he walked out with tears in his eyes.

He wandered through the quiet morning streets, not wanting to go home. Then he needed a bathroom. He was passing the Alta church, thinking there must be one in there, but a service was in progress. He thought of Kaskie's lab, a place he'd always liked, and when he got to the building, he took the stairs two at a time. Suddenly, he was alone in a large bathroom, where he banged open the stalls, finding none of the toilets clean. Kids. He took paper towels from over the sinks and set to work cleaning a toilet seat carefully, folding the paper over it as his own mother had taught him and Pony to do, then he wondered if anyone had demonstrated this to Jane. He shrugged, trusting that Mary probably had. Overall, she was a pretty good mother. He had been lucky. So lucky. He stepped out, then turned back to flush not only his own but all the others. He left the bathroom roaring like a waterfall.

It had been almost a year since Owens visited the lab. Noah's time line, filled with entries, had grown to twelve feet.

"Hey, pal," Noah said, not sure what to expect. Owens had grown a beard and was wearing a flannel shirt. "You want to go take a drive and see the trees?"

Owens nodded, and Noah grabbed his jacket from a peg on the way out. He poked his head into Louise's station, to tell her he was leaving.

"You know what I like?" Owens said. "Those trees you see on all the boulevards in Paris. What are those?"

"Horse chestnuts, I think."

"They're very beautiful," Owens said. "Did you know it takes an olive tree thirty years to bear fruit?"

"That's why agriculture is always associated with peace." Noah took out his keys and unlocked the van. "After the—what was it?— the Peloponnesian War, the farms were ruined and people had to go to the cities. Cultivation takes patience. Hey, I discovered one good thing about call waiting today." The two friends shared an animosity for telephone innovation. "I was having an interminable conversation, this guy going on and on, and then my phone beeped."

Owens' attention lifted. "We should make you a little tool that'll replicate the noise, so you can just push a button and it shoots through the line."

Kaskie gulped air. Owens was still Owens.

In the park, fog was blowing off, and the sky was shot with sun. Owens stretched out of the van slowly, as if just emerging from a long convalescence. It was a weekday morning. In the midst of bikers, girl runners, kids on blades and bursts of athletic color, Owens spotted a bride. She stood stiffly in a dress with a full lace veil, holding a bouquet. Around her, kids in light clothes zoomed on skateboards. A small party surrounded the incongruous bride.

"Filipinos, I guess," Noah said. "They're speaking Tagalog."

Owens decided that he was like the Filipino bride, having what was most important to him in public, so apparent as to be foolish to the hundreds who risked nothing but only played the better part of the soft day. Looking at the red-leafed trees, he considered what to do. "I'm going to sell all my Genesis stock tomorrow," he finally said. "I think the value'll rise, but to stand by rooting for them would be too conflicted a life. I'll sell all but a dollar's worth, so I can still get the annual report." A smile flickered under his lips. It would cost them between seven and eight dollars to produce and mail him that report.

The two men stood admiring a Japanese maple. "That must be what—seventy years old?" Owens said. "You can't buy a Japanese maple that old."

You probably could, Noah thought, but he was glad his friend didn't know that.

A boy on a skateboard skidded to a stop. "Are you Tom Owens?"

Owens smiled quizzically. "Why?"

"Because if you are—oh, man, you saved me. What you did is incredible."

Owens grabbed the boy's hand. He asked his name and age, then told him where he lived and said that if he ever had any problems to just come up and knock on his door.

OWENS OUT! he remembered, as he did a hundred times a day. "It must've been really tough for Jane," he said, "all the kids and teachers at school seeing." And she having to walk the still-straight line.

When the election results came in, later that night, the candidate whom Owens' five advisers had supported lost, and he wondered, for a moment, if he could have won.

A year after Owens sold out, Genesis stock soared, because of NT12. He'd been right all along. Only late.

Two Parties

◄ ◄ ◄ ◄ ◄

*N*oah attacked history, on his time line, in much the same way he'd searched for his gene—catholically, generously, going at the problem from as many angles as he could think of. He realized it would be hard to describe his approach as elegant. In the late fall and early winter, he took on another project in this manner, and that was love.

By now he had his heart set on Louise, but he was willing to admit it didn't look good. And on his friends' advice, he'd decided to give her—or them—a deadline. If nothing happened by the new year, he'd forget it. And then, if nothing happened with anyone else, he'd try to make himself feel more for Rachel. She came down to his lab frequently now. Her face, in newly adopted makeup, seemed flush with the pride of discovery. *He* was the discovery, Noah knew, not any gene. She felt she'd spotted him early, understood what he had in him even when he was apparently floundering, and now the world could tell too.

And that was all true. But Rachel was a type of girl who'd always

334

been drawn to Noah—maternal, laplike. Lonely as he was, he wanted to choose, not be chosen.

Noah splurged, spending the tenure raise he didn't yet have on a new pair of boots. It was hard to find shoes in his size that were at all stylish. At least they'll last, he said to himself.

A week before Christmas, Noah had two parties on the same night: one out of obligation, the other for fun. He invited Louise to the better one.

She couldn't decide what to wear. All her clothes seemed stained or out of fashion. She hadn't bought anything new since she'd started breeding her flies. She went to the ladies' room down the hall, took off the final outfit and put on jeans again, with her old heels and a black sweatshirt. She unhooked her earrings and washed her face. She was someone who never felt like herself adorned. It came from growing up in Michigan and hanging up her white blouse every day after school before running outside to play in fields.

"I don't feel like going," she told Noah. "I want to do nothing."

"Come on; it's Christmas and you're a Christian. You shouldn't stay here."

"I'm sick of Christmas." She'd decided to stay away from things that pick and harm, like parties where she didn't meet men or else found assholes.

"You're in a rut," Noah's sister had said. He was always in the lab with Louise, and nothing happened. He half thought of inviting Rachel. When his sister came home, he would tell her everything. She would smooth it all out, with her large hand.

"Not me," Noah said to Louise. "I've got a new scarf and I'm going."

If Louise had said yes, he told himself, he would have got out of this somehow. He was a chaperon at the annual winter prom for crip teens. They had a rock band, and the kids were dancing in wheelchairs. The whole thing put Noah in mind of bumper cars, but he stayed at the edges of the gym, filling flimsy Coke cups and talking to his old friend Ed, from the agency days. He hadn't spoken to Ed for ages, but they were like that. They'd go years without talking, and then they'd have an essential conversation.

Ed pulled a square bottle from behind him in the chair and poured into two paper cups. "This'll help," he said.

"So, Ed, tell me about sex," Noah said. Ed was paralyzed from the chest down, a T-five paraplegic, but he'd been married and divorced. He had a kid.

"What do you want to know?"

Noah swallowed. "That's my problem. I don't even know what I should know."

"When I was in the hospital I was a boy, in a big room with all paraplegics. We were miserable. And then they put one quadriplegic in with us. He was one of the first. There were no quadriplegics until twenty-five, thirty years ago. They died. Sir Ludwig Gartman created an operation. That one man, the quadriplegic, kept all of us happy. He didn't feel his body at all."

It was different to be born with a disease than to have a car crash, Noah knew that. He'd never had to relearn the world. He'd never had to adjust to the dimensions of a chair. It grew with him. He could judge a theater aisle instantly. Noah's disease felt to him natural. Ed was someone whom Noah considered crippled. *That guy is really disabled,* he'd thought on first seeing him, but he wasn't then, when you knew him.

The kids on the floor were riling up, their arms wild, chairs spinning, doing wheelies, stopping and starting. Noah looked at his watch. He'd been here three hours. He could go now, to the tree-trimming party Jane and Mary were having with Julie and Peter.

"Leaving early?" Ed said.

Noah pushed out a hand for a high-five. "Yeah, bud."

Ed clasped his hand. Like a lot of paras, he had incredible strength in his hands. But this touch was more of a squeeze, gentle, a search and a question. "This is sex," he said.

Noah wheeled along the street, looking for a liquor store. It was a cold night, sharp with every breath. He wasn't sure now that he wanted to go. He'd bought a coat-hanger angel for the Christmas tree, but he wanted to bring a bottle too. What was the name of that red wine? Well, he'd ask: What could they recommend for under ten? This was the first Christmas party he could remember, besides the elementary school assemblies and office gatherings with cartoned eggnog.

Louise had given him a new red plaid scarf. The wool, when he pulled it up to his mouth, turned wet with a faint rind-edge of cold around the warm.

He had to buy new gloves. He used them up fast; the wheels burned right through. He had certain duties in life, and he'd tended them. He'd found tiny gold earrings, stars for Mary and crescent moons for Jane, and sent them in the mail. He'd woken early to beat the line at the post office. You took numbers now, like in a butcher shop. I'm celebrating Christmas, he'd told himself, waiting his turn. The woman ahead had three stacked boxes releasing a faint cloud of sugar. He liked to think of Jane and Mary opening the brown boxes, not being able to wait, then having the shiny new things to wear. They needed him less now, but he knew Owens would never give the shimmery small luxuries that would make them feel rich for the day.

When he arrived, both the bungalow and Julie's cottage were brightly lit. Jane was wearing his earrings when she opened the door. The party was here in the cottage, she explained, but she'd take his coat over to the bungalow. Mary's bed was for coats, and Jane's room was where they'd put the babies. Noah went with Jane up and down plywood ramps and tossed his coat onto the pile on Mary's bed.

Back in the cottage, Julie and Mary moved in a frenzy through the kitchen, searching for the nutcracker. Ordinarily frugal, but not tonight, Julie finally sent Peter out for a new one. At this point, if things were lost, they were just buying them; charging, apparently. Looking at Peter, you could see he was the kind of guy who would go and go.

Noah recognized the man in a black-and-white photograph framed on a sideboard. "That's Niels Carradine. Is he related to somebody here?"

"He's Julie's father," Jane said, as Olivia and Huck joined them. "Isn't it nice she has all these pictures?"

"Well, I think it's a little strange," Olivia said. "They have all these pictures of her father around the house but none of her and Peter."

Jane wished Owens were here to see how comfortable chairs and sofas made a house.

"Her father's dead." Huck shrugged. "She sees Peter every day."

"Her father was a famous physicist," Jane added.

"Now, why can't we live like this," Mary muttered in the next room, marveling at the vase of flowers.

"Oh, no." Julie's voice carried. "We didn't invite Tim. What do I do now?"

Mary and Julie seemed fonder of each other tonight, gifted with a buoyant humor. They were in this together, and their mutual dependence gave them a sense of invincibility or at least communion. The contours of their individual lives blurred as they opened wine bottles. Bags mounted in the kitchen; an ebullience took hold. They were still cooking, with music on.

When Noah asked if he could help, Mary told him she'd taken Jane riding at a stable in the foothills and that on the bench where the mothers sat she fell into conversation with a woman who knew him.

"I'm trying to think who has a daughter."

"Oh, no. She was there with her niece."

Mary looked young to him tonight, her breasts still girl-like in a plain wash-slumped tee shirt, but her mouth was ringed with lines, her chin just beginning to give. He supposed his would, too, soon. The thought of these women, watching their supple-backed, virgin daughters, like beautiful new versions of themselves, just pressing into womanhood, made him feel that he was missing his life.

"Anyway, I invited her."

"What's her name?"

"Rachel Gottlieb."

Just then the aunts arrived, carrying small patent-leather purses and wearing hats. The hostesses tended to them, fighting them out of coats and leading them to the good chairs.

"Isn't it a magnificent tree," Amber pronounced.

They enlisted Noah to check the lights for the one bad bulb. To have something to do with his hands was a relief. The tree was by the front window, a bowl of clementines on the table. It was harder to enjoy himself, knowing that Louise was agitated, still working.

"Omigod, what about ice!" Julie called. "Who can we call to bring ice?"

Almost every new person brought an ornament and walked over to put it on the tree. Several people said that the coat-hanger angel was lovely, and Noah hoped that someone tall enough would lift it to the top, where there was no star.

Amber explained that when Julie was a girl, they'd given her an antique angel every year, so when she was eighteen and left home she had this gorgeous collection.

Noah hated this kind of party, where everyone was standing. He was stuck in the sit-down corner with the old aunts.

"That's a spruce, isn't it?" Ruby said. "We always have a noble fir."

"I pruned it today," Peter offered.

"Pruned it? I've never heard of anybody pruning a Christmas tree," Amber said to Noah. "Have you ever heard of such a thing?"

"No," he said. "I'm Jewish."

"Well, I never did either," Amber said. "Bah. Pruning a spruce."

Across the room, three beautiful girls stood near a wooden bowl of ornaments. Noah felt like Owens, who'd plan out whole parties but then let other people have the fun. During one of his Genesis parties, they'd talked for an hour outside in the parking lot. He suddenly missed Owens, then turned to the old teachers. "I'm going to get a drink. Can I get you something?" Noah asked, thinking how much harder it was to wheel away from someone than to drift off, walking.

"No, no, we're just fine," Ruby said, lifting her eyes to the tree.

Noah shoved a window open, leveraged himself up out of his chair onto the ledge, wind riffling his hair. Drinking again, from the bottle, he was in a crazy mood, full of abandon. Then he saw Julie. He hoped she wouldn't say anything to him about her friend with the O.I. child. This was his daily guilt. Julie was actually quite pretty, though until now he'd always thought she was too thin. He never would have guessed she was Niels Carradine's daughter. Niels Carradine was one of the German-Jewish physicists everyone in the generation before Noah envied. Hundreds of guys had become physicists because they wanted to emulate those men. And Carradine died famously young when an ocean liner went down.

"Congratulations," Julie said, coming towards him. "I hear your discovery's going to lead to a cure for Alzheimer's."

So she knew about his gene. Noah had always tried to stay away from disease, preferring to study fundamental biology. Even so, it now seemed to come down to disease and cure anyway. But since he'd had some success, he minded less. He lifted the bottle to his mouth and threw his head back. For some reason, he wanted her to see him out of his chair like this, drinking.

"How's motherhood?" Earlier, she'd been carrying her little girl, dressed as an angel, wings made of cotton balls pasted on cardboard.

"Coco's great. But I don't know. I still don't feel like myself again yet." She laughed. "It's only been two years."

"You look like yourself. Better, even." She'd definitely gained weight. He offered her the bottle and heard himself laughing. With the back of his knuckles he'd touched her chest. Her skin, between the shirt lapels, was warm.

By the tree, someone had persuaded Ruby to take the pins out of her bun, and the hair fell in a coil down past her waist. She and her sister were trying to convince Jane to go into teaching. "You get your summers, a month for Christmas and a sabbatical every seven years so you can travel."

"Not the most money," Amber said, with a firm nod, "but the best life."

"Every seven years?" Jane said. "I'm going to travel more than that!"

Then she and another girl her age started dancing together in a corner, in their tights, shoes kicked off. They looked silly and happy, no different, really, from the kids in the gym, ramming chairs. *Don't change!* Noah wanted to call out to them.

"There's something I have to tell you, Julie. You have a friend whose baby has what I have." Noah's hand gestured down at himself.

Julie bent towards him, listening. All of a sudden, the party was still going on around them but they were having a quiet conversation.

"Anyway, she called a long time ago and I never called her back. I'm sorry. I would like to meet the child."

"I shouldn't have given her your number without asking you first. I was just . . . I didn't know what to say. And I know how hard you've been working."

"No, it wasn't that. It was me. I'm not big on the crip network." He laughed his raucous laugh again, but she didn't smile. "But I'm not proud of it. I'm changing."

"The girl's here tonight. Do you want to see her?"

"Yes. And I should talk to her mother later."

"Follow me."

Noah left the bottle, now empty, on the ledge and, lowering himself into his chair, rolled after Julie out the back-door ramp, under pines. When they entered the bungalow, Noah noticed animal tracks on the dusty floor. They went through the dim room to Jane's bedroom, where the nursery was set up. It was dark because the children were sleeping. But soon their eyes adjusted to the orange glow of a night-light. Noah recognized Julie's daughter, an angel a half hour ago, asleep with her arms above her head.

"There's the girl," Julie said.

In a brightly colored plastic fold-up crib, her head turned sideways, the girl slept under a hand-knit blanket. Her breath made a tiny even whistle, like any child's.

All of a sudden, Noah felt sick. "Excuse me," he said, rolling back quickly. He moved his chair down the hall to the room where the coats were piled, just to sit still. He shoved the window up so a blast of sharp air came in. He wanted it to stop his reeling. Then Julie came in and sat on the bed. She touched his wrist. "Are you okay? Should I get you some water?"

"I'm a little wasted," he said.

His arms strong, he swung, landed, wriggled, then they were on the bed together amidst the piled coats.

He was lying on a coat and could feel a button poking him in the back, but his head was still revolving, and before he could twist and move the coat, it was happening—what he'd wanted so long and thought about countless times, but now too soon. "My husband's over there." Julie sat up, pushing her soft suede boots off with the fork of her toes. "I'll shut the door."

She crossed the room, then returned. He rubbed her heaving back in circles. She turned up in a yawn, knelt over him, her patterned legs on either side, and she was kissing him, and it was not what he'd imagined, but rougher, her tongue sandpaper like a cat's, and he worried about not knowing how. He tried to do what she did back. She was unbuttoning him, murmuring, and her hand moved on his buckle in the strange gray light.

"Does this hurt?" she whispered.

Her patterned tights bunched at her ankles, an accordioned mural, and he wanted to tell her to wait, he was going too fast. But he felt numb and his body flew ahead, complying without him; it was too late to master himself. Suddenly, a baby cried in the next room, and Julie stiffened. Her head tipped, still. "It's not mine," she said. He saw her leg, where the thigh joined, and it was like the pictures he'd seen all his life, and a noise leapt out of his chest, a long pulled rickety chain.

He felt bruised, sensitive. She arched her head back, beautiful, so he could see her neck. They were still on top of the coats. A piece of her hair was in his mouth. The baby was screaming now.

"I'd better go," she said. She sat on the edge of the bed and lifted her legs, one at a time, toes pointing, to pull up her tights.

"Wait," he said.

She put a finger to his lips. "Shhh. Thank you." Then she kissed his forehead, and after she left he felt a weight there, like a coin.

What he'd wanted to say was that she had to help him down. Now he'd have to slide or wait for someone to come in. Once, he was left out on a blanket in the sun, grass pricking through the thin wool and the low world buzzing around him. That was his first memory of being stopped. He also waited in hallways, in rooms. People said, "Just wait here, I'll be right back." He was stationary. But he hadn't lived that way. He was an early crawler.

He tossed his clothes down to the floor first, then slid off slowly, hanging on to the little white tassels on the edge of the bedspread. When he came out of the room, Rachel was walking towards him, dressed up, her mouth dark with lipstick. She knew something was wrong, because she looked down when he said hello. He felt moved by her trying to look pretty; and sorry: Rachel was just arriving, and he was leaving.

Rolling down the sidewalk, he thought of the world outside that was never Christmas. On Main Street the homeless shuffled with their cups; the hospital at the end was always open and every night the same. Louise was probably fierce in a fit of calculation, mad because she hadn't gone and now the party was over.

Years from now, he thought, Julie would listen for his name. They would be part of a secret network of kindness, watching for each other in silent ways. She knew, wild as he'd been on the windowsill with the long green bottle, that he was losing his virginity to her on top of the coats. She had been with him as if she were unwrapping a package.

He went not home but to the lab. Louise was still there, sternly working. She pretended not to notice when he came in.

"We've got to talk," he said.

"About what?"

"You know what."

And they began. It took a long time, and then, from the lab door, which he'd locked, came an insistent knocking. Louise stood up to see.

"Leave it," Noah ordered.

"Who is that?"

"Never mind."

"I know anyway." And then she sighed, and like a dutiful child raised up her arms and pulled off her tee shirt. She wasn't wearing a bra.

"You're just doing this because of Rachel. What do you really want?"

"Enough, I think."

He was afraid to ask more.

She was also frightened. "I don't want to lie. I mean, this isn't like it was with Andy. But it's some things that wasn't. It's different."

"That's good enough for me. But you need to decide if it'll be enough for you."

She awkwardly bent down to kiss him, there at the drosophila station, cradling her bare, cold breasts in her arms.

"What would you want if you could have one thing?" she asked.

"For years, like I told you, all I wanted was to walk. It wouldn't be that anymore."

"What is it now?"

"Same as you. To be a scientist."

But that was a lie, too, an old truth that had stopped being true only a few hours earlier. Julie's act of curiosity and charity, a proof of her own wildness and the variety of life, had brought back a linked train of a thousand memories. Noah loved to be touched. All he wanted now was Louise and love.

Later, Rachel slipped a long, painstaking letter under the lab door. Louise, as she left at dawn, marked the white envelope with her high heel.

To the Moon

❖ ❖ ❖ ❖ ❖

"*O*rdinary civilians will be going to the moon in our life-time," Owens said, standing on the back porch, looking up at the night sky. "They've actually got a list at NASA, and I'm on it. I had the chance to sign up a few years ago. I put down myself and my wife."

"And who will that be?" Jane asked.

He shrugged. "You can probably come along."

"No, thanks. I'll be in college."

Who would get to be his wife was the eternal question of Jane's childhood. Spanning the years, it had yielded a good deal of pleasure, as she and her mother pondered why and why not Olivia. To both of them, it had seemed like a long talent search.

Sometimes it seemed an unfair trick of life that Mary wasn't eligible even to try. Only now, as she sat below her father on the porch, did it seem the slightest bit unnatural that her mother had entered those discussions with so much fervor.

Ever since Olivia had been pregnant, Jane had believed Owens would have more children. Every day when he didn't was a day she wouldn't have had to worry as much as she did. She understood that when the bad news came, she would feel the sorrowing relief of a long rain. It was so much work to keep track of the inevitability, every day counting the not yet. She felt afraid of Olivia, her towering—maybe she would be the new mother. But Jane was even more afraid of someone she didn't know.

That night, Mary was sitting in a Western Civilization class at Grass Valley Community College. The teacher was finishing a long explanation Mary had already lost the gist of. She'd wait until he started another one, and then she'd concentrate from the beginning.

So many times, it seemed to Mary, she'd been outside this door, quietly thinking she deserved to get in but receiving no answer. Now an answer had come: a typed yes from Eliot Hanson, as easy as a letter, ordinary, a transaction that stopped nothing in the world. So why, now, did she feel small?

Her leg seemed white under the standard metal desk, her skirt flimsy. The lights in this room were the kind that hurt your eyes. Students slouched and fidgeted in the chairs around her. There was no college momentum, she thought, no program here.

She went back to daydreaming about the tent. A friend of Julie's had hired her to plan a two-year-old's birthday party. She would rent farm animals, a small goat, an old horse and chickens from the road where she grew up. She'd paint a small green circus tent with flowers.

Eliot Hanson, who hadn't seen Owens for almost a year, still devoted a great deal of thought to his client's life. Owens did not confide in him; in fact, he tried not to have to talk to him at all, so Eliot had to glean what he could from the bills he paid and the purchases he arranged. With a kind, paternal interest, he tried to reconstruct the currents of event and affection from this trail of receipts.

This morning, he'd closed his office door and sat with Owens' December folder, then written a large check pertaining to Olivia. Owens had ordered her a car. "Her Bug's in and out of the shop all the time, and I think one of these days it's gonna just die." He'd first wanted black, then he'd called to change it to forest green. This was the first expenditure of any kind that Eliot had linked to Olivia.

But Eliot had managed money long enough to understand that large expenditures could as easily signal an end as a beginning. His predecessor, Kellogg Hooper, had given him the advice: "Before people divorce, they do one of two things. They either buy a house or have a child."

Eliot's wife, Hazel, said it wouldn't be Olivia. She was too guileless, Hazel thought, and lacked the sophistication to run a romance its full course. Romance, like most other feelings, was something Owens wanted to be entirely natural. But as any older woman and some men could have told him, romance cannot survive in nature on its own.

Mary di Natali had made an appointment to come in. To have all possible information on the table, Eliot put in a call to Owens' travel agent, to ask about the South Pacific. "Has he decided if Jane's going? Three tickets. A-OK."

Since Owens left Genesis, his bills had shot up. Though they were well within the range of what he could comfortably afford, Eliot nevertheless read them as a warning sign. It was pretty clear Owens needed something to do all day. The South Pacific was another example.

In an interview Eliot had read a few years before, Owens talked about going back to school. But it was hard to picture him sitting at a small desk, listening to a lecture with nineteen-year-olds. He needed a job, but who would hire him? His only experience was being boss. Maybe he'd reconsider public office, but Eliot wasn't going to encourage that. "Good money after bad" was another phrase popular with Kellogg Hooper, who'd accompanied the words with a sour downturning of the mouth.

No, it won't be Olivia, Eliot decided. His quiet conclusion had nothing to do with his wife's assessment, which seemed to derive from the way Olivia dressed. Eliot remembered Hazel's glance when the top of Olivia's tee shirt left two inches bare above the crenulated band of her jeans. Hazel was a bit of a prude. From Eliot's point of view, it was timing. Owens couldn't possibly get married when he had nothing to do all day.

And if Olivia wouldn't be permanent, who would be?

Jane would, and the child had to be protected. Jane's mother was a more complicated consideration, but that was why he looked forward to meeting her. He'd heard a great deal about her but wanted to make a determination for himself.

At ten o'clock, his secretary announced that Mary di Natali was there, with a Julie Carradine. Eliot frowned. She'd said nothing about bringing anyone along; moreover, Eliot hadn't mentioned this meeting to Owens. But there was no time to think. The two women walked in and took seats on the other side of his desk.

"I'm Julie Carradine," one said, extending her hand. She explained that she and Mary were friends and neighbors. "I was a lawyer until a few years ago"—she laughed—"and now I have the hardest job I've ever had, and that's a two-and-a-half-year-old daughter."

Wary as Eliot was of meeting with Mary's lawyer, he instinctively trusted Julie. She had a simple manner he appreciated, and the bearing of someone whose duties in life had never yet risen to the level of her capacity. Perhaps nothing had called her passions or temper into her work, so she remained graciously calm. Just now she was explaining the precariousness of Mary's position, her concern for Jane's college education. Owens, she pointed out with a sharing smile, didn't like to talk about the future. While Julie spoke, Mary's face hung like a dour mask. Mary, it seemed, could not laugh about Owens.

"I understand perfectly why you'd want to know Owens' intentions for Jane's future," Eliot said.

One edge of Mary's lip lifted, and the eye on that side squinted.

The fact was that Jane's college and graduate school expenses were already secured and accounted for, though Eliot wasn't at liberty to reveal these arrangements. It was a complicated fiscal instrument involving Owens' will. Once, when Eliot suggested a standard trust fund for Jane, Owens had looked at him aghast. "It would detune her life," he'd said. Apparently, Owens' conviction that Jane should know nothing of her future inheritance, so as not to taint her middle-class freshness, had the additional benefit of causing Mary consternation.

Eliot had somehow to set Mary's mind at ease without disclosing any confidential particulars. After a few vaguely consolatory remarks left Mary's face hanging blank and suspicious as before, he turned instinctively to Julie.

"Let me put it this way. I have a daughter too, and I know just how you're feeling. And to be honest, I'd have the same concern if I thought there was any chance that Jane's future was threatened. But let me put your mind at ease. Whatever he says or will not say, Owens is going to do right by Jane."

Julie glanced at Mary. "Well, good, that's reassuring," she said calmly. "Of course, anything we could do by way of written guarantees would be helpful."

"I don't think that's going to be possible, and it's not necessary. You really don't have to worry about the money for Jane's education going anywhere. I can promise you that personally."

"All right," Julie Carradine said. "That's good enough for us."

Mary, whose mouth had been closed for some time as if worrying the pit of something, suddenly lifted her head. "But it's not only about Owens and Jane. There's a lot that's Owens and Mary too." She looked hunted, cornered. "He's paying for my college, but it would take years to get a degree, and degrees in art don't mean anything anyway. What's needed is help with my business. If I could buy tents and start painting them."

Julie explained that Mary had planned three children's parties: she'd painted the tents and brought the animals, baked cakes and made the favors. "There's solid business in that," Julie said, then smiled. "I know I'm going to hire you."

"Let's put it this way," Eliot said slowly. "We could talk to Owens and explain the relative merits of starting a business versus going back to school. Or we could do something easier. Right now you're sending me the tuition bills and I'm paying them directly. Instead of that, I could just figure out the cost of a semester, counting tuition and fees and books, and send you a check."

"That sounds best," Julie said. "You don't even have to involve him."

Mary mumbled, "He could do a lot more to help me keep her."

Eliot saw from Julie Carradine's bent neck and scratching glances at the floor that she too felt startled.

"Tell me what you mean," he said gently.

Looking from one to the other, as someone unsure which to distrust more, Mary spoke in a rambling, plaintive voice for almost ten minutes. What emerged most vividly was a fury with Owens for not sharing his fruit.

"Does he want the good fruit, the cherries and big strawberries, just for himself, or does he want his daughter to have it too? Because I can't afford it on what he gives me."

Of course, what Mary was saying wasn't literally true. Eliot wrote the checks. Surely she could afford fruit.

"She's over there half the time already. Pretty soon she'll always want to be there. I can't keep up. I don't even know the names of half his fruit."

"Well, maybe this isn't a matter for Eliot," Julie said softly.

Mary recoiled.

"That's right," Eliot said. "There we get into the realm, I'm afraid, of personality, and what you and Tom decide between yourselves. I think we can all agree it would be nice if he'd send Jane home with a basket of peaches or whatever it is he's got there. But that's the kind of thing we just have to leave up to him."

The two women stood, Mary still shaking her head, and Eliot encouraged them to call again if any problems arose concerning Jane. He had determined for himself that Mary di Natali was not a conniver, as Owens had suggested. She was a flustered woman who needed shelter. Jane, Eliot had sensed a long time back, was a gift Owens would someday fully recognize. And as a father, Eliot understood in a deep way that you couldn't look after the interests of a child without considering her mother.

Since losing Genesis, Owens had become a believer in vacations. And this particular trip over the holidays held the advantage of avoiding family, to which neither he nor Olivia truly belonged.

Air on the island felt easy on their arms, and as they stepped down from the plane, an adipose native woman presented them with orchid leis. Due to her lingering status as a child, Jane received many more gifts besides. First, a man behind the tiki stand wove her a hat made of long grass. On a dive, Olivia—seeming even more opulent underwater, her hair fanning out three feet—picked up a perfect shell and put it in Jane's hand. Later, Jane joined a group of very young native girls, who were learning the constructive art of grass-skirt-making. Women in muumuus tied white string between palm trunks and set the girls to work, leaf by leaf. It turned out you tied the pampas leaves like men's neckties. Jane felt patient to learn on both accounts, for a grass skirt now and because a man's tie would be a cute accessory to her wardrobe at home. Owens had so many ties he didn't wear anymore.

The days bagged, lacking definition, and it seemed one could live a whole life without accomplishing anything or even minding. The listing hours in the rope hammock, the suck of the ocean, still and gurgling, and clean-bellied afternoons spent swimming lulled them into a false state of summer. In the dining room at breakfast time, birds flew in freely off the pearled sea. Jane watched for progress on the twin clock of her skin and hair. About this, as everything else, Owens had peculiar theories. "The sun is good for human beings. You don't need sunblock. We're not meant to be inside buildings."

"It's bad for you, Owens," Jane said. "Doctors proved it."

"It causes cancer," Olivia added.

He remained calm and quizzical when no one took his advice, and after he'd burned himself beet red he reluctantly began wearing shirts and rubbing in the reviled lotion he still claimed not to believe in. "I think people burn because we're not outside enough. Our bodies aren't used to it."

Once, in high school, he almost froze to death in Yosemite, Jane's mother had told her. He always wanted to be part of nature, but the feeling didn't seem to be reciprocal.

Jane learned to make her fingers precise and useful in the long dipping boredom of afternoon, for no purpose other than distraction. She and Olivia spent hours braiding each other's hair into hundreds of tiny braids, then floating and letting it dry into a soft halo.

They watched Owens swimming into the waves like a long, awk-ward bird.

There was only one girl Jane's age, who wore a gold ankle bracelet. Jane stared at her when she thought the girl wouldn't notice, in the outside shower. Jane studied the way her thighs squared off at the top; maybe that was the way thighs were supposed to be. And there was a cute boy who sailed the sunset cruise boat. When she could, Jane fol-lowed him aimlessly, just for something to do.

Early one morning, she hiked to the cove where they kept the up-turned rowboats. Sometimes she saw him out rowing at this still, calm time of the day. Turning the corner, she saw parts of legs—the girl and him on the sand. The girl's nipples looked different; where Jane's were tiny and pink, she had brown circles. Jane kept thinking she hadn't re-ally seen. She walked in the other direction, stiff and conscious of how her butt looked from the back. Hours later, they were in the water, the girl's hair flattened against her head like a dark bathing cap, her two hands on the bobbing shelf of his shoulders.

When Owens and Olivia debated a helicopter ride to a volcano, Owens said, "And Jane hasn't had her life's fulfillment yet," and she tried to keep her cheek from ticking. Now this other girl was having hers.

When they left the island, a hula dancer presented each of them with a double-shell necklace, the kind Jane'd had the patience to string only long enough for an ankle bracelet. Olivia gave Jane her necklace, so Jane had two. As they boarded the plane in the tiny airport, Jane mar-veled that the kids had all the presents, not the adults. She supposed this was because a lot of the parents here were rich like Owens and the kids already understood that they might never be able to afford a life like this on their own and so they were saving souvenirs.

Owens had already told her she would not inherit. She sighed; he was always offering her his life, but not to keep. She even knew what he'd say if she said that: Life isn't to keep, he'd say, and raise his eyebrows.

Olivia's black Volkswagen finally died, so she was riding her bike to the hospital and back.

On Saturday, Owens picked up the new car and persuaded her to accept it. He showed her the various features, shining in the strong, late-morning light. When he demonstrated how the convertible top went down, she smiled.

"This is real progress," he said to Jane, having for so long convinced himself that Olivia was not only immune to but actually repelled by money. Jane knew better. As they explored the new car, his voice fast and excited, Jane heard him laugh and realized it was the first time in almost a year.

He and Olivia were talking about a baby shower. Karen Croen was pregnant and she knew from the amniocentesis that the baby was a girl. She and Dave promised to name her Olivia Rose. They'd told Olivia when she came home from the South Pacific, and this seemed to give her unaccountable joy.

Jane could tell Owens found it poignant, her pleasure in this, because he truly couldn't understand himself why any such thing would make her happy. He'd already stood godfather to five children, but he'd made it to the christening only once. That was for Shep and Lamb's girl, Minna.

"Minna graduated from high school last spring," he said. "I got a little card inviting us to a party. But that was when Exodus was falling apart."

"Where's she going to college?"

He didn't know, and Jane wondered whether her parents had the money to send her where she really wanted to go or to the best place she got in. Once, long ago, he'd meant to tell them that money shouldn't be a consideration, that Minna should choose whatever school she wanted and he would help. But now the decision was already made, acceptances filed, and a life started.

"Did you ever give gifts to your godchildren?"

"No."

"Not even Minna?"

He shrugged.

"Do you write them letters?"

"Yeah, I know. Their parents are probably thinking they made a big mistake."

Or else, Jane thought, they hoped some obscure advantage would come to their kids later on, as she and her mom always had. But Shep and Lamb didn't seem to expect anything.

Olivia had already wrapped two presents for the baby. In addition to the tiny ring that was supposed to have been given to her as a child, she'd found a wreath for the baby's head, made of dried bud roses.

"I think you're doing it the right way," Jane said.

"I do too," Owens said, "but I couldn't have done it. There were too many ceremonies, too many babies, people I didn't really know."

"So you should have said no to those people and just been really good to the one who mattered."

"You mean Minna."

Jane hadn't meant Minna. She had meant herself.

"When Frank and I were just starting out, we went to a sperm bank a couple times, because they paid us. And once, a woman who worked there said to me, 'I'm not supposed to tell you this, but you have eleven kids.' " He sighed. "I wish now I hadn't done that."

This was about as close as he came, Jane figured, to apologizing.

"What made you change your mind about Jane?" Olivia asked, reading in bed, wearing a tee shirt and underwear. He moved around the room, still dressed.

"What do you mean?" It is a difficult circumstance to live with someone who doesn't believe in your goodness, and Owens had endured that irritation for some time now. He'd made adjustments to it, as to a physical pain.

"Well, when she came to Alta, you said you were going to be nice but you didn't think she was yours. And now you obviously do. So what happened?"

"Livia, when she came here I didn't know her. And Mary can be pretty loopy."

"I sometimes wonder, what if Jane had had problems?"

They had reached a strange plane in their relationship. They each said things they knew to be wrong and couldn't stop themselves, thinking, I can't help it. Neither of them doubted for long that they would break up, but neither knew when one of them would feel the strength.

Owens left the room. It was dusk, still early enough for bike rides outside, families walking.

She followed. Olivia had long felt herself to be on an investigative journey, as if there were some evidence yet to be found that would determine conclusively whether he was better or worse than she feared. What she went over, again and again, was his change towards Jane. She needed to know why he loved her. "I think we should talk about this. It matters if we ever have children."

He didn't answer, only lowered his head to his arms. For some reason, he remembered the day Mary told him she was pregnant. He'd never told her that they would stay together. The weird thing was, she just went away. And the problem seemed gone. But then it would bob up at stray moments, and years later he finally understood: this would never go away.

That was how he felt now about Olivia. He doubted they could ever make it better anymore, but she existed in him like a permanent thread-line pain.

One evening in April, Olivia ran the twenty-one-day-old convertible into a copper beech. She was lucky, so lucky, to be fine. The tree was over a hundred years old.

They became careful with each other, then matter-of-fact. A few days later, she flew to Asia. He called her there, in the middle of the night. "I really cared about you. I want you to know that."

Every day, they broke up again, on different continents, over the phone.

There are things you know about a man you don't know you know until they're useless, Olivia understood in Singapore. How far he swings his arms when he walks. Olivia looked for him, from behind, in a crowd. She always saw one small part of him and then felt disappointed.

Eliot Hanson arranged for a check to be sent to Olivia. Owens had vacillated wildly over the amount. He'd decided on twenty-five thousand, finally, as a kind of token. Eliot was particularly sad, for no reason, as he sealed the envelope. He himself had married into money.

He felt a certain vicarious victory when the check was returned, by certified mail, a few days later. He took it upon himself to visit Olivia, to urge her to accept this or some larger form of compensation. She refused to discuss it, merely shook her head and shut the door.

Three Regrets

⊰⊱⊰⊱⊰⊱⊰⊱

*D*uring the month of May, Owens asked more than a hundred people who they thought was more beautiful, Olivia or Eve Peck. It was his particular talent to ask with such searching depth in his eyes that people shuddered. They didn't want to get the wrong answer, but they had no idea and they didn't really care. Most of them had had enough of Olivia but didn't know Eve Peck.

At seven o'clock one Thursday evening, Eliot Hanson stopped by the house. After a few minutes of conversation about marks, yen and T-bills, Owens asked the question. There was nothing lighthearted in his face.

"Oh, I don't know about that," Eliot said. Eliot knew Olivia, the flash of her long hair. She was tall, straight up and down, usually wearing faded jeans. Eliot knew from his wife, Hazel, how difficult jeans were to fit for women. They seemed to shop around a great deal for them, and even then they had them nipped in and let out, shortened.

More than a few times, Eliot had seen Olivia walk out in a huff.

He'd met Eve Peck only once. She was slimmer, Indian-featured, beautiful in a way that would last. She seemed intelligent and kind.

"Come on, really. Tell me what you think."

"I don't know either one of them, Tom."

"Well, you know Olivia."

"Yes, and she's always been very nice to me."

"And what do you think of Eve?"

"I like her too, so far as I know."

Eliot had not driven all the way down to Alta to discuss the relative material dimensions of Olivia and Eve Peck. It was time, he'd decided, to inform Owens about his mother. "Sit down," he said, and handed Owens the file.

He then began to explain the contents in his annoyingly thorough way, to the point where the greatest mystery of Owens' life had, in the course of half an hour, begun to bore him. Eliot was still on the woman's sophomore year of college, information he'd gleaned from computer searches.

"Cut to the chase," Owens said.

Owens wished for a moment that he could ask this woman, his mother, whom he should marry. But she was only twenty-three when she died, younger than either Olivia or Eve.

Olivia's small life song: Nobody else will believe, but I was the one who said no. Twenty years later, her children would know that he begged, "We'll change our socks and we'll change our shoes," but she was the one to say no.

> *No one will ever believe*
> *that I was the one who said no.*
> *He came to me and begged with rings*
> *but I was the one who said no.*

Twice Owens found a young guy at Olivia's new cottage, who disappeared into the garage when he came and turned Olivia's bike upside down, to fix. As they argued Owens heard the wheels outside, whirring.

-◄-

Driving home after divesting himself of Owens' mother and her large file, Eliot Hanson thought of his wife's legs. Hazel was short, five feet nothing, but sturdy. Her legs reminded him, sweetly, of a panda, but he felt agitated because Owens had in all probability made a negative assessment of Hazel. Not only was she short but she was covered with freckles.

There were views of her he found beautiful. Hazel had fine tapered fingers. Great strong arms. But Hazel looked like most women in jeans. When they were dating they had fallen into the habit of having real meals, including a dessert, at Hazel's apartment. Every night, she did the dishes. She often changed clothes and would stand washing at the sink in her long kimono. One night, there, he asked her.

Later, for years and years, the story was told to friends: "I was just washing the dishes, and he said, Well, maybe we should get married."

He hadn't had a ring or anything. Owens already owned an extraordinary ring; Eliot knew because he'd had to liquidate some treasury notes. That had been more than a year ago now. As was his habit, Eliot worried whether Owens had taken sufficient care to protect the stone, and he made a note to himself to check on the computer tonight whether the item and its appraisal had been included under any insurance policy.

Hazel had been so happy it rang out of her face. Then she served dessert. After she cleaned up, they always had tea and dessert.

"I'm getting old enough to have things I regret. I really regret three things. I regret not working harder with Livia, because I could've made that work. And I regret the way things ended at Genesis. I should never have hired Rooney."

Jane was waiting for the third thing, the one he'd saved for last. It had to be her. Even as old as she was, she felt her cheeks blush. She hoped he wouldn't see and wanted him to look at her.

"And I regret not spending more time with my mom before she died."

In her stunned disappointment, Jane babbled. "Even if you had spent more time, you'd probably always feel that."

"No. I didn't even take off a week. I really could have."

That was different and true. There was nothing she could think of to say then. She searched her mind, the way she'd scribble all over a piece of paper, and she discovered nothing. So she shut up.

Her first ten years, she wasn't even a regret. She could forgive him. She had been ready to. She was only waiting for him to ask.

"I don't want to blow it with Eve," he whispered. "You know I've got the ring."

"Is it the same one you had for Olivia?" Jane said.

He didn't answer. He was finding it generally more difficult to manage his child as she became older. In fact, he had two rings in his possession. "How should I ask her?"

"Put it on her finger while she sleeps," Jane whispered, "so she wakes up engaged, like in a fairy tale."

He did just that, with his mother's ring, and Jane knew she'd never get the credit.

On Owens' wedding day, for the second time in his life Alta was given snow, but he wasn't there to see it. With Jane, he and his bride flew to Italy, where they would be married in Assisi, in a chapel he'd read about but never seen.

Mary spent the day cooking, the snow falling in fine lines outside. She kneaded bread again and again, pounding hard between rises. At five o'clock, Olivia came over with a bottle of wine. They ate the food he would rather have been eating, toasting the end of some long epic in their lives.

Here

━◄─◄─◄─◄─◄

*L*ight fell pink in their house. The old windows had a drop of gold in them. Roses bloomed outside the windows, and you could smell them. There were insects too. Good insects, crickets and ladybugs. Owens had purchased ten thousand and released them into the yard.

There are roses outside.

I can just go outside and pick roses if I want.

Why didn't I get a start like this?

Why wasn't I born now?

When the baby was born, Jane had wanted to move in with Owens and Eve. Owens offered Mary a trip around the world and presented her with a globe to plan her itinerary. He suggested she pick a pursuit—butterflies, birds, astronomy—to structure her journey. She went to a Viennese psychiatrist, who said, capaciously spreading his arms, "It sounds like they're trying to get rid of you."

Eli was like a child with Owens: impressed, always trying to please. They decided to send him along too. So now they were traveling with a woman who claimed to have been on the last plane out of China in 1949 and was going back for the first time. Every week, Jane received postcards from their adventure.

"She says her life would be different, not different but a lot better, if I'd never been born."

"You know, Jane," Eve cautioned, "people say a lot of things in fights that they don't really mean."

"I know. But she's right. Her life *would* be different."

No one could say anything to that.

"We paid good money for our house, and we have a right to sleep in it!" Owens hung out his upstairs window and yelled down to the teenage boys sitting on the hood of a car, pitching empty beer cans into a metal drum in which they'd lit a fire. The people across the street were having a party.

He planned to go over the next day, knock on the door and state his views.

Jane just pulled a pillow over her head.

For Easter, Owens decided they should work in a soup kitchen, but when Eve called the listings in the yellow pages, it turned out all the soup kitchens were full up.

"We have lots of volunteers round the holidays," said the man Owens asked at the old Auburn church.

"Well, this is Tom Owens. Could you please call me if anybody cancels."

And sure enough, they got in off the waiting list. The organizers set Jane up at the apple cider, which she ladled to mumbled gratitude, as much for her young face as for the warm styrofoam cups she handed out.

A man about Owens' age settled over his dinner with an amazed look on his face, his long arms rested on either side of the place mat. He face bowed down to inhale the steam. "What a wonderful meal," he said.

Owens put his head down in his own folded arms; given his tastes in food, he couldn't eat anything here. He finally looked up, to see Eve showing two old men the baby. All he wanted to do was protect that child, so newly risen, it seemed, she could dent. Love of the one conquered love of the many. But he'd been raised by a woman who didn't give birth to him; he himself was unowned. What he lived for now was her: her fresh, unimprinted love. He felt such gratitude to Eve for being able to love him. Olivia had tried and been unable.

The baby spit up on Eve's clean blue-and-white striped shirt. Eve was young, with a young mother's strength and courage. Jane was always surprised that she didn't get only the best clothes. She didn't seem to buy much at all, from what Jane saw, not even furniture. Jane watched what she did carefully, because Eve was the first woman she really knew who'd gone to college and done everything, like a man. Noah's friend Louise was like that too, but she seemed mad all the time. Julie had been a lawyer, but Jane knew she cared more about her house and the details, like dishes and placemats. Eve made it all look easy. And when something spilled, she didn't worry. Her engagement ring was too big and she'd never had it made smaller. She just wore it every day with a piece of yarn.

Owens felt a primitive pride. His success allowed him to give his family a good house and simple clothes and a dinner to come home to every night. He could offer them this forever, and that was what mattered now.

Owens had discovered that he liked to bake, and he was quite proud of his bread.

"Whenever I pass this place," he told Jane, "I always think of Olivia."

They were on a side street Jane had walked probably a thousand times already in her life. On the corner was the antique store where Amber had once bought her the Chinese painted pillbox she'd lost in the American River, and across the street was the drugstore where Noah Kaskie had taken her for hamburgers when he found her that first day here. Owens was pointing at a plain downtown hotel. "Because that's where her mother blew her brains out."

"With a gun?"

"Yup. She had a gun."

They stood looking at the building, which Jane had seen for years but never before taken even a fraction of a second to consider. The top floor no longer had the raised letters pronouncing its name, but their stencils remained legible. Jane knew Alta by now as the place she'd grown up in and was dying to leave, ticking, counting the months and days before she could go free; but occasionally, for a moment, she could imagine herself later, the new person she would become. This hotel too she would add to her collection of monuments that marked the education of her youth.

A teacher at school had helped her fill out the long pages of application to the college in New England she'd seen only pictures of—a town of brick buildings covered with ivy, everyone riding bikes and wearing corduroy and sweaters. She had forged a parent's signature, tracing from an old Genesis annual report she'd found in the local library. Every day she had to be home first to get the mail, and yesterday the letter had come.

From a pay phone, she'd called Eliot Hanson. If she was going to go to New England, he would have to pay.

She didn't know how to ask them; once, they'd agreed together she should never go to school. So she'd told Noah first.

"Why didn't you stay back East? Do you think the quality of life's better here?"

Noah had shrugged. "Quality of sidewalk. You should go."

Now she and Noah picked up Owens at his house and then continued on their walk.

"So what do you think?" Noah asked. "You going to run for something?"

Jane looked at her father, eager for the answer. She'd wanted to ask him that too.

"Naw. You can't go making a fool of yourself on roller skates if you're a senator or something. I'm sick of representing things. I want to just be a goof. I think that'll be a lot funner. No, I'm glad history's passed me by."

"Look over there," Jane said, when they finally wound back home. The neighbors in the yellow house across the street seemed to be having another party. People slowly moved over the lawn in long ballroom dresses.

"She's a debutante, the daughter," Jane said. "But what is that exactly?"

"Oh, it's a horrible little club," Noah said, "set up so the upper classes can guarantee that their children marry into the upper classes."

"No, Jane," Owens said. "I don't think that's what it's about with our neighbors. Their daughter has some hearing problems. She's actually pretty deaf. And they want her to have as normal a social life as possible. So I think that's why they have all these parties. They figure if they have a lot, people will maybe invite her to theirs."

Noah snickered. The deaf, in his experience, were often snobs.

They all came to Jane's graduation. For that day, the old teachers turned up, carrying rich Mason jars of preserves they'd made from fruit picked at night in Alta's parks. Old stragglers, single people from her years over the mountains, came too. Bixter handed her a puppy from her bucket, its eyes still closed. Eli had castanets on his fingers, Olivia brought a bouquet of daffodils.

For those who knew her earlier in her life, what had become of Jane was amazing though also a sorrow, not because she was lost to them forever but because she had ceased to engage their deepest interest. These were people who had been willing to fight for her survival, and now she had not only survived but was thriving. To many of them, what was rare and best in her bloomed only in shaded obscurity; her odd clarity, her frangibility, her allowance for their small comforts and predilections, had not long survived her drive over the mountains. That soft-fingered child was somewhere buried, another victim of the frontier. She had survived, in ways most of them had not, and they carried their losses everywhere behind them, jangling like a string of tin cans.

The diction of Jane's new family was High English. They whistled Mozart, roller-skating under the full dark trees or pushing the stroller. Since the valley had become rich, most of the old houses had been refurbished and some of the bungalows had been torn down and replaced with structures built out to the lot lines. Fathers could be seen through yellow windows, sitting down to read. If you asked any one of them how his day was, his answer was apt to be "Great!"

So the old ones gave their gifts and bowed away after the ceremony, and Jane settled the strange assortment in a bag, holding the puppy under her dress. She sighed. These were precious oddments she had no use for, typical of her mother's friends.

"Did you see Ozzie's father over there? He was all proud, saying, 'Attaboy. That's my boy.' He gave him a thousand-dollar bill."

"What does his father do?" Mary asked.

"Counterfeiter," Owens said.

Owens was still famous. A woman he didn't know walked up to him and said, "Oh, I'm so glad you shaved off your beard. It was really ugly."

He shrugged and said, "I'm speechless."

Another of his theories concerned summer. He decided Jane should do nothing. He wanted her to sleep late and slouch around the house. Pick roses and put them in vases if she wanted to.

Weekdays, between the hours of nine and five, Alta reverted to its long-ago memory and lived in Spanish. Gardeners tilled yards and dispensed water they would never own. Soft religious women held babies too young to talk, feeding them things their mothers disapproved of, because they knew what God wanted with children, and it was quiet and graceful repose.

Owens could be counted on to believe in love, not only his own but yours too, if you told him so. It was his supreme value in life, even when he'd worked twenty hours a day. For him, it was the slender everything.

He believed in Jane's loves when she was too young to really have any. And he was loyal.

He sang:

> *I'm just that man*
> *whose sperm fertilized the egg—*
> *half your chromosomes—*
> *who made sure you weren't a man.*

Or, into the telephone, calling Eliot Hanson, "We're sitting around in the foyer, trying to call our favorite lawyer. . . ."

This was embarrassing but also consoling. The way he was.

-+-

They ate at six o'clock and walked at seven. They fell asleep at nine-thirty or ten, and beyond the screenless windows crickets sounded their two notes under the dark stateliness of the old oaks and a tilted moon like an ironic earring.

Owens knew odd facts—for example, that Mount Whitney is the highest point in America, Death Valley the lowest, and California has both. He loved to explain things to Jane, small things that were part of the everyday world but that would neither come up in ordinary conversation nor help her get into graduate school.

He pointed at the triangular device he was pushing the baby in.

"Why does it stop so evenly, Jane?" He always quizzed her to make sure she understood.

One night, she asked him about his youth.

"I wrestled for six months over whether I was going to start Genesis. I knew I wanted to do it but just not then. I wanted to wait. I thought maybe I should go and join a monastery. But I also knew that was the time." He looked at her as he did only with Eve and, sometimes, her. "I knew it was going to be really big."

They walked with that for a moment, then Owens stopped at a bush of open roses. He cupped one and dunked Jane's head down to smell. She loved thinking of her parents together, sharing a bed that had white sheets and no blanket, never made. She pictured it in an empty room, with one chair.

"You know, rock and roll started here. The Grateful Dead was here. *The Whole Earth Catalog* started here. It's hard to explain, but it was really wonderful here then. It was—well, I want to say the sixties, but the sixties were really the seventies. You could date it with *Sergeant Pepper.* It's like the universe cracked open for a little while and a certain number of people got out, some of the brightest people in the world. Chemists and poets and philosophers.

"I feel lucky to have been in it. I wouldn't trade it for anything. It was like, it was like this. . . ." He swept his arm off the handle of the baby carriage, "This time of night in summer, about seven o'clock, a little balmier than right now."

The Dance

*T*o Noah's wedding, Jane wore the first dress her father had finally bought her. He'd taken her to the fifth floor of Alta's old department store, where she'd carried dresses to the assigned room and walked out in her rubber shoes and thick socks, the flimsy fabric tickling her knees. They'd agreed on the dress; it was black and sleeveless. And every time Jane wore it, she felt the thrilling bareness again as air tangled around her legs and scarfed inside the armholes. By now, she owned many dresses. Eve took her shopping and let her pick out what she wanted. One thing Jane liked about Eve was that even though she didn't care much about clothes herself, she didn't make Jane feel bad because she did. Still, once Jane could wear anything, she found she was most comfortable in the jeans and tee shirts of her childhood.

The wedding was outside, in the stunted orchards adjoining the Copper King's mansion, and Jane had flown home for it. Home: it slipped over you like a dress when you stepped outside the airport doors into the transparent weather and saw the ridge of pines with palms. She found her father the way he'd become: outside, in his garden, the infant girls at his feet. The oldest was standing now, wearing overalls, bending the corn.

He was a man who could have only girls. In this epoch of genetic understanding, everyone knew whose fault this was. He could have eleven more children in the next twenty years, all daughters, he said, and that would be fine. "It's a lot more important than work," he told Jane and winked, handing her the warm bundle.

He'd given away the cars and made a regular triangle between the college library, the farmers market and home. "I find, as I get older, what I care about most is I love watching things grow."

Only now, living away, Jane began to understand how many kingdoms there were. His was not the first or the largest. A lot of other people, even in college, tried to be showy. And the East counted all kinds of things she'd never even heard of, or heard of only in bad ways from old-fashioned books. But in the sphere of home, very little was enough, and probably, all over the country that was once a frontier, they were all emperors to their children: a chicken in every pot and a king in every living room.

Louise, Noah's bride, had silver-gray hair and a dress that was absolute white, dimming the fog as it sailed up the mountains, snagging on pine.

Jane remembered the first time she had come to this place. What if it had been empty, as it was now? She would've lived off the stunted orchards and vagrant gardens, with the hulking walk she'd had in the mountain town.

The ceremony was over; and they were beginning to serve food. It was just dusk, and people Jane didn't know—scientists maybe—were crowding around Noah. She wandered through the whole wedding and found no boys her age.

But the Copper King's mansion had not been empty. Her father lived in three cold rooms, and Noah found her and saved her for him. She'd always wanted to know her father, the way she knew her mother, and now she did. But with her mother it was still different. She and her mother had always had the bird time of day. About now, they stopped wherever they were, together or apart, and stood still in the new dark, looking outside and listening to the trees. Her mother sometimes relaxed, almost alone, even with Jane. "Listen to the birds," she'd say, without ever expecting an answer. "Smell the lavender."

She wanted Jane to hear every sound and see every beauty she did. She didn't expect conversation. In fact, if Jane said something, it startled her. This must have begun when Jane was newly born, long before she could talk. Her mother spoke to her when she took long walks pushing the stroller.

"Hey, I brought you some chow," Owens said, handing her a bowl and sitting down next to her. "There wasn't much we can eat. These carnivores."

Jane sometimes ate a hamburger at school and regular things like cheese he didn't believe in, but her father always assumed she was as pure as he was. Now she had acne and often felt the craving for the clean taste of his vegetables. Jane ate the bowlful of rice, picking out the broccoli with her fingers. She used a spoon, not a fork, and pushed the rice into the spoon with her other thumb. This was one of the things her mother, glancing from two tables away, knew her by. They ate in silence under a canopy of rustling, cheeping birds.

Then, on the big black-and-white floor inside the tent, people were beginning to dance. Jane bit her lip. She wanted to. A long time ago, before she came to Alta, she knew how to dance. In the mountain town, it had been all she cared about, and for years she'd watched grown-ups dancing. Having studied this evolution, she now saw each stage of her parents visible here. The tuxedo dance her father had done with Olivia on marble floors, each of them as tall as the other— Louise's mother was waltzing that same way, with a man in a white jacket and an orthopedic shoe. And her mother and Eli swinging in a folk turn, as they had in the desert, with opposite hands meeting in the middle—a dance of people who didn't know steps but felt love. Back East, the old bells would sometimes ring from church steeples, summoning the rare devout from their shaded streets: Olivia had that air to Jane now, slightly out of date, without the constituency and power she once had.

Then the music changed, and they were all hopping, dancing rock and roll, as Owens and Eve had goonily after Jane's graduation. Little children jumped on the floor, a boy in a fancy blue satin suit. Eve danced neatly; she told Jane she'd learned from copying black women in jazz clubs. Owens was a goof, his legs far apart, stomping like a bear. Julie and Peter reminded her of Minna and her father on the kitchen floor. Huck was dancing now with her mother, bending her backwards.

But there was no one to ask Jane to dance. Noah and Louise were sitting holding hands. Jane didn't want to split them. Noah couldn't dance, and Louise didn't seem as if she wanted to.

Then a man introduced himself. "I know you," he said. "You were born on my farm in Oregon."

Jane had always thought she'd someday meet this man and asked him if he'd like to dance.

"Oh, no, sweetie," he said. "I don't dance." He winked. "I would if I was twenty years younger."

Maybe she could dance alone, or else grab the hand of that little boy in the blue satin suit.

A waiter came by and handed around champagne in tall swirled flutes. Jane sipped the top and felt froth in her nose.

Finally, she asked her father.

He stood up and took her hand, but then the music changed again, into a circle dance, the vine step. Jane knew that from Bixter; it was easy. She leapt up with her father, then looked over at Louise and Noah and said, "You guys should come too, even if you just clap."

Then she broke two hands and joined in, around and around, faster and faster. Everyone was rising from the tables, the sky patched in a faceted circle the quicker she went, stumbling a little, her heart heavy but aloft, and she saw people clustering around Noah as he danced with his hands, clapping overhead. Someone tore the chain and led his line under another bridge of hands so the circles intersected and twined inside each other like a seashell. The grandmother across from her was light on her feet, and Eve kicked off her heels to dance in her stockings, while the music kept building more and more, and Jane was sweating but it was a clear blue night and now this was fun. And all of a sudden, two guys stamped a chair in the center of the circle and everyone kept going, frenzied as some kind of pipes or harmonica burst, high and shrieking, crazy into the music. Jane heard the pop of a champagne bottle just over her right ear and felt some of the froth land on her wrist, wishing she could lick it, the sweet and the salt, but she couldn't stop now. She was in until it was over, and then in the center her father and Huck and Frank and some men she didn't know were lifting up the bride in her long white dress and Noah in his chair, and they were raised high in the air by a crowd of tuxedoed men for a long time, Noah still holding his flute of champagne. He threw out a white cloth, a handkerchief, and in the excitement, he tossed the champagne too, which arched up and then rained on them all.

The white cloth had two tiny spots of blood, like a bite. Jane watched her father. If he weren't down, she wondered, would I be up? It was a question she'd asked herself before. If he hadn't lost, would he love her? She looked around the night, considering this sliding register. She was becoming an adult.

This was not really the first dress. The first real dress was the uniform for school, when they'd finally let her go. Ruby had patiently hemmed it, while Jane stared at her new self in the mirror. Then, with the wool jumper over a white blouse and knee socks, she'd stood outside the pink-brick public school, carrying a notebook. A bell rang and the front hall began buzzing with footsteps, as she'd imagined for years, and she hurried to get into the crowd.

Acknowledgments

I'm grateful for the generous intelligence of my friends Allan Gurganus, Rob Cohen, Cristina Garcia, Lewis Hyde, Jeanne McCulloch, Ileene Smith, Ben Watson, Binky Urban and my editor, Gary Fisketjon. I would also like to thank Pamela Bjorkman, of Caltech, Lucila Cordero Nual, Roy Schafer and Mathew Soyster. The MacDowell Colony and the Rockefeller Foundation's Bellagio Study Center offered sanctuary during the writing of this book.

Most of all I want to thank my family—especially my husband, Richard Appel, for his jokes, editing, understanding, patience and the ever endowing wisdom that comes from having fun along the way.